'Tis the
in
it's a

Penn
and Judy Christenberry invite
you to three very special

Winter

weddings

Against a beautiful backdrop of brilliant
white snow, tendrils of ivy and scarlet
holly berries, each wedding brings joy
and happiness to the bride and groom –
the perfect Christmas present. But read
on to discover the passion, mystery and
emotional heartache it's taken to get
these couples to say 'I do' . . .

PENNY JORDAN

Penny Jordan has been writing for more than twenty years and has an outstanding record: over 130 novels published including the phenomenally successful **A Perfect Family, To Love, Honour and Betray, The Perfect Sinner** and **Power Play** which hit *The Sunday Times* and *New York Times* bestseller lists. Penny Jordan was born in Preston, Lancashire, and now lives with her husband in a beautiful fourteenth-century house in rural Cheshire.

Look out for novels by Penny Jordan in Modern Romance™!

GAIL WHITIKER

Originally hailing from Pembrokeshire, Gail Whitiker now lives on beautiful Vancouver Island on the west coast of Canada. When she isn't indulging her love of writing, you'll find her enjoying brisk walks along the Island's many fine beaches, or trying to catch up on her second love, reading. She wrote her first novel when she was in her teens, and still blesses her English teacher for not telling her how bad it really was.

JUDY CHRISTENBERRY

Judy Christenberry has been writing romances for over fifteen years because she loves happy endings as much as her readers do. A former high school French teacher, Judy devotes her time to writing. She hopes readers have as much fun reading her stories as she does writing them. She spends her spare time reading, watching her favourite sports teams and keeping track of her two adult daughters.

Winter
weddings

Three brand-new Christmas novels

Penny Jordan   Gail Whitiker

Judy Christenberry

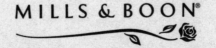

MILLS & BOON®

*MILLS & BOON and MILLS & BOON with the Rose Device
are registered trademarks of the publisher.*

*First published in Great Britain 2002.
Harlequin Mills & Boon Limited,
Eton House, 18-24 Paradise Road, Richmond, Surrey TW9 1SR*

WINTER WEDDINGS © Harlequin Enterprises II B.V., 2002

The publisher acknowledges the copyright holders of the
individual works as follows:

Christmas Eve Wedding © Penny Jordan 2002
A Scandalous Courtship © Gail Whitiker 2002
Snowbound Sweetheart © Judy Christenberry 2000

ISBN 0 263 83661 4

59-1102

*Printed and bound in Spain
by Litografía Rosés S.A., Barcelona*

Contents

CHRISTMAS EVE WEDDING   9
by Penny Jordan

A SCANDALOUS COURTSHIP   199
by Gail Whitiker

SNOWBOUND SWEETHEART   505
by Judy Christenberry

Christmas Eve Wedding

by
Penny Jordan

Dear Reader,

When I sat down to write this book, with its Christmas background, I wanted to include in it something of what I love about the festive season. So I chose to combine my memories of a recent trip to New Orleans with the magical world depicted in the Christmas windows of our large department stores.

I'm sure I'm not alone in admiring the layouts of special "Christmas" themed windows in shops and stores with their backdrops and wonderful luxurious gift ideas. Looking into them I find myself picking out imaginary presents for my family and friends, anticipating their excitement and pleasure when they receive them – my gifts given with love to those closest to me.

But of course Christmas isn't just about giving material "things" to those we love. It's much more about giving ourselves and showing them how much we care and value them, and so I hope you will enjoy reading how Christmas for Jaz and Caid results in the ultimate gift: each other's love. I always want "happy ever afters" for my characters and I wish you the same this Christmas.

Penny Jordan

Look out for more Penny Jordan books, coming soon in Modern Romance™.

CHAPTER ONE

A LITTLE hesitantly Jaz pressed the button for the lift to take her to her hotel bedroom. She was alone in the dimly lit foyer apart from the man who was also waiting for the lift. Tall, broad-shouldered, and subtly exuding an aura of very male sexual energy. Being alone with him sent a frisson of dangerous nervous excitement skittering over her skin.

Had he moved just that little bit closer to her whilst they waited, blocking her exit and hiding her from the view of anyone walking past the lift bay so that only he knew she was there, or was she imagining it? Like she had 'imagined' that look he had just given her body...her breasts...

And had he noticed the treacherous reaction of her body to his sexually predatory glance? The taut peaking of her breasts, the sudden soft gasp of her indrawn breath. Could he tell that recklessly she was in danger of actually becoming physically excited, not just by his presence but also by her own thoughts?

There was an awesome sexuality about him that made her tremble inside with arousal and guilt.

Was it possible he guessed what she was thinking? Was that why he had moved closer to her?

Colouring up self-consciously, Jaz looked away from him, determined to focus her thoughts elsewhere. She pondered on what had brought her to this hotel in New Orleans in the first place.

On the other side of the city her godfather would

9

be going through the final details of the sale of his exclusive and innovative English department store to the American family who had been so eager to buy it, to add to their own equally prestigious and larger chain of American stores. They needed the store to give them an entrée into the British market.

She knew that her own job as the store's display co-ordinator and window designer was totally secure, but it had been a struggle for her, and a test of her determination and resolve to prove herself and succeed in her chosen career.

Her parents, loving and caring though they most certainly were, had initially been shocked and disbelieving when their only child had been unable to share their commitment to the farm she'd grown up on, and had instead insisted on making her own way in the world.

They had been very reluctant to accept her decision to go to art college, and Jaz knew that it was really thanks to the intervention of her godfather, Uncle John, that her parents had finally taken her seriously. Thanks to him too that she now had the wonderful job she did have.

It was no secret that her parents still harboured the hope that she would fall in love with someone who shared their own lifestyle and ambitions, but Jaz was fiercely determined never to fall in love with a man who could not understand and did not share her feelings. She felt that the right to express the artistic side of her nature had been hard-won, and because of that it was doubly precious to her. She was ambitious for her talent, for its expression, and for the freedom to use it to its maximum capacity, and she knew how impossible that would be if she were to marry a man like her father, kind, loving and generous though he was.

To further validate her ability she had recently been head-hunted by a top London store, but she had chosen to remain loyal to her godfather and to the unique and acclaimed store which had originally been begun by his grandfather.

Now in his late seventies, her godfather had been for some time looking for a worthy successor who would nurture the store's prestigious profile, and although at first he had been dubious about selling out to new owners on the other side of the Atlantic, a visit to New Orleans to see the way the Dubois family ran their business—a trip on which he had invited Jaz to go with him—had convinced him that they shared his own objectives and standards. Since he had no direct heirs to pass the business onto, he had decided that the best way to preserve the traditions of the store was to sell it to the like-minded Dubois family, a decision Jaz herself fully endorsed.

As the lift arrived and the doors slid open Jaz's thoughts were snapped back into the present. She couldn't help snatching an indiscreet look at the man waiting to step into it with her, her heart bumping against her ribs as she acknowledged the buzz of sexual excitement she had felt the moment she had seen him. Was it the fact that she was out of her own environment, a stranger in a different country, that was encouraging her to behave so recklessly? Or was it something about the man himself that was making her touch the tip of her tongue to her lips as she stared boldly at him, her female senses registering his sexy maleness?

Just the thought of being alone in the lift with him

was filling her mind with all manner of forbidden erotic scenarios. A wanton inspection of his body verified just how completely male he was. A soft, dangerous lick of excitement ran over her as her senses reacted to the way he was looking at her, silently responding to the fact that she had looked at him for just that little bit too long, challenging him in a way that was wholly female to show her that he was equally wholly male.

'Seen something you like, hon?' he asked her as the lift door closed, trapping Jaz inside the intimate space with him.

Apprehension curled feather-soft down her spine. She knew that what she was doing was totally out of character, but for some reason she didn't care. There was something about him that brought the secret ache deep within her body to a wire-sharp intensity that could not be ignored.

Refusing to back down, she met his amused look head-on, tossing her head as she replied huskily, 'I might have done.' She had been warned before her visit that New Orleans was home to a very dangerous type of sexually attractive man—men who never refused to gamble against fate or to take up a challenge. And she held her breath now, wondering how he would respond. She couldn't resist glancing into the mirrored wall to her side to take another peek at him.

His shirt was unbuttoned at the throat, exposing an exciting 'V' of male flesh. Impulsively she took a step towards him. She wondered how it would feel to caress that flesh with her lips, to taste and tease it until he had no option but to reach for her and—

She could feel her body melting with arousal. Everything about him tormented her senses in ways she had never imagined. Just looking at him made her want him. She could feel her face burning, her heart racing at the explicitness of her own thoughts and fantasies. She felt shocked by them.

Her heart thumping, she continued to study him. Over six foot, with very thick rich brown hair just touched with honey-gold where the fierce heat of the sun had lightened it. In the close confines of the lift she could smell the cool expensive tang of his skin. Everything about him looked expensive. From his clothes and his haircut to his elegantly discreet watch. Everything apart from his hands which for some reason, whilst immaculately clean, were slightly callused. Her stomach lifted and clenched with female excitement at the thought of those hands, so tellingly male, pressed against the soft femininity of her own skin.

She had started to breathe too fast, betrayingly fast, she recognised as his glance locked on her mouth.

'Go ahead,' she heard him urging her shockingly. 'Go ahead, hon, and do what you want to do. And you do want to, don't you?' he guessed, his voice dropping until it was a low sexy murmur, as rawly sensual as though he had actually caressed the most sensitive parts of her body with the rough male heat of his tongue.

Somehow she had actually put one hand against his chest!

His skin was warm and tanned, with tiny lines fanning out from his eyes. His eyes...

Her breath locked in her chest and another wave of sensual dizziness filled her. She had never, ever seen eyes so blue before. It was a denser, deeper, stronger blue than the bluest sky she had ever seen, the colour so intense that she felt her own golden-brown eyes must look totally insignificant in comparison.

'I can't,' she responded shakily, too lost in her own desire to conceal what she was feeling from him. 'Not here.' Her voice faltered and fell to a husky whisper. 'Not in the lift.' But as she spoke her gaze went betrayingly to where his jeans were now visibly straining against the tautness of his arousal.

'Liar!' he taunted her softly. 'I could take you here and now. And if you want me to prove it—' His hand was already reaching for the buckle of his belt.

Jaz felt dizzy with the aching intensity of her fevered longing. Impulsively she moved even closer to him, and then stopped.

The knowing smile that accompanied the look he was giving her brought a deep flush of colour to Jaz's skin.

He had the whitest, strongest teeth, and it was hard not to imagine him biting them into her skin with deliberate sensuality. A fierce, shocked shiver ran through her at the explicitness of her own thoughts, and she moved a little uncomfortably, shifting her weight from one foot to the other.

'Careful, hon,' she heard him warning her. 'If you keep on looking at me that way I guess I'm just going to have to give you what those big eyes of yours are asking me for. In fact...'

Jaz shook her head and tried to deny what he was saying, but it was too late for her to say or do anything. He had moved so quickly, so light-footedly for such a big man, and he had somehow imprisoned her against the back of the lift, his hands planted firmly either side of her as he lowered his head until his lips were resting on hers.

The feeling of being surrounded by him, by the heat of his body, the weight of it that was almost resting on her, the scent of it that filled the air around her, was so intensely erotic that she felt almost as though he had laid her bare and actually touched her. She shuddered as he placed his hand on her breast, caressing it through the fine silk of the dress she was wearing. He bent his head and she turned her own to one side, then cried out in protest as she felt his lips caressing her nipple through the fine silk.

Swooningly Jaz closed her eyes. She ought not to be doing this. It was so dangerous. Common sense told her that. But her hand had already gone to his groin, seeking, stroking, needing the hot hard feel of him to prove to her that she was not alone in the savage almost frightening urgency of her need. The sensation of him swelling fiercely beneath her touch soothed her fractured ego, just as the sudden rough acceleration of his breathing brought her a swift feminine surge of triumph. She was not alone. He wanted her as much as she wanted him!

The lift shuddered to a halt and the door opened. Immediately she pushed past him.

They stepped out of the lift together, Jaz aware that her face was burning hotly and that her legs felt so weak they were barely able to support her. What if they had remained in the lift for longer? Would he…? Would she…?

As she turned away from him she heard him saying softly to her, 'Let's go to your room.'

Helplessly she stared at him. He was a man totally outside all her previous experience—which she had to admit was less than worthy of any kind of comparison. She had always led an unfashionably sedate kind of

life, compared with the lives of her peers. Her battle
to prove to her parents how important her chosen career path was to her had not left her with time to indulge in the sexual experimentation of other girls her
age.

But it was a life which suited her and which she
had always been very happy with. Sexual adventures
of the kind that involved kissing tall, dark, handsome
men in lifts were not something that had ever remotely
interested her—or if they had she was certainly not
prepared to admit it publicly, she hastily amended, as
she wordlessly led the way to her hotel bedroom with
her head held high but her heart thumping frantically
in a mixture of excitement and apprehension.

It was only when they reached the door that qualms
of conscience made her hesitate. She turned to him as
she searched in her bag for her key.

'I don't think—' she began, but he had taken her
bag from unresisting fingers and was reaching out to
draw her into his arms. In the same movement he slid
open the door.

'What is it that you don't think, hon?' he asked her
with male emphasis. 'That you don't want this?'

Jaz's whole body shook in the hard embrace of his
arms as he bent his head and kissed her, a long, slow,
lingering kiss that melted her bones and her will-
power. They were inside the room, now and he had
closed and locked the door, all without letting go of
her, and now in the soft darkness he was still kissing
her. Though what he was doing to her mouth was
more, much more than merely kissing it. What he was
doing was...

Jaz shuddered convulsively as his hands touched her
body lightly, delicately, knowingly... This man knew

women… He knew them very, very well. She could feel it in his touch…feel it in him. His tongue caressed her lips, as though he sensed and wanted to soothe her fears, circling them slowly and carefully, until the delicate pressure of his tongue-tip became not soothing but frustrating, tormenting…making her want…

The darkness seemed to increase her awareness of him, of the hot, musky male scent of his body. It made her doubly aware of the feel of his skin against her as she felt the roughened rasp of his jaw on her cheek, and the corresponding texture of his jacket sleeve against her bare arm. She was almost intoxicated by the cool fresh hint of cologne he was wearing.

In her mind's eye she could see him in a very different environment from that of her hotel room—the Bourbon court had been exited from France to New Orleans, and it didn't take much imagination on Jaz's part to picture him at Versailles at the height of the Sun King's reign. How well he would have fitted into that sophisticated and splendid milieu; his sexuality would have driven the court ladies into swooning fits of desire—would have had much the same effect on them as it was having on her right now!

He was like no other man she had ever met, dangerous and exciting, and she was drawn to him in a way that both shocked and thrilled her.

His teasing kiss was beginning to aggravate her. He was treating her like a girl, not a woman—not like the woman she knew she could be with him. All fire and passion, need and hunger. A woman to whom nothing else mattered more than her man, the feelings and desires they were generating and creating between them. Her made her feel… He made her feel alive, primitive, sensual—all woman! His woman!

Reaching up, she wrapped her arms around him, boldly tangling her tongue with his, drawing him into a kiss of fierce passion.

'Uh-huh, so that's what you want, is it?' he demanded thickly against her mouth as he responded to her. 'Well, in that case, hon—'

Jaz gasped as he picked her up as easily, as though she were a child, making his way sure-footedly towards the bed like a mountain cat.

As he laid her down he was already undressing her, and she made no move to stop him. She had known the moment they stepped into the lift together that this was going to happen. Had wanted it to happen. As it had happened with this man so many times since she'd arrived in New Orleans. She positively longed for Caid's now familiar touch.

Moonlight streamed in through the unclosed curtains, silvering her exposed breasts. She gasped in pleasure as he touched them, running the slightly coarse pad of his fingertip round the exquisitely sensitive flesh surrounding each pouting nub.

Excitement, as hot and sweet as melting chocolate, filled her with shocked pleasure. Her body arched like a bow as she offered her breasts to him in the silent heat of the shadowy room, its stillness broken only by the raw tempo of their aroused breathing.

This was what she had been imagining them doing in the lift—she'd been picturing their naked bodies entwined in the still heat of the Louisiana night.

Fiercely she reached for him, her fingers tugging at buttons and fastenings, not stopping until she was able to touch the hot skin that held the muscled tautness of his naked body.

Just touching him unleashed within her a driven

hunger she was half afraid to recognise. It was far, far outside the boundaries of her normal emotions. A reckless and alien, dangerous and wild wantonness that refused to be controlled or tamed.

As he reached for her, covering her body in fierce, rawly sensual kisses, she sobbed beneath the onslaught of her own response—which was immediate, feral and unstoppable.

Passionately they clung together, stroking, touching kissing, devouring one another in their mutual driving need. In the moonlight Jaz could see the scratches she had scorched across his back, and in the morning she knew her own body would bear the small bruise-marks of his hotly male demands on her, his desire for her. Then perhaps she would wonder at her own behaviour, but right now her thoughts were elsewhere.

'Ready, hon?' he demanded as he gathered her closer, so close that she could feel the heavy thud of his heart as though it were beating within her own body.

Wordlessly she answered him with her body, lifting her legs to wrap them tightly around him as he thrust into her.

The sensation of him filling her, stretching her, made her shake with almost unbearable pleasure.

Each movement of his body within hers, each powerful thrust, increased the frenzy of need that was taking her higher, filling her senses with the immensity of what was happening. And then abruptly the fierce, breath-catching ascent was over, and she was cresting the topmost wave of her own pleasure, surfing its heights, awed by the power of what she was experiencing. She cried out unknowingly, clinging to the body covering her own, feeling the male release within her; her body accepting the satisfaction of knowing it had given him completion whilst her exhausted senses relaxed.

Caid leaned up on one elbow and gently tickled the impossibly delicate curve of Jaz's jaw with his fingertips. She was so tiny, so fragile, and yet at the same time so breathtakingly strong, this Englishwoman who had walked so unexpectedly into his life and his heart.

He had had his doubts—one hell of a lot of them, if he was honest—and with good reason. But then he had overheard her godfather talking to his mother about her background, and Caid had started to relax. Knowing that she came from farming stock—that she had been raised in a country environment and that her role within the store was simply a temporary one she had taken on to show her independence until she was ready to settle down and return to her roots—was all he had needed to lower his guard and stop fighting his feelings for her.

Which was just as well, because there was no way he could stop loving her now. No way he would ever contemplate settling down with a girl who did not share his deep love of country living and his determination that their children would be raised on his ranch, with their mother there for them, instead of travelling all over the world in the way his own mother had done. She had never been there when he had most needed her, and his parents finally divorced when his father had grown tired of his mother's constant absences, her single-minded devotion to the family store. Caid had never been in any doubt that the store mattered more to his mother than he did. She had always been frank about the fact that his conception had been an accident.

As a young boy Caid had been badly hurt by his mother's open admission of her lack of maternalism. As a teenager that hurt had turned to bitter resentment and as Caid had continued to grow his resentment had become an iron-hard determination to protect his own children from the same fate. Like many people who'd experienced a lonely and painful childhood, Caid had a very strong desire to have his own family and create the kind of closeknit unit he felt he had missed out on.

One of the most painful episodes of his childhood had been the time when his mother had not even been able to be there for him when his father—her ex-husband—had been killed in a road accident.

Caid had been eleven at the time, and he had never forgotten just how it had felt to be taken to the mortuary to identify his father... How alone, how afraid and how angry with his mother he had felt.

He had made a vow then that there was no way anything like that was ever going to happen to his kids. No way!

Consequently he had been very wary of becoming emotionally involved, despite the number of women who had tried to coax and tempt him into falling in love with them.

Until now... Until Jaz.

He had walked into the restaurant where the family, including his mother, was having dinner with Jaz and her godfather, and the moment he had set eyes on her he had known!

He had known too, from Jaz's dazed expression and

self-conscious pink-cheeked colour, that she was equally intensely aware of him.

It hadn't taken him long to skilfully detach her from the others, on the pretext of showing her the view of the Mississippi from the upper floor of the restaurant, and even less time to let her know how attracted he was to her.

That his behaviour had been somewhat out of character was, he recognised, an indication of just how strong his feelings for her were.

Ironically, he had almost not met Jaz at all.

Although Caid had now established a workable and accepting adult relationship with his mother, one of the legacies from his childhood was his intense dislike of the family business. Had he been able to do so he would have preferred to have nothing whatsoever to do with the stores at all. However, that simply wasn't possible. His maternal grandfather had left him a large portfolio of shares in the family business, which he held in trust, and as a further complication his mother had put emotional pressure on him to take on the role of the business financial adviser, following the completion of his Masters in Business Studies, claiming that if he didn't she would never be able to believe he had forgiven her for his childhood.

Rather than become involved in painful wrangling Caid had given in, and of course the family had insisted that he further his role as financial adviser on their proposed purchase of the English store his mother was so keen to acquire—to add to the portfolio of highly individual and specialised stores already operating in Boston, Aspen and New Orleans.

Unlike the rest of his mother's family, Caid's first love was the land, the ranch he had bought for himself and was steadily building up, financed by the money he earned as a much sought-after financial consultant.

But he had come to New Orleans, protesting all the way like a roped steer, and thank heavens his mother had persevered, insisted on his presence. Because if she hadn't...

The sexy smile curling his mouth deepened as Jaz opened her eyes.

'Mmm, that sure was another wonderful night we spent together, ma'am,' he teased her softly.

As he had known she would, Jaz started to blush. It fascinated him, this delicate English colour of hers that betrayed her every emotion, and made him feel he wanted to wrap her up and protect her.

'You'd better go,' Jaz told him unsteadily. 'You know we both agreed that we wanted to keep this...us...to ourselves for now, and my godfather will be expecting me to have breakfast with him. Your mother has arranged for us to visit her warehouse this morning.'

Jaz gave a small soft gasp as Caid leaned forward and covered her mouth with his own, kissing her into silence, and from silence into sweetly hot fresh desire.

'Are you sure you want me to leave?' he asked, breathing the words against the sensitivity of her passionately kissed mouth whilst his hand pushed aside the bedclothes to mould round her breast.

As she struggled to keep her head and behave sensibly Jaz breathed in the intoxicating warm man-scent of Caid's skin and knew she was fighting a lost cause.

Much better simply to give in, she acknowledged giddily as Caid started to kiss her again, gathering her up in his arms and rolling her swiftly beneath him.

'Oh!' Just the feel of his naked flesh against her

own was enough to prompt Jaz's soft betraying gasp, swiftly followed by a second and much more drawn out murmur of female pleasure as Caid made his intentions—and his hungry desire for her—very clear.

In terms of days they had known each other for very little time, but in terms of longing and love it felt to Jaz that they had known one another for ever.

'A month ago I never dreamed that I'd be doing anything like this,' she gasped as Caid's hand stroked her body.

'I should hope you didn't,' he growled mock-angrily.

'After all, a month ago we hadn't met.'

Immediately Jaz's eyes filmed with tears.

'Hon… What is it? What's wrong? What did I say?' Caid demanded urgently, cupping her face with his hands, his expression turning from one of amusement to anxious male concern.

'Nothing,' Jaz assured him. 'It's just that… Oh, Caid… If I hadn't come to New Orleans—! If we hadn't met—! If…I hadn't known…'

'You did come to New Orleans. We did meet, and you do know. We both know,' Caid emphasised rawly. 'I know, Jaz, that we were made to be together, that you are perfect for me. Perfect,' he repeated meaningfully, glancing down the length of her body and then looking deep into her eyes.

Jaz could feel her toes curling as she looked at him. The way she felt about him still totally bemused and awed her. She had never thought of herself as the kind of woman who fell head over heels in love at first sight, who behaved so rashly that nothing would have stopped her sharing Caid's bed or his life once he had told her how much he wanted her there.

It still made her feel giddy with happiness to know that Caid, who was surely the epitome of everything she had ever imagined she could possibly want in a man, had fallen in love with her. Caid was exactly the kind of man she had always secretly hoped she might meet: sophisticated, virile, sexy. A man who shared her world, who understood how important it was for her to be able to give free rein to her artistic nature; a man whose background meant that he would know instinctively why she preferred to stroke the sensual silkiness of rich velvet than to rub down the hind-quarters of a horse. And why she could spend hours, days, wandering in delight through an art gallery, whilst the delights of a cattle market left her cold.

'Will you be joining us this morning?' Jaz asked him.

Caid shook his head and Jaz tried to conceal her disappointment. As excited as she was at the thought of seeing behind the scenes of the store, so to speak, she knew it would have been an even more wonder-fully fulfilling experience if Caid had been there with her.

She knew that his mother had overall control of all the buying for the stores, and that she travelled the world seeking out new and different merchandise to tempt their discerning customers, but it was through Caid's eyes that she wanted to see the Aladdin's cave she suspected the warehouse would be—in Caid's presence that she wanted to explore a part of the world he had made it clear they were going to share.

'We can meet up this afternoon at the house,' Caid said once they were both dressed. 'You and I have talking to do and plans to make,' he told her mean-ingfully.

'Uncle John and I are flying home tomorrow,' Jaz reminded him.

'Exactly,' Caid acknowledged. 'Which is all the more reason for you and I to make those plans.'

CHAPTER TWO

JAZ smiled excitedly as she hurried towards the luxurious house in the centre of the French Quarter of New Orleans, where Caid was staying for the duration of his visit.

He had given her his spare key to the house the same night he had declared his love for her—a week to the day after they had first met—and now, as she turned it gently in the lock and opened the door to step inside the house's hallway, Jaz wondered how on earth she was going to cope tomorrow morning when she was due to fly home—without him!

Already, secretly, she had fantasised about the life they would live together—the children she hoped they would one day have. A boy, a miniature Caid, patterned on his father, and a girl, to fill the home they would share. Suddenly it struck her that she did not know where Caid's permanent home actually was!

Not that it mattered, she assured herself. After all, she knew all the really important things about him... Like the fact that he slept on his right-hand side and that he was such a light sleeper that if she so much as brushed the lightest of kisses against his skin he was immediately awake—even if on one occasion he had fooled her into thinking he wasn't, and she had betrayed herself, giving in to her female longing to relish the secret intimacy and pleasure of touching and exploring him whilst he slept.

Hastily Jaz dragged her thoughts onto more mundane things. She knew that Caid had been to college in Boston, where his family also had a store, and that his work as a financial consultant required a certain amount of travel.

'Fortunately I can work from any base, so long as I have a computer,' he had told her, adding jokingly, 'And my own plane.'

Did 'anywhere' mean that he was thinking of basing himself in her hometown, Cheltenham?

Or did he have somewhere else in mind? Jaz had been thrilled when his mother had sought her out privately to tell her how much she admired her work.

'It could well be that there are opportunities for you to branch out rather more after the takeover,' she had told Jaz, excitingly. 'Would you be interested? It could mean a change of scenery for you.'

'I'd be very interested,' Jaz had replied dizzily.

'Good,' Caid's mother had approved.

Had Caid perhaps hinted to his mother that Jaz might possibly work in one of their American stores?

He had told Jaz very comprehensively how well suited he thought they were, and she certainly felt the same way. She had deliberately refrained from saying too much to him about her job once she had realised who he was, not wanting him to think that she was trying to make a good impression on him out of some ulterior career-driven motive, but she had mentioned to him that she had known where her life lay from being a young girl.

The speed of their relationship and her own love for her parents had kept her from saying anything to him about the problems she had experienced as a child— as yet—but she knew that with his family background he would completely understand and sympathise with how she felt.

From the house's stately drawing room a corridor led to its other rooms, and from her end of the hallway Jaz could see the door that opened into Caid's bedroom was ajar. Instinctively, Jaz knew that Caid had reached the house ahead of her and was waiting for her. It was all she could do to stop herself from breaking into an undignified run and rushing into the bedroom to throw herself into his arms.

When she pushed open the bedroom door she saw that she had been right.

Caid was lying on the bed, a thin sheet pulled up to his waist, the rest of his body exposed as he lay back in the bed, his arms raised and his hands folded behind his head.

Hungrily Jaz's gaze feasted on him. There was, after all, no need for her to try and hide her feelings from him. After all, Caid understood her desire, her arousal...her love.

'Miss me?' he whispered as she hurried unsteadily towards the bed.

'Mmm...' Jaz admitted. 'But the warehouse was wonderful. I thought our buyers at home were good, but your mother is in a class of her own.'

'Tell me about it!' Caid agreed cynically, but the grimness in his voice was lost on Jaz, who was reliving the awe and excitement she had felt when she had toured the New Orleans store.

'I know that she personally approves everything that your buyers source.' Jaz shook her head. 'How on earth does she do it? She must be totally dedicated.'

'Totally,' Caid agreed tersely.

Frowning a little as she caught the sharpness of

his voice, Jaz looked at him. 'What's wrong?' she asked him.

'Nothing,' Caid responded firmly, smiling at her as he added softly, 'Apart from the fact that you've got far too many clothes on and we're wasting too much time talking.'

'You said you wanted to talk,' Jaz reminded him. 'To talk and make plans,' she emphasised.

'Mmm…and so I do,' Caid agreed. 'But right now you're distracting the hell out of me and making me want you so damn much that the way I need to communicate with you has suddenly become much more personal and one on one. You haven't said hi to me yet,' he told her softly.

'Hi…' Jaz began, but Caid immediately shook his head.

'No. Not like that. Like this.' Swiftly he reached for her, his mouth starting to caress hers.

'Oh, *that* kind of hi.' Jaz managed to find the breath to tease him.

'That kind of hi,' Caid agreed, releasing her mouth to look into her eyes.

Jaz could feel the heat spreading through her body. She started to quiver, and then to tremble openly. She could see from the look in Caid's eyes how much he was enjoying her helpless response to him.

Well, he would pay for that enjoyment later, when she tormented him the way he was tormenting her right now.

'I've never met anyone who shows her feelings so clearly and so openly,' Caid told her quietly. 'I love that honesty about you, Jaz. I don't have any time for people who cheat or lie.'

For a second he looked so formidable, so forbidding, that Jaz felt unsettled. To her he was the man she loved, but she could see that there was another side to him—a fiercely stubborn and unforgiving side, she suspected.

'I love the way you show me your feelings,' she heard Caid saying. 'The way you show me how much you want and love me. Show me that now, Jaz.'

Jaz didn't need a second invitation.

The heightened sound of Caid's breathing accompanied the speedy removal of her clothes, until her progress was interrupted by Caid's refusal to allow her to complete the task unaided, his hands hungrily tender against her body as they exchanged mutually passionate kisses and whispered words of love.

The heat of a New Orleans afternoon was surely made for lovers, Jaz reflected languorously a couple of hours later as she lay in Caid's arms, enjoying the blissful aftermath of their lovemaking. After all, where better to escape the heat than in the shadowy air-conditioned coolness they were enjoying?

'Time to get dressed,' Caid murmured as he leaned over to kiss her.

'Dressed? I thought we were going to talk,' Jaz reminded him.

A sexy smile crooked his mouth.

'We are!' he confirmed. 'Which is why we need to get dressed. If we stay here like this, talking isn't going to be what I feel like doing,' he added, in case Jaz had missed his point. 'I can't wait for us to be married, Jaz, or to take you home with me to Colorado—to the ranch. We can begin our lives together properly there. With your background, you'll love it, I'll get you your own horse, so that we can ride out together, and then, when the kids come along—'

'Your ranch?' Jaz stopped him in a shocked voice. 'What ranch? What are you talking about, Caid? You're a businessman—a financial consultant. The stores…'

'I am a financial consultant,' Caid agreed, starting to frown as he heard the note of shocked anxiety in Jaz's voice. 'But that's what I do to make enough money to finance the ranch until it can finance itself. And as for the stores…to be involved in the stores or anything connected with them is the last way I would ever want to live my life. To me they epitomise everything I most dislike and despise.' His mouth twisted bitterly. 'I could say that I have a hate-hate relationship with them. Personally, I can see nothing worthwhile in scouring the world for potential possessions for people who already have more than they need. That's not what life should be about.'

Jaz couldn't help herself—his angry words had resurrected too many painful memories for her.

'But living on a ranch, chasing round after cattle all day, presumably is?' she challenged him shakily.

With every word he had uttered Caid had knocked a larger and larger hole in her beliefs, her illusions about the kind of relationship and goals they shared. Jaz recognised in shocked bewilderment that Caid simply wasn't the man she had believed him to be.

'The stores aren't just about…about selling things, Caid,' she told him passionately. 'They're about opening people's eyes…their senses…to beauty; they're about… Surely you can understand what I'm trying to say?' Jaz pleaded.

Caid narrowed his eyes as he heard the agitation

and the anger in Jaz's voice. From out of the past he
could hear his mother's voice echoing in his six-year-
old ears.

'No, Caid. I can't stay. I have to go. Think about
all those people I would be disappointing if I didn't
find them beautiful things to buy! Surely you can understand?'

No! I don't understand! Caid had wanted to cry, but
he had been too young to find the words he wanted to
say, and already too proud, too aware of his male
status, to let her see his pain.

But he certainly wasn't going to make the mistake
of holding back on telling Jaz how he felt.

'I thought we were talking about us, Jaz! About our
future—our lives together. So why in hell's name are
we talking about the stores?'

'Because I work in one of them, and so far as I am
concerned my work is a vitally important part of my
life.'

'How vitally important?' Caid demanded ominously, his voice suddenly icily cold.

Jaz felt as though the ground that had seemed so
safe and solid was suddenly threatening to give way
beneath her, as though she was rushing headlong into
danger. But it was a danger she had faced before,
wasn't it? Listening to Caid was in many ways just
like listening to her parents—although Caid's anger
and bitterness was a frighteningly adult and dangerous
version of parental emotion.

She felt intensely threatened by it—not in any physical sense, but in the sense that his attitude threatened
her personal freedom to be herself.

As she looked at him, remembering the intimacy
they had just shared, the love he had shown her, she

was tempted to back down. But how could she and still be true to herself?

'My work is as important to me as it gets,' she told him determinedly. Though what she was saying was perhaps not strictly true. It was not so much her job that was important to her as the fact that it allowed her to express her creativity, and it was her creativity she would never compromise on or give up. 'As important,' she continued brittly, 'as you probably consider yours to be to you!'

'Nothing—no one on this earth—could ever make me give up the ranch!' Caid told her emphatically.

'And nothing—no one—could ever make me give up my...my...work,' Jaz replied, equally intensely.

Silently they looked at one another. The hostility in Caid's eyes made Jaz want to run to him and bury her head against his chest so that she wouldn't have to see it.

'I can't believe this is happening.' Caid's voice was terse, his jaw tight with anger.

'If I had known—'

'You did know,' Jaz interrupted him fiercely. 'I have never made any secret of how much my...my creative my work means to me. If I had thought for one minute that you might not understand...that you were a ...a farmer...there is no way that—'

'That what? That you'd have jumped so eagerly into bed with me?'

'I was brought up on a farm.' Jaz struggled to explain. 'I know that it isn't the kind of life I can live.'

'And I was brought up by a mother who thought more of her precious stores than she did of either my father or me. I know there is no way I want a woman—a wife—who shares that kind of obsession.

I want a wife who will be there for my kids in a way that my mother never was for me. I want a wife who will put them and me first, who will—'

'Give up her own life, her own dreams, her own personality simply because you say so?' Jaz stormed furiously at him. 'I don't believe I'm hearing this. Just what kind of man are you?'

'The kind who was fool enough to think you were the right woman for him,' Caid told her bitingly. 'But obviously I was wrong.'

'Obviously,' Jaz agreed chokily, then emphasised, '*Very* obviously!' And then added for good measure, 'I hate farming. I loathe and detest everything about it. I would never ever commit myself or my children to…to a man as…as selfish and narrow-minded as you certainly are. My creativity is a special gift. It means—'

'A special gift? More special than our love?' Caid demanded savagely. 'More special than the life we could have shared together? The children I would have given you?'

'You don't understand,' Jaz protested, her voice thickening with tears as she forced herself not to be weakened by the emotional pressure he was placing her under. If she gave in to him now she would never stop giving in to him, and she would spend the rest of her life regretting her weakness. Not just for herself but for her children as well.

But still she tried one last attempt to make Caid see reason, telling him huskily, 'When I was growing up I knew how important it was for me to fulfil the creative, artistic side of my nature, but my parents didn't want to accept that I was different from them. If it hadn't been for Uncle John I don't know what would have happened. I had to fight far too hard for my right to be me, Caid, ever to be able to give it up for anyone…even you.'

What he hadn't understood as a child Caid certainly understood now, he acknowledged bitterly. Once again, the most important person in his world was telling him that he wasn't enough for her, that she didn't love him enough to want to be with him for himself.

'I thought after what I'd been through with my mother I'd be able to recognise another woman of her type a mile away,' he growled angrily. 'And perhaps I would have done too, if I hadn't heard your precious Uncle John talking about you and saying that your family expected you to return to your roots and settle down to the life they'd raised you in.'

The accusation implicit in his words that somehow she had actively deceived him infuriated Jaz, severing the last fragile thread tugging on her heartstrings.

'My parents might want that, but it certainly isn't what I want, or what I ever intend to do. And if you misinterpreted a conversation you overheard, that's hardly my fault. If marrying a farmer's daughter is so important to you, why didn't you say so?'

'Because I believed that what is important to me was equally important to you,' Caid told her bitingly. 'I thought that you were the kind of woman strong enough to find her fulfilment in—'

'Her husband and her children? Staying home baking cakes whilst her big strong husband rides his acres and rules his home?' Jaz interrupted him scathingly. 'My God. If your father was anything like you, no wonder your mother left him! You aren't just old-fashioned, Caid, you're criminally guilty of wanting to deny my sex its human rights! We are living in a

new world now. Modern couples share their responsibilities—to each other and to their children—and—'

'Do they? Well, my mother certainly didn't do
much sharing when she was travelling all over the
world buying "beautiful" things,' he underlined cynically. 'She left my dad to bring me up as best he
could. And as for her leaving him—believe me, he felt
he was well rid of her. And so did I.'

Caid started to shake his head, his eyes dark with a
pain that Jaz misinterpreted as anger.

'My mother was like—'

'Like me?' She jumped in, hot-cheeked. 'Do you
feel you'd be well rid of me, Caid?'

Broodingly Caid looked at her. Right now he ached
to take her in his arms and punish her for the pain she
was causing them both, by kissing her until she admitted that all she wanted was him and their love, that
nothing else mattered. But if he did he knew he would
be committing himself to a life of misery. After all, a
leopardess never changed her spots—look at his
mother!

The look he was giving her said more than any
amount of words, Jaz decided with a painful sharp
twisting of her heart that made it feel as though it was
being pulled apart.

'Fine,' she lied. 'Because I certainly think that I will
be well rid of you!!'

She could feel the burning acid sting of unshed
tears. As angry with herself for her weakness as she
was with Caid for being the cause of it, she blinked
them away determinedly.

'I'm a woman with needs and ambitions of my own,
Caid, not some…some docile brood mare you can corral and keep snugly at home.'

'You—' Infuriated, Caid took a stride towards her.

Immediately Jaz panicked. If he touched her now, held her…kissed her…

'Don't come any closer,' she warned him, her eyes glittering with emotion. 'And don't even think about trying to touch me, Caid. I don't want to be touched by you ever again!'

Without giving him any chance to retaliate she turned on her heel and fled, almost running the length of the house and not stopping until she was halfway down the street, when the heat of the New Orleans late afternoon forced her to do so.

It was over. Over. And it should never have happened in the first place. Would never have happened if she had for one minute realised, recognised, just what kind of man Caid was.

She had been out of her depth, Jaz acknowledged miserably, in more ways than one.

The only consolation was that, thanks to Caid's practicality and insistence on protecting her, there was no chance there would be any repercussions from their affair. And for that she was profoundly thankful! Wasn't she?

CHAPTER THREE

'YOU want me to go to England and find out what's happening?' Caid stared at his mother in angry disbelief. 'Oh, no...no way. No way at all!' he told her, shaking his head.

'Caid, please. I know how you feel about the stores, and I know I'm to blame for that but you are my son, and who else can I turn to if I can't rely on you? And besides,' she continued coaxingly, 'it would hardly be in your own financial interests for the stores to start losing money—especially not right now, when you've invested so much in modernising the ranch and buying more land.'

'All right, Mother, I understand what you're saying.' Caid stopped her grimly. 'But I fail to see why a couple of personnel leaving the Cheltenham store should be such a problem.'

'Caid, they're going to work for our competitors.'

'So we recruit better and more loyal employees,' Caid responded wryly. 'Which departments are we talking about anyway?' he asked, as casually as he could. So far as he was concerned, he told himself, if one of the people who had left was Jaz then so much the better!

It was over four months since Jaz had walked out on him after their fight. Over four months? It was four months, three weeks, five days and, by his last reckoning, seven and a half hours—not that he was keeping count for any other reason than to remind himself how fortunate he'd been to discover how unsuited they were before he had become any more involved.

Any more involved? How much more involved was it possible for him to have been? Hell, he'd been as deep in love as it was possible for a man to be!

Irascibly, Caid started to frown. He was growing a mite tired of being forced to listen to the mocking taunts of his unwanted inner voice. An inner voice, moreover, that knew nothing whatsoever about the realities of the situation!

So what if it was true that there had been occasions when he had found himself perilously close to reaching for the phone and punching in the English store's number? At least he had been strong enough to stop himself. After all, there was no real point in him speaking to Jaz, was there? Other than to torment and torture himself—and he was doing one hell of a good job of that without hearing the sound of her voice.

His frown deepened. By now surely he should be thinking about her less, missing and wanting her less—especially late at night...

'Caid...come back... You're miles away...'

His mother's voice cut into his private thoughts, mercifully rescuing him from having to acknowledge just what was on his mind late at night when he should have been sleeping.

'The employees who have left are both key people, Caid: loyal personnel who had worked for the store for a long time. I'm concerned that their decision to leave will reflect badly on us and on our ability to keep good staff. Not to mention our status as a premier store. The retail world is very small, and it only needs a whisper of gossip to start a rumour that we are in danger of losing our status as market leader...' She gave him a worried look. 'I don't need to tell you what that is likely to do to our stock.'

'So two people leave.' Caid shrugged. He knew his mother, and the last thing he needed right now was to have his time hijacked on behalf of her precious stores.

'Two have left so far, but there could be more. Jaz might be next, and we really can't afford to lose her, Caid. She has a unique talent—a talent I very much want. Not just for the Cheltenham store but for all our stores. It's in my mind to appoint Jaz as our head window and in-store designer once she has gained more experience. I'd like to have her spend time working at each of the individual stores first. Caid, we mustn't lose her, but I'm very much afraid we are going to do so. If it wasn't for this stupid embargo the doctors have put on me flying I'd go to Cheltenham myself!'

Caid watched as his mother moved restlessly around the room. It had come as just as much of a shock to him as it had to his mother to learn that a routine health check-up had revealed a potentially life threatening series of small blood clots were developing in her lower leg. The scare had brought home to him the fact that despite everything she was still his mother, Caid recognised grimly. The clots had been medically dispersed with drugs, but his mother had been given strict instructions that she was on no account to fly until her doctor was sure she was clear of any threat of the clots returning.

When she saw that he was watching her she told him emotionally, 'You say that you've forgiven me for…for your childhood, Caid, but sometimes, I wonder…I feel…' When she stopped and bit her lip, looking away from him, Caid suppressed a small sigh.

'What are you trying to say?' he asked her cynically. 'That you want me to prove I've forgiven you once more by going to Cheltenham?'

'Oh, Caid, it would mean so much to me if you would,' she breathed.

'I don't—' Caid began, but immediately she interrupted.

'Please, Caid,' she begged urgently. 'There isn't anyone else I can trust. Not when I suspect that the root cause of the problem over there is the fact that your uncle Donny has appointed his own stepson as chief executive of the store,' she told him darkly. 'I mean, what right does Donny have to make that kind of decision? Just because he's the eldest that doesn't mean he can overrule everyone else. And as for that dreadful stepson of his... Jerry knows nothing whatsoever about the specialised nature of our business—'

'I thought he was running a chain of supermarkets—' Caid interrupted.

The constant and relentless internecine war of attrition waged between his mother and her male siblings was a familiar ongoing saga, and one he normally paid scant attention to.

'Yes, he was. But honestly, Caid—supermarkets! There just isn't any comparison between them and stores like ours. Of course, Donny has done it to appease that appalling new wife of his... Why on earth he marries them, I don't know. She's his fifth. And as for Jerry... There's no way he would have ever got his appointment past the board if I hadn't been in hospital! There's nothing Donny would like better than to get me completely off the board, but he'll never be able to do that...'

'Mother, aren't you letting your imagination rather

run away with you?' Caid intervened. 'After all, it is as much in Uncle Donny's interest as it is in yours to have the business thrive. And if Jerry is as bad as you are implying—'

'As bad! Caid, he's worse, believe me. And as for Donny! Well, certainly you'd think with four ex-wives to support he'd be going down on his knees to thank me for everything that I've done for the stores. But all he wants is to score off me. He's always been like that…right from when I was born…they all were. You can't imagine how I used to long to have a sister instead of five brothers… You'd think after all I learned about the male sex from them I'd have had more sense than to get married myself. You were lucky to be an only child, Caid—'

She stopped abruptly when she saw his expression. 'Caid, please,' she begged him, returning to her request. 'We can't afford to have this happen. We desperately need Jaz's skill. Do you know that her window displays for the Christmas season are so innovative that people go to the store just to see them? She has a talent that is really unique, Caid. When I think about how lucky we are to have her… We mustn't lose her. I've got such plans for her…'

'Mother—' Caid began resolutely.

'Caid, don't turn me down.'

Grimly he watched as his mother's eyes filled with tears. He had never seen her cry…never.

'This means so much to me…'

'You don't have to tell me that!' Caid responded dryly, and yet he knew that despite his own feelings he would give in. After all, as his mother had just pointed out, he couldn't afford to see the value of his trust fund stock in the business go down—not now, when he had so much tied up in his ranch. And that, of course, was the only reason he was going, he reminded himself firmly.

'Jaz, I'd like to have a word with you, please.'

Jaz's heart sank as she saw the store's new chief executive bearing down on her. Since returning from New Orleans things had been far from easy for her. She knew that she had been fully justified in everything she'd said to Caid, and that there was no way there could have been a relationship between them, but that still didn't stop her missing what they had shared, or dreaming about him, or waking up with her face wet with tears because she ached for him so much. The last thing she had needed to compound her misery had been the unwanted interference in her work of someone like Jerry Brockmann.

After meeting Caid's mother, and listening to her enthuse about the Cheltenham store and her objectives for it, she had never expected that they would be saddled with a chief executive who seemed to epitomise the exact opposite of what Jaz believed the store was all about. Already the changes he had insisted on making were beginning to affect not just the staff, but their customers as well.

Jaz had lost count of the number of long-standing customers who had commented unfavourably about the fact that the store was no longer perfumed with the specially made room fragrance she herself had chosen as part of the store's exclusive signature.

'What the hell is this stuff made of?' Jerry had complained, as he'd chaired the first departmental heads meeting after his arrival. He'd thrust the bill from the manufacturers beneath Jaz's nose. 'Gold dust? It sure costs enough. Why the hell do we have to scent the damn place anyway? Are the drains bad or something?'

'It creates the right kind of ambience. It's what our customers expect and it encourages them to buy designer fragrances for their own home,' Jaz had replied quietly, trying to ignore his rudeness.

It had been soon after that, and before Jerry had chaired his next meeting, that the chief buyer for their exclusive Designer Fashion Room had announced that she intended to leave.

'He says that he plans to cut my budget by half!' she fumed furiously to Jaz. 'Can you believe that? After what you said about the New Orleans store and its management I'd been putting out feelers to a couple of new up-and-coming designers to see if I could tempt them to let us stock their stuff—and now this! If I stay here now I'm going to totally lose my credibility.'

Jaz felt acutely guilty as she listened to her, and tried to smooth things over, but Lucinda refused to be appeased. She had already handed in her notice she informed Jaz angrily.

Even worse was Jaz's discovery that her closest friend on the staff was also planning to leave.

'But, Kyra, you've always said how much you loved working here,' Jaz protested.

'I *did*,' Krya emphasised. 'But not any more, Jaz. Jerry called me in to his office the other day to inform me that he thinks we should go more downmarket with our bed and bath linens. He said that we were catering for too small a market.'

'Didn't you explain to him that the mass market is so well covered by the multiples that we couldn't possibly compete with them, that it's because we supply only the best that we've got our Royal Warrant?'

'Of course I did,' Kyra had responded indignantly. 'But the man's obsessed by mass sales. He just can't seem to see that this isn't what we're all about. Anyway, the upshot of our ''discussion'' was that I completely lost it with him and told him what he could do with his mass market bedding *and* his job!'

'Oh, Kyra,' Jaz sympathised.

'Well, as it turns out I've done myself a favour, because I've got a friend who works at Dubai airport—that represents the real luxury end of the market—and she says there's a job for me there if I want it.'

'I'm going to miss you.' Jaz sighed.

'Well, you could always leave yourself,' Kyra pointed out. 'In fact,' she added, 'I don't know why you don't. It can't be for any lack of offers. Oh, I can understand that whilst John still owned the store you must have felt bound by loyalty to him. But now...'

'Perhaps I *should* think about leaving,' Jaz agreed huskily. 'But not yet. Not until—'

'After the Christmas windows?' Kyra supplied ruefully, shaking her head.

Jaz's devotion to her Christmas windows was well known throughout the store.

'It wouldn't be fair,' Jaz told her gently.

'You should think more about being fair to yourself than being fair to other people,' Krya chided. 'Which reminds me. I haven't liked to say anything before, but you haven't been your normal happy self since you came back from New Orleans, Jaz. I don't want to pry, but if you need someone to talk to...?'

'There isn't anything to talk about,' Jaz told her firmly.

'Or anyone?' Kyra persisted gently.

Jaz couldn't help it; she felt the tears stinging her eyes, the emotion blocking her throat, but she managed to deny it to Kyra.

And it was true—in a way. After all, what was the point in talking about Caid?

'Excuse me if I'm coming between you and your private thoughts, Jaz,' she heard Jerry saying sarcastically to her. 'But am I right in thinking that you are supposed to be working?'

Pink-cheeked, Jaz apologised.

'I've been going through John's files and I can't seem to find any budget forecasts for your department.'

Jaz forced herself to ignore the hectoring tone of his voice.

'Traditionally, my department doesn't work to a budget—' she began to explain, but before she could continue Jerry interrupted sharply.

'Well, in future it damn well does. And by in future, Jaz, I mean as of now. I want those forecasts on my desk by close of business tomorrow afternoon.'

He had gone before Jaz could either object or explain, leaving her hot-faced and resentful, her only small consolation the knowledge that it wasn't just her who was suffering.

Since Jerry's arrival the whole atmosphere of the store had changed—and in Jaz's opinion not for the better!

'Jaz, I thought you said the American stores were wonderful, very much on our wavelength. How can they be when Jerry's so obviously trying to turn the store into some kind of dreadful pile-it-high-sell-it-cheap place?' one of the department heads had complained.

'I don't understand what's happening any more than you do,' Jaz had been forced to admit.

'Can't you speak to John?' another of the buyers had urged her.

Jaz had shaken her head. 'No. He isn't very well…his angina is getting worse.'

So much worse, in fact, that on his doctor's advice John had had to move out of the pretty three-storey townhouse adjacent to the store, where he had lived virtually all his life.

For security reasons the Dubois family had insisted on buying the house, along with the store, but John had been granted a long lease on it which allowed him to rent it from them at a peppercorn rental. Jaz knew how upset he had been when his doctor had told him that the house's steep stairs were not suitable for a person with his heart condition.

Luckily he also owned a ground-floor apartment in a renovated Victorian mansion several miles away from her parents, and he was now living there under the watchful eye of his housekeeper.

To Jaz's delight, John had offered her the use of the townhouse in his absence, knowing that Jaz was in between properties herself, having sold the flat she had previously owned and not as yet being able to find somewhere she wanted to buy.

'Are you sure the Dubois family won't mind?' she'd asked John uncertainly when he'd made her his generous offer.

'Why should they?' he had demanded. 'And besides, even though it's not strictly mine any longer, I would feel much happier knowing that the house is occupied by someone I know and trust, Jaz.'

Her new home certainly couldn't be more convenient for her work, Jaz acknowledged; even if right now that work was becoming less and less appealing. But there was no way she could allow herself to leave. Not until after Christmas!

She had started planning this year's windows right after last Christmas, and had come back from New Orleans fired up on a mixture of heartbreak and pride that had made her promise herself that this year's windows would be her swansong—proof that she was getting on with her life as well as a way to show every single member of the Dubois family just how damned good she was. And then she would stand up and announce to them that there was nothing on this earth that would persuade her to go on working for a family of which Caid was a member.

At first she hadn't been sure just what angle to go for—she'd already done fantasy and fairytale, and she'd done modern and punk only the previous year. But then it had happened. Her idea to end all ideas. And the miracle of it was that it was so simple, so workable, so timeless and so...so right.

The theme of her windows this Christmas was going to be Modern Womanhood, in all its many guises. And her modern Christmas woman, in defiance of everything that Caid had thrown at her, was going to be the hub of her family and yet her own independent and individual person as well! Each of the store's windows would reflect a different aspect of her role as a modern woman—and each window would be packed with delectable, irresistible gifts appropriate to that role. Right down to the final one, where she would be shepherding her assembled family to view a traditional Nativity play, complete with every emotion-tugging detail apart from a real live donkey.

Everyone thought that the high point of her year were those few short weeks before Christmas, when her windows went on display, but in fact it was actually those weeks she spent working on the ideas and designs that she loved best.

This year she had spent even more of her time plotting and planning, drawing out window plans and then changing them. Because she needed to prove to herself that she had made the right decision…because she needed to find in the success of achieving her own targets and goals something satisfying enough to replace what she had lost?

No. She simply wanted to do a good job, that was all…of course it was!

Now her ideas and her plans were almost all in place; there was only one vital piece of research she still needed to do, and her arrangements for that were all in hand.

Jaz was a stickler for detail, for getting things just right. She needed a real-life role model for her 'modern woman'. A role model who successfully combined all the elements of her fictional creation: a woman who was loved and valued by her partner and yet someone who had her own independent life. She needed a woman who acknowledged and enjoyed fulfilling her own personal goals, but still loved her children and her family above all else. A woman, in short, Jaz had dreamed of being herself—until Caid had destroyed those dreams.

Luckily, though, there was someone she could model her 'modern woman' on.

Jamie, her cousin, was in her thirties, ran her own business, and lived in a wonderful country mansion with her adoring husband and their three children.

In fact, if there was anyone Jaz might have been tempted to tell, about Caid and his unreasonable, appalling attitude, it would have been Jamie. But she had sternly refused to allow herself to be so pathetically self-indulgent.

However, what she had done was invite herself to spend a couple of days with Jamie and her family, so that she could observe them at close quarters and re-affirm to her own satisfaction that she had caught the mood of her 'model family'.

And soon when the whole of the retailing world was gasping over her genius, she would have the satisfaction of knowing she had made the right decision—that she had been true to herself.

CHAPTER FOUR

SUNSHINE in England, in autumn! Caid scowled. Right now there was no way that sunshine fitted in with his mood. It was all very well—and no doubt would earn him Brownie points in the cashbook of life—to have impulsively decided to give up his first-class aircraft seat to a worn-out young mother carrying a fractious baby and travelling economy, but right now he was paying the price for his generosity and suffering the after effects of having spent the night with his six foot tall, broad-chested body stuffed into the confines of a too-small economy class seat.

Not that the blame for his current black mood could be laid totally at the feet of a lost night's sleep...

As he got into his hire car, ready for the drive from the airport to Cheltenham, he tried not to think about the last time he and Jaz had been together...the way they had made love so passionately before the awfulness of their ensuing row drove her out of his life...

It was almost lunchtime when Caid arrived in Cheltenham, and he had been wandering around the store, studying its workforce and its customers, for over an hour before anyone realised who he was. And that had only been when, to his own surprise, he had been tempted to buy a pretty antique fan for his great-aunt, who collected them, and had paid the bill with his credit card.

By chance it was the head of the department who

had served him, and immediately recognised his name, discreetly and excitedly sending one of the juniors to alert Jerry to the fact that Caid was in the store.

Jaz paused on her way up the wonderful Gothic staircase that led from the ground floor of the store to the Designer Fashion Room, trying not to dwell on her latest altercation with Jerry. She concentrated instead on the pleasure and pride that looking down into the heart of the store always gave her.

Caid's mother had told her that she had been so very impressed with the unique layout Jaz had designed for the store that she wanted to adapt it for the American stores.

On the fashion floor clothes were displayed flung over antique brocade-covered sofas and hung on screens, and the cosmetics department, which sold only the most exclusive brands, was housed in a 'boudoir'. The building's original dining room had been redecorated in Georgian red, and was home to a display of the upmarket china, stemware and silver the store sold. It was these details that made the Cheltenham store so unique—a uniqueness that Jerry seemed for some unfathomable reason determined to destroy, Jaz reflected unhappily.

From her vantage point she looked automatically over the ground floor, and then tensed, as she recognised the man walking across it.

Caid. It couldn't be, but it was. Caid was here…in Cheltenham. He had come to tell her that he was sorry, that he realised how wrong he had been.

No firework display on earth could have come anywhere near matching the glorious exultant shock of brilliant explosive joy she was experiencing right now,

Jaz acknowledged as she started to hurry down the stairs towards him, her eyes shining with a mixture of love and emotional tears.

'Caid!' As she cried his name he looked at her, his expression unreadable and controlled. How could she have forgotten just how dangerously and excitingly male he was? Her heart started to do frantic back-flips in reaction to her feelings.

'Caid!' She had almost reached him now! 'Caid,' she repeated. Her fingers brushed the sleeve of his suit jacket as she reached out to him, waiting for his arms to open and gather her close. There would just be time for her to look eagerly at his mouth before it covered hers, and then...

'Caid—hi. Why didn't you come straight up to the office? Donny said you were flying in today.'

Jaz froze as she saw Caid looking past her, through her, to Jerry, who was holding out his hand to greet him. Who was saying that *he* had been expecting him. Who had *known* that Caid was due to arrive. Which meant, she told herself nauseously, that Caid had not come here to see her at all, as she had so stupidly thought.

'What are *you* doing down here? Shouldn't you be working?'

Locked in the painful realisation of the truth, it was several seconds before Jaz realised that Jerry's loud-voiced criticism was directed at her.

Her face flaming, she saw that Caid was now looking directly at her. And it certainly wasn't love she could see in his eyes, she acknowledged miserably.

'Gee, Caid, you just wouldn't believe what I have to put up with from these people. I hate to be critical of your mom, but I have to say that Donny was right to question the buying of this store. I mean, the over-heads! And the administration!' Jerry had started to shake his head. 'They don't have the faintest idea. And as for time-wasting!' He raised his voice pointedly as he flared up at Jaz. 'I thought I told you to go and work on your budgets. Have you done them, or is this your way of telling me that you don't know how to draw up a budget?'

Jaz could feel her face starting to burn with anger as well as pain and embarrassment as she was forced to stand and listen to Jerry insulting her.

'You said that the budgets had to be on your desk tomorrow afternoon,' she reminded him.

For some reason Caid had moved, was now standing closer to her. She could feel the bitter little tug of pain on her heart as she reflected that not so very long ago she would have automatically assumed he had moved closer to her in order to protect her. But after the way he had just looked at her—and then through her—she was under no such illusion! No doubt he was relishing hearing Jerry criticise and humiliate her.

'See what I mean?' Jerry appealed to Caid, totally ignoring Jaz. 'Back home I would have had those budgets by now—no question. These people haven't a clue, Caid. And if you ask me the whole place is over-staffed anyway. If this store is going to turn in a profit one hell of a lot of changes need to be made—starting with getting rid of unproductive staff. Anyway, wel-come on board. It will be good to have some decent down-home support here. Come on up to the office…'

'I'll be with you in a minute,' Jaz heard Caid saying to Jerry.

Jerry frowned as his mobile phone started to ring. 'It's Donny,' he told Caid.

'That's fine. You come on up to the office when you're ready.'

Caid waited until Jerry was out of earshot before turning back to Jaz, but the moment he did so she wheeled round on her heel and started to walk away from him.

'Just a minute!' he cautioned her, automatically reaching out to grab her arm and stop her leaving.

She was so fine-boned that his fingers closed easily around her arm.

Eyes glittering with pride and anger, she turned on him, demanding furiously, 'Let go of me at once.'

'Not yet,' Caid refused. 'Is Jerry always like that?' he asked frowning.

'In general, do you mean, or just with me?' Jaz challenged him.

'Does it make any difference?' Caid shot back.

'I don't know—you tell me.' Jaz gave an angry little shrug. 'And whilst you're about it perhaps you can tell me why you want to know! Is it out of concern for the morale of the staff? Or perhaps because it would give you some kind of pleasure to know that it was just directed at me? After all, we both know that it would give you a great deal of satisfaction to see me being punished, don't we? A man like you could never tolerate knowing that a woman would prefer to be on her own and have her career rather than live in the middle of nowhere as your possession.'

Jaz had no idea why she was behaving like this, other than a hazy recognition that it had something to do with her reaction to seeing him here in the store— that coupled with the knowledge that she had been about to make a complete and total fool of herself before she'd realised he had not come here to see her.

But, whatever the reason for her verbal attack on him, she couldn't afford to back down now—and what was more she had no intention of doing so!

'Or is your concern on another level altogether? Motivated by a fear that the Dubois Corporation could be sued for condoning the harassment of its employees?' she continued.

'Now, look here—'

As he inhaled savagely above her, Jaz felt Caid jerk on her arm, drawing her closer to his body. Frantic to break free—not because she was afraid of him, but because she was afraid of herself and what the proximity between them might do to her—Jaz reached out with her free hand and clawed the exposed wrist of the hand gripping her arm.

'Why, you little she-cat,' Caid breathed in disbelief as they both stared at the red weals her nails had left against his skin.

Against his will he could feel himself reacting to her—and to her anger. Earlier, listening to Jerry verbally abusing her, it had been all he could do to stop himself from grabbing the other man by his jacket lapels and demanding that he leave Jaz alone. But now...

Now it was Jaz he felt like grabbing and holding—until he silenced her venom with his mouth.

Instinctively Jaz jerked back from him. He mustn't touch her, mustn't breach her defences. But the heat she could see shimmering in his eyes wasn't caused by desire, she recognised; it was caused by fury.

'Let go of me, Caid.' she demanded in a low voice. 'People are staring. And besides, I've got work to do...remember?'

As he turned his head to glance round Jaz seized

her moment and took advantage of his slackened grip on her arm to pull away from him.

Grim-lipped, Caid watched as she made her escape. His eyes felt gritty and sore, but the adrenalin was pumping round his veins.

For a minute, when he had first seen her, his urge…his need to go to her and claim her, to beg her to give him—them—a second chance, had been fiercely intense! In fact if Jerry hadn't been there he doubted he would have been able to stop himself from taking hold of her! Why couldn't she see that they were made to be together? Why couldn't she realise that he was right? If she had loved him enough she would have done, he reminded himself bitterly. And there was no way he intended to allow himself to give a single damn about a woman who didn't love him one hundred per cent…no, one hundred and fifty per cent. Because that sure as hell was the way he had been prepared to love her!

It was almost an hour since she'd walked away from Caid, but she still hadn't stopped starting up nervously every time she heard footsteps in the corridor outside her workroom.

The budgets she had come here expressly to work on had not progressed beyond a few mere notes. Right now it was a battle to think of something as mundane as what she was going to have for her supper this evening, never mind anything more demanding. Right now her every single thought was occupied by one Caid Dubois!

Not that he deserved or merited the exclusive attention of her thoughts any more than he deserved her love. Anyway, what love? she challenged herself, her body stiffening. She didn't love Caid. She was over him. How could she not after the way he had behaved towards her? After he had shown her how overbearing and selfish he was—after he had made it plain to her how unimportant he considered *her* dreams and ambitions to be.

No way could she ever ever love a man like that.

No, she told herself firmly, what she was feeling now was anger against herself because of the stupid way she had reacted when she'd first seen him. Thank goodness she'd come to her senses and had been able to show him exactly how she did feel about him!

How could she possibly have thought he'd come to see her when it was so obvious that he had not? But what *was* he doing here?

Had Jerry been sent here to do a clean sweep of the store's original personnel in such a way as to avoid any claims against the Dubois Corporation? Surely that was a far-fetched, indeed almost paranoid suggestion?

Jerry had made it very clear Caid was here to back him up. And, given Caid's reaction towards her, it seemed obvious to Jaz that he would enjoy making life as difficult and unpleasant for her as he could!

Well, she certainly wasn't going to give way…to allow herself to be pushed out of a job she loved. When she left the store—*if* she left it—it would be on her own terms and in her own time. Not because she was running scared from anyone, and most especially not from Caid Dubois.

She looked at her watch. Today was supposed to be her half-day, but it was almost halfway through the afternoon now.

At times of crisis in her life she had always sought

and found solace and escape in her work. So stuffing the pieces of paper on her desk into a drawer, she got up. She would go next door, to the privacy of her temporary home, and work there—safely away from Caid and any temptation…

Temptation? What temptation? No way was she in danger of any kind of temptation, she assured herself firmly. Unless it was the temptation to tell Caid Dubois just how lucky she considered herself to be in having found out what an unbearable, unappealing, stubborn, selfish, sexy, impossible and arrogant specimen of the male sex he was!

Jaz grimaced angrily to herself. Not even a long soak in the bath, whilst listening to the soothing sound of her special relaxation tape had managed to calm the turbulent effect on her senses of seeing Caid.

Pulling on her bathrobe, she went into the spare bedroom.

She hoped that working would keep Caid out of her head and her thoughts. And out of her heart?

Angrily she pushed the taunting little question away. He wasn't in her heart. She had locked him out of it and she intended to keep him locked out!

She had work to do, she reminded herself, and working was very definitely a far healthier and more constructive thing to do than brooding on what had happened at the store.

Jaz opened the portfolio containing the sketches she'd made for the Christmas window displays.

The first window would depict the woman in her home as she studied her Christmas present list. She would be surrounded by gifts she had heaped up on the floor, along with wrapping paper and ribbons.

After all, what better way to display the range of gift wrappings available in the store? On a small table in prominent view would be a photograph of her family, so that those looking into the window could see whom she had bought the gifts for.

Jaz smiled as she studied her drawings. So far so good. As yet she had merely outlined where the pile of gifts was to go—the textbooks, the laptop computer and the student pass, the golfing equipment and a cookbook of quick meals for one—but these gifts were not traditional. No, in her desire to show the complexities of this 'modern family' and its life Jaz had chosen to be slightly controversial. The student gifts were for the woman's mother-in-law, who had always secretly yearned to finish her education, and the cookbook was for her father-in-law—a hint that with his wife back studying he would need to learn to be more self-sufficient. The golf paraphernalia was destined not for the woman's husband, or her father, but for the second of her sons, whose dreams were of becoming a world-class golf pro.

To facilitate the onlookers' ability to recognise all this, Jaz had come up with the idea of depicting in other windows a member of her 'family' with two thought bubbles—one showing what he or she expected traditionally to receive and the other showing what they really longed for—as they gazed at their private dream surroundings, designed to echo their true desires.

It was a complex and ambitious scheme, but Jaz knew it was going to work. She knew too that it would be thought-provoking and cause interest, which would be good for the store and—she hoped—good for their customers, who would hopefully be tempted to be more adventurous in their choice of gifts!

In the final window she was giving in to sentimentality, she knew, in having her family viewing the traditional Nativity scene. But she hoped that this would show their customers that her modern woman, depicted in each window trying to balance her career, family life and home responsibilities, was still in touch with the realities of life. And that was why in her Nativity scene Jaz intended to highlight the presence of the infant Jesus's mother.

It was only where the woman's gifts *from* her family were concerned that she was having a problem. So far she had been toying with the idea of having the 'family' present her with beautiful antique and modern boxes, each of which would contain that member's feelings—'joy', 'love', 'happiness'—but ruefully she admitted to herself that she still needed to work on this concept.

Discarded drawings and notes covered the spare bedroom's bed, and in one corner of the room was a small mock-up of her first window. Only the staff who worked directly with her were allowed to know the content of the windows before they were opened to public view, and that was another reason why Jaz had been so pleased to be invited to make use of John's house, so conveniently situated right next to the store…

Still fuming after his argument with Jaz, Caid left the store and headed for his temporary home, determined to rest and *not* think about her.

At such short notice it had proved impossible for him to find suitable accommodation in Cheltenham, but when he had pointed this out to his mother she had accused him of looking for excuses to back out of going.

'You can stay with John—like I would have done,' she had told him firmly.

'He told me when he was over here that his house has two large bedrooms, each with its own bathroom, and that he'd be delighted to have any of us stay whenever we choose. All we have to do is ring and let him know.'

'Okay.' Caid had capitulated, knowing when he was beaten.

He had only been in the store a couple of hours, but it was already obvious to him that Jerry was causing a good deal of unrest and unhappiness amongst the staff. And as for the way he had spoken to Jaz...

Caid frowned at he mounted the three stone steps that led to the front door of John's house. Why couldn't he stop thinking about Jaz? She was clearly not what he wanted. Jaz was a committed career woman, in no need of his championship or support.

Career women. He reached for the door-knocker. Why did his life have to be plagued by them?

Jaz made a small exasperated sound as she heard someone knocking on the front door. She wasn't expecting anyone and she was hardly dressed for visitors.

Ignoring the knocking, she concentrated on what she was doing.

Outside in the street, Caid grimaced in irritation, and then reminded himself that John was an elderly man with a heart condition—who surely should not, he recognised frowningly, be living in a three-storey building!

He reached for the knocker again, and this time banged it just a little bit louder and longer.

Jaz gave a small feline growl of resentment as she heard the door-knocker a second time. The visitor—whoever he or she was—plainly wasn't going to go away.

Getting to her feet, she opened the bedroom door and headed for the stairs.

Caid was just beginning to question whether his mother might have given John the wrong date for his arrival, when the house door was suddenly pulled open.

Only it wasn't John who was standing in the hallway glaring belligerently at him; it was Jaz.

'You!'

'You!'

CHAPTER FIVE

CAID was the first to recover and break the tense atmosphere of spiky silence. 'I'd like to see John,' he announced in a clipped voice.

'John?' Jaz let her breath escape in a small, secret, leaky sigh of relief. For a moment she'd thought that Caid had actually come to the house to continue the argument they'd been having in the store.

'Yes, John,' Caid agreed sardonically. 'He lives here—remember? And so for the next few weeks shall I be. Now, if you would kindly tell him that I'm here?'

'What? No!' Jaz started to shake her head in fierce denial. 'No!' she repeated. 'You can't stay here.'

Caid had had enough. He told himself it was jet lag that was making him feel the way he was feeling right now, and nothing at all to do with Jaz. 'Give me one good reason why not.' he demanded ominously.

Jaz reminded herself that it was anger that was making her shake inside, and absolutely nothing else. 'Because *I* am living here,' she told him. 'John invited me to,' she hurried on as she saw the way Caid's eyes were narrowing as he looked at her. 'When his angina got worse he moved away—and he didn't say anything to me about *you* staying here,' she informed him defiantly.

'Well, he sure as hell didn't mention anything to me about *your* presence,' Caid retaliated grittily.

'No—you can't come in,' Jaz protested angrily as Caid picked up his bag and shouldered open the front door, making his way inside before turning round in the confines of the long narrow hallway and closing it firmly.

'No?' he challenged Jaz in a deliberately exaggerated drawl. 'So who's gonna make me leave, honey? You?'

'Don't you dare call me that,' Jaz protested in a suffocating voice.

'Why not?' Caid taunted her. 'I don't remember hearing you complain before. Far from it. In fact, as I remember, you seemed to kinda like it—leastways that was the impression you gave me!' he told her with a deliberately insolent look that made Jaz burn with fury.

'If there's one thing I loathe and detest more than a man who believes that a woman should be subordinate to him, it's a man who behaves like a boorish, insensitive male brute, so desperate to prove just how wonderful he is that he tries to boast about…about imaginary sexual conquests! All it does is prove how *un*sexy he is!' Jaz burst out.

'Imaginary? Oh, no.' Caid told her softly. 'There's no way what happened between us—the way you gave yourself to me—was "imaginary". And as for me being unsexy…you know, honey, some men…might just be ungallant enough to think that that's a kinda come-on…an encouragement…a challenge thrown at them so that they feel they have to prove their sexuality.'

'How dare you say that?' Jaz breathed. 'No way would I give any man—and most especially you—any kind of come-on. I don't want anything from you, Caid, other than to have nothing more to do with you. You can't stay here!'

Was it really possible than he had grown taller,

broader, more…more of everything male than she remembered?

'I don't have any option,' Caid told her shortly. 'There isn't anywhere else.'

Jaz frowned. She knew how busy the town was at certain times of the year. But there was no way she was going to allow Caid to force her into giving up the house to him—at least not until she had spoken with John.

'Why don't you go and share with Jerry?' she suggested nastily. 'I've heard that he's taken a whole suite at the Grand Hotel—'

'Room with Jerry? I'd as soon move in with a polecat,' Caid drawled and then stopped and subjected her to a look that made Jaz's whole body burn from the top of her head right down to the toes she was currently curling into the carpet.

'Is it a British custom for a woman to answer the door in her bathrobe? Funny… Back home we also consider that to be kind of giving a man a come-on…'

'I wasn't expecting anyone to call,' Jaz defended herself, adding hotly, 'And I wouldn't have answered the door if—'

'If you had known it was me?' Caid supplied for her. 'And yet somehow or other I got the impression a little earlier on today that you were all too ready to give me a warm welcome.'

Jaz gasped in furious indignation.

So he *had* noticed!

Well, now it was time he was made to notice something else.

'That was a mistake,' she told him haughtily. 'I thought…'

'You thought what?' Caid encouraged her.

'I thought you'd come to your senses and wanted to apologise to me,' Jaz told him, revealing her pretty teeth in a nasty smile.

'Me, apologise to you?' Dark flags of angry male pride burned against Caid's taut cheekbones. 'Now, let's get one thing straight,' he told her savagely, 'there's only one reason I'm here and it has nothing to do with apologising to anyone for anything...'

'I see. So why exactly are you here?' Jaz challenged him.

Caid looked briefly away, guarding his expression from her. He could scarcely tell her right now what his mother wanted him to do. The mood she was in she was more than likely to hand in her notice right here and now...

'I can't say,' he told her coolly. 'It's family business...'

Jaz's heart jumped. So she had been right!

Feigning a casual attitude she was far from feeling, she shrugged and started to turn away from him, saying, 'There's no need to be secretive, Caid. I've already worked out for myself why you're here—and I might as well tell you right now that you're wasting your time! We've got laws about that kind of thing in this country!' she threw at him wildly. She wasn't sure if what she was saying was strictly true, but she was determined to show him that she was not going to be intimidated.

Grimly Caid listened to her. After hearing the way Jerry had spoken to her he couldn't pretend to be surprised that she was determined to leave, but he knew his mother. She would expect him to do far more than simply passively accept Jaz's decision without making any attempt to persuade her to change her mind.

He just never learned, did he? Caid reflected in self-disgust. From the moment he'd been born his mother had relentlessly turned his life upside down. If he'd listened to his own instincts he would never have agreed to come to Cheltenham in the first place. But now that he was here there was no way he was going to give up a comfortable bed on Jaz's say-so.

'Where are you going?' Jaz demanded sharply as Caid picked up his bag and headed for the stairs.

'To bed,' he drawled promptly.

'Oh, no, you aren't. Not here!' Jaz denied.

One foot on the first stair, Caid turned round, breathing in rather pointedly as he told her with exquisitely polite steeliness, 'I thought I'd already made myself plain on this one, Jaz. Where you choose to sleep is your affair, and likewise where I choose to sleep is mine. Right now I choose to sleep here. If you don't like that, then don't let me stop you finding yourself a bed somewhere else.'

Somewhere else! Jaz glared at him.

'John offered this house to me, and I am not moving out unless he asks me to,' Jaz told him, incensed.

How dared Caid expect her to give up the house for him? Let *him* find somewhere else to stay.

Caid put down his case, folded his arms across his chest and looked at her. 'I have just flown across the Atlantic, and I am in no mood for an argument. I need a bed and eight hours' sleep, and I fully intend to have both.'

'Maybe you do, but you are not going to have them in this house,' Jaz told him furiously.

'Oh, yes, I am!' Caid corrected her flatly. 'In this house and right now.'

'There's no way I am moving out of here until John

tells me to,' Jaz repeated. Her colour was high and so was her temper. He was trying to bully her. Well, he wasn't going to. No way. And besides, she had no-where else she could go at such short notice, other than her parents' home.

'My God, but you like to live dangerously, don't you?' Caid grated savagely. 'Don't push me too hard, Jaz. Because if you do you might get far more than you bargained for. Right now it wouldn't take very much for me to—'

'To what?' Jaz challenged him recklessly. 'To treat me the way you did in New Orleans?' Bitterly she started to shake her head. 'No way. No—'

'I don't seem to remember you doing any objecting at the time,' Caid interrupted her grimly. She might be claiming that she didn't want him now, but she hadn't faked her sexual response to him when they had been lovers. And if she continued to push him hard enough, he might be sorely tempted to prove that to her.

'Why don't you take a walk into the town?' Jaz threw at him. 'You might find it's a good way of eas-ing your temper as well as finding yourself a hotel room.'

That was it! Caid had had enough. More than enough!

Advancing on her, he told Jaz through gritted teeth, 'Don't push your luck. Because right now the only way I'd like to ease my temper is by taking hold of you and—'

Caid knew how dangerously volatile the situation had become. He was also aware just how much of his anger was being fuelled by emotions he should not be feeling. Jaz was deliberately trying to incite him.

Things were going too far. Jaz knew that, and suddenly she felt very vulnerable. The sex between them had been so potent, so overpowering. Would she really be strong enough to resist him if he should...?

'You wouldn't dare,' Jaz breathed.

Somewhere at the back of her mind a cautionary little voice was warning her that the mood had shifted from anger to excitement and arousal. Why couldn't she control her feelings around Caid?

'*No?*'

The very softness of his voice was enough to send alarm scudding through her. He had closed the distance between them, was already reaching for her, imprisoning her with arms that bound her to him whilst his mouth plundered hers with a furious refusal to be denied.

A hot, raw agony of longing seethed through her, enveloping her in mind-blowing waves of aching need. She was so hungry for him, for his touch, his mouth, for the feel of his body. With a little whimper Jaz reached out to touch him—and then stopped, her body freezing in self-disgust and horror.

'No!'

Her choked denial pulled Caid up short and reminded him of just what the situation between them was. But he couldn't shake the red-hot image branded into his mind of the two of them together, her naked body held fast against his, whilst he punished her for each inflammable word that she'd spoken. For refusing to see things his way, refusing to be the woman he needed and wanted her to be.

'You're right, Jaz. You can't be the woman I want. The woman I thought you were.'

The bitterness in Caid's voice shocked Jaz. Somehow it was far more painful for her to hear than his anger. The feeling of desolation and loss that suddenly rushed over her from out of nowhere, swamping her with its intensity, frightened her. Instinctively she struggled against it. There was no way she was going to allow herself to be dragged back into the black hole of despair and heartache she had suffered on her return from New Orleans. The very thought made her shake from head to foot with fear. She now realised she'd never really admitted just how deep the pain had been.

Caid was the first man she had truly loved, trusted and believed in. She'd committed herself to him heart and soul. Every now and again, in her darkest moments, the thought tormented her that he would be the only man she would feel all those things for. But Jaz prided herself on her own inner strength. She had needed that strength when she was growing up, and now she needed it again.

Love at first sight, a meeting of hearts, souls and minds, a sharing of goals in a love that would last a lifetime. That was what she had believed she had found with Caid. But she had been so very, very wrong.

No matter how fragile and appealing Jaz might look in her bathrobe, with her hair casually tied back and her face flushed and free of make-up, he knew what she really was, Caid told himself angrily. A more stubborn, wrong-thinking, argumentative, independently sassy woman he had yet to meet. Why the hell had nature decided to give her such a tempting, sensual body? The kind of body that made him ache in a hundred different ways... She had the tiniest waist, wonderfully curving hips, and long, long slim legs. And as for her breasts... Couldn't she have also been given a personality he would have found equally irresistible, equally in tune with his?

Giving in just wasn't something that existed in Caid's emotional vocabulary—after all, his mother had never given in to his pleas for her to stay with him, had she? Compromise wasn't a word he normally recognised either, but right now...

Caid closed his eyes.

The thoughts he was having at this moment were as unique to him as they were dangerous.

Instinctively he fought to eject them, in the same way he had fought all his life to maintain his hard-won emotional independence.

If there was anywhere else at all where he could spend the night he knew he would be high-tailing it out of the house right now. Just being weak enough to admit to the thoughts he was having made him furiously angry with Jaz, for being the cause of them, and even more frustrated with himself. But there wasn't anywhere else. He already knew that.

Why on earth didn't she simply walk past him and leave? Jaz asked herself miserably.

All right, so it would take her a couple of hours to drive to her parents' farm...and a couple of hours to drive back again for work every day, she reminded herself grimly. But at least at home with her parents she would be safe...

Safe from what? she challenged herself. Safe from her own thoughts? Mentally she derided herself. What was she going to do? Leave them behind her here in the house?

Anyway why should she give in to Caid? Why

should she be bullied by him? Uncle John had given *her* the use of the house.

'You can say and do what you like. I'm not leaving,' she told Caid flatly.

'Don't tempt me,' Caid growled.

Jaz flashed him a bitter look, but before she could say anything to her horror she felt her eyes suddenly began to sting with tears.

From what felt like another lifetime she could hear the echo of Caid's voice, whispering throatily to her, 'You tempt and torment me in a thousand ways, each of them uniquely pleasurable, each of them uniquely you.'

That had been the first night they had met…the first time he had kissed her…

'I'm going down to my car now, to get the rest of my stuff,' Caid warned her grimly. 'And when I come back…'

'You'll do what?' Jaz challenged him, grateful for the reviving surge of fury that had obliterated her earlier misery. 'Throw me out bodily? If you dare to lay so much as one finger on me—'

She stopped as she saw the way he was looking at her.

'Funny how things change,' he drawled, but Jaz could see the hot anger banked down in his eyes and wasn't deceived by the slow softness of his voice. 'Not so very long ago you were begging me to lay one hell of a lot more than a finger on you, honey, and when I did I don't recall you objecting—unless it was to tell me that you wanted even more.'

His smug, sure male confidence made Jaz want to physically tear it from him and jump up and down on it until it was as damaged and battered as her own pride.

If she hadn't been convinced before of just how much better off she was without him she should be now, and she told herself grimly. Only the most callous and uncaring of men could say something like that.

'Nothing to say?' he mocked her.

Fiercely Jaz blinked away the threatening tears. To cry now, in front of him, would be her final humiliation. But she couldn't bear the way he was destroying the bittersweet memories which only now she was being forced to acknowledge she had foolishly clung on to.

'If you think you can bully me into giving in and doing what you want, Caid, you're wrong,' she told him quietly, before turning her back on him and heading towards the master bedroom.

Furiously Caid watched her. She had a way of getting under his skin and making him itch that no medical team in the world could possibly find a cure for.

She had meant what she said to Caid about not being bullied into leaving, Jaz decided as she heard the front door close behind him. No matter how much pain it might cause her to stay here, under the same roof as him. From a practical point of view the house had two bedrooms, after all.

Deep down inside Jaz knew that her decision, her obstinacy and her pride, had nothing whatsoever to do with the house at all, but one hell of a lot to do with that idiotic way she had reacted when she had first seen him in the store earlier.

How could she have been stupid enough to think he

had come to see her? To have wanted him to have come to see her!

How could she possibly love a man who was just…just a…a hatchet man, who had both supported and enjoyed the floor show Jerry had given as he'd tried to manoeuvre her into leaving?

He had shown her just how little she meant to him. Now he was going to be shown that he meant nothing whatsoever to her! Less than nothing! Less than less than nothing!

Furiously, she pulled open the doors of the wardrobe she was using and started to remove her clothes, knowing that it would be far easier to transfer them to the other bedroom, which she was using as a workroom, than to move and re-set up her work. Both bedrooms were the same size. It was simply that the spare bedroom had a good strong northern light which was much better for her work.

There was one thing that did concern her, though, and that was the fact that Uncle John had made no mention of his invitation to Caid to her. She knew how concerned her parents had been earlier in the year, when the stress of the sale of the business had caused John to become a little bit forgetful on occasions, and the last thing Jaz wanted to do was to upset her godfather. But her forehead started to pucker into an anxious little frown.

Silently Jaz looked at her bedside clock. Four o'clock in the morning! She had been awake since one, and prior to that she had hardly slept, her mind too full of painful, angry thoughts to allow her to relax.

Her heart was thumping in heavy anxious thuds

whilst her head seethed with frantic, desperate thoughts.

No way was she going to be forced to leave the job she loved and had put so much into. Her windows for this year were going to be her best ever! But she knew that there was equally no way she could do her best work, give of her best, for a concern that did not value or appreciate her.

It hurt to recognise that the praise Caid's mother had given her, the interest she had shown in her, had not been genuine. Perhaps she just wasn't up to the world of big business, she acknowledged unhappily.

She turned over onto her side and tried to summon sleep, but it was totally impossible.

Perhaps if she got up and made herself a soothing hot drink that would help.

Quietly Jaz made her way to the kitchen and switched on the kettle.

In New Orleans Caid had teased her about how deeply she slept, tucked up against his side, burrowing into his warmth and staying there until he kissed her awake in the morning.

He had laughed too, at her shyness the first morning he had shared a shower with her, whispering that he couldn't believe she was being so prim when the previous night she had so passionately abandoned herself to him. But then, when she had reluctantly explained that he was the first man she had shared so much intimacy with, and that the total sum of her previous experience had been nothing more than a fumbled rite of passage with an equally virginal fellow student, something she had felt she had to do rather than something she'd overwhelmingly wanted to do, his laughter had died. And the tenderness with which he had treated her had brought emotional tears to her eyes.

And now tears were suddenly stinging her eyes again, at the memory of that tenderness.

Her hands trembling, Jaz reached for the cup of herbal tea she had made for herself, and then gasped in shock as it slid through her shaking fingers, spilling hot tea on her bare skin before crashing to the floor and breaking.

Almost boiling, the tea had been hot enough to cause serious burns, and the shock of her pain made her cry out sharply.

Caid heard Jaz cry out as he lay motionless and wide awake in his bed.

By rights he ought to have been asleep, and he had determinedly been putting the fact that he was not down to jet lag rather than admit that it could in any possible way be because of Jaz. But the minute he heard her cry he was out of bed and on his feet, reaching for his robe and pulling it on.

Two minutes later Jaz was shakily trying to insist to him that she was perfectly all right as he knelt at her feet, commanding her tersely not to move as he picked up the broken shards of crockery.

'Look, I can do that myself,' Jaz protested.

She wished he would not kneel so close to her, nor block her exit from the kitchen with his male bulk. His hair was shiny and tousled, and for some reason as she looked down at the top of his head she ached to reach out and stroke her fingers through it.

His body had that clean soap smell she still remembered, and his bare feet were so much larger than her own, his skin so much browner... As he stood up to dispose of the broken cup she gave an involuntary shiver, which he immediately registered and reacted to with a frown.

'Please go back to bed,' Jaz begged him stiffly. 'I can clean up the rest myself.'

Her fingers were covering her arm where the burn was beginning to throb painfully.

'It's four o'clock in the morning.' Caid told her, ignoring her to reach for a cloth to mop up the spilled tea. 'Just what exactly were you doing making tea?'

'Perhaps I happen to like a cup of tea at four in the morning,' Jaz told him sharply. 'Not that it's any business of yours!'

'Not unless you spill it all over the place and wake me up,' Caid agreed dryly, conveniently ignoring the fact that he had been very far from asleep.

'I'm sorry if I disturbed you,' Jaz apologised insincerely.

'You don't disturb me, Jaz!' Caid told her silkily. 'Not any more. But something obviously disturbs *you*, if you need to be making yourself cups of tea in the early hours. The Jaz I remember slept like— Something bothering you?' he taunted unkindly, as Jaz suddenly tried to push past him, and his hand reached for her arm to stop her.

The moment his fingers closed over her burned skin Jaz let out a whimper of pain, and her face paled so quickly that Caid's frown deepened.

Removing his hand, but still blocking her exit from the kitchen, he studied her arm. He could see that her skin had been badly burned and looked very sore, with a blister already starting to form where the hot tea had scalded her.

'That needs some attention,' he told Jaz firmly.

'Yes, I do know,' Jaz agreed angrily. 'It is after all

my arm. And if you will just get out of my way that is exactly what I am going to give it.'

She just hoped that John had something in his bathroom cupboard she could put on the burn. It was now beginning to feel very uncomfortable.

'You can't manage to dress it by yourself,' said Caid. 'You'd better let me deal with it.'

Him? Touch her? No way! Jaz opened her mouth to tell him as much and then closed it again, her objections forgotten as her glance inadvertently dropped to his body. His robe had come open whilst he had been cleaning up the mess, exposing the hair-roughened warmth of his chest.

A dizzying wave of sensation swamped her. It must be the pain of her arm that was making her feel like this, she said to herself, as she tried to drag her gaze from his torso and discovered that she couldn't. She could still remember how wonderful it had felt—he had felt—that first time she had touched his naked body…

Caid's family had taken her and John out for dinner, and John had stayed on at the restaurant to continue talking business whilst she had opted to walk back to their hotel. Caid had offered to escort her, insisting that she ought not to walk through the streets of the French Quarter on her own.

The evening had been hot and sultry. They had walked slowly through the streets, talking to one another. She had known by then just how she felt about him, and, although he had been discreet about it, Caid had shown her by his attentiveness towards her that he shared her desire.

They had come to a quiet shadowy corner and Caid had drawn her to him, telling her thickly, 'If I don't kiss you soon I am going to go crazy.'

And then he had covered her lips with his and kissed her with such urgency and intensity that Jaz had been oblivious to anything and anyone but him. When he had kissed her exposed throat and shoulder she had shuddered in hot response, unable to resist slipping her hand inside the unfastened neck of his shirt. And then somehow one thing had led to another.

Before they had finally broken apart his shirt had been unbuttoned right down to the waist and her breasts had been aching so much for the touch of his hands that when they had finally reached her room, and Caid had pushed her up against the bedroom door the moment he had closed it, she had actually helped him to tug down the top of her dress...

'Jaz—you aren't going to faint on me, are you?'

Abruptly she dragged herself back to the present, fiercely swallowing against the tears of self-pity she could feel filling her eyes.

In the bathroom, Caid dealt quickly and efficiently with her burn—dressing it and then bandaging it in a far more effective way than she could have managed herself, she was forced to acknowledge.

As a rancher he was, of course, very self-sufficient—would be well used to dealing with minor medical crises. She, on the other hand, was not used to dealing with the touch of the man she had thought loved her but who she had discovered did not. And the effect it was having on her was thoroughly unsettling.

Jaz had just got back into bed, and was about to switch off her bedside lamp, when the door opened and Caid stood in the doorway.

Her heart leapt, then skidded to a frantic halt before slamming against her breastbone.

Caid had come to her room. What…?

'I've made you a fresh cup of tea.'

Wordlessly Jaz stared at him, wondering why on earth so prosaic an action should make her want to cry so badly.

Grimly Caid strode through the store. He had barely slept at all the previous night, knowing that Jaz was so close to him, that only a mere wall separated them, and that there was nothing apart from his own will-power to stop him from going to her and—

He was here to work, he reminded himself angrily, not to waste his time thinking about Jaz. He had been so furious with her when she had refused to quit the house, his fury partially driven by shock and partially by jet lag-induced exhaustion. Just seeing her had made him ache to take hold of her, show her just what her stubborn refusal had destroyed. But somehow he had made himself keep his distance from her, had gone down to his car to collect his bags.

He had returned to find Jaz standing in the middle of the bedroom floor, the bed in front of her stacked with clothes and other personal possessions she was in the process of removing from its cupboard and wardrobes.

At first he had thought that she'd given in and she was going to move out, and his heart had slammed against his ribs before doing a very slow and uncom-fortable somersault that in no way could he pretend to himself constituted a victory roll.

The thought that she was leaving had created a good

many complex feelings inside him, but not one of them had come anywhere near approximating triumph!

As he had stood there watching her she had looked antagonistically at him and grabbed a handful of underwear from the drawer she had just pulled open, telling him belligerently, 'I can't stop you from staying here, if you're going to be ungentlemanly enough to insist on doing so, but there is no way I am going to move out, and no way you can make me! Anyway, it just so happens that the house has two bedrooms.'

'And you, being the altruistic human being that you are, are moving your stuff out of this one for me?'

Desperate to ignore the relief seeping like venom through his veins, Caid had made his voice as deliberately cynical as he could.

'Not for you,' Jaz had corrected him immediately. 'But *because* of you. And my work is in the other room.' She had given a small dismissive shrug as she had told him, 'It makes more sense to move my clothes rather than my work.'

As she had spoken she had made her way forward to the door, carrying the huge pile of clothes she had picked up off the bed.

Unable to stop himself, Caid had responded bitterly and unchivalrously. 'Yeah, after all—as I have good cause to know—removing your clothes is something that comes easily and unimportantly to you. You sure enough removed them pretty fast for me.'

Jaz had gasped and gone white, her voice a whispery thin flicker of raw sound as she'd responded, 'Thank you, Caid. You've just confirmed everything I already know about you. How lucky I am to have you out of my life.'

And she had walked past him with her head held

high, for the entire world as though she were the innocent party!

When she had left Caid had glanced down at the floor and seen the delicate lacy garment she had dropped. Bending down, he had picked it up. It was a tiny fragile cream lacy thong he'd last seen adorning Jaz's body. There were women who could wear thongs and women who could not, and when it came to Jaz—well, Jaz's delicious derrière would stop the traffic. Fully clothed!

Following her through the door, Caid had crossed the corridor and pushed open the half-closed door of the other bedroom. When she had seen that he had followed her, her mouth had compressed, her eyes widening and then darkening with anger.

Her eyes really were the most extraordinary colour, Caid acknowledged now, shimmering through a thousand different shades with each of her emotions. When she was aroused they turned the colour of molasses; when she was complete and satisfied they glowed pure gold...

What the hell was he thinking about? he derided himself, dragging his renegade thoughts away from the treacherous quicksands of Jaz's sensuality and his own reaction to it.

'What are you doing in here?' Jaz had demanded sharply, glowering at him.

'You dropped this,' Caid had replied, dangling the tiny scrap of cream lace from his finger.

If he was honest, there was a part of him that had taken a grim sort of pleasure in her reaction. Her skin had flushed the colour of a Colorado sunset in winter. She had given a small, sharp gasp and then reached out to snatch the thong from him.

'Give it to me. It's mine,' she insisted, when Caid had stepped back from her, his a hand closing round the lace.

'Funny how little it takes to turn a man into a fool,' Caid had responded as he'd tossed the lace to her.

Caid had known as he spoke that he was being ungallant, that he was delivering a low blow and descending to the kind of depths he would never normally have stooped to, but just holding that intimate scrap of female apparel, remembering how good things had been between them, how good they still could have been between them if only Jaz would see sense, had filled him with such a burning sense of outrage and anguish that he hadn't been able to stop himself.

Somehow the memory of Jaz in his bedroom, wearing that same lacy nothing, her breasts bare as she leaned over him whilst he lay on the bed watching her, desire and what he had so foolishly believed was love darkening her eyes, had driven him to do it.

He had heard quite plainly the hiss of her indrawn breath, and the sound that accompanied it. Her face had gone paper-white, as though she had been dealt a mortal blow, and he had had to battle against the urge to tell her that he hadn't meant it, that it was only his pain that was driving him to say such things, only the ache of his need for her tormenting his body that was sending him crazy.

Unable to trust himself to stay in her bedroom any longer, he had turned on his heel without waiting for her to make any response and quickly headed back to his own room.

*   *   *

Tiredly Jaz pushed her hair off her face, mentally acknowledging that the monthly heads of department meeting, fraught though it had been, was not the real cause of her low spirits.

When she had refused to give up the house to Caid she had not fully realised what the stress of sharing living accommodation was going to do to her. It was bad enough that she was spending hours when she should have been asleep lying awake, knowing that he was there in the next room to her, but what was even worse was the destruction of her self-respect, the impact of their unwanted physical proximity.

It was barely three days since he had arrived, and every morning she promised herself she would tell him that she did not wish to have her breakfast in the same room as a half-naked man, that if he had to wander around the kitchen wearing nothing other than a towel draped carelessly around his hips, then he should do so when she was not there. And every morning she had found that she just could not bring herself to end the silence between them, or to betray her real feelings with an unwanted stammer or, even worse, a vivid blush.

She had become so on edge that she was starting at every sound, tensing her body with anxiety, and she knew that she was already perilously close to breaking point without the added pressure of the problems she was facing at work.

Jerry had taken an aggressive stance right from the start of the meeting—which, to Jaz's relief, Caid had not attended—humiliating one of their most senior departmental heads by querying his monthly sales figures and then boastfully comparing their turnover to that of the supermarket chain he had run in America.

Then it had been Jaz's turn to be denigrated and criticised.

'These supposed budget figures you've given me,' Jerry began. 'This is what I think of them.'

And then he ripped them up and threw them in his wastepaper bin.

'Trash. Which is what I'm going to say when I report back to my stepfather. Your department is trash, unless you come up with something to prove me wrong and change my mind. Hey we all know you were John's blue-eyed girl—his *god-daughter*,' he emphasised, 'but John isn't here any more.'

His implication that she had been accorded special privileges because of her relationship with John infuriated Jaz, but not as much as his unsubtle suggestion that she just wasn't up to her job.

'My job is to make sure that the store draws in the maximum amount of customers,' she started to say, just as the door opened and Caid walked in.

It was obvious to Jaz from the hard-eyed look Caid gave her that he supported Jerry's antagonistic stance towards her, but then what else had she expected?

'I detest the stores,' he had told her in New Orleans, but obviously he didn't detest them enough to pass up the opportunity to witness her public humiliation.

'You wouldn't be trying to tell me how to do my job, would you?' Jerry demanded ominously. 'I hope not, since it's obvious to me that you aren't that good at doing your own.'

It took all Jaz's will-power not to look at Caid or react to Jerry's inflammatory and unfair criticism in the way she suspected he wanted her to.

To Jaz's relief the store's manager came to her rescue, saying quietly, and very bravely, 'Jaz's Christmas window displays in particular bring an enormous amount of extra business to the store—past sales figures from all departments prove that—and in fact they've become something of a local cult and get us a lot of free publicity.'

'Well, that's as may be,' Jerry blustered, 'but there's still the little matter of her budgets. And, speaking of window displays, I'd like to know just what her plans *are* for these supposedly wonderful Christmas windows. I would hate our customers to discover that they can't buy anything they see in the windows because it's merely some arty display piece and we don't have it in stock.'

Jaz's face stung at this slur on her professionalism. It was true that she liked to keep her windows a secret—it helped to build up a sense of Christmas excitement—but of course she checked beforehand that they would have in a large stock of whatever she featured, and she was scrupulous about only using store stock.

Jerry's attack on her was both unprofessional and unfair, and after the meeting ended she edged her way out of the room—past Caid, who was standing by the wall. His stance was that of a man expecting and ready for trouble, and she couldn't stop herself letting off steam by hissing furiously to him, 'You're really enjoying this, aren't you, Caid?'

Jaz tensed now as, almost as though she had conjured them up by her thoughts, she saw Caid and Jerry walking towards her. She quickly turned on her heel and headed for the lift to take her down to the basement and the cubbyhole that was her workroom.

Caid frowned as he watched her go. He'd just spent the best part of an hour on the phone to his mother, who had rung to demand an up-to-date report on what was happening.

As Jerry complained about the store Caid listened in silence. He hadn't cared much for Jerry when he had first been introduced to him, and now he liked him even less. Right now he wasn't sure if the man was just plain unfit to be in charge of the store, or if he was deliberately trying to cause anxiety and mayhem amongst the staff.

As he had said to his mother, in answer to her anxious question, 'What's happening? I wish I knew! The jury's still out on just what Jerry is trying to do here, Mom, but whatever it is isn't doing the store any good.'

'What do you mean, the jury is still out?' She responded indignantly. 'Caid, it's perfectly obvious what he's trying to do. This is Donny's way of attempting to discredit me. Oh, I know him so well. This has his trademark all over it... Oh, I just wish I could be over there.'

Caid heard the energy and frustration humming in her voice.

'Quit being a control freak, Mom,' he told her wryly. 'It isn't good for your blood pressure.'

'Me a control freak?' She responded immediately. 'That's good coming from you, Caid. And at least I'm not so judgemental that I can only see everything and *everyone* in black and white. You remind me so much of your grandfather. He was just like you...stubborn! That man would never admit he could possibly be wrong about a single thing. I can still remember how he was when I told him that your father and I should never have married.

'"You're a female, Annette," he told me, "and it's a female's job to make her marriage work." Just like you, Caid, he thought I should stay home and play house, defer to your father in everything—just so long as your father deferred to *him*, of course.'

Caid listened in silence. He already knew the sorry saga of his parents' marriage, and the fact that his grandfather had put pressure on them to marry because there was a distant family relationship. As well as having the family name, his father had also had a handful of family shares.

Familiar though the story was, it still irked him to be told he was like a man who by all accounts had been an unpleasantly dictatorial and narrow-minded patriarch to his family.

'It's good to know we share such a high opinion of one another, Mom,' he told her warningly.

He heard her sigh travelling along the miles separating them.

'Oh, Caid,' she protested. 'I know what personal unhappiness can do to a person, and I don't want that to happen to you. You are my son, after all…'

When he made no response she sighed again, before asking him, 'Have you spoken to Jaz yet? Have you told her how much we need her to stay?'

Caid cursed under his breath as he heard the anxiety and the persistence in his mother's voice.

'No. Not yet,' he told her curtly. Though talking about Jaz reminded him of something he needed to discuss with his mother. 'You did check with John that it was okay for me to use his spare bedroom, didn't you?'

'Yes, of course I did. He said it would be fine,' she responded promptly.

'Uh-huh. And did he happen to mention that he'd been told by his doctor that his heart condition means that it isn't wise for him to live there at the moment? And that because of that he'd offered the house to Jaz?'

There was a small telling pause before his mother acknowledged the truth. 'Well, yes, he did say something about it, now that you mention it.'

'And you didn't think to tell me?'

'Well, no.' Caid was quite plainly able to hear the defensiveness his mother's voice. 'I mean, neither of us thought that the pair of you would mind sharing... As John said, the house has two bedrooms.'

'You thought we wouldn't mind, but you didn't think we ought to be offered the chance to make up our own minds?'

'Caid, you said yourself that you couldn't get a hotel room—and like John said he could hardly ask Jaz to move out. The last thing I wanted was—'

'To give me an excuse to refuse to come here?' Caid guessed. 'Well, let me tell you—' He stopped abruptly, realising what he'd been about to say was too personal.

And as for his mother's comment about not thinking he and Jaz would mind sharing! If she believed that then she should see the look Jaz gave him every morning when he walked into the kitchen after his shower. It was a look that said quite plainly just how infuriated she felt about having him there. But he was sure she felt nowhere near as infuriated as he did about having to share his living accommodation with her.

And he wasn't just infuriated, if he was honest—

and Caid prided himself on his honesty. It irked him more than he wanted to admit to be forced to admit that physically he still reacted to her, still wanted her!

'Caid, please be nice to Jaz.'

'Be nice to her?' Caid exploded. 'Have you any idea—?' He began, and then stopped, slowly mentally counting to ten before telling his mother grimly, 'What I intend to do is find out what Jerry is doing, and deliver your message to Jaz. And then I'm getting on the first flight home. And nothing and no one is going to stop me!'

CHAPTER SIX

JAZ tensed as she heard Caid let himself into the house early the following afternoon. Involuntarily her glance was drawn to the sketch she had just done, supposedly of the male partner for her windows woman. Her husband, the father of her children, her lover and her best friend—a man who was genuinely her partner in every single way. The kind of man a woman could trust and rely on and yet know at the same time that he cherished her individuality and her independence. The kind of man who was fully prepared to take his share of the chores and the child rearing. The kind of man who was still macho and male enough to allow himself to resort to a few sensual caveman type tactics when the mood allowed. In short he was the kind of man that every woman secretly wanted.

So why, why, why had she sketched him with Caid's familiar features?

'Jaz?'

As Caid rapped on her door, she snatched up the drawing, hiding it behind her back.

'There's something I want to talk to you about,' Caid announced brusquely as he pushed open Jaz's bedroom door.

Out of the corner of his eye he could see the piece of paper she was screwing up behind her back and then letting fall in a small ball to the floor.

'You're wasting your time,' she told him fiercely,

then frowned as they both heard someone knocking on the front door.

Caid cursed mentally under his breath at the interruption. So far as he was concerned, the sooner he said what had to be said to Jaz the better. As he'd said to his mother, he couldn't wait to be on a plane back home.

When Jaz hurried away to answer the door Caid absently put the ball of paper he had retrieved into his pocket before following her.

As she went downstairs Jaz was acutely conscious of Caid's more leisurely pace behind her. They reached the narrow hallway virtually together, and Jaz fought to ignore the effect Caid's proximity was having on her body.

The door-lock was slightly stiff, and as she tussled with it Caid reached out to help her. Jaz exhaled sharply as their fingers touched, recoiling from the contact.

'Leave me alone. I can manage,' she told Caid fiercely.

But it took Caid's stronger, surer fingers to release the mechanism that for some reason her fingers had been too tense to manage.

Silently they stared at one another, Jaz's expression mutinous, Caid's mocking, until Caid pulled open the door.

'Jaz—I thought you'd be here.'

As Jaz stepped back into the hallway Jamie, her cousin, accompanied by her two younger children, swept inside like a warm and busy whirlwind, dispensing hugs and kisses to Jaz at the same time as instructions to her children, her chatter only coming to a breathless halt when she saw Caid.

One eyebrow rose speculatively she looked from Jaz to Caid and then back again.

'This is Caid Dubois,' Jaz introduced him weakly. 'He's here to—'

As Jaz floundered for an explanation Caid quickly stepped in, smiling at Jamie with a warmth that immediately made Jaz want to stand between Caid and her cousin. How dared Caid look at Jamie like that in front of her? How dared he look at another woman like that? Ever?

As she battled with the shock of her own searing jealousy she heard Caid explaining pleasantly to Jamie, 'I'm here on family business.'

'Family business?' Jamie frowned, then her face cleared as she exclaimed, 'Oh, Dubois, of course! It's your family who have bought the store. How do you like Cheltenham? Where are you staying?'

In typical Jamie fashion she was firing off her questions without waiting for any answers.

'I haven't had time to see much of the town as yet,' Caid responded easily. 'And I'm staying here. John was kind enough—'

'Here?' Jamie exclaimed. 'With Jaz?'

'Jamie...' Jaz pleaded in a slightly choked voice.

'Jaz and I are co-tenants,' Caid interjected smoothly. 'John seemed to think that neither of us would mind sharing the house.' He gave a small shrug.

There was a telling pause whilst Jamie looked from Caid's impenetrable and very dominant alpha-male face to Jaz's slightly flushed and much more vulnerable one.

Please, Jamie, don't say anything, Jaz was mentally begging her cousin, knowing how outspoken, not to say outrageous her cousin could be at times.

To Jaz's relief, when Jamie did speak it was only to say easily, 'I expect John was pleased to think that Jaz would have the protection of a male presence in the house. He's very sweetly old-fashioned like that.

'I hope we aren't disturbing you, Jaz,' she continued with a smile, after Caid had asked to be introduced her two children. 'We're here on a mission to book our Christmas trip to Aspen,' she informed them both, 'and to try to persuade Jaz to come with us this year,' she added with a meaningful look in Jaz's direction.

'My husband, Marsh, is a very keen skier,' she explained to Caid, 'and once he discovered just how good American snow is we couldn't keep him away. Last year for the first time we spent the whole of Christmas and the New Year staying at a marvellous lodge complex not far from Aspen. I desperately wanted Jaz to come with us—she's much more of an outdoorsy type than I am—but there was no way I could drag her away from her precious windows.'

'I'd love to come, but you know how it is,' Jaz told Jamie with a shake of her head. 'As soon as Christmas is over the windows have to be prepared for the sales. It seems unfair to go off and leave others to do it.'

'That's so typical of you, Jaz.' Jamie sighed ruefully. 'You are far too conscientious. I know how important your work is to you, but there are other things in life, you know! Caid, do you ski?' Jamie asked.

'I do—weather conditions and livestock permitting,' Caid responded laconically.

'Caid owns a ranch in Colorado.' Jaz explained reluctantly to her cousin.

'Oh, you farm!' Jamie exclaimed beaming. 'Then you'll have a lot in common with my husband, and with Jaz's father. Have you taken Caid home with you yet, Jaz?'

Jaz shook her head. Her exuberant cousin, in her normal way seemed about to adopt Caid into their family circle. Jaz mentally cursed the fact that she had not taken the opportunity to explain the situation before Jamie had met Caid.

'You must go,' she was now telling Caid enthusiastically. 'Jaz's father breeds world-famous cows—doesn't he, Jaz?'

'My father owns two very highly rated Holstein breeding bulls,' Jaz explained quietly.

'You'd never think that Jaz comes from a farming background, would you?' Jamie laughed as she gave Jaz a teasing look.

'No, I wouldn't,' Caid agreed with a coldness Jaz prayed her too-curious cousin would not pick up on and question.

'Remember when you used to help clean out the bull-pens to earn enough money to pay for your art materials, Jaz?' Jamie was asking with a rueful and reminiscent shake of her head.

'I remember,' Jaz agreed, her own voice now nearly as terse as Caid's had been.

But luckily Jamie's suspicions weren't aroused.

'Is there any chance that you can come down to the Soda Fountain with us?' she asked Jaz. 'It's been half-term, and I promised the kids a treat.' She turned to Caid. 'My husband, being a farmer, works from home, and devoted though he is he likes his own space every now and again. Allied to that we've got our family elders living with us, and after five days of two boisterous children they're ready for a break too.'

'You've got three generations living under the same roof?' Caid asked, looking impressed.

'Three generations and a few add-ons,' Jamie agreed, laughing. 'Jaz thinks I'm crazy. She says she'd hate to live my life.'

'Yes, I'm sure she would,' Caid agreed grimly, giving Jaz a cold look as he smiled warmly at Jamie, announcing, 'Personally, I think you re to be admired, and your husband and family envied.'

'We want the Soda Fountain,' Jamie's children began chanting, bringing a halt to the adult conversation. And as Jaz absorbed Caid's praise of her cousin she angrily tried to deny the sharp twist of pain in her heart.

Why should she be jealous of Caid praising Jamie? She didn't want to love a man who felt and thought as Caid did!

Angrily Caid watched as Jaz turned her back on him to talk to her cousin's children. What kind of fool was he for noticing how much such a cherishing role suited her, when he already knew that Jaz was just too stubborn to admit that she might be making the wrong choice?

The Soda Fountain, like the caviar and smoked salmon bar in the store, was famous in its own right. Generations of children had enjoyed its sodas and ice creams, and it had been at Jaz's suggestion that it had been updated and redecorated just prior to the Millennium celebrations.

'I should be working—' Jaz began, but to her surprise Caid cut across her.

'I thought it was your half-day?' he said simply.

'Yes, it is but—' Jaz agreed, caught off-guard.

'Why don't you come with us too?' Jamie invited Caid.

On the point of refusing, Caid saw Jaz's anxious expression. 'I'd love to,' he accepted, ignoring the mutinous look of angry resentment Jaz was giving him. 'I've been wanting to have some lime ice cream ever since I arrived—it's always been one of my favourites!'

As they all made their way to the store Caid watched the speed with which Jamie's children left their mother's side to be with Jaz. It was plain that they adored her from the way they vied for her attention, but what surprised him even more was how natural and loving she was with them. Narrow-eyed he watched the three of them together. After the declarations she had made to him about her plans for the way she wanted to live, he had imagined that she would find it difficult to relate easily to children. And yet here she was, cuddling and teasing these two youngsters in a way that was totally uninhibited and relaxed. A way that made him feel...

'Jaz will be a wonderful mother.'

Jamie's affectionate comment, thankfully bringing his dangerous thoughts to a halt, prompted Caid to say bitterly, 'Do you think so? In my experience career women do not make wonderful mothers. At least not so far as their children are concerned.'

Jaz and the children had already reached the Soda Fountain, but Jamie stopped and frowned a little as she studied Caid.

'Do I sense a man who believes that a woman's place is in the home?' she challenged him, with a small smile.

'I'm certainly a man who believes that a child—children—need a mother like you. One who is there for them one hundred per cent of the time,' Caid acknowledged curtly.

'Like me?' Jamie raised her eyebrows and shook her head. 'One hundred per cent of the time? No way could I ever do that. In fact Jaz is far more of an ideal mother than I could ever be. My children have virtually had to bring themselves up—with a little help from their grandparents and their father. Oh, yes, I've done my bit, but—as I explained to Marsh when I agreed to marry him—there is no way I could live without my own space and the freedom to do those things that are important to me.

'I ran my own business and, like Jaz's mother, I'm a keen rider,' she explained. 'I demand a husband who is prepared to accept that there are times when his needs have to come second to my own. And that's what modern marriage should be all about, in my view. Both partners respecting and accommodating one another's needs. Despite what they say, love is not always enough. Mind you, it certainly helps. If I didn't love Marsh as much as I do, there's no way I'd ever have agreed to having his parents living with us—and yet as it happens it's turned out to be one of the best decisions we ever made.'

Caid listened to her grimly. This wasn't what he had expected or wanted to hear at all.

'Jaz!' Jamie called out to her as they reached the Soda Fountain. 'I've just had a great idea. Why don't you and Caid come over to us for dinner, I know that Marsh would really enjoy meeting you,' she told Caid warmly.

Appalled by her cousin's suggestion, Jaz immediately shook her head in denial, protesting, 'I don't think—'

Immediately Caid cut her off. 'Thank you I'd like that,' he accepted, giving Jaz a grim look as he did so.

'Wonderful! How about the end of next month?' Jamie beamed. 'My in-laws will be away then which will give us more room for guests.'

'That's fine by me,' Caid concurred.

'Good. You could drive down together on a Friday evening, stay over for dinner on Saturday, and travel back on Sunday.'

'I'll be looking forward to it,' Caid assured her politely, whilst Jaz looked on in furious disbelief.

What on earth did Caid think he was doing? Her cousin's home was virtually her only retreat—somewhere she could be totally herself and allow both sides of her nature to emerge without fearing that someone was going to use one of them against her.

Even now, whenever she went home, her parents still took the slightest indication of any enjoyment on her part of anything remotely connected with their lifestyle to mean that they had been right all along. Why couldn't the people who claimed to love her best simply accept that it was possible for her to enjoy some aspects of a country lifestyle and yet at the same time need to fulfil herself artistically?

Unlike her visits home, her visits to Jamie had never made her feel on edge and defensive, or anxious and conscious of a sense of pain and loss because she could not be the daughter she knew her parents had really wanted her to be.

Which was why it was so very important to her that the man she loved—the man who loved her—

Jaz swallowed hard. She mustn't start thinking like that now, when Caid was only a few feet away from her. Only she knew just what it had cost her to walk away from him in New Orleans, and only she would ever know!

Somehow, from somewhere, she would find the strength to deal with Caid's presence in her cousin's home. But she still couldn't help feeling angrily resentful that Caid had accepted Jamie's impromptu invitation primarily to spite her!

Out of the corner of his eye Caid watched Jaz. Whilst he and Jamie had made their way to the circular champagne and smoked salmon bar in the centre of the food hall, which was situated in the original basement kitchen of the building, Jaz had elected to remain at the Soda Fountain with Jamie's two sons—where she was quite plainly enjoying herself, Caid noted.

How the hell was it possible for one small woman to be two so very different people? Caid wondered savagely. Jamie was right, Jaz was a natural-born mother and just the sight of her right now with Jamie's two boys was stirring instincts, desires in him, which had nothing to do with logic or reality and one hell of a lot to do with a much more basic male instinct—like picking her up and kissing the breath out of her and then… Why the hell was he tormenting himself with impossible images of Jaz with his child in her arms?

'You can't put that in there!' Jaz almost shrieked.

'Oh, I think you'll find that I can,' Caid corrected her with soft menace as he glanced from her face to the very large piece of fresh meat he had just placed on the empty central shelf of the fridge. 'There are two of us living in this house, Jaz,' He reminded her. 'And if I want to put my food in this fridge…'

The look he was giving her was both implacable and intimidating, Jaz acknowledged, but she had her own weapons for dealing with a man who couldn't take advice and believed he always knew best.

'Anyway,' he continued contemptuously, 'There's plenty of room left for that rabbit food you eat.'

Jaz could feel her temper starting to rise.

'That's typical of you, Caid, to start criticising me, blaming me for your own pigheadedness. And as for my "rabbit food" as you choose to call it, I shall hardly be able to eat it once your meat has dripped blood all over it—which is why for health reasons it is normally considered safest to put meat on the lowest possible shelf in a fridge. That's all I was going to say to you. But of course no one can tell you anything, can they, Caid? No one apart from *you* can possibly have a valid opinion about anything—'

'If you're trying to pick a fight with me,' Caid interrupted her coldly. 'let me warn you—'

'No,' Jaz broke in sharply. 'Let me warn *you*, Caid. Let me warn you that you had no business accepting Jamie's invitation.'

'No business?'

Jaz tensed as she saw his thunderous expression, but she wasn't going to back down. As he slammed the fridge door shut and came towards her she tried to make herself stand her ground, but to her chagrin she realised she was retreating from him, backing away until the feel of the wall behind her told her that she couldn't go any further.

'This is what marriage to you would have been like, isn't it, Caid? You giving the orders, making the rules.

You expecting everything to be done your way. You demanding that your needs always come first. It isn't because of any children you might have that you want your wife at home under your thumb all the time,' she told him with biting scorn, 'it's because you can't bear the thought of not being in control. Because you're so selfish and stubborn that you can't allow anyone other than yourself to be right about anything. Well, go ahead and give yourself food poisoning, then. I don't care. Why should I? I feel very sorry for the woman who does eventually make the mistake of marrying you. Thank goodness it won't be me.'

'Have you finished?' Caid demanded with ominous anger.

When Jaz turned away from him without making any response she heard him saying savagely under his breath, 'My God, but you know how to wind me up! Does it give you a kick?' he taunted her. 'Pressing all the wrong buttons because you can't press the right ones any more?'

Jaz gave a small furious gasp of female outrage. 'How can you say that?' she breathed indignantly. 'When you…when you—?' To her chagrin her voice had developed a small betraying hesitation, and she knew too that her face had begun to burn. Taking a deep gulp of breath, she said quickly, 'When you touched me—'

'Touched you?' Caid threw back his head and laughed. 'My, but you are naïve, aren't you? You might know where to put meat in a fridge, Jaz, but when it comes to knowing about the male sex… Shall I spell it out for you? I'm a man and I simply have a man's needs!'

It wasn't the indifference in the small shrug he gave

as he turned away from her that hurt, Jaz told herself fiercely. And it certainly wasn't hearing him spell out the fact that he didn't love her any more. After all, she didn't love him, did she?

No! It was just… It was just…

Pinning a bright smile on her face, she told him in the most dismissive voice she could manage, 'Your needs are of no interest to me, Caid, and neither are you!'

There! That should reassure him that there was no danger of her making a lovesick fool of herself over him.

But Caid's reaction was anything but one of gratitude, Jaz acknowledged apprehensively, as he suddenly closed the distance between them and demanded, 'No? Then what does this mean?'

Struck dumb with horrified embarrassment, Jaz stared at the sketch he had thrust under her nose. The one she herself had drawn and discarded! The one depicting him in the role of her windows husband and father, complete with winsomely adorable children carrying his unmistakable likeness and an even more doting wife.

Bitterly Jaz wondered what could possibly have possessed her to put down on paper such a potentially betraying and feeble-minded set of images.

'Nothing to say?' Caid taunted her.

Hot-cheeked with discomfort, Jaz demanded huskily, 'Where did you get that? It's mine. Give it to me.'

As she made it to snatch the paper from him, Caid held it up out of her reach.

'So you did draw it,' he commented with satisfaction.

'It means nothing,' Jaz denied passionately. 'You don't mean anything to me now, Caid. You never really did,' Jaz lied wildly, desperate to protect herself.

Caid's expression hardened, making her heart miss a couple of beats and her body shake apprehensively. Unable to move, Jaz watched as Caid stood menacingly over her. Why had she said that? She had pushed him too far, but pride was refusing to let her back down.

'Oh, didn't I?' Caid demanded savagely.

Her words had raked his pride, exposed the raw nerve endings of the emotions he had been fighting to bury. They goaded him beyond the already overstretched limits of a self-control worn thin by night after night of knowing how close she was, of knowing just how much he still wanted her and knowing too, that he must destroy his feelings for her. Rationality was replaced by primitive male instinct.

'Well, let's just put that to the test, shall we?' Caid suggested in a voice so soft Jaz couldn't believe it had the power to savage her.

Trapped between Caid and the wall, she tensed her muscles defensively, pride flaring in her eyes as she silently dared him to touch her. But Caid was beyond recognising such subtle signals. His hands grasped her wrists, pinioning her arms on the wall, whilst he lowered his head towards her.

Jaz could feel his hot breath on her skin, could smell its scent of mint. It was heart-searingly familiar. Helplessly Jaz turned her head one way and then the other as she fought to avoid the unwanted domination of his mouth. But she already knew it was a lost fight.

The weight of his body imprisoning hers against the wall felt like a merciless physical brand. Instinctively she closed her eyes, wanting to blot out the sight of him. But instead by some dangerous alchemy her senses were suddenly sweeping her back to when they had first met, when she had wanted him beyond reason and sanity, when just to be within sight of him had been enough to melt the flesh from her bones and make her body respond to him on a thousand different levels.

Like ice cracking under immense pressure, her emotions forced a fissure in her self-control. Every sense she possessed reacted to him, reached for him, ached despairingly for him. Her whole body was acting as though it was outside her own control, her emotions overwhelming her.

Feverishly she waited for the taste of Caid's kiss, knowing with a sense of helpless desperation just how much she wanted it. How much she wanted him. His mouth touched hers—hot, angry, demanding—and fiercely she responded to it, her anger against herself as well as against him. They kissed with fury and pain, with disillusionment and destruction, until the room was filled with the charged sound of their breathing.

Jaz shuddered as she felt Caid's arousal. Her own body was equally vulnerable. Her breasts ached for his touch, and that sensation deep down inside her that only he could arouse was a slow throbbing torment.

She wanted him to pick her up and carry her to his bed, to remove the restriction of their clothes as speedily as he could—in any way he chose. She didn't care how he did it, just as long as she could feel his flesh against her own. She was so hungry for him, so much in need of him that her whole body shook with it. It was as though she had a fever that only he could cool—a wound that only he could heal.

Tormentedly she pressed her lips against his throat, his jaw, his mouth, desperately prising the hard lines of his mouth apart with her tongue-tip.

Beneath his hand her breast swelled and ached. She couldn't wait for him to remove her top, to touch her the way he had done in New Orleans when she had shivered convulsively, her body arcing in hot, shocked delight at the feel of his work-hardened fingertips caressing the wanton sensitivity of her nipples.

'Admit it, Jaz,' Caid was groaning against her skin. 'Right now you're as hungry for me— For us—as I am for you.'

His words shocked her back to reality—and self-loathing.

'No!' she denied in panic, pulling away from Caid. 'No. No, I'm not.'

Silently Caid let her go. But she could imagine what he must be thinking. How much he must be enjoying his triumph and her own humiliation!

Half an hour later, as she stood in the bathroom of the house, her fingers pressed to her kiss-swollen mouth, she wondered how on earth she was going to survive what was happening to her.

She couldn't still love Caid. It just wasn't possible. She *mustn't* love him.

A small sob of panicky despair closed her throat.

Grimly Caid wondered what the hell he was doing and why he didn't just make good his earlier threat and get on the first flight home. Surely it wasn't because his body was aching for a woman he knew it would be crazy for him to still love?

The air in the room still held her scent, accentuated

by the heat of their shared sexual urgency. No matter what Jaz had tried to say, she had wanted him as much as he had done her; been as hungry for him as he for her. Oh, yes, Jaz had wanted him… His nerve-endings felt exposed, raw, a restless urgency burning through him.

He took a step towards the kitchen door and then stopped. So he had proved that sexually Jaz wasn't averse to him—what did that mean? Turning round, he walked over to the fridge and opened the door.

Removing his steak, he started to clean the shelf he had placed it on, and then meticulously washed Jaz's salad and fruit before packing them back in the salad crisper and returning his meat to the fridge—on the lowest shelf.

CHAPTER SEVEN

'AND you've written here under Special Effects an amount of £5,000. But so far as I can see there is no breakdown of just what these "special effects" are going to be—nor any past receipt evidence to support this expenditure.'

Caid compressed his mouth as he listened to Jerry hectoring Jaz about the budget she had produced for him. It was plain from the angry flags of colour flying in Jaz's cheeks and the hostile atmosphere in the office just what her own and Jerry's feelings were.

Even now Caid wasn't sure just why he had insisted at the last minute on being included in the one-to-one meeting between Jerry and Jaz. It certainly didn't have anything to do with any protective male concern for Jaz. Why should he feel either protective or concerned for a woman who cared more about her career than she did about him?

'Where exactly is this money going to go? Or can I guess?' Jerry sneered openly.

Jaz gasped in outrage as she correctly interpreted his accusation. 'If you are trying to suggest that I would do something underhand or dishonest—' she began immediately.

'All I'm asking for is proof of what the money is to be spent on,' Jerry told her smoothly. 'If you don't like or can't comply with my request—'

'Jerry, that's enough.'

The sharp incisive interruption of Caid's angry

voice caused Jerry's face to burn an unpleasantly angry colour.

'Hey, Caid. I'm the one in charge here,' he began, but immediately Caid overruled him.

'My uncle may have appointed you, Jerry, but in my book—and I'm sure in the family's as well,' he told him meaningfully, 'I think we both know that my authority ranks way above yours. If, historically, Jaz has not been asked to provide budgets for her department, then so far as I am concerned she certainly doesn't need to now.'

Reaching across the desk, Caid picked up the folder Jaz had brought in with her. 'Thank you, Jaz. You can go,' he told her as he handed it back to her.

'Now, wait a minute!'

Jaz could hear Jerry blustering furiously as Caid opened the office door for her. But no matter how angry Jerry was at Caid's interference he couldn't be anywhere near as angry as she was herself, she decided as she blinked away the tears of fury and humiliation that were burning her eyes.

How dared Caid belittle her like that? How dared he interfere? And for what purpose, when she already knew that he wanted to see her leaving his family's employment every bit as much as Jerry did?

Downstairs in her workroom, she flung the folder into a drawer, her face still burning.

What Jerry had just tried to imply was an insult— an insult that hadn't just infuriated her but had hurt her as well, and all the more so because Caid had witnessed it.

Reluctantly she acknowledged that her resolution was beginning to waver, that she was beginning to ask herself if the price of staying on at the store was one she was going to be able to pay. Wouldn't it be much easier to give in; to hand in her notice and leave? It wasn't as though she wouldn't be able to find another job.

But she liked this job. She reminded herself stubbornly and she wasn't going to be pushed out of it just to suit the Dubois family! And she certainly wasn't going to be patronised by a certain arrogant member of it who, for reasons best known to himself, had suddenly decided to act as her defender!

Her angry resentment was still bubbling hotly inside her half an hour later when Caid pushed open the door to her small domain.

'Why did you do that?' she challenged him. Her workroom felt cramped at the best of times, but now, with Caid in it, it was unbearably claustrophobic. How was it possible for a man she knew hadn't been anywhere near the great outdoors within the last twenty-four hours to smell somehow of huge open spaces, cool, clean air, and that indefinable something which her senses recognised as being uniquely Caid?

'Why did I do what?' Caid responded. 'I came down here to talk to you about something, Jaz—'

'Something?' Jaz interrupted him wildly. 'What kind of something? If you're expecting me to shower you with gratitude because of the way you belittled me upstairs in front of Jerry—'

'I *belittled* you? Now, just a minute—!'

'Yes, belittled me,' Jaz insisted. 'I don't need you to protect me or come to my rescue, Caid. I'm perfectly capable of dealing with Jerry on my own. You had no right to interfere.'

'No right?' Caid stared at her. 'Do you really think that I'm the kind of man who just stands to one side and allows a person—any person—to be bullied like that? Just because you...'

'Just because I what?' Jaz demanded. Colour burned in her face and her hands were clenched into two tight, defensive little balls. 'Don't think I don't know what you're trying to do with all this pseudo-sympathy and protection.'

Jaz could hear the emotion shaking her body beginning to infect her voice. 'I've been there before, Caid, with my parents. But at least I knew when they tried to undermine me that they were motivated by love. But you! You just can't wait to see me fall, can you, Caid? You'd do anything and everything within your power to bring me down and humiliate me. To have me down on my knees begging you to take me back just for the satisfaction it would give you. Well, it's never going to happen. I could never, ever commit myself to a man who can't accept me as I am. You wouldn't expect me to change the colour of my eyes because you preferred blue to brown, would you? Or dye my hair, cut off an arm? But you obviously think it quite acceptable to expect me to deny part of my personality, part of my most sacred inner self.'

'Don't be ridiculous. You're overreacting,' Caid told her curtly.

'I am not being ridiculous,' Jaz stormed. 'In wanting me to give up my career to conform to your idea of what a woman should be you are every bit as guilty of trying to bully me as Jerry is. But you can't see that, can you? You're too stubborn to *want* to see it! You want me to be less of the person I am, less of the woman I am, and I can never ever do that. Oh, why, *why* did you have to come over here?' Jaz demanded.

Bleakly Caid looked at her down bent head. The

angry explosion of words she had hurled at him felt as though they had embedded themselves in his pride, like so many pieces of shrapnel, tearing him to pieces.

He had come down to Jaz's workroom anticipating that she would be in need of some comfort and reassurance—wanting to let her know that no matter what might lie between them she was assured of someone on her side, to take her part, and that she need have no fears of Jerry whilst he was there.

The reality of her reaction could hardly have been more different.

Bitterly he told her, 'As to my reasons for coming here…' Shaking his head, he added coldly, 'I doubt that they are something you would be able to understand.'

As he finished the solitary meal he had just eaten in a nearby restaurant Caid glanced at his watch. It was ten p.m. now. If he found himself a quiet bar and had a drink he need not return to the house until gone eleven, by which time hopefully Jaz would have gone to bed. And tomorrow he would be driving down to stay with John.

He and Jaz had been studiously ignoring one another since their argument in Jaz's workroom, and this morning Caid had telephoned John—ostensibly to thank him for allowing him the use of his spare room and to invite himself down to spend a couple of days at John's apartment so he could take him out for a thank-you dinner, but in reality simply so that he could get away from Jaz. Because if he didn't he didn't think he would be answerable for what might happen.

*　　*　　*

Jaz forced her lips into what she hoped would pass as a natural and genuine smile as she slowed her car down ready to turn into the drive that led to her parents' property. She had said nothing to Caid about her visit to her parents, but after all why should she?

The land on which her father raised his pedigree stock had been in his family for many generations, and Jaz felt she wouldn't have been the person she hoped she was had she not felt a small rush of pride and belonging as she drove towards the pretty manor house.

As she continued down the drive she glanced over at the stable block. Jaz enjoyed riding—but as a relaxing hobby, that was all. She had never shared the competitive instinct which had taken her mother to the top of her chosen career, but that did not stop her loving and admiring her mother for all that she had achieved and for the determination and dedication she gave to training and teaching her young hopefuls.

At least here she would be spared having to see Caid, she reminded herself. She usually took pride in her strength of mind, her resilience and her self-control—but right now...

The atmosphere between them had become so dangerously hostile and tense that Jaz was actually starting to feel physically sick with nerves at the thought of having to come face to face with Caid. The way he was making her feel was even beginning to affect her work.

Right now, she acknowledged shakily, each and every one of her defences had become frighteningly weak. He made her say and do things that were totally the opposite of the way she normally behaved. It frightened her to know she was so out of control. But what frightened her even more was the way she couldn't stop herself from thinking about him, from obsessively going over and over everything he had said to her.

It was obvious he didn't love her any more. Her face burned as she remembered the way he had taunted her about using her for his sexual satisfaction.

She needed to put some distance between them and this was the perfect way of doing it because there was no way Caid would turn up at her parents', as he had done at the store, standing there, and filling her with foolish hope and delight, when all the time…

No, here with her parents she was totally safe!

Caid frowned as he listened to John explaining that he had organised a small treat for him.

'I couldn't help feeling that you would be bored stuck in my small apartment, so I rang Helena and asked if we might stay with them for the weekend.'

Caid checked him. 'Helena?'

'Yes. Helena and Chris—Jaz's parents. They only live a few miles away, and you'll be much more comfortable there than here.'

John was suggesting that they spend the weekend with Jaz's parents? In Jaz's home?

She hadn't been in the house when he had returned from the store to pack his bag, so he had left her a curt note, explaining that he was going away for a couple of days.

His immediate response to John's suggestion was to refuse to go, but he argued with himself. To do that would be unfair to John—and bad manners as well. After all, it wasn't as though he was afraid of going, was it?

An hour later, as he stowed John's overnight case

away in the boot of his hired car and made sure the older man was comfortably installed in the passenger seat, Caid acknowledged that it didn't matter where he was, just so long as he was away from Jaz.

If he were to come face to face with her right now he didn't think he could be responsible for his reaction. But then he wasn't going to come face to face with her, was he?

CHAPTER EIGHT

'DARLING...you've made good time! You look pale, though. You need some fresh air,' Jaz's mother reproved. 'It's almost time for lunch. John's here, by the way. He's staying for the weekend.'

As she followed her mother into the kitchen Jaz tried to relax.

Coming home always put her on the defensive, but she knew now that the determination not to be undermined she felt with her parents was nothing when compared to the fierce need to defend her independence that gripped her when she was with Caid.

Caid! As she walked it the kitchen she closed her eyes for a second. She had come here to escape him, hadn't she? So why was she letting him dominate her thoughts?

'Darling, why don't you do through to the sitting room?' her mother suggested. 'The others are in there, and you know what Dorothy's like about serving meals on time. You might warn your father that she's on the warpath.'

Dorothy was the linchpin of the household, the person who held everything together, acting as cook-cum-housekeeper-cum-secretary to her parents, running the household and devoted to them.

Leaving her mother to remove the outdoor clothes she was wearing, Jaz made her way along the hall to the sitting room. As she pushed open the door she could see her father and John.

'You run cattle yourself, then, do you, Caid.' Jaz heard him asking interestedly.

Freezing in disbelief, she stood in the open doorway. This couldn't possibly be happening. She was imagining it. She must be. She had to be. Caid could not possibly be here. He *must* not be here!

'Jaz…come on in. Don't just stand there. I don't know!' Jaz could see her father shaking his head wryly. 'Are you sure she's as good at this job of hers as you're always telling us she is, John?' he asked John as he turned towards him. 'Only she's always been such a daydreamer…'

'She's exceptionally good at her job—and exceptionally gifted as well.'

Jaz heard John defending her gently. But for once all her attention was not focused with painful intensity on the usual underlying parental criticism. How could it be when Caid was standing less that five feet away from her, his expression shuttered and austere, only the grim tension of his jaw giving away the fact that she was as unwelcome a sight to him as he to her?

'Mother said to warn you that Dorothy is about to serve lunch,' Jaz told her father, managing from somewhere to summon a brightly false smile for him before deliberately ignoring Caid and stepping past him to give John a warm hug.

She could almost feel Caid's cold, concentrated gaze turning her spine to ice.

'Jaz—I didn't realise you were going to be here.' John greeted her with warm enthusiasm.

'Oh, you know what Jaz is like,' her father broke in jovially. 'Head always in the clouds. But then that's these arty types for you. Can't really understand what it's all about myself.'

'What what is all about, dear?' Jaz's mother enquired, coming in to shepherd them all into the dining room.

'This arty thing of Jaz's,' Chris Cavendish replied, shaking his head. 'She had every opportunity to join a farming life. But all she wanted was this art business.'

Jaz could see the way Caid was frowning as he looked from her to her parents, and her face started to burn with a mixture of angry pride and embarrassment.

'Caid's family own the store that Jaz works for,' Jaz's mother reminded her husband as she ladled soup into everyone's bowls.

'Maybe so, but Caid's like us—he's a rancher,' Chris informed her approvingly.

'Well, I have to admit we were disappointed when Jaz told us what she wanted to do,' she sighed. 'We tried to talk her out of it—for her own sake, of course—but she can be amazingly stubborn.'

Jaz tensed, her spoon clattering against the plate as she put it down with a small bang.

'I don't think that Caid is interested in hearing about my failings,' she said grittily to her mother.

'I think Caid already knows how gifted you are, Jaz,' John intervened quietly. 'I know for a fact how impressed his mother was with your work.'

It was on the tip of Jaz's tongue to demand to know why, if that was the case, she was now being bullied into handing in her notice? But mercifully she managed to restrain herself.

She couldn't bring herself to look at Caid, but she knew how much he must be enjoying hearing her parents criticising her. A childish desire to claim that she wasn't hungry any more and get up and run away threatened to turn her into the child her parents always treated her as. Fiercely she resisted it.

Dipping her head, she concentrated on drinking her soup.

Grimly Caid surveyed Jaz's downbent head. An unfamiliar and discomfiting insight was challenging him to take note of what was happening. Logically he knew he should be applauding and supporting the opinions he had just heard Jaz's parents voice, but instead...

Jaz realised that her father had started to engage Caid in a discussion about livestock. Relieved not to have to defend herself any further, she lifted her head—only to realise her mistake.

Caid might be listening to her father, but he was staring right across the table at her. And the look in his eyes was one which...

A brilliant surge of colour seared Jaz's skin. What was Caid doing? He had no right to look at her like that. As though...as though...

'Goodness, Jaz, you look flushed,' her mother commented solicitously. 'I do hope you aren't coming down with something...'

Something? Did dying dreams, shattered illusions and a breaking heart count as 'something'?

Caid's gaze had locked with hers, refusing to let it go. Desperately Jaz struggled to escape from its searching intensity; from the ignominy of what she was having to endure.

Just as soon as lunch was over she made her escape, heading for the barn which housed her mother's free-range poultry. She carried Dorothy's egg basket over her arm.

An hour later, with the basket almost full, she put

it down. It was warm inside the barn, and she took off the jacket she was wearing, putting it on top of the basket before going to climb the ladder that led to the barn's hayloft.

As a girl this had always been one of her favourite retreats. Her special sanctuary where she had come when she'd felt as though life and its problems were becoming too much for her to bear. From its windows she could see right across the fields to the hills. It was the place she'd come to think her private thoughts, dream her private dreams.

She had certainly never needed its sanctuary more than she needed it now, Jaz acknowledged as she headed for a small window, curling up beneath it on the soft hay.

'You look angry, Caid.'

Caid started as John spoke to him. They had finished lunch and the older man had announced that he was going upstairs to rest. Caid had offered to carry his bag up for him and the two of them were now standing outside the room John was going to occupy.

'I hadn't realised that Jaz's parents—' he began tersely, then stopped when John sighed.

'They love her, of course—very, very much. And I don't mean to gossip, but it's no secret that in their eyes Jaz doesn't fit their idea of what a child of theirs should be. That made life very hard for Jaz when she was growing up. I can remember her as a little girl.' He smiled ruefully. 'She desperately wanted to please them, to be what they wanted her to be, but whenever she could she would try to show them how important it was to her to follow her artistic urge. They couldn't understand...

'That hurt her. Badly. And she had to fight very hard for the right to fulfil her own destiny. Too hard I sometimes think, for a person of her loving temperament. Her parents taught her that a temperament like hers could be used against her. She wanted to please them because she loved them, and I'm afraid that they tended to use that love to try and make her do as they wanted—but for the best of motives, you understand. They genuinely believed that she would be much happier living the same kind of life as them. They couldn't understand how it might make her feel trapped and cheated, how it would deprive her of a part of herself that was so very important to her. Of course that's all in the past now, and naturally they are very proud of her.'

'They treat her as though she were still a child,' Caid objected grimly. 'Patronising and without respect.'

Leaving John to have his rest, Caid went back downstairs. He was finding his own reaction to what John had said even more disturbing than John's actual disclosures.

But the fact that he had suddenly discovered there might be a valid reason for Jaz's attitude didn't mean that he had changed the way he felt about it!

'Yes, I'm very pleased with the results of our breeding programme,' Jaz's father confirmed to Caid an hour later as they walked towards the kitchen.

Naturally, in view of their shared interest, Jaz's father had offered to show Caid his stock—an offer that Caid had been unable to resist accepting. During the course of their conversation it had become plain to Caid that Chris Cavendish did love his daughter, though it was equally plain that he could not understand her.

'Of course,' he'd confided to Caid, 'her mother and I haven't given up hope that she'll come back to her roots. You should have seen her when she was young. She loved feeding the calves…' He'd shaken his head and sighed.

'Look, I've got a couple of phone calls I need to make,' he said now. 'Please, make yourself at home and feel free to have a look around if you wish.'

Thanking him, Caid watched as he walked back to the house before turning to study the vista in front of him.

This land so unlike his own fascinated him, and he walked over to the fence to study it better. Hens scratched busily in the dust of the yard, beyond which lay an old timber-framed barn. There was a date carved over the opening and he walked over to inspect it more closely.

As he entered the barn he saw the basket on the floor beside the ladder, and Jaz's jacket folded neatly over it. Broodingly he studied it. He knew it was Jaz's because he recognised it. Picking it up, he let the fabric slide through his fingers. It felt soft and warm, like Jaz herself—sensuous, perfumed. He eyed the ladder, then came to a decision.

He might have come here to get away from her, but now that they were here together perhaps it would be as good an opportunity as any for him to deliver his mother's message to her and make a plea on her behalf.

Determinedly he started to climb the ladder, frowning as it creaked beneath his weight. Jaz had apparently climbed it safely enough, he reminded himself.

He was well over three quarters of the way up when he heard an ominous cracking sound. Caid held his breath and waited, hoping that he was wrong and that it didn't mean what he feared it did. But then, as he held firmly onto the ladder and tried to make up his mind what to do, he heard the wood crack again, and this time he felt the ladder start to buckle and slide away as it broke beneath his weight.

Grimly he reached up and managed to grip hold of the loft floor above him, intending to haul himself up…

Jaz woke up with a start. She didn't know how long she'd been asleep but what she did know was that she'd been dreaming about Caid. Dreaming about the time they had shared in New Orleans, the way things had been between them before…

Her eyes dark with remembered emotions, she turned her head and then blinked dazedly as she saw Caid's head and shoulders framed in the opening to the loft.

'Caid…'

Her eyes widened. It was almost as though she was still locked in her dream. Caid was here… She could feel herself beginning to tremble with longing and need…

'Jaz, the ladder's snapped,' she heard Caid telling her abruptly, and his words brought her shockingly back to reality.

Immediately she was her parents' daughter, brought up from birth to deal with this kind of emergency. Getting up, she hurried across to him, quickly recognising the danger he was in. There was no way he could go back down the broken ladder, and the floor was too far below for him to jump down safely. The only thing he could do was haul himself up to safety in the loft. But to do that he would need her help.

Determinedly she braced her body and instructed him briskly, 'Give me your hand. If I hold onto this beam, and you hold onto me, you should be able to lever yourself up here.'

Jaz hoped she sounded more confident than she felt. She weighed just under eight stone, and Caid, she suspected, weighed over half as much again—at least. If she lost her grip on the beam they could both end up falling and injuring themselves. The floor of the stable was flagged in Cotswold stone, and Jaz hated to think what a fall from such a height might do to the human body.

Clenching her teeth, she wrapped her free arm around the beam whilst Caid gripped her wrist. Closing her eyes, she prayed silently, her whole body flinching when she heard the sound of the broken ladder crashing to the floor and felt the sharp pull of Caid's weight on her body.

'Jaz, it's okay. You can open your eyes.'

Her whole body went limp with relief as Caid released her wrist. When she opened her eyes he was kneeling on the floor of the loft in front of her.

Caid had made it! He was safe!

Yes, he was safe, but *they* were trapped up here together in the hay loft until someone realised they were missing and came to look for them, Jaz recognised distractedly. And that wouldn't be until at least dinner-time!

'You've got hay in your hair.'

Jaz made to pull back as Caid reached towards her.

'Hold still,' he commanded matter-of-factly, securing her arm with one hand whilst he reached out to pluck the pieces of hay from her hair.

Jaz could feel the warmth of his breath on her skin. She could see the tanned hollow of his throat. Her chest felt dangerously tight, constricting her breathing and depriving her of oxygen—which must be why her thoughts had become a dislocated haphazard muddle and why her heartbeat was echoing noisily in her own ears.

'Caid...'

She had meant her voice to sound strong and distancing, dismissive, but instead it was a soft, shaken sound that had exactly the opposite effect from the one she had wanted.

Instead of releasing her Caid moved closer to her, looking down at her mouth.

'No, don't!' Jaz whispered, reaching up with her free hand to push him away.

'No, don't what?' Caid murmured, capturing her hand and holding it within his own, rubbing his thumb lightly against the softness of her palm so that she shuddered violently.

Don't kiss me! she had wanted to say. But it was already too late. Already his mouth was feathering hers in the lightest and most tempting of kisses.

It's just sex, she tried to remind herself. That's all he wants you for. He doesn't love you. You must not... But her body was swaying into his, curving to meet its hardness, her muscles softening, her body yearning, opening.

'Jaz...'

Just the way he breathed her name was enough to make her moan achingly.

His hands cupped her face.

'Look at me.' She heard him demand roughly. 'Look at me, Jaz, and tell me that you don't want me.'

'I can't... I can't...' Jaz told him in anguish.

His nose rubbed tenderly against her own and his thumb tip stroked the softness of her lips.

Automatically she parted them, flicking her tongue softly against his skin, feeling him shudder in response against her.

'Why do we fight when we could be doing this?' Caid groaned hoarsely as he gathered her up against him.

'I don't know,' Jaz admitted dizzily. And right now it was the truth—she didn't! She didn't know anything apart from the fact that she had just been dreaming the most wonderful dream about him and now he was here, and she was here, and the way he was holding her, touching her, kissing her, was melting away all the bad times and taking her back to when they had first met. Right now that was the only place she wanted to be, she acknowledged.

'Don't deny me,' Caid was begging her. 'Don't deny this...don't deny us, Jaz.'

And then he was touching her mouth with his, capturing it in a kiss of searing domination and demand.

Jaz felt her whole body go limp as her desire to reject him was overwhelmed by a far stronger and more elemental need. Her heart smashed against her chest wall and her legs went so weak she was forced to lean on Caid for support. Her lips parted eagerly, greedily, whilst her poor embattled mind fought and lost its lonely fight for resistance.

This was what she hungered for, longed for, ached for, in that secret part of her heart she had refused to acknowledge existed. Caid's touch, his warmth, his kiss. His body…

Mindlessly Jaz clung to him, returning his kiss, oblivious to everything but the feelings driving her.

She could feel his excitement as she pressed herself against him, as hungry for him as she could feel he was for her. She opened her mouth to the searching probe of his tongue, wrapping her arms around him as though she would never let him go.

Her head swimming, her heart pounding, her whole body a delirious mixture of longing and excitement, Jaz marvelled that she had been able to live so long without him.

Greedily she pressed tiny kisses against his jaw and then his throat, almost high on the taste and the feel of him. This was her lover, her man, her destiny… And her body, her senses, her heart flatly refused to listen to any pathetic whining from her head. This was love; this was now; this was Caid.

In the heat of the hay-sweet privacy of the barn they tugged impatiently at one another's clothes in between increasingly passionate kisses, two equals in their longing and love for one another.

Jaz felt Caid shudder as he released her breasts from confinement, cupping them with his hands whilst he gazed down at them in absorbed wonder.

She had never felt so proud of her body, her womanhood, never felt so strong and empowered by its desirability.

She could feel the fine tremble of Caid's fingers as he touched her, circling and then tugging gently on her taut nipples whilst her breasts swelled eagerly against his hands. Daringly she leaned forward and brushed her lips against his own body, flicking her tongue against one hard flat nipple in both a caress and a subtle invitation. The hard male body, which it now seemed to her she had known and loved for a thousand hidden and shadowy past lifetimes, trembled with heart-aching vulnerability beneath her touch. How she loved to see him like this. Reduced in his need for her to the same level of intoxicated adoration as she was by him.

There was, she reflected dreamily, no pleasure on earth greater than the liberty to enjoy the body of one's beloved. To reach out and touch it…him…to stroke and kiss him as she was doing now, running her fingertips hotly down the line of silky dark hair that disappeared beneath his belt and following that journey with her lips.

She heard Caid groan and then suddenly she was lying on her back against the hay, with Caid leaning over her, looking down at her, his blue eyes so dark with passion they were almost black.

His gaze locked with hers, he began to unfasten his jeans. Jaz could feel herself starting to tremble slightly and then to shake. The pain of the months without him overwhelmed her, and there were tears in her eyes as she leaned forward to touch him in all the intimate ways they had so fleetingly shared.

'No—wait!' she heard him say, his voice thick, slurred and distorted by his desire for her.

He had just begun to pull down her jeans, burying his face in the smooth swell of her stomach as he kissed her skin, his breath hot with passion, his kisses sending exquisite needle-sharp darts of fiery pleasure through, her.

'Are you sure you can live without this?' he was demanding thickly.

'Without us? Because—'

'Jaz—?'

Abruptly Jaz came to her senses, the betraying response she had been about to make freezing on her lips as she heard her father's voice calling her name.

What was she *doing*? Her face stung with shame and anger. She knew that Caid didn't love her any more. So why on earth had she behaved so—so...?

Her face burned even more hotly as Caid handed her her clothes and called out to her father, 'We're up here, Chris!'

Whilst he was speaking Caid was quickly dressing himself. Miserably Jaz looked away from him.

The shock of hearing her father's voice had brought her very sharply back to reality. Her hands were trembling as she fastened the last of her shirt buttons. She felt so angry with herself, so ashamed. What could she have been thinking of?

'Jaz...Caid...' Jaz could hear the relief in her father's voice. 'Your mother was just about to insist I sent out a search party. She was convinced that you must have had an accident.'

'Well, we have, in a manner of speaking,' Caid answered her father ruefully before Jaz could speak. 'I'm afraid I've damaged your loft ladder beyond repair.'

'The loft ladder? Oh...' Jaz could hear the consternation in his voice. 'Dammit! I should have warned you. We've got a new one on order. It's fortunate that neither of you were hurt. Hang on a minute whilst I go and get another ladder.'

As she watched him hurrying away and out of sight Jaz knew there must be a hundred different things she should say to Caid. But the stifling silence of the barn and the weight of her own misery made it totally impossible for her to speak.

'Jaz?'

She froze when she heard Caid say her name. How dared he sound so tender, so dangerously warm, so much as though he actually cared about her, when she knew that he did not? When he himself had proved to her that he no longer loved her!

'Whatever it is you're planning to say, don't. Because I don't want to hear it,' she told him grittily, each word hurting her as though it was a piece of sharp glass being ripped across her throat.

To her relief her father had returned, bringing with him a set of long ladders.

Caid went down first, waiting halfway down for her and reaching out with his hands to steady her. Immediately Jaz recoiled from him, telling him stiffly, 'I can manage by myself, thank you.'

The coldness in his eyes as he turned away from her closed her throat with painful emotion.

Why was life punishing her like this? What on earth had she ever done to deserve what she was suffering now?

'I'm afraid Jasmine won't be down for dinner,' Jaz's mother apologised several hours later, when Caid and John joined her in the drawing room. 'She sends her apologies. She's got a migraine.'

CHAPTER NINE

'IS THAT all you're having to eat?'

Jaz could feel the tiny hairs on her skin prickling antagonistically in response to Caid's sternly autocratic question as he looked at the salad she had prepared for her evening meal.

'Yes, it is,' she agreed, adding belligerently, 'Not that it's any business of yours.'

Ignoring her warning, Caid pointed out disapprovingly, 'All you had for breakfast was a cup of coffee. It's a proven fact that in order to operate at maximum capacity the human body needs a proper protein breakfast—and, since you work for a company in which I have a financial interest, I can legitimately insist that I have every right to—'

'Will you stop behaving as though you're my father?' yelled Jaz. 'When will you all realise that not only am I capable of making my own decisions but also that it is my right to do so. How would any of you like it if I denied you that right?'

'I am not behaving like your parents,' Caid insisted, his voice harsh with his own immediate response to her accusation. 'Just because they refused to allow you to be yourself when you were growing up, Jaz, it doesn't mean you have to hang on to some paranoid belief that no one else will either.'

'No?' Jaz challenged him. 'I don't know how you have the gall to make a statement like that,' she told him witheringly. 'At least my parents were motivated by love. Unlike you! I know exactly what you're trying to do, Caid, and why you're so determined to wrongfoot and undermine me! It's obvious that this is yet another attempt to coerce me into handing in my notice!'

Caid stopped her. 'What the hell are you talking about?'

'Oh, come on, Caid,' Jaz derided. 'You know full well what I mean.'

'No!' Caid corrected her, placing his palms flat on the table as he looked at her. 'I don't know what you mean at all.'

'Of course you do,' Jaz insisted, refusing to be intimidated. 'You've made that clear. And I've told you that there is no way I am going to be bullied into handing in my notice just because it suits the Dubois family to get rid of some of this store's existing personnel. Jerry has made it more than plain what he's been sent here to do. Well, let me tell you—'

'Now, just a minute—' Caid began ominously.

'It's no good, Caid.' Jaz stopped him sharply. 'I realise how very…satisfying it must be from your point of view, to be here not just witnessing but also being instrumental in putting me in my place—seeing me get my come-uppance as it were. And I can see how from your blinkered point of view you must be looking forward to gloating over the fact that the career I chose over being with you is about to come to an abrupt end. But it isn't quite like that. For one thing I can get another job. In no way am I dependent on the Dubois family. Yes, foolishly I did perhaps assume that your mother meant what she said when she hinted that there might be the potential for promotion for me within the business. But it wasn't my career that came between us…it was your attitude.'

'Now, see here—' Caid began sharply.

Jaz could see the fury smouldering in his eyes, turning them a dangerously dark shade of blue, but she wasn't going to allow herself to be intimidated. 'No, Caid!' she told him determinedly. 'It's time you listened to *me*. Before you start relishing the taste of the revenge you obviously think you are getting at my expense, there are one or two things you ought to know! The first is that I have no intention of handing in my notice until I am ready to do so. The second is that I'm glad you have done what you are doing. Because it totally confirms to me how right I was to end our relationship.'

'To end it? You mean like you were doing in your parents' barn?' Caid interrupted stingingly.

Jaz met the look he was giving her with pride and defiance.

Shrugging as nonchalantly as she could, she told him, 'So I felt like having sex? What's wrong with that?'

'One hell of a lot, if you want to convince a man that what you were doing was purely sex,' Caid told her softly.

Jaz didn't like the way he was watching her. It made her feel as though he was just waiting for her to betray herself so that he could pounce like a cat on a mouse. And no doubt when he did he would toy with her and torment her as cruelly as any hunter with its prey, inflicting wound after wound on her emotions until she was incapable of protecting herself any longer.

'That isn't something I feel any need to talk about,' she told him, assuming an expression of haughty disdain. 'It happened, but it doesn't have any real relevance in my life.'

'You mean like I don't?' Caid suggested.

'Exactly,' Jaz agreed in triumph.

'But you told me you loved me and you wanted to spend the rest of your life with me,' Caid reminded her softly. 'You cried out to me that you had never known such pleasure could exist; you begged me…'

White-faced, Jaz tried to blot out what he was saying and the images he was conjuring up—shockingly intimate and private images that now turned her face as hotly red as it had been tormentedly pale.

'That was before I knew what you were really like…before I realised that you would never allow me to truly be myself,' she burst out. 'I can't live like that. I've already tried for my parents and I can't do it—I won't do it. And I won't give in and resign from my job either, Caid, no matter what kind of pressure you and Jerry put on me.'

'Can I have that in writing?'

Jaz stared at him. What kind of Machiavellian sleight of hand was he trying to work on her now?

'Excuse me?' she asked.

'You heard me, Jaz. I want it in writing that you don't intend to leave. Or rather my mother does.'

'Your mother?' Now Jaz was confused.

'Yes, my mother,' Caid confirmed grimly. 'Contrary to what you obviously believe, I did not come over here either to try and get you to resign or to gloat over any potential loss of your job.'

Jaz shook her head. 'I don't believe you,' she told him flatly. 'Why else would you be here?'

An unfamiliar hesitancy held Caid silent for a second before he made any response. But Jaz was too wrought up to be aware of its significance, or to question it as he told her shortly, 'Filial duty and financial prudence, I guess.'

Something in the slightly hoarse sound of his voice and the way he looked away from her alerted Jaz's intuition to the fact that he wasn't being totally honest with her.

'No,' she repeated firmly. 'Although I don't know what you think you can achieve by lying to me at this stage of things!'

'Lying to you?'

Jaz flinched as she saw the fury in his eyes.

'Now let me tell you—' He stopped; cursing under his breath as his mobile suddenly rang.

Taking advantage of the interruption Jaz hurriedly left the kitchen.

'Tell me what, Caid?'

Caid heard his mother's voice enquiring in bemusement as she caught his muttered imprecation against Jaz and her departure, across the transatlantic telephone line.

'Nothing, Mom.'

'I've got some wonderful news, Caid. You'll never guess what! Donny and Number Five are getting a divorce, and he's as good as admitted that she was pushing him to try to get me off the board. Anyway, to cut a long story short, Donny is ringing Jerry right now to tell him to pack his bags and go join his mother. There is one small problem, though...'

'Whatever it is, I don't want to hear about it,' Caid told her. 'The minute this call is over I'm calling the airline.'

'Well, yes, I can understand how much you must want to get back to your ranch, Caid. But surely it won't hurt to stay there just a little while longer, say a week or so? Only it's going to take a few days to appoint a replacement for Jerry. We've got someone in mind, of course—the current assistant chief executive of the Boston store. Oh—and have you spoken to Jaz yet, by the way?'

'Yes. I have,' Caid told her tersely. 'You can stop worrying. It seems that Jaz has no intention of leaving, nor of being coerced into leaving.'

'Coerced into leaving? What on earth do you mean?'

Caid cursed inwardly as he realised he had let his feelings get the better of him. 'It's nothing,' he denied brusquely. 'Just that Jaz thought because of the way Jerry has been treating her that the family wanted to get rid of her.'

'What? Oh, Caid! You told her how much I want her to stay, I hope?'

'I did,' Caid confirmed.

'I think I'd better speak with her myself,' he heard his mother saying. 'I'll give her a ring now. You will stay there until we can sort out the new appointment, won't you, Caid?'

'You've got ten days,' Caid told her firmly.

Ten days would take him just to the other side of their dinner engagement with Jamie and Marsh. Caid knew that he should have cancelled—and of course the only reason he was not doing so was out of good manners. It had nothing whatsoever to do with Jaz!

Impatiently, Jaz stared at the sketch she was working on. Why was it that when she tried to alter the features of her woman's partner, and make him as physically unlike Caid as she could, the image staring back at her from her drawing board simply did not convey the emotions she wanted to project?

She had just ripped the sheet from the board when the phone rang.

The shock of hearing Caid's mother's voice on the other end of the line made her voice crack slightly as she responded to her greeting.

'I've just been speaking to Caid,' she said, and that made Jaz's heart lift and then drop with anxiety. 'Jaz, I'm so sorry about what's being happening,' Annette Dubois apologised.

'The very last thing we want is to lose you. In fact...'

As she listened to what she was being told Jaz's anxiety gave way to surprise, and then bemused relief as Annette explained briefly what was going to happen.

'Caid will be delighted to be able to get back to his ranch.' She laughed. 'He's probably been acting a bit like a grizzly with a sore paw, but there just wasn't anyone else I could trust in the way I trust him who could take my place and sort out all the problems in the UK store. I specifically asked him to persuade you not to leave. No doubt he'll be counting the days now until he gets on that flight. Now, tell me about your plans for the Christmas windows, Jaz.'

Forcing herself to focus, Jaz did so, but it was hard to talk about her work when she was still trying to absorb the fact that she had got it wrong about Caid's purpose in coming to the store. So she had made a mistake—got things wrong! Well, that was hardly surprising, was it, given Caid's own attitude towards her? If she had misjudged him he had brought that on himself, hadn't he? And for her to be thinking of apologising… No way was she going to do that!

'I take it that you have spoken with my mother?'

'Yes,' Jaz responded to Caid's worryingly smooth voice and calm question.

'And of course you now realise that at no time was I in any way looking to "gloat" over—'

'All right, Caid,' Jaz interrupted him defensively. 'So I got that wrong—but it was hardly all down to me, was it? I mean you made it plain enough in New Orleans how you regarded…' Jaz pressed her lips together firmly and shook her head.

'I don't want to discuss this any further. There just isn't any point,' she burst out when he remained silent.

She could see the condemnation in his eyes…the contempt. Remembering what he had been saying to her before his mobile had rung she lifted her head and admitted, 'I can't pretend that…that sexually there isn't…that I don't…' Biting her lip to stop it from trembling, she shook her head.

'Look, the kind of life I want to share with my…with someone…is about much more than just sexual desire. I want…I need to feel that the person closest to me understands my emotional needs as well as my physical ones, Caid, even if he can't share them. I need to feel that he supports me, that he is strong enough to allow me to be me, that when he can't agree with me he can at least attempt to compromise.'

'Compromise? You mean like you do?' Caid demanded harshly.

Jaz looked away from him. Why was it that they couldn't be together without verbally ripping into one another? Or physically ripping one another's clothes off?

'Your mother said that you'd be flying home just as soon as you could arrange it,' she told him in a clipped voice, changing the subject.

'That's right,' Caid agreed in an equally distant tone. 'I've already booked my flight. I leave on the Tuesday after your cousin's dinner party.'

Jaz's heart did a double-flip.

'You still intend to go to that?'

'It would be bad manners not to do so,' Caid told her coldly.

CHAPTER TEN

ANXIOUSLY, Jaz studied the clothes she had put out to pack for the weekend visit to her cousin's.

When Jamie had rung earlier in the week to check on the arrangements she had informed Jaz that she'd invited some of their neighbours to join them for dinner on the Saturday evening.

'Alan will be there,' she had told Jaz. 'He's bringing his new girlfriend. She's not really our type, but apparently his mother approves of her. Alan asked to be remembered to you, by the way. If you ask me he's got quite a thing about you, Jaz,' she had teased.

Alan Taylor-Smith was one of Jamie and Marsh's closest neighbours and Jaz knew him quite well. Although she liked him as a person, she had never been particularly attracted to him.

'What about your other guests?' she had asked, ignoring Jamie's comment.

'Newcomers to the area, from London. He's a musician and she's a TV producer. A very glamorous couple—think cool and Notting Hill. Oh, and get as glammed up as you like. I thought we'd make a really special occasion of it.'

As glammed up as she liked! Well, the dress she had decided to wear for the dinner party was certainly glamorous, Jaz acknowledged as she studied it uncertainly. She had happened to be there when the fashion buyer had been overseeing the unpacking of an order.

'Jaz, you have to see this!' she had called out.

'These clothes are from a new designer and I think they'll be a sell out over Christmas. Just look at this dress.'

The dress in question was a mere sliver of damson-coloured silk velvet, cut on the bias and dipping right down at the back almost to the point of indecency!

'Try it on,' the buyer had urged her. 'It's the perfect colour for you and you've got the figure to wear it.'

Even now Jaz wasn't entirely sure just why she had ended up buying it. It was far more daring that anything she would normally have worn. Of course the fact that the dinner party would be the final time she and Caid would be together had nothing whatsoever to do with it...

Despite the buyer's amusement, Jaz had refused to follow her recommendation and not wear anything beneath the dress.

'But you can see for yourself that briefs spoil the gown's line,' the buyer had complained.

'No way am I going anywhere without my knickers—VPL or no VPL!' Jaz had retorted sturdily.

As a compromise she had bought for herself a couple of pairs of ridiculously expensive pieces of silk nothings which barely showed through—and the pedicure in the store's beauty salon she had just managed to squeeze into her busy schedule meant that her toenails were now painted in one of the season's hottest new shades, which just happened to tone perfectly with her gown.

For the rest of the visit Jaz had packed a spare pair of jeans and a couple of tops. Her cousin might be able to muster a dinner table of guests any hostess would envy, but she was still a countrywoman at heart.

It was four o'clock, and they were due to leave at

six. She hadn't seen Caid all day, and half of her was hoping that he would change his mind and not go to her cousin's. But the other half...the other half was rebelliously determined to overrule Jaz's stern disapproval and show him on this final time they would spend together just what his stubbornness was costing him!

When he walked away from her she wanted him to carry an image of her that would torment him every bit as much as her memories of him were going to torment her.

Quickly showering, she hesitated before getting re-dressed. With time in hand before they were due to leave, Jaz succumbed to the nervous impulse dictating that she try the dress on one more time before she packed it—just to make sure it looked alright...

Caid checked the time as he let himself into the house. The door to Jaz's bedroom was half open, and he could hear Jaz moving about inside the room. He had sourced half a dozen bottles of a particularly rare red wine he hoped Marsh would enjoy, to take with them, but he needed to check with Jaz to find out if Jamie preferred chocolates or flowers.

In her bedroom, Jaz slipped into the minute piece of underwear she had bought to wear under her dress. It would show through the fine silk velvet, she knew, but there was no way she intended not to wear it. Frowningly, she went to lift the dress off its hanger.

Caid knocked briefly on Jaz's bedroom door, pushing it open as he called out, 'Jaz—I want to—'

Freezing as she heard his voice, Jaz turned towards the now open door, glancing wildly from it to the dress that was still out of reach, a couple of feet away. She could feel her face turning a deep shade of hot, self-conscious pink as Caid looked at her.

'I just wanted to try on my dress for tomorrow night,' she heard herself explain defensively. 'I wasn't sure...'

With the delectably sexy sight of Jaz's virtually naked body in front of him, stirring up as it did all manner of erotic and demanding memories and longings, Caid was not really able to focus on what she was actually saying—nor make an immediate connection between her alluring state of semi-undress and the slither of silk velvet hanging up behind her on the wardrobe door!

Somehow, instinctively, deep down inside, Jaz could almost feel what Caid was thinking. What he was wanting!

Without moving, she watched and waited as he looked at her.

No, there was no mistaking that hot, dangerous look of male arousal she had glimpsed in his eyes before he had managed to tamp it down.

Recklessly, she wanted him to do more than just look at her. Much, much more. Perhaps her own feelings were so acutely intense because she knew how soon they would be parting for ever! Whatever the reason, she was immediately aware of her own sharp thrill of tension, and of the highly sensually charged effect on her of having him standing there looking at her. Her body was trembling in the grip of a dangerous surge of longing so immediate that it shocked her.

Quickly she tried to counter-balance what she was feeling. Taking a step back from him whilst holding up her hand, she denied huskily, 'Caid! Don't! Stop!'

Even as she spoke Jaz could hear her own words

repeated inside her head. But this time in a remembered soft, broken litany of love and helpless desire, as she had lain beneath him in the shadowy privacy of her hotel room, begging him achingly, as he loved her, 'Caid! Don't stop... Please don't stop!'

It was like being swamped by the uncontrollable forces of nature; thrown into a maelstrom over which she had absolutely no control.

As Caid came towards her, her body quivered in helpless arousal. His eyes were the deepest, darkest most passionate colour she had ever seen them, and as their gazes locked Jaz felt totally unable to drag hers away.

Dizzily she acknowledged that there was something volatile and erotically alluring about the visual impact of his dark business-suit-clad body contrasting with her virtual nakedness. She believed in total equality between the sexes, in total honesty and trust, and yet here she was being hotly turned on by the knowledge of her own vulnerability to Caid through her semi-nakedness.

His hands felt cool and powerful as they closed around her upper arms, drawing her to him, but when Jaz opened her mouth it wasn't to deny him, but to take as eagerly and hungrily as he was giving the bittersweet physical passion of his kiss.

She made him feel more angry that any other human being he had ever met. The sheer stubbornness of her refusal to see what she was denying them infuriated him to the point where...

Beneath his hands Caid felt Jaz quiver, as though she could sense what he was thinking.

That small betraying gesture shattered his self-control. Unable to stop himself, he ground his mouth hotly and urgently against hers, driven by a deep, gut-tearing need to absorb every bit of her as deeply into himself as he could.

Wrapped tightly in Caid's arms, her mouth fused hotly to his, Jaz had to grit her teeth against the low, moaning sob of pleasure and need burning in her throat. His hand touched her breast, cupping it, and she cried out in an urgent frenzy of pleasure. The savage burn of her own inner anguish engulfed her in pain. She wanted him so much. Just this one last time…just to give her something to cling to for comfort…even if it was only a memory….

'No!' Caid denied them both fiercely, thrusting her away from him.

As he stared at her, torn between his hungry need of her and his pride, Caid fought to control his breathing. He was dangerously close to the edge and it would take very little to push him over. What he wanted, with an intensity he could only just hold at bay, was to take Jaz and lay her on the bed so tempt-ingly close at hand, to allow himself the sweetly sav-age pleasure of tasting every inch of her exposed skin, to caress her until she was crying out to him in need, until nothing could stop her from wrapping those slim, sexy legs around him as she urged him deeper and deeper within the moist intimacy of her body.

But most of all what he wanted was not only to have her body, but to have the infinitely more precious gift of her heart. For her to tell him that nothing else, nothing in this universe or beyond, was more impor-tant to her than him, that her love for him was so powerful, so comprehensive that he and it came before everything else in her life.

What he wanted, Caid recognised, was to receive

from Jaz the totality of a love that would eradicate for ever that cold, hurting place in his heart where a young boy's fear of not being loved still tormented him. What he needed from Jaz was not just her love, but proof of her love. And she could not give him that...

Jaz took a deep breath as she saw Caid walking towards her. She had just finished stowing her luggage in the boot of her car, and she was fiercely determined that not so much as by the smallest quiver of a single eyelash was she going to betray to Caid just how much what had happened between them in her bedroom earlier was still affecting her.

They were in the car, and she had driven several hundred yards down the road, when she suddenly remembered that she had left her big coat behind on her bed. Well, she wasn't going to go back for it now and invite Caid's criticism of her for forgetting it in the first place.

After all, it was Caid's fault. If she hadn't been so busy torturing herself about what had happened between them...

She had tried frantically to convince herself that he was totally responsible, totally to blame, that she herself had done nothing to encourage his unwanted touch and his equally unwanted kiss, but her conscience would not allow her to do so. Shamingly she had to acknowledge that she had been within a few pulsebeats of ignoring the fact that he simply wanted her for sex. Another second of that fiercely demanding kiss, of his touch on her skin, and she would have been all melting compliance, begging him to go on.

Only her pride was keeping her going now—her

pride and her determination to show him that he meant as little to her emotionally as she did to him!

Coolly ignoring Caid, Jaz gradually increased the speed of her little compact car. She had saved up for it herself, refusing her father's offer to buy her something larger. Now, though, seeing the way Caid had to hunch himself up into the passenger seat, she acknowledged that it was perhaps a little on the small side. Certainly this enforced intimacy was making her far too acutely aware of Caid sitting alongside her.

Being familiar with the country route to her cousin's, Jaz had chosen to use that rather than the motorway. Her cousin lived to the west of the ancient town of Ludlow, right in the heart of the Welsh marches, and good manners obliged her to turn to Caid as they approached the town, and tell him stiltedly, 'Jamie won't be serving supper until late this evening—I normally stop here in Ludlow on my way to see her; you might like to see the town—it's very old.'

It was the first time she had spoken directly to him since they had set off.

'Good idea,' Caid agreed coolly, 'I'd like to stretch my legs.'

'I'm sorry if my car isn't up to American standards,' Jaz answered back with immediate defensiveness.

They had had a sunny day, but the evening air was crisp and sharp, hinting at an overnight frost. As she got out of her car Jaz could smell the familiar scent of winter in the air and huddled deeper into her jacket.

By the time they had walked out of the car park and up the hill past the castle Jaz was shivering, wishing that she had turned back for her thicker coat.

Refusing to check to see whether or not Caid was

following her, she hurried through the market square and down a little side street to her favourite Ludlow coffee-shop-cum-wine-bar.

An hour later, when they left, having had a coffee during which they had barely spoken to one another at all, Jaz shivered in the cold night air.

It was a good twenty-minute walk back to where she had parked the car. Frost had already started to rime the ground, sparkling in the light from the clear sky. It was beautiful to look at but far too cold to be out in without the protection of a warm coat.

Within seconds of stepping outside Jaz felt her teeth start to chatter. Automatically she started to walk faster, gasping out loud as they turned a corner and she was exposed to the icy air being channelled up the hill they had to walk down to reach her car.

It was too late to try to conceal the open shivering of her body. Caid had seen it.

'Wait,' he told her cursorily.

At first Jaz thought that he was going to offer to give her his jacket, and she had the words of self-denial and refusal all ready to say. But to her consternation instead he closed the small gap between their bodies, reaching out with one arm to tug her firmly against his side, inside the jacket he had unfastened, so that she was pressed up close against his heart whilst the warmth of his body soaked blissfully into her chilled flesh.

However, when she realised that he intended them to walk back to the car like that, with her body pressed up close against his, just like the love-drugged pair of teenagers she had just seen crossing the grass in front of the castle, pausing every few steps to exchange passionate kisses, Jaz struggled to pull herself free. Caid refused to let her go.

The young lovers had disappeared into the protective shadows of the castle's mighty walls, but Jaz was oblivious to their disappearance. Pain had snatched her up in its grim claws, squeezing the love out of her heart until it dripped like lifeblood into the vast emptiness of the dark despair she was fighting to deny.

The walk to the car felt like hours. With each step they took Jaz was more and more aware of Caid's body next to her own.

Yes, she said to herself as they finally reached the car and he let her go. So far as she was concerned Tuesday could not come fast enough. Surely once the Atlantic Ocean was safely between them she would be able to get on with her own life?

'Well, are you going go tell me what's wrong or am I just going to have to guess?'

Mutinously Jaz turned away from Jamie, whom she had offered to help with dinner preparations.

'Nothing's wrong.' she insisted, and then to her horror she promptly burst into tears.

'It's Caid, isn't it?' Jamie guessed, coming over to her.

'No. It's got nothing to do with him. Why should it have?' Jaz fibbed defensively, before whispering, 'Oh, Jamie!'

Jamie simply stood and looked at her. 'Tell me about it?' she invited.

Half an hour later, when she had finally stopped speaking, Jaz looked at her imploringly. 'You do understand, don't you?'

'Yes, I do,' Jamie acknowledged sadly.

*   *   *

'These logs are just about the last of the trees we lost in the year before last's bad gales,' Marsh informed Caid as they stood in front of the drawing room fire, waiting for the other dinner guests to arrive.

Caid had barely seen Jaz since their arrival the previous evening; both of them had been keeping an equally determined distance from one another.

Marsh handed him a bourbon, and saw his look of appreciative surprise. 'Jaz told us it was your drink,' he told Caid with a smile.

The newspaper he most liked to read and a whole pot of coffee, strong enough to stand a spoon up in and boiling hot, had also been brought to his room this morning by one of Jamie and Marsh's children. It was exactly what he most enjoyed early in the day, and now he'd been given his favourite drink. They were not fortuitous coincidences, as he had assumed, but the result of Jaz's observations.

For Caid, that kind of detailed knowledge about a person's tastes equated not just with caring about them but with caring *for* them as well. It certainly wasn't the kind of thing he expected from a woman who prized her own freedom and independence above all.

He started to frown.

'Speaking of Jaz, I hear that you got to see her father's Holsteins. I have to tell you that that is a real compliment. He's very protective of them and pretty choosy about who he shows them to.'

'Fine beasts,' Caid responded enthusiastically, and before too long the two men were deep in a discussion about livestock. But although outwardly he was listening to what Marsh was saying, inwardly Caid was thinking about Jaz.

*   *   *

Jaz tensed as she heard the soft rap on her bedroom door, but when she went to answer it was only her cousin standing outside, her eyes widening appreciatively as she saw what Jaz was wearing.

'Wow!' she exclaimed approvingly. 'You look stunning.'

'You don't think it's too much, do you?' Jaz asked anxiously as Jamie studied her.

'It will certainly be too much for the men.' Jamie laughed. 'If I'd known you were going to be wearing something like that I wouldn't have gone to so much trouble with the food. They'll scarcely notice what's on their plates with you in front of them! What do you wear underneath it, by the way?' Jamie teased. 'That fabric is so fine…'

'The briefest little thong I could find,' Jaz admitted ruefully. 'And our buyer didn't even want me to wear that. You can actually see it,' she added, pointing out the faint line in the fall of her gown to her cousin.

'Only just!' Jamie assured her. 'Are you ready to come down? The others are just about due to arrive.'

'Give me five minutes,' Jaz told her.

As luck would have it she was halfway down the stairs when the other dinner guests arrived—and, as Jamie had predicted, the arrested and approving gazes of both male guests went immediately to her as she stood poised there.

Their female partners' glances were equally immediate, but assessing rather than admiring.

'Jaz, come down and meet everyone,' Jamie instructed, explaining to her guests, 'Jaz is my cousin.'

'Jaz!' Alan enthused, stepping forward and kissing her for just a little bit longer than was really necessary.

'Aren't you going to introduce me, Alan?'

'Jaz—Sara,' Alan introduced obediently.

Everything about Alan's new girlfriend was sharp, Jaz reflected as Alan introduced them. Her voice, her nose; her chin, her fashionably thin body, and even her cold china-blue eyes.

No, you don't like me, do you? Jaz reflected as she correctly interpreted the look she was being given, and the determinedly proprietorial way in which Alan's girlfriend was gripping his arm.

To Jaz's relief the television producer and her husband were much more sociable—a pair of thirty-somethings confidently at ease with themselves and, Jaz guessed, very socially aware.

'Do you work? Are you here with a partner, or on your own?' Myla Byfleet, the TV producer, quizzed Jaz with open interest.

'You'll have to forgive my wife,' Rory Byfleet apologised with a grin. 'She used to be a reporter.'

'Jaz is the window and display designer for Cheltenham's largest department store—you may have heard of it,' Jamie explained with a smile. 'She's here with Caid Dubois, whose family have bought the store,' she added diplomatically, ignoring the look that Jaz gave her.

'I should have guessed you're artistic,' Myla complimented Jaz warmly as they all went through to the drawing room, adding, 'I love your dress! You look stunning.'

'Doesn't she just?' Alan agreed enthusiastically. As he spoke he reached past her, ostensibly to push the drawing room door open wider for her, but as he did so his hand brushed her hip and lingered there briefly.

Ruefully aware of Sara's sour glare in her direction, Jaz moved away from him. If this was the kind of reaction her dress was going to provoke, she knew she was going to regret buying it.

One man was obviously immune to its allure, though, she recognised as she saw the way that Caid was frowning at her.

Deliberately she kept her distance from him as Jamie reintroduced everyone. With a speed and obviousness that Jaz would have thought out of character, Sara began flirting openly with Caid, her voice girlishly high as she exclaimed that she adored American men. Watching them together, Jaz felt an immediate pang of angry jealousy.

Barely listening to what the woman just introduced to him was saying, Caid continued to glower at the man who had ushered Jaz into the room.

Caid had seen the way he'd touched Jaz, his hand lingering on her hip. Did she have any idea just what she looked like in that dress? It clung to her skin as fluidly as water, rippling provocatively with every movement she made. It was, Caid suspected, impossible for her to be wearing the slightest thing underneath it. But then she turned towards Marsh, accepting the aperitif he was handing her, and Caid saw the discreet line that just marked the fabric—and remembered what she had said to him about trying on her dress.

Heat shot through him—a fierce, elemental surge of possessiveness and knowledge. Without the slightest effort he could see her as she had been in the house, her body naked apart from her the tiny scrap of fabric that had tantalised and tormented him so much.

He was barely aware of finishing his drink or sitting down at the table. All he could think about was Jaz.

He wanted to take her somewhere very private and slide that sexy, distracting and dangerous dress from her even more distracting and dangerous body. Then he wanted to hold her, touch her, kiss every single inch of her until her voice was a paper-thin whispering sob of pleasure, begging him to satisfy her need.

Jamie had seated Alan on Jaz's right, whilst Caid sat opposite her. Despite the presence of his girlfriend, Alan was making full use of his proximity to flirt openly and fulsomely with Jaz.

Since Jaz knew him, she refrained from treating him as coolly as she would have done had he been a stranger to her. The truth was that she felt slightly sorry for him. His bossy mother was itching for him to get married and produce grandchildren, so she could dominate them in the same way she had done him, but she was equally determined to choose her own daughter-in-law. And poor Alan had a penchant for exactly the type of woman his domineering mother least wanted as her son's wife. To judge from the fact that he was dating Sara, Jaz guessed that his mother now had the upper hand.

Generously she made allowances for Alan's heavy flirting, telling herself that the poor man was probably trying to make a last desperate bid for freedom.

Beneath the table Alan had started to stroke her leg.

Immediately she moved out of his way, shaking her head at him in discreet admonition. Across from her, Sara was shooting Jaz a bitterly resentful look, at the same time moving closer to Caid, her hand fixed firmly on his arm as she turned to smile at him.

The Byfleets were recounting a mildly ribald anecdote about a minor media personality. Politely Jaz listened and smiled though out of the corner of her eye she could see Sara whispering something to Caid. Sara's glass was already empty, and so was Alan's. To judge from the looks they were exchanging, Jaz guessed that angry words had been exchanged between them prior to their arrival.

'So you work in a store? Oh. Yes, of course—Alan's mother has mentioned you,' Sara informed Jaz dubiously, making it abundantly plain that whatever Alan's mother had had to say about her, it had not been complimentary. 'And *your* family now owns the store,' she whispered to Caid in a false 'little girly' voice.

How could any man be taken in by that kind of thing? That kind of woman? Jaz wondered irritably.

'Actually, Sara, Caid is a rancher,' she told the other girl coolly.

But if she had been hoping to deflect Sara's interest away from Caid with her statement it had backfired on her—and badly, Jaz recognised, as Sara's eyelash-batting went into double time.

'A rancher? You mean like in cowboy films? Oh, how exciting…and…and romantic! Sort of noble.'

'I think you must have got the cowboys mixed up with the Indians,' Myla Byfleet told Sara, laughing. 'You know—the noble savage sort of thing,' she explained carefully, exchanging an ironic glance with her husband.

Obviously Sara appealed to Myla as little as she did to her, Jaz recognised, but, whatever the other women around the table thought about her, Caid quite obviously thought she was wonderful.

In her own way, Sara certainly seemed determined to dominate the dinner table conversation, and to demand all the available male attention for herself—especially Caid's!

Forcing herself to ignore Caid's rapt concentration on Sara, Jaz joined in the conversation going on between the Byfleets.

She laughed when Rory Byfleet told her admiringly that she had a wonderfully musical voice, and it was the sound of that low husky laughter that drew Caid's fixed gaze to her.

'Oh, I do wish I was more like Jaz.' Sara sighed helplessly at his side. 'I do so envy women like her...'

'You do? Why?' Caid felt obliged to ask.

'Well, she's a career woman, isn't she? Men like that type of woman, don't they? They find them dangerous and exciting. All I've ever wanted to do is fall in love and have babies—stay at home and look after them and my husband.' She gave another soft sigh. 'I'm boring, I know, but that's just how I feel. Of course, Alan's always had a thing about Jaz,' she added, less softly, both her voice and her gaze sharpening as she looked across the table to where Alan was still trying to engage Jaz's attention.

'I suppose it gives her a bit of a kick to encourage him. She's that kind of woman, isn't she? It's so hard for someone like me to compete with someone like her. But Alan's mother says I would make him a good wife, and I think that in his heart Alan knows that as well. I know it's old-fashioned of me, but I believe that a woman's role is to love and support her husband and her children.'

Catching this artless declaration from the other side of the table, Jaz could feel her ears starting to burn.

Sara couldn't have found a better way to gain Caid's

attention and approval! Well, she was welcome to him! Very welcome!

To Jaz's relief the evening finally came to an end. She had barely eaten or drunk anything, and now she was feeling so on edge that her head had actually begun to pound with tension.

As everyone began to exchange goodnights, Alan made a lunge towards her, obviously intent on kissing her. Immediately Jaz moved slightly to one side, so that his kiss landed against her cheek, rather than on her mouth, but she was still too late to stop him from enveloping her in a tight and embarrassingly sexual embrace.

Firmly disentangling herself, she stepped back from him just in time to see the lingering kiss that Sara was sharing with Caid.

The sickening wave of jealousy and pain that struck her was so strong that it actually physically rocked her on her feet.

Jamie, witnessing that small betraying movement, reached out and put a hand on her arm, saying quietly, 'You look exhausted. Why don't you go up to bed?'

'And leave you to clean up? No way.' Jaz shook her head, turning her back on Caid as Marsh finally closed the front door on the departing dinner guests.

Normally this was the part of Jamie's dinner parties that Jaz relished—the relaxing winding down after the event, when she and her cousin could talk intimately about the party and the guests whilst they worked companionably and efficiently together to clear everything away. But tonight...! No way did she want to discuss the intimacy that Caid and Sara had shared with anyone!

* * *

In the end all four of them cleaned up from the dinner party together—Jaz and Jamie hand-washing the expensive dinner service Jamie and Marsh had been given as a wedding present, whilst the two men did everything else.

'I've got a favour to ask you tomorrow,' Jamie confessed when the four of them had finally finished. 'You know the cottage we let out on the edge of the estate?' she asked Jaz. 'You pass it when you drive back.'

'Yes, I know the one,' Jaz confirmed.

Running an estate the size of Marsh's was an expensive business, Jaz knew, and her cousin and her husband did everything they could to find ways to maximise the estate's revenue. Letting out empty estate cottages to holidaymakers was one of them. This particular cottage, which had originally, in Victorian times, been the home of one of the estate's many gamekeepers, was very isolated, and a favourite location for people wanting a romantic hideaway.

Jamie had focused on this aspect of the cottage when she had refurnished it for visitors. The main bedroom possessed an enormous four-poster bed, complete with gorgeous bedlinen. And real fires burned in both the bedroom and sitting room grates—backed up by modern central heating. As part of the package she sold to visitors Jamie ensured that on their arrival they would find the fridge stocked with all manner of foodie luxuries, specially chosen with both their preferences and their status as lovers in mind.

'I've promised to take Chester over to see a friend of his tomorrow afternoon,' Jamie told her, 'and I was wondering if on your way back to Cheltenham you could possibly stop off at the cottage with the food for the guests who are due to arrive on Monday evening.'

'No problem,' Jaz assured her, only too happy to be able to help.

She had studiously ignored Caid whilst they had all been cleaning up and now, as she kissed her cousin and Marsh goodnight, she deliberately kept her back to him.

Her head still ached—even more painfully, if anything—though fortunately she had some painkillers with her that she could take. They would put an end to her headache, but what about the pain in her heart? No medication on earth could ease that...

'Sorry we had to seat you with Sara,' Marsh apologised to Caid as he offered him a final nightcap. 'Dreadful woman. I fought like hell against Jamie when she told me that no way was she going to be a stay-at-home wife—I'd envisaged her playing the same supportive role Sara seems to favour—but Jamie made it clear that she had other ideas.

'No career, no relationship. That's what she told me. At the time I thought I was being quite the hero to give in to her, but every time I come across a woman like Sara I realise what a narrow escape I had.

'Imagine having to live with a woman like that, who has no identity of her own, no thoughts, ideas, no personality, and who spends most of her time working out how best to manipulate you and everyone else into doing what she wants whilst maintaining her chosen role of doting subservience?'

'What's that you're saying?' Jamie enquired, as she caught the tail end of Marsh's comment.

'I was just saying how lucky I am that you saved me from a fate worse than Sara,' Marsh teased her.

'Worse than Sara? Is that possible?' Jamie grimaced. 'Poor Alan. I do feel sorry for him—especially knowing what a thing he's got for Jaz.'

'A "thing"? What "thing"?' Marsh began in bewilderment, but behind Caid's back Jamie shook her head, warning him, and like the observant and intuitive husband he was Marsh recognised her silent message.

Oblivious to the looks that Jamie and Marsh were exchanging, Caid put down the drink he had been holding unfinished.

'I think I'll go up, if you don't mind,' he announced abruptly.

'What was all that about?' Marsh enquired plaintively, once he had gone. 'What did you mean, Alan has a "thing" for Jaz?'

'Well, perhaps I exaggerated a little.'

'Hmm!'

Jaz had just swallowed down the second of her painkillers when she heard the knock on her bedroom door.

Going to open it, she saw Caid standing outside.

'Can I have a word?'

He looked and sounded so formidable that she automatically stood back from the door.

As she did so the light from the room fell across her body, revealing the sheer delicacy of her dress.

'I must say you looked very impressive this evening,' Caid told her coldly. 'But then of course you don't need me to tell you that, do you? Who exactly were you dressing for, Jaz, or can I guess?'

'Well, it wasn't for you!' Jaz lied.

'No, I think I managed to work that out for myself.

Have you no compassion for others? No respect for their feelings?'

Jaz raised her hand to massage the pain in her temple. This was the last thing she needed right now.

'Whatever it is you want to say, Caid, I don't want to hear it!' she told him stonily.

'No. I'm damn sure you don't! But you sure as hell are going to!' Caid responded grimly.

Jaz could see how furiously angry he was, but for some reason, instead of alarming her, her recognition of his anger only served to add to the savagery of her own righteous sense of betrayal.

'Have you any idea of the damage you were causing back there during dinner?' Caid challenged her. 'The hurt you might have been inflicting?'

'What?' Jaz exclaimed, her voice taut with disbelief and incredulity. 'On who?'

Caid's mouth compressed.

'On Sara, of course,' he told her tersely. 'She's desperately in love with that—with Alan. God knows why. And she's equally desperately afraid that she will lose him. Personally I think she'd be better off if she did. Why on earth a woman like her wants a man like that, who doesn't respect her, doesn't realise how lucky he is—'

'Well, Alan might not but you obviously do,' Jaz interrupted him. 'But then of course she is your type, isn't she? Your perfect woman! Did you tell her that? You should have done. From the way she was behaving my guess is that she'd be only too delighted to ditch poor Alan if she thought you would be willing to take his place.'

'What the hell are you talking about?'

Jaz stared at him. She took a deep breath as she

tried to control the fury rushing through her in a dangerous riptide.

'Isn't it obvious?' she threw at him savagely. 'I mean, Sara was hardly behaving like a loving and faithful girlfriend, was she?'

'She was very distressed,' Caid countered. 'Naturally for pride's sake she didn't want Alan to see how upset she was.'

'Which was no doubt why she gave you such a lingering goodnight kiss—even though Alan was nowhere in sight,' Jaz shot back.

Her head was pounding so badly now she was afraid she might actually be physically sick. Just thinking about the passionate kiss she had seen Sara give Caid was threatening to shatter what was left of her composure.

'Lingering? You call that a lingering kiss?' Caid derided.

'Well, it certainly looked that way from where I was standing,' Jaz countered.

'I don't care how it looked,' Caid denied. 'And besides, the best way to judge a kiss in my book is to experience it—feel it. Like this…'

Jaz realised just too late what he intended to do, and by then she couldn't evade the fierce pressure of his mouth as it came down on hers. But the punishment, the harshness she'd automatically steeled herself to resist never came. Instead Caid was softly stroking her lips with his—caressing them, teasing them, making her feel…making her want…

Helplessly she swayed closer to him, unable to stop her lips from parting as he ran his tongue-tip along them, easing them open, dipping into the soft, moist warmth of her mouth, slowly caressing her tongue, biting gently at her lips and then running his tongue over their kiss-bitten sensitivity.

Over and over again Caid brushed her mouth with his own, stroking her lips with his tongue, one hand cupping her face whilst he drew her closer to him with the other.

Mindlessly Jaz gave in to her emotions.

'Now that,' Caid told her rawly when he finally lifted his mouth from hers, 'is a lingering kiss!'

White-faced, Jaz pulled back from him.

Reaching for the bedroom door, she slammed it shut, leaving Caid standing on the other side.

Taking a deep breath, Jaz leaned against the door she had just closed whilst the tears she could no longer control filled her eyes and rolled painfully down her face.

Frowning, Caid stared at Jaz's door. The savagery of his own pain and jealousy shocked him. After one last look at the firmly closed bedroom door he made his way back to his own room.

CHAPTER ELEVEN

'AND you're sure you don't mind calling at the cottage with the food?' Jamie checked, having looked from Caid's set face to her cousin's shockingly pale one.

'Not in the least,' Jaz confirmed in a brittle, too bright voice that matched her equally forced smile.

They had all just finished Sunday lunch, although Jaz had barely been able to eat more than a mouthful or so of her own. Her headache might have gone, but it had left in its place the deepest, blackest sense of despair and anguish that she had ever known.

She and Caid had totally ignored one another during the meal, and she suspected that he must feel the same abhorrence at the thought of sharing the car journey back to Cheltenham as she did.

An hour later, with Jamie's delicious home-cooked gourmet meals and other food packed into cool bags in the back of her car, Jaz paused to give her cousin a final hug, before heading towards her car.

Silently, his face drawn into grim lines, Caid followed her.

Jaz frowned as she saw the way the wind was beginning to whip the bare branches of the trees into a fierce frenzy, its unforecast strength scooping up piles of dead leaves and flattening the grassy pastures on either side of the road.

The morning's weather forecast had given slight a gale warning, but this looked as though it was going to be far more severe than the forecast had threatened. Automatically she switched on her car radio, to try to get an update, but all she could hear was the crackle of static.

Sensing her concern, Caid broke the silence which had lain bitterly between them since the start of their journey to demand, 'Is something wrong?'

'Not really. It's just that the wind seems to be getting very strong,' Jaz responded stiffly.

Out of the corner of her eye she could see the sudden quirk of Caid's eyebrows, and heard the slight amusement in his voice as he drawled, 'If you think this is strong you should see some of the twisters we get back home. And in the winter the wind can blow up one hell of a snowstorm.'

Jaz didn't bother to make any response; she was too busy gritting her teeth against the way the wind was now buffeting her small car as she took the turn-off into the long and winding unmade-up road that led to the cottage.

Right at the furthermost boundary of the estate, it was nestled in the heart of a small pretty wood, overlooking a good-sized natural pond which was the habitat of a variety of wildlife.

Skilfully, Jamie had utilised this charming setting to create an artlessly wild garden for the cottage—which in actual fact was really more of a small four-square Victorian house than a mere cottage.

As she parked her car outside Jaz was disturbed to see how increasingly wild the wind had become, causing the branches of the trees around the cottage to thrash frantically. She could feel the car rocking, and was unable to suppress the small gasp of alarm that rose to her lips.

Jaz could see the frowning look Caid gave her as he thrust open the passenger door, but unlike her he did not have seared into his memory pictures of the destruction caused by a certain other gale, which had shocked the whole country with the devastation it had caused.

A little nervously she too got out of the car, flinching as the branches of the trees beat frantically against the sky. Caid was already opening the boot of the car, and, reminding herself of just why they were here, Jaz reached in her pocket for the spare set of keys to the cottage and hurried up to the front door.

As she opened it the scent of Jamie's home-made pot-pourri soothed and enveloped her. The cottage felt warm, thanks to its central heating.

As she looked back towards the car she saw that Caid was starting to remove the food carriers.

In view of the weather Jaz was glad that they wouldn't need to spend very much time there. No longer, in fact, than it would take to put the food safely in the fridge and leave a welcome note and a bowl of fruit for the incoming guests. The truth was that the sooner they were on their way the happier she would be—and not just because of the storm that was threatening outside. No, the real danger was within herself: the fear of what even the smallest degree of physical intimacy with Caid might do to her self-control.

Even as her thoughts formed, Jaz could hear how the gale was increasing in intensity. As she crossed the hallway, leaving Caid to follow her inside, she tensed at the sudden and breath-catchingly eerie silence that made the tiny hairs on her skin lift in atavistic warning.

Instinctively she turned towards Caid, who was now

standing on the other side of the hallway, listening as intently as she was herself.

The storm wasn't over, she knew that, but even though she was prepared for it, the sudden high-pitched whistling of the wind as it picked up again at a terrifyingly high speed, made her flinch.

From outside they could hear the sharp cracking noise of wood splintering whilst rain spat viciously at the windows.

'What the hell is happening out there?' Caid demanded, striding towards the door.

Jaz went to follow him, but as she did so she heard a door banging somewhere upstairs, as though a window had been left open.

As Caid disappeared through the open front door, Jaz headed for the stairs.

The cottage had two smaller bedrooms in addition to the large master bedroom suite, and a huge bathroom, with a sensually luxurious spa bath. It was in one of the two smaller rooms that Jaz found the window which had been left slightly open and quickly closed it before turning to hurry back downstairs.

She was just about to step into the hall when she heard it—a horrible renting, a savage cacophony of sounds, that had her running for the front door and tugging it open, her heart leaping in frantic panic and hammering against her chest wall as her worst fears were confirmed.

The storm had brought down a huge tree which had fallen right across the lane, completely blocking it—and crushing her car.

For a few seconds shock froze her into immobility. She could see the bright patch of colour that was her car beneath the tree's heavy branches, just as she could see the huge hole in the earth where the tree's roots had once rested. But the whole scene seemed to be being relayed to her with her senses in slow motion, so that though she saw it, she somehow could not quite comprehend it.

Her gaze panned the whole scene slowly, several times, and then abruptly focused on the dark blur that was Caid's jacket, just visible on the ground between her crushed car and the heaviest part of the uprooted tree. Caid's jacket! The jacket which Caid had been wearing when he had walked out of the hall a few minutes ago! Caid's jacket... The jacket he had been wearing. The jacket with his body inside it...

Jaz started to run, brushing aside the branches that tore at her clothes and hair, pushing them back as she fought to get to Caid, sobs tearing at her throat as her fear for him shook her whole body. Ignoring the cold wet sting of the small whippy branches as she climbed through them, she cried out Caid's name in frantic panic.

Only now, when the fear of losing him had stripped bare her emotions, could she truly see how much she loved him. As she focused on his jacket she knew with a sudden blinding flash of insight, in a way she had refused to recognise before, that he was quite simply the only man she could ever love.

She had almost reached him, but the branches were thicker now, and more tangled, too heavy for her to move. She would have to—

'Jaz!'

Disbelievingly, Jaz stood still. She could hear Caid calling her name. But the sound was coming from behind her, not from the frighteningly still dark mass of the jacket she had been working her way towards!

'Jaz!'

Stronger now, and more urgent, the commanding tone of Caid's voice forced her to turn round.

The sight of him standing just outside the open front door of the cottage filled her with a feeling that was at once both so joyous and so humbling that she found it impossible to give it a name. More than relief, it was a sense of profound gratitude so intense that it blurred her eyes with tears.

Slowly at first, and then more quickly, she made her way back, his name a shaky tear-stained gasp, blown away on the gusting wind. 'Caid—you're alive. You're safe...'

It was Caid who was walking towards her now, reaching out to extricate her from the final tangle of branches until she finally she stood beside him, trying to push the damp hair off her face with numb fingers, unaware that the moisture on her face was not rain but her own tears.

'Oh, Caid... Caid...'

Unable to stop herself, she threw herself into his arms, shaking from head to foot as he opened them to enclose her. 'I thought you were hurt...dead...' she whispered chokily as her body shook with the ferocity of her emotions. 'I saw your jacket...'

'It caught on a branch whilst I was collecting some extra logs for the fires—I noticed that they needed some. I took it off, and then the wind must have blown it into the tree,' Caid said, his voice as thick with emotion as her own.

Her emotions overwhelmed her. To her own shame and disgust tears filled her eyes once again.

'Jaz—' Caid began, but she shook her head.

'It's nothing—I'm not crying,' she denied shakily.

'Not really.' She made to pull away from him, but Caid refused to let her go.

'You're in shock,' he told her curtly. 'I saw what had happened. That's why I went back inside—to tell you and ring Jamie. You nearly gave me heart failure when I came back and saw you crawling through those branches.'

Suddenly Jaz was trembling so violently that her teeth were chattering; the trembling turned into a deep intense shaking as shock and relief fought for control of her emotions.

'Come on—let's get back inside,' she heard Caid telling her.

Was it her imagination, or had his arms tightened just that little bit more around her?

As she started to move away from him, to walk back to the cottage, she felt the resistance of his hold. A brief silent questioning look into his face brought an answering equally silent shake of his head. Gratefully Jaz sank back against him, allowing him to guide her back to the house and revelling in the sensation of being so close to him.

With the door closed against the still howling gale, the warmth of the cottage embraced her, permeating the numbness of her shocked body.

'I'd better warn you that we're here for the night,' Caid told her ruefully. 'When I spoke to Marsh he said that he doesn't feel it's safe enough to send anyone out tonight to lift the tree. He reckons it would be dark before he could get anyone here…'

Listening to him, Jaz closed her eyes, and then wished she hadn't as behind her closed eyelids she saw the mental image she had recorded of the moment she'd looked across at her car and seen what she had believed to be Caid's trapped, broken body beneath the full weight of the tree.

Tears filled her eyes and splashed down her face.

'I thought you were there…under the tree,' she whispered, pulling herself free of Caid's arms to look up into his eyes, her own huge and dark with emotion. 'I thought… Oh, Caid…Caid…'

'Shush…it's all right,' Caid comforted her, and he drew her back into his arms, holding her as carefully as though she were a small hurt child.

The intensity of her emotion made him ache with love for her, and at the same time the raw nakedness of her pain made him want to hold her and protect her for ever.

'What happened to us, Caid?' Jaz asked him chokily. 'Why did it all have to go so wrong?'

Her fears had stripped away from her any desire to pretend any longer that she didn't care.

'I don't know,' Caid admitted sombrely. 'But what I do know is how much I want to make it all right, Jaz. How very, very much I want to start again…to tell you and show you just how much I still love you.'

'You love me?'

She had said it with all the shining joy and hope of a child discovering that there was a Father Christmas after all, Caid recognised, looking down into her eyes and seeing there the love and bemusement he could hear in her voice. But before he could reassure her she suddenly reached up and pulled his head down towards her own, kissing him with frantic anguished passion, her face wet with tears.

Fiercely Caid struggled between logic and love. Logic told him that they should be talking through their problems, but with Jaz's mouth pressed so hun-

grily and so sexily against his, how the hell was he
supposed to think about logic?

'Hold me, Caid! Love me!' Jaz demanded in between feverish kisses. 'I need to know that this isn't
a dream, that this is real, that *you* are real, not...'

As she started to shudder, unable to put into words
the fears that had filled her earlier, Caid knew there
was no way he wanted to resist her.

'I've never stopped loving you,' he told her rawly,
cupping her face in his hands and looking down deep
into her eyes as he kissed each word into her mouth,
spacing them slowly apart so that the kisses between
them grew longer and more intense. 'And as for holding you...' He went on in a husky dangerously male
voice, 'Jaz, no way can I hold you right now and not
make love to you,' he admitted thickly.

For a second Jaz hesitated, but she knew that if she
were to close her eyes she would see again his jacket
lying beneath the fallen tree, feel again the agonising
sensation of believing he was dead.

'Then make love to me,' she answered him softly.
'Make love with me, Caid.'

Silently they looked at one another. Even the air
around them seemed to be holding its breath, as
though something beyond it was waiting, hoping...

'Jaz...'

As he moaned her name Jaz took Caid's breath into
her own lungs, digging her fingers into the hard muscles of his shoulders and then the back of his neck as
they kissed one another with passionate abandon. She
couldn't stop touching him, running her hands over
his flesh, his body. A tiny gasp of tormented longing
locked in her throat as their need for one another
burned out of control.

Blindly she tugged at the fabric of Caid's shirt, its buttons, anything that was stopping her from reaching her longed-for goal of feeling his skin beneath her touch. She was heedless of the impatient help that Caid himself was giving her as he ruthlessly wrenched buttons from fastenings, ignoring the tearing sounds of destruction he was causing to his shirt.

Even more than Jaz wanted to touch him, he wanted to be touched by her. To be kissed by her, welcomed by her into the soft, sweet mystery of her wholly womanly and beloved body.

His hands cupped her breasts, tugging at her own clothes. White streaks of heat shot through her, and Jaz gave a small, thin cry of desperate longing, burying her face against his throat as her body convulsed into his touch.

On the floor she could see Caid's shirt, and her own top, although she had no knowledge of just how it had got there. She moaned as Caid bent his head, easing her breast free of her bra to caress it with the hot sweetness of his mouth.

'Not here,' Jaz heard Caid protesting huskily, lifting his mouth from hers only to rub his thumb against her softly swollen lips whilst he watched her aching reaction to his touch with a look that said he simply could not bear not to be touching her. 'Let's go upstairs—so that I can really enjoy you. So that we can really enjoy one another,' Caid begged her.

As she listened to him a long, slow shudder of response passed through Jaz. Silently, she nodded her head.

It was Caid who picked up the clothes they had discarded, and Caid who halfway up the stairs turned to Jaz and held her against his body, devouring her mouth in a kiss of such intimate passion that its intensity and promise made Jaz's eyes sting with emotion.

Like her, Caid seemed reluctant to speak—perhaps because he was afraid of damaging or destroying what was happening between them, Jaz reflected, as Caid led her to the door of the main bedroom and then opened it.

They kissed with hungry, biting little kisses, unable to get enough of one another, unable to control their shared longing to touch and taste every belovedly familiar, ached-for part of one another.

A stream of discarded clothes marked their progress to the huge four-poster bed, and now they stood body to body at the foot of it, Jaz naked apart from her silky briefs.

'I love you. I have always loved you. I shall always love you,' Caid told Jaz as he kissed her closed eyelids, the curve of her jaw, the soft readiness of her mouth, and then the pulsing hollow at the base of her throat, whilst his hands moulded and shaped her willing nakedness for their shared pleasure.

His own body, taut and naked, virile, visibly mirrored the desire beating through Jaz. Achingly she reached out to touch him, but Caid stopped her, and instead dropped to his knees in front of her, sliding his hands beneath the silky fineness of her briefs and slowly removing them, whilst his lips tormented her with hotly erotic kisses placed with hungry sensuality against her naked flesh.

He had loved her intimately and sensually in the past, but this, Jaz knew, was something else—something richer. This was a total giving of himself, a revelation of his need and vulnerability, almost a worship of all that she meant to him, a form of loving that somehow went way beyond even the wildest shores of desire.

When his tongue finally stroked against the innermost places of her sex, for a heartbeat of time both of them went still, sharing a special communion, a special bonding in a place that was totally their own.

Tenderly Jaz reached out and touched his downbent head, catching her breath as her own sensual response to his intimacy suddenly crashed through her. Her fingers slid to his shoulder, sweat-slick with the heat of his arousal, and her sob of pleasure was sharp and high.

She had to touch him, taste him, feel him again where he belonged—deep, deep inside her.

As the words of love and longing poured from her Caid responded to them, gathering her up and placing her on the bed, his own moan of raw triumphant pleasure when she reached for him, stroking the length of his erection whilst she studied him with eager hungry eyes, joining the soft aching words of praise she was whispering against the pulsing fullness of him.

'I want you inside me, Caid. Now! Please, please now!'

'Are you awake?'

Instinctively Jaz burrowed tightly into the warmth of Caid's body before answering him.

'Yes, I am,' she admitted.

It was too early yet for dawn to have begun lightening the sky, but plenty late enough for the fire Caid had lit to have burned down to mere ashes. Jaz gave a small shiver at the metaphorical parallels her thoughts were drawing. She didn't want to acknowledge them any more than she wanted to acknowledge the purpose she could hear behind Caid's question.

'Last night was wonderful,' she whispered to him, stroking her fingertips along his chest, ruffling the soft hair lying there. '*You* were wonderful,' she added.

'Wonderful? But not wonderful enough for you to change your mind and come back to America with me? Is that what you're saying?' Caid guessed.

Jaz could feel the happiness seeping out of her. She didn't want to have this discussion. All she wanted was to lie here with Caid and keep them both enclosed in their own special world, here beneath the bed-clothes.

Their special world? A world as fragile as a glass Christmas tree bauble, as ephemeral as a soap bubble? That was their world. In the real world their world could not survive. Like their love?

Tears pricked her eyes. She so much wanted things to be different. For Caid to be different...? Jaz closed her eyes. She loved so many, many things about him. His strength, his warmth, his honesty. But she could not live the life he wanted her to live with him.

'I love you more than I can find words to tell you, Jaz. There is nothing I want more than for you to be my wife and the mother of my children. What we have between is just so good.' Caid groaned, kissing the top of her head and tightening his hold on her. 'So very, very good. Come back with me when I fly home. At least give the ranch a chance. If I can't persuade you that you'll love living there with me and our kids in oh, say ten years, then you can come back.'

His voice was warm and teasing, but Jaz did not make the mistake of forgetting that the issue he was raising was very serious.

'Caid, I can't,' she interrupted him firmly. 'No matter how much I might want to, I couldn't go anywhere until after Christmas.'

When he started to frown, she reminded him, 'My windows, Caid. They're the focal point of my working year. There's no way I can walk away and leave them. No way at all. Not for anyone.'

'You could fly out for a few days. For Christmas and New Year at least,' Caid argued crisply.

Jaz shook her head.

'No, Caid.' Her voice was equally crisp. 'Not even for Christmas. I shall be working right up until the last minute on Christmas Eve, and then even before the store opens again I shall be going in to help the others get ready for the sale—and that includes redressing the windows. You know what you're asking is impossible, Caid. Not even my parents…'

Caid looked at her.

'Your parents? Yes, I can see how hard it must have been for you growing up, Jaz, and how…how hurt you must have felt at times, how alone. But surely that makes what we have even more special? I know it does for me, which is why— Look, Jaz can't you see?'

Jaz could hear the frustration and the stubbornness in his voice and her heart went cold—cold but unfortunately not numb, so that she could still feel every sharp agonising vibration of the pain she knew was lying in wait for her.

The temptation to give in, to tell him that she could be what he wanted, was frighteningly strong. But Jaz knew that she could not give in to it.

Taking a deep breath, she answered unevenly, 'No, Caid. Can't *you* see? Can't you see that this issue goes much further than just you and I?'

'No. I can't see that. What do you mean?' Caid
challenged her. He had already shifted his body, so
that now there was a chilly little distance between
them in the bed, and now he removed his arms from
her. Ostensibly so that the could prop his head up and
look at her, but to Jaz the withdrawal of the warmth
of his body and his arms was very symbolic.

'What I mean,' Jaz told him, hesitating as she tried
to choose her words extra carefully, 'is that I am not
just thinking of this as an issue that involves you and
I. I have to think about the lessons I learned as a child,
Caid—just as much as you have to think about yours.
My parents love me dearly, I know that, but I also
know how it feels to be a child who is not allowed to
be their own person and to follow their own life path.
I don't want that for my children—our children.'

She could see the way Caid was frowning at her as
he absorbed what she was trying to say.

'But I would never do that to my kids. Never.'

'Caid, you can't say that,' Jaz argued quietly. 'What
if we had daughters? What if they wanted to be high-
flying career women? How would that make you feel?
How would it make them feel if the father they loved
disapproved of their ambitions? And even if you
didn't...if you were able to give them the right to be
themselves that you could not give me...what kind of
effect do you think it would have on any child to witness a relationship between his or her parents which
sent out a clear message that it was not acceptable for
a woman to be anything other than a wife and a
mother? I can't marry you and not have children, Caid.
But neither can I give my children a father who could
not accept and respect them and me as individual human beings.'

'Jaz, please...' Caid implored her. 'I can't change the way I am. The way I feel.'

'No, Caid,' Jaz agreed quietly. 'I don't suppose you can.'

'You know my flight is booked for tomorrow morning?' Caid warned her. 'This is our last chance, Jaz.'

'Yes, I know that,' Jaz agreed woodenly. 'I can't do it, Caid,' she burst out, when she saw the way he was looking at her. 'I can't mortgage my—our children's future happiness to buy my own. I can't. And I don't think that you'd be able to either. This problem isn't going to go away...ever. It would always be there, confronting us. Separating us. I can't live like that—and, more importantly, I can't love like that.'

'Where are you going?' Caid demanded sharply as she moved away from him and got out of bed.

'It's morning,' she told him flatly, directing his gaze towards the window. 'The storm has gone now. It's blown itself out, Caid. It's time for us to move on. To go our separate ways.'

She could cry later, Jaz told herself. After all, she would have the rest of her life to cry for Caid and their love!

CHAPTER TWELVE

'I WISH you would change your mind and join the rest of us in Aspen for Christmas, Caid.'

'I can't. It's a busy time at the ranch,' Caid answered his mother brusquely.

'Besides, Christmas is a time for kids, and I don't have any.'

'Kids and families,' his mother corrected him gently. 'And you do have one of those.' She smiled ruefully as she got up from the chair she had been sitting on in the large kitchen of his ranch. 'I can still remember the Christmas you were four. We'd got you a toy car, but you ignored it and spent most of the day playing with the box it came in instead.'

Caid gave her a bleak look.

It was just over two weeks since he had left England—and Jaz—and there hadn't been an hour, a minute, a single second during those weeks when he hadn't been thinking about her...wanting her.

That last night they had shared together would stay in his memory for ever. No other woman could or would ever take her place, but he couldn't go back on what he had said to her, nor alter his feelings. But knowing that didn't stop him longing for her.

'The Christmases I most remember,' he told her curtly, 'are the ones when you weren't there. Remember them, Mom? There was the one you spent in Australia—you sent me photographs of yourself and a koala bear—and then there was the time you were in India, sourcing embroidered fabrics, and then China, and—'

He stopped and shook his head, bitterness drawing deep grooves either side of his mouth.

He only had to access those memories to know how right he was to feel the way he did about his own marriage.

'Caid, listen to me!'

As Annette Dubois turned her head towards him Caid saw the pain in her eyes.

'When you were a child—'

'You had your work and that was way, way more important to you than I was. Your need to express yourself came first. You—'

'Along with the koala bear I sent airline tickets for your father to bring you to me,' Annette interrupted him. 'It was all supposed to be arranged. I'd organised a special barbecue on the beach with some other kids for you... But your father changed his mind at the last minute. That's how it was between us.

'When I was in India I tried to get back, but I was hospitalised with dysentery. In China...well, by the time I went to China I'd begun to give up. But I did send you a video of myself, telling you how much I loved you and how much I wished I could be with you. I guess you never saw it! You see, Caid, by then I'd realised that no matter what I did, how much I tried to be conciliatory, to find ways to persuade your father to allow me to have you with me, it was just never going to happen.'

'Dad allow you? Oh, come on, Ma. I was there. I heard him on the phone to you, pleading with you to come home. ''Don't worry, son,'' he used to promise

me. "I'll speak to your mom and tell her how much
we need her here."'

'Oh, Caid... I promised myself I would never do
this, but...your father and I should never have married—'

'I've heard it all before, Mom.'

'Some of it...but, no, you haven't heard all of it,
Caid. By the time you were born we both knew that
our marriage was all washed up. I would have gone
for a divorce before you were born—raised you on my
own. But my father persuaded me not to. Afterwards...
Well, I guess I was so desperate to prove that I could
support the both of us, and to show big brother Donny
that I wasn't going to be sidelined out of the business,
that I over-compensated.

'My plan was that I would take you with me when
I travelled, but the family were horrified at the idea of
me taking a new baby into some of the remote areas
I was going to, and I guess they frightened me enough
to think that perhaps you were safer at home. But then
when I came home I found that I was being eased out
of your life, that your father was making decisions that
should have been made by both of us.

'Those phone calls you just mentioned, for in-
stance—' she shook her head '—there never were
any—not to me. Your father knew how much I loved
you, Caid. How important you were to me. You see,
after you were born the doctors told me that I couldn't
have any more children, so he blackmailed me into
letting him play the role of good father whilst I was
forced into the position of bad mother!'

'You could always have given up your job,' Caid
pointed out coldly.

'Yes, Caid, I could. But you see, I had inherited the

fatal family stubbornness—just like you—and I thought I could make everything work out. By the time I was ready to admit that I was wrong it was too late. Had I been less stubborn, less determined to see everything as black or white, no doubt your father and I could have reached a compromise. And do you know what hurts me most, Caid? Not what I have lost, but what has been lost to you. I know we've mended our broken fences, and that we now share a good relationship, but whatever I do I can never give you back those lost years, that lost love. But you must never think that I didn't care, Caid, that you weren't in my mind every single second. You were my child. How could you not be?'

When Caid wouldn't meet her eyes, she changed the subject.

'I managed to persuade Jaz to tell me about her Christmas windows. She is very, very talented. She'd been interviewed on national TV the day I spoke to her—a contact she'd made through her cousin apparently. The final window is just so special! Did she discuss the theme she was using with you when you were over there?'

'No,' Caid replied curtly. He turned away from his mother to look out across the snow-covered land beyond the window, so that she wouldn't see his expression.

'Well, she took these photographs and sent them to me. Would you like to see them?'

As desperately as Caid wanted to refuse, he knew he couldn't without arousing his mother's suspicions.

'I loved this touch,' Annette chuckled a few minutes later, when the photographs were laid out in order on Caid's kitchen table. 'To have dressed the man—the husband and father of the family—in such very American clothes is a really unifying idea that subtly underlines our ownership of the store.'

Caid froze as he looked at the photograph his mother was pointing to. The window dummy was dressed in denim jeans and a white tee shirt underneath a designer label shirt. Just like the man Jaz had drawn in the sketch he had picked up off the floor—the man who had borne such a remarkable physical resemblance to himself.

'And look at these,' his mother was commanding excitedly. 'I mean in our modern consumer-driven world, when we're all so hungry for something meaningful, what could mean more than the gifts this woman is being given?'

Unwillingly Caid studied the photograph. Beautifully presented gifts were being handed to the window woman by her family.

Caid tensed as he read the handwritten notes, Jaz had placed in each of the open gift boxes.

Love… Joy… And there, tucked away in so small a box that he almost missed it, an extra gift that the man was handing over. Inside it, in writing so small he could barely read it, Jaz had written the word, *Acceptance.*

As she slipped unobtrusively into the crowd of Christmas shoppers admiring her windows, Jaz wondered why she didn't feel her normal sense of thrilled pride.

It was true, after all—as the local paper had reported—that this year she had outdone herself.

Annette Dubois had raved excitedly about Jaz's work, but all the praise and excitement in the world couldn't warm the cold despair from her heart. In her bleakest moments Jaz feared that nothing ever would.

'They look wonderful, Jaz.'

Startled, Jaz turned her head to see Jamie smiling at her.

'I've come to do some last-minute bits of shopping,' Jamie explained. 'We fly out to America tonight. I must admit, I'm not really that keen on going. I'd prefer to stay at home and then go somewhere lovely and hot in January. You know me, I hate the cold and I'm definitely no skier. But Marsh loves it, and so do the kids, so we agreed to compromise. Aspen this Christmas, but next year we're going to stay at home and Marsh is going to take me to the Caribbean in January.'

Nervously Jaz waited as her luggage was checked in. Her flight left in just under an hour, and she still wasn't sure she was doing the right thing. It had been the conversations she'd had with Jamie that had done it—that and the unendurable pain of longing for Caid.

Compromise. Could they do that? Would Caid even want to try? She hadn't warned him what she was doing. She had been too afraid that she might not have the courage to go through with it, that she might change her mind. And besides...

He might refuse to see her. He might tell her that he did not want to compromise...that he preferred to live his life without her rather than give even the smallest bit of ground.

Her whole body shook.

What was she doing here? She couldn't go through with it... She was a fool to even be thinking that anything could be different. But it was too late to change her mind now. Her luggage had been checked in!

Was he crazy for doing this? Caid had no idea. He only knew that it was something he had to do. And anyway, there was no going back now. Blizzard conditions had been forecast for the part of the state where his ranch was; there was no way he could get back.

His flight for Heathrow didn't leave for another four hours.

In his suitcase he had the Christmas gift he had carefully wrapped for Jaz.

Would she accept it? Would she accept him? Would she accept that he had come to realise there was a need for change within himself? That they had something so important, so precious to share with one another, that there had to be a way they could make it work? That listening to his mother had softened his iron-hard implacability? Given him the key to turn in the rusty lock of the prison wall he had constructed for himself out of stubbornness and the ghost of his childhood fear of losing the people he loved? And, even if she accepted the genuineness of his willingness to change, would that be enough?

Gritty-eyed and exhausted, Jaz stared at the desk clerk in disbelief.

'What do you mean,' she faltered, 'there are no flights to Freshsprings Creek? I'm booked on one...'

'I'm sorry, all flights to that part of the state have been cancelled due to weather conditions,' the clerk told Jaz politely. 'There's a blizzard out there. No planes can get in or out. Everything is grounded until the weather clears.'

'But I have to get there,' Jaz protested. 'Is there another way…train? Road…?'

The desk clerk was shaking her head, giving Jaz a pitying look.

'Honey, like I just said, there's a blizzard. That means nothing moves. Nothing.'

Absently, Caid glanced at his watch. Another half an hour and he would go through to wait for his flight. He glanced round the terminal building and then froze.

Over by the enquiry desk a familiar figure was speaking with the clerk. It looked like Jaz. But it couldn't be. Could it?

'Please, you don't understand. I have to get there,' Jaz was begging the clerk. 'You see—'

Helpless tears of frustration blurred her eyes as she recognised then the impossibility of explaining to this stranger just why she was so desperate to get to Caid.

'Perhaps I can help?'

'Caid?' Jaz stared up at him in disbelief. 'Caid! What—? How—?'

Colour tinged her face, drawing out its tired pallor, her eyes huge and dark with emotion.

Caid looked away from her and glanced towards the announcement boards.

'They've just called my flight,' he told her.

'Your flight?' Jaz went white.

'Listen,' Caid demanded.

Straining her ears, Jaz heard a voice announcing that the international flight for London, Heathrow, was now boarding.

'You're going home?' Jaz whispered in shock.

'No,' Caid told her softly, shaking his head as he

relieved her of the bag she was clutching and took her in his arms. His voice was suddenly muffled as he whispered, 'I am home, Jaz. Now. *You* are my home. My heart. My love. My life. I was on my way to see you. To tell you…to ask you…to see if we could…'

'Compromise?' Jaz offered hesitantly.

Silently they looked at one another.

'There's a decent spa hotel a few miles from here. We could book in there—at least until the weather clears,' Caid suggested. 'Then we could…talk…'

As lazily and sensually as a small cat, Jaz stretched out her naked body, revelling in the warmth of Caid's She had no idea just how long they had been asleep, but it was dark outside now.

Contentedly she leaned over and kissed the top of his bare shoulder, grinning when he immediately wrapped his arm around her and turned to look at her.

'Still love me?' he asked her softly.

'What do you think?' Jaz teased back.

'What I think,' Caid told her, his expression suddenly serious, 'is that I don't know how I ever thought I could possibly live without you. I was an arrogant fool…'

'No.' Jaz corrected him tenderly. 'You were a wonderful, but very stubborn man.'

'We *will* make it work,' Caid promised her. 'I know it won't always be easy. But if we—'

'Compromise?' Jaz smiled.

During the long hours of the fading day, when they had talked everything through with one another, it had become their private buzzword.

'Jaz, I want you more than I want life itself. I love you totally and absolutely, without conditions or boundaries. And nothing—*nothing*,' Caid stressed emotionally, 'will ever change that. I love you for the woman you are. I love every bit of what you are. Every bit, Jaz,' he added emotionally. 'I will never come between you and your career, I promise.'

'And do you also promise that you won't regret any of this?' Jaz asked him, searching his gaze.

'The only thing I could ever regret now is being fool enough to let you go!' Caid answered rawly. 'I guess what my mom had to say made me see a lot of things in a very different light. But even without that I couldn't have gone on much longer without you.'

'Like me with my windows. They matter. They matter a lot. But every time I looked at that mannequin all I could see was you.'

'Well, I have to tell you that ranchers do not wear designer shirts.' Caid laughed.

'Will the blizzard stop in time for us to spend Christmas together at the ranch?' Jaz asked him eagerly.

'It might. But there's something important we have to do before I take you home with me,' Caid informed her.

Jaz frowned. 'What?'

'Well,' Caid murmured as he bent his head to kiss her, 'winter hereabouts lasts a good long time… Once the snow settles it could be well into March before it lifts, and that's a lot of cold dark nights when there won't be much to do except snuggle up in bed together. And if we do that…I want us to get married, Jaz,' he told her abruptly his voice suddenly becoming much more serious. 'Now. Not next year, or maybe some time, but now—just as soon as we can. Are you ready to make that kind of commitment to me? Do you trust me enough to believe what I've said about being willing to change?'

Jaz took a deep breath.

'Yes,' she told him softly. 'Yes, I do...'

'I DO...'

'Are they married yet, Mummy?'

Jaz could feel the ripple of amusement spreading through their guests as they all heard Jamie's youngest son's shrill-voiced question.

Pink-cheeked, she was glad that only she could hear Caid growling to her, 'Once we are I'm taking you away from this lot. Somewhere very, very private just as soon as I can.'

Their arrival in Aspen a few days earlier, followed by Caid's announcement that they were getting married, had been all it needed to have the focused determination of the Dubois family, plus some hefty input from Jamie, swinging into action.

So much so, and so effectively, that here she and Caid were on Christmas Eve, exchanging their vows in the fairytale setting of Aspen, surrounded by the love and approval of both their families.

Jaz's dress had been specially flown in from the Dubois store in Boston, a dozen junior members of the Dubois family had rushed to offer their services as her bridal attendants—and Caid had declared that he wished he had simply flown her to Las Vegas and married her in some drive-through wedding chapel.

'You may kiss the bride...'

'You wait,' Caid promised softly to Jaz as his lips brushed tenderly against hers. 'Once we're on our own

I'm going to show you how a man really wants to kiss his bride.'

'Will it be a lingering kiss?' Jaz dulcetly teased him back.

And then they were finally alone, in a wonderfully private suite at the luxurious hotel Caid had booked for them.

'Come here,' Caid demanded throatily, reaching for her.

Willingly Jaz went to him, looking enquiringly up at him as he handed her a small, carefully wrapped gift.

'What's this?' she asked.

'Your Christmas present,' Caid told her. 'I was going to give it to you when I reached Cheltenham.'

A little uncertainly, Jaz unwrapped it. He had already given her the most beautiful engagement and wedding rings, and a pair of matching diamond earrings, but she could tell from the tense set of his shoulders that this gift was something special.

Very carefully she lifted the lid from the box and then removed the layers of tissue paper.

Right down in amongst them was a small scrap of paper.

Jaz's heart started to beat unsteadily.

Her fingers were shaking as she took out the paper.

'Read it,' Caid urged her.

Slowly, Jaz did so.

Written on the paper was one single word. *Acceptance*.

'Oh, Caid.' Tears blurred her eyes and trembled in her voice as she flung herself into his arms. 'That is the most wonderful, the most precious…the best present you could have given me,' she told him. 'I shall treasure it for ever.'

'And I shall treasure *you* for ever. You and our love,' Caid promised.

✳ A Scandalous ✳
Courtship
by
Gail Whitiker

Dear Reader,

One of the joys of writing historical romance is the ability to step back in time and experience different ways of life. The Regency period has always been my particular favourite, and I've had countless hours of enjoyment living in grand houses and attending elegant soirées and balls as I follow my characters through their journeys towards love. Because after all, finding that one special person in life is what really matters, whether you're a lofty lord or a struggling governess.

The idea for *A Scandalous Courtship* first came to me several years ago, and evolved from a single thought. What if a baby was left abandoned in a carriage and claimed by a lonely, titled lady who was desperate for a child to love? Would she take the baby home without telling anyone and raise it as her own? If she did, what would happen when the child came of age and found out she wasn't who she'd always thought she was? More importantly, how would the man she loved react to the news—a man who'd grown up believing she was someone else entirely?

I hope you enjoy Hannah and Robert's story. It's a story of love and courage, and of the willingness to make sacrifices; gifts made all the more special at this festive time of the year.

I enjoy hearing from my readers. If you have a minute, stop by my website at www.gailwhitiker.com or visit: www.millsandboon.co.uk.

Happy Holidays!

Gail Whitiker

Look out for more books by Gail Whitiker in Mills & Boon Historical Romance™!

CHAPTER ONE

April, 1813, London

IN THE spacious confines of a room dedicated to the sport, two gentlemen took up their positions under the watchful eye of a third, a tall, silver-haired gentleman, who stood quietly to one side. Garbed in the requisite attire of the fencing school, the young men raised their foils and silently saluted their tutor. Then, following his sharply delivered command of *en garde*, they turned to face each other and assumed their positions for the assault and lesson about to begin.

The gentlemen had been friends for many years. Originally introduced as boys at boarding-school, they had gone on to complete their educations at Oxford, and then to take up their respective places in society. They were both fine-looking men who, despite the three-year difference in their ages, shared a similar outlook on life. They were both well travelled and extensively read, they both belonged to the requisite number of select gentlemen's clubs, and they both enjoyed the privileges of life to which birth and money had entitled them.

Physically, however, the resemblances were fewer. The younger man was fair-haired and blue-eyed, with a countenance that was pleasing, but unlikely to cause a lady's pulse to quicken in anticipation of sinful pleasures or amorous indulgences. He might be looked upon as a jovial brother; one who could be counted upon to be amusing rather than exciting, and to accomplish things by affability rather than through authority.

By contrast, the older gentleman was neither fair nor sweet-tempered, but was possessed of such striking features as to make any lady turn to take a second look. Dark of hair and swarthy of complexion, he was everything his youthful friend was not. His features were sharp, his appearance suggesting a certain roguish elegance that most women found distinctly appealing.

The two gentlemen had studied with Monsieur Rochefort for several years, and while it was evident that their lessons had been well learned, it was equally apparent that their skills were not evenly matched. Even to the most casual of observers it was clear that the darker man had the advantage. He was more muscular in build, and lighter on his feet than his slender opponent, but it was his unquestionable finesse with the long, tapering sword that gave him the true advantage.

When he had scored his fifth hit of the match, Monsieur Rochefort held up his hand to signal a halt to the bout. 'Lord Winthrop has scored the greatest number of hits in the time allotted, Mr Stanford. Would you care to continue the engagement?'

The younger man shook his head. 'Not today, *monsieur*.' He removed his mask and grinned with good-natured resignation. 'I know when I am beaten, and there is no need to belabour my weaknesses. I know what they are and shall endeavour to improve them.'

The tutor smiled as he turned to regard the darker

gentleman. 'And you, Lord Winthrop? Are you satisfied with the day's work?'

Robert Edward, fifth Viscount Winthrop, nodded his agreement as he let the foil drop back to his side. 'I am, *monsieur*, thank you. But perhaps I could see you the day after tomorrow so that we might continue work on my compound manoeuvres.'

The elderly gentleman inclined his head. 'As you wish, my lord.' Then with an elegant bow he left them, moving to take his place at the opposite side of the room where another pair of swordsmen awaited his expertise.

'Dash it all, Winthrop,' James Stanford said as he pulled off his gloves. 'I thought I'd improved enough to give you a good match, but it's damnably clear that you are still the superior swordsman.'

The man so addressed put down his foil and clasped his friend on the shoulder. 'You're too impatient, James. Timing is crucial in this sport. You must anticipate your opponent's moves and be ready for them. *You* are too busy recovering from your last parry to think about deflecting my next one. Besides, you were trying to exorcise anger today, and that never improves the reflexes.'

Stanford sighed as he accepted a cloth from the young lad standing nearby. 'Perhaps, but can you blame me for being angry? My life is about to go completely awry and there is nothing I can do to prevent it.'

Accustomed to his friend's viewing of every parental intervention in his life as a catastrophe, Robert chuckled. 'You're exaggerating again, James. Your parents are not *ordering* you to marry Lady Constance. They are simply suggesting she is a better choice than

the young lady with whom you seem to fancy yourself
in love.'

'I do not *fancy* myself in love! I *am* in love!'
Stanford cried. 'Madly so, and with an angel whom
even you were moved to call extraordinary.'

'She is a beauty, to be sure, but without the social
acceptance so critical to our world, she cannot hope
to make you a worthy bride, nor you an enviable al-
liance,' Robert said calmly. '*That* is what your parents
object to, my friend. I dare say your father would be
happy enough to see you set her up as your mistress—'

'I say, Winthrop, have a care.'

'I have all the care I need. Miss Blazel is a charming
young woman, but she is a dancer. A very lovely and
talented dancer, I admit, but a dancer nonetheless, and
therefore totally outside our social circle. You have no
knowledge of her background or family connections,
and as the next Viscount Stanford it behooves you to
be mindful of such things, lest some disreputable rel-
ative suddenly turn up at your door claiming your new
viscountess as his long-lost sister, or, worse, his errant
wife!'

Stanford gave a snort of disbelief. 'I assure you,
Suzette has never been married. And I'm quite sure
she comes from a perfectly respectable family.'

'Ah, but you cannot say you are *absolutely* sure,
can you?' Robert countered, smiling in a way that only
a few close friends were ever permitted to see. 'And
in that small measure of ignorance lies the greatest risk
for disaster. No, I fear I must side with your parents
on this, James. Miss Blazel is not a suitable young
lady for you to gift with your coronet. Enjoy her if
you will, but do the intelligent thing and choose your

bride from amongst those more suitable, with backgrounds and families that are known to you. The other way only presents the potential for heartache and ruin.'

'Huh! Easy enough for you to say,' Stanford muttered as he shrugged on his exquisitely tailored cutaway coat. 'Your heart isn't being wrenched in two the way mine is. In fact, given the circumstances, I wonder I am even considering your advice this time.'

Robert frowned as they headed for the door. 'Why would you not consider it?'

'Because *you* are not in love. And while our situations are similar, in that we both require wives, I do not see you rushing to do the *intelligent* thing, as you would so blithely have me do.'

'Our situations are not the same at all,' Robert objected. 'You like the idea of being married. I do not. And even if I did I would certainly not be hasty in my selection of a bride. I would take my time and make sure I knew the lady well before asking her to marry me. I dislike making mistakes, James, and I should hate to discover I had made a very serious one when it was too late for me to do anything about it.'

'But you're not likely to do that, are you?' Stanford countered amiably. 'Because for all your dashing good looks you're such a calm, level-headed fellow that when you do finally choose a wife, nobody doubts that she will be anything but perfect. She will be chosen from the right circles and there will not be so much as a hint of scandal attached to her name.'

Robert slid his friend a quizzical glance. 'Is that such a bad thing?'

'Of course not. It's just that…well, what I'm trying to say is…oh, hell, I'm not sure I know *what* I'm trying to say any more,' Stanford said in frustration.

'I just wish my parents would leave me to get on with my life, rather than attempt to wear me down with their incessant badgering. Why not just let me make my own decisions, the way your mother does you? The Viscountess doesn't seem to care what you do or with whom you do it.'

'That is only because I haven't given her any cause to worry about what I do or with whom I do it,' Robert drawled as the two stepped out of the house and into the bright afternoon sunshine. 'I dare say that if all she heard was that I was chasing Cyprians from one end of London to the other, she would have posted up from Sussex long before now.'

'But that's just it. She *wouldn't* hear anything like that because you don't get up to the kind of antics that would cause a mother embarrassment, or that would force her into making decisions for you under the guise of doing what was best.'

Robert sighed as he abruptly drew to a halt, compelling his friend to do the same. 'Look, James, the only way your parents are going to start letting *you* make decisions of your own is by demonstrating your ability to make them with some degree of intelligence and common sense. All *I'm* asking you to do is think very carefully before making a choice that will most surely affect the rest of your life.'

'But I *have* thought about it. I love Suzette, and she loves me. I cannot imagine spending the rest of my life with *anyone* but her.'

'Isn't that what you said about Miss Lucille Clapshaw this time last year?'

A heated blush stained the younger man's cheeks. 'That wasn't the same at all! My feelings for Suzette are nothing like what I had for Lucille—'

'Of course they are, because you're a gullible fool when it comes to a pretty face and a sweetly turned ankle,' Robert said in a conversational tone. 'You fall in and out of love like a green lad fresh from the country, and I'll wager here and now that if you were to meet a young lady who was even lovelier than Miss Blazel, and of whom your parents approved, you would forget about your dancer in the blink of an eye.'

'Never!'

'Are you willing to put money on it?'

Stanford stared at his friend in disbelief. 'You're not serious.'

'I most certainly am.'

'Impertinent fellow. I've half a mind to call you out.'

'I wouldn't, if I were you.'

'No. I suppose that would be the height of stupidity,' Stanford muttered as they walked on, 'given that you're as skilled with a pistol as you are with that damned blade. But even if it were possible for me to forget Suzette, where do you expect me to find this...paragon of virtue? I have attended all the salons in London and have even braved several evenings in the company of the mighty patronesses, without once having spied a society chit who takes my fancy.' His eyes narrowed as he glanced at his friend again. 'I say, Winthrop, what secrets are you keeping? What aren't you telling me?'

'Only that I am aware of certain plans which involve a delightful young lady of good family coming up from the country to spend a few months in London.'

'Is she pretty?' Stanford asked, intrigued in spite of himself.

'Would I have brought it up if she were not?'

'Well, no, but—oh, now, wait a minute. You're not referring to your sister, are you?'

'My sister!' Robert's head snapped round. 'Why on earth would you think I was talking about her?'

'Because she lives in the country and, from what little you've told me, is of an age to be married.'

'Of an age she may be, but I would hardly put her forward as a candidate for marriage to *you*. For one thing, I barely know the girl. We've spent most of our lives apart, and I have no idea whether she's a milk-and-water miss or a veritable hoyden. Although, given Mama's influence, I find it hard to credit she would be either,' Robert said, more to himself than to Stanford. 'However, I would certainly not deign to meddle in her personal affairs or try to form an attachment for her with any gentlemen of my acquaintance here.'

'Has she ever expressed a desire to come to London?'

'No.'

'But surely she wishes to be married?'

Robert shrugged. 'As much, I suppose, as any young lady. But if she is not inclined to do what is necessary, why should I? The last correspondence I received from her led me to believe that she was quite happy staying in the country. In fact, she said something about being happier tending Mama's gardens than she was in cultivating her own.'

'Oh, I say, that's good.' Stanford grinned. 'Obviously possesses a decent sense of humour.'

'Does she?' Robert flicked his friend a sardonic glance. 'Perhaps I *should* introduce the two of you, if that is your idea of wit.'

'Steady on, Winthrop, I merely said I found the remark amusing, not that I was interested in meeting her. As I recall, you said she was somewhat ungainly the last time you saw her.'

'Did I? Well, to be fair, she was only thirteen at the time, and what girl of thirteen is not?'

'Suzette is sixteen and there is nothing ungainly about her,' Stanford said in defence of his ladylove. 'In fact, when she dances, her body moves with the most exquisite grace, and she has the loveliest long legs—' He broke off, abruptly reminded of what his friend had accused him of only moments before, and gruffly cleared his throat. 'Yes, well, never mind that. You were trying to convince me of the suitability of this *other* young lady, whom I have now concluded is not your sister, and whom you honestly believe I should meet. Yes?'

'Indeed.'

'Very well. If you feel that strongly about it, arrange a meeting at a time and place of your choosing, and I shall be there, just to show you that I am capable of making decisions with some degree of intelligence and common sense,' Stanford said, mimicking Robert's words and tone of voice. 'But do not hold it against me if I fail to find her as delightful as Miss Blazel.'

'I shall not hold it against you, but I do believe the undertaking to be worthwhile, if only to show your parents that you are intent on heeding their advice. Hopefully, that will bring about an end to what you call their incessant badgering. Which they only do, I might add, because they are concerned about you.'

'Yes, I know,' Stanford agreed with a grudging sigh. 'Talking of parents, isn't it about time you paid a call on *your* mother?'

'I suppose.' Robert tipped his hat to an attractive young lady and her companion as they passed by. 'Her sixtieth birthday is but a week away.'

'Sixty? I say, what a splendid age.' Stanford likewise tipped his hat and then winked at the ladies, eliciting the most satisfactory of blushes in response. 'Is she still in good health?'

'She has been, though of late my sister's letters have been filled with news of a most disturbing cough.'

'Well, then, what better tonic for her than to have you arrive home unexpectedly? A delightful surprise for them both, I should think.'

It would be a surprise indeed, Robert thought as he walked in silence beside his friend. Pity only one out of the three of them would find anything to be happy about it in it.

Gillingdon Park, Sussex

The rippling notes of a minuet echoed around the music-room, bringing a smile of pleasure to the face of the elderly lady sitting on the brocade sofa opposite the pianoforte. 'Oh, Hannah, that was lovely. I vow I have never heard you play the piece better.'

The young lady seated at the instrument sat back with a smile of satisfaction. 'Yes, I think I am finally ready to say that I have triumphed over that difficult bit in the middle, Mama, and not a moment too soon. I vow it is one of the most intricate pieces I have ever attempted. Now, what shall I regale you with next? A light and frivolous dance, or something of a more classical nature?'

'Something light and frivolous, I think, my dear,' Lady Winthrop said. 'I am not in a mood for anything cerebral this afternoon. What about *A Lady Came A Calling*? It has such a lovely tune and you play it so well.'

'Very well. And, speaking of a lady coming to call, I saw Mrs Branksmuir in the village today,' Hannah said as she searched for the piece of music. 'She asked me to pass along her regards and to say that she is looking forward to seeing you when you are more inclined to receiving visitors.'

'Humph. As if I would *ever* be inclined to receiving one such as that.'

Hannah frowned as she placed the music in front of her. 'I thought you liked Mrs Branksmuir.'

'Oh, I suppose I do well enough, but she can be such an interfering busybody at times,' Lady Winthrop muttered. 'She gossips about everyone and everything, and most of the time there is not a hint of truth to anything she says.'

'Nevertheless, she did seem genuinely concerned when she enquired after your health.'

'Of course she would appear concerned, because she knows it is the polite thing to do. Elizabeth Branksmuir would naturally open the conversation with a question about me before launching into the subject she *really* wished to discuss.'

'Which was?'

'Why, her daughter's engagement, of course. Which I, for one, refuse to comment upon and which I see no reason for her to gloat about. After all, Elizabeth knows that the only reason Mr Twickenham proposed to Frances was because *you* would not have him,' the Viscountess said smugly. 'Philip has always held you in the highest regard, and Elizabeth Branksmuir knows very well that you could have been engaged to him years ago had you been so inclined.'

Hannah's lips twitched. 'Perhaps, but how could I have taken Philip seriously after all the things we did together as children? It is far easier for me to think of him as a knobbly-kneed boy with whom I climbed trees and chased rabbits than as a handsome gentleman intent on courting me.'

'Of course it is. Why do you think I tried to discourage you from engaging in such unladylike activities at the time? Even then I feared you might form just such an opinion. I, on the other hand, liked Philip and have always thought he would make you an excellent husband.'

'Perhaps, but it would be very hard for me to see him in a romantic light after what has passed between us,' Hannah said, setting her fingers to the keys. 'Do you remember the time he came to see you after I pushed him into the pond?'

Lady Winthrop hooted. 'Gracious, how could I forget? What a spectacle he made, dripping water and green muck all over my floor.'

'Poor Philip. He truly was annoyed, wasn't he?'

'He was, but I think he was more angry with *me* for not punishing you the way he felt I should than he was with you for having committed the deed.'

Hannah smiled as she tilted her head to one side. 'Why did you not punish me?'

'Because I suspected the only reason *you* were not the one dripping green muck all over my floor was because you were the quicker of the two.' A twinkle appeared in the depths of Lady Winthrop's clear grey eyes. 'You always were the most argumentative pair.'

'There, you see,' Hannah said triumphantly. 'Philip and I have been at odds with one another for years, whereas he and Miss Branksmuir have been polite to each other almost from the start, which is why I think they will get on so well together. I certainly cannot imagine Philip wishing to push *her* into a duck pond! And while we are on the subject of unacceptable behaviour, have you heard from Robert?'

'Robert?' The Viscountess glanced at her in surprise. 'No, why? Should I have heard from him?'

'Well, I thought you might. Your birthday is next week, after all, and I thought he would have written to tell you when he was coming.'

Lady Winthrop's mouth curved in a smile, but her eyes were filled with shadows. 'I doubt Robert will have any time to spare for us this year, my dear. The Season is already underway, and you know what a popular gentleman he is. Especially with ladies who have marriage on their minds.'

'But it is your birthday!'

'Yes, but that has not been reason enough for him to come home in the past. However, I think it is time we discussed *your* going up to London,' Lady Winthrop said briskly. 'You will be one-and-twenty this year, Hannah, and it offends me to listen to Elizabeth Branksmuir prattle on about her daughter's good fortune whilst you sit here and pay no attention to your own.'

Seemingly unconcerned, Hannah turned the page. 'Never mind, Mama. I am not in the least troubled by Miss Branksmuir's good fortune. If it gives her mother pleasure to dwell on her daughter's engagement, of what concern is that to us? Truth be told, I suspect Frances is anxious to get out from under her mother's domineering hand, and I certainly cannot blame her for that. I, however, have no wish to leave you here alone, and would certainly not do so when you are feeling so poorly.'

'Nonsense! Sally is here and quite capable of looking after me. And you needn't worry about having to travel up to London on your own. You can take Sarah with you, and you will stay with Prudence in Cavendish Square. You know how delighted she and Alice will be to have you.'

'*They* may be delighted, but I'm not so sure Sir Roger will welcome the presence of another female in his house.'

Lady Winthrop chuckled. 'Pay no mind to your uncle, Hannah. I learned a long time ago that he is far more amiable than he likes to let on, and a good deal stronger than he appears. My sister can be rather formidable when she chooses, but I am quite convinced Roger only acts the part of the downtrodden husband because it suits his purposes to do so. But with Alice having made her come-out this year there would be plenty of opportunities for the two of you to be out of the house. Judging from my sister's letters, Alice is enjoying herself immensely with the endless round of soirées and routs the Season has to offer.'

'Of course she would enjoy herself.' Hannah finished the piece, and then got up to join her mother on the sofa. 'Cousin Alice has always enjoyed going to parties and indulging in the aimless chatter expected of young ladies at such gatherings.'

'And you do not?'

'I do not enjoy being looked upon as a blue-stocking simply because I choose to express opinions which necessitate the use of one's mind.'

'But that is generally the nature of polite conversation, my dear. A surfeit of wit and an absence of intellect.'

Hannah's mouth pulled into a grimace. 'Then I dare say there would be little point in my moving in society at all, since those whom I do not offend I would surely embarrass. But let us speak no more of London,' she said, brightening. 'Let us talk of your birthday festivities, for I think achieving such a fine age and looking as lovely as you do demands a celebration!'

Lady Winthrop leaned over to place an affectionate kiss on her daughter's cheek. 'Dear Hannah, you bring me so much joy. You always have.' She hesitated, and then sighed, her smile fading as her expression grew troubled. 'Which is why I think it is time we talked about matters of considerable importance.'

Hannah rolled her eyes. 'Mama, I have already told you I have no wish to go to London—'

'This has nothing to do with London, child. What I must say to you will have a far greater effect on your life than a Season in London ever could.'

Puzzled by the note of concern in her voice, Hannah reached for her mother's hand and held it gently between her own. 'Now, remember what the doctor said, dearest. You are not to trouble yourself with anything until you are feeling a little stronger.'

'I know that, child, but Dr Blake has not the issues on his mind I have!' Lady Winthrop said in agitation. 'There are things you must know. Things I should have told you and Robert years ago, but which were difficult to say, and which only grew more difficult as the years went by. I was never sure the time was right.'

'Are you so sure the time is right now?'

A tremor touched the Viscountess's mouth. 'I fear I cannot wait much longer. I know I am not in the best of health, my dear, and you must know the truth before it is too late. You *must*!'

There was an ominous ring to the words, and hearing it, Hannah gave her mother a forced smile and a tense nod of consent. 'Very well. Then let us speak of it in the morning when you are feeling more rested. You have already spent too much time with your embroidery this afternoon. Your eyes are heavy and you are starting to droop, like a pretty flower in need of water. I shall ring for Sally and have her take you upstairs. Then tomorrow, after breakfast, we shall talk about this most important matter. Would that be all right?'

'I suppose it will have to be.' Lady Winthrop sighed. 'I admit, I am feeling a little weary this evening.'

'There, you see. And I have likely made it worse with all my playing.' Hannah crossed to the bell-pull and gave it a sharp tug. 'I should have known better.'

'Never! Listening to you is a pleasure, my dear. Yet another area where Frances Branksmuir is to be found lacking,' the Viscountess muttered. 'I have heard her play the pianoforte and she does it exceedingly ill.'

'Obviously Philip does not care that his future wife is not musically inclined,' Hannah said, her ever-present smile finding its way back to her lips.

'What's this I hear about future wives?' asked old Sally, appearing in the doorway. 'Have I gone and missed news of your engagement, Miss Hannah?'

'Nothing so momentous, Sally,' Hannah assured her mother's elderly companion. 'Mama and I were simply talking about Mr Twickenham and Miss Branksmuir.'

'Ah. And a fine wife she'll make him too.'

'A fine wife? What do you know, you old fool!' Lady Winthrop grumbled. 'Frances Branksmuir isn't half the young lady Hannah is. The girl can barely hold a tune, her skills upon the pianoforte are non-existent, and she is forever complaining about the weather being too hot or too cold.'

'Be that as it may, the girl has a right to a good marriage,' Sally replied, seemingly undaunted by her mistress's criticism. 'And if Miss Hannah doesn't want Mr Twickenham, why shouldn't Miss Branksmuir have him?'

'Well, that just goes to show how much sense *you* have, Sally Taylor!' the Viscountess said in exasperation. 'Perhaps if Miss Branksmuir had kept her distance, Mr Twickenham would have courted Hannah and we would not be having this conversation now. Which I'm surprised I am even entering into if that is the extent of your common sense.'

'I've all the sense I need for dealing with the likes of you,' Sally said with nary a blink. 'Now, take my arm and come upstairs. I'll have no more of this silliness.'

Hannah carefully hid her smile as the two ladies headed for the stairs, bickering all the way. It was an unusual friendship to say the least, but it was one Hannah had no intention of interfering in. Sally may have started out as her mother's maid, but she had become much more than that in the years since.

Several of the ladies in the village had respectfully suggested that Hannah hire a younger, more deferential companion to look after the Viscountess, but Hannah had told them it would be a waste of time. Her mother would never replace Sally. The irascible Yorkshirewoman had been with her since the early days of her marriage, and as outspoken as she was, Hannah knew the woman's gruffness hid a heart of gold. Besides, Sally's devoted care and attention had become even more important in the last few weeks, given how frail the Viscountess had become.

It was a worrisome time for all of them—and for Hannah in particular. It was also the reason she was so anxious that her brother come home for *this* birthday, if for none other. Unfortunately, she suspected that her mother was right. With the Season underway, it was unlikely that Robert would take time from his busy schedule to pay a visit to his mother and sister in Sussex.

Hannah had seen very little of her brother during her life. Already twelve and away at school when she'd been born, he had become little more than a name to her. By the time she was eleven, Robert had already been leading the life of a dapper young gentleman about town. He had inherited the title of Viscount Winthrop upon his father's death, and with his dashing looks and charming manner had become a most sought-after gentleman by London hostesses and matchmaking mamas.

Still, he had written to her for a while, Hannah admitted. Or rather, he had answered, in a somewhat haphazard fashion, the letters her mother had insisted she write to him. But even she could not remember the last time he had sent her a reply. Indeed, Hannah wouldn't have bothered to keep up the correspondence but for the fact that she wanted Robert to be aware of the state of their mother's health.

But why did he not keep in touch with them, or make any effort to visit his mother? He knew the Viscountess's health was failing. Was he truly more concerned with his life in London than he was with the welfare of his family in Sussex?

It certainly seemed that way, Hannah thought darkly. She couldn't remember the last time he'd been home for Christmas, or when he'd bothered to stop by to celebrate one of his mother's birthdays. Certainly he had never acknowledged any of *hers*. It was almost as though he was ashamed of them. As though they didn't exist.

Ironically, both the Viscountess and Sally had repeatedly tried to defend him. They'd said he was a gentleman intent on making his way in the world, and whose affairs kept him occupied in London.

Hannah had her own opinions about that. It might have been affairs that were keeping him in London, but she doubted they were strictly of the business kind. However, because it was her nature, she had been willing to give him the benefit of the doubt.

But not any more. If Robert hadn't come home by Wednesday next—the day they celebrated the Viscountess's sixtieth birthday—she would be forced to conclude that her brother was as thoughtless and selfish as time had proven him to be, and she would wash her hands of him completely. She would not forgive him for ignoring their mother's birthday, no matter what the justification. Because London would be there next year.

Hannah had a sinking feeling their mother would not.

CHAPTER TWO

THE stately old clock in the hall had just chimed three when a frantic knocking at her door roused Hannah from the depths of sleep. 'Yes, who is it?' she murmured, struggling to sit up.

'It's me, miss. Sorry to wake you so late, but her ladyship's in a very bad way.'

The sound of Sally's voice had Hannah out of bed within seconds. She reached for her shawl and, throwing it over her shoulders, hurried to open the door. 'That's all right, Sally. Has the doctor been called?'

'Yes, miss. I sent young Ned to fetch him.'

'How bad is it?' Hannah asked as they hastened towards her mother's room.

'I fear it's one of her worst spells so far, Miss Hannah. I tried to settle her down before coming to get you, but she wouldn't have it.' The old maid cast her an anxious glance. 'Told me his lordship was standing in the corner of the room again, looking just the way he always had, and that he was waiting to take her away.'

Hannah pressed her lips tightly together. Her mother's coughing fits had indeed been getting worse over the past few weeks, but it was the delirium which accompanied them that was the more upsetting. For brief periods of time, her mother seemed to lose all touch with reality. She started rambling about people and places that didn't exist, or that she hadn't seen in years, and she was constantly seeing the ghost of her dead husband, John, standing in her room. She claimed he was waiting to take her to heaven.

The doctor had been called, of course, and each time he'd administered a dose of laudanum to help settle her down, but the effect was only temporary, and it did nothing to prevent further attacks. Worse, he could not say what was causing the attacks, which meant he also couldn't suggest any ways to prevent them. But they all knew that the Viscountess was slowly slipping away.

'She's so very frail,' Sally whispered, dashing tears from her eyes. 'I don't think her poor heart can stand much more of this.'

'Then we must pray for her, Sally,' Hannah said, refusing to dwell on the possibility that Sally might be right. 'Pray that the good Lord isn't planning on taking her from us so soon.'

'I don't know I've much faith in the good Lord's planning, miss,' Sally muttered. 'He took her husband long before it was time, and if your mother thinks his lordship's calling to her now, I don't know there's much we'll be able to do to stop her from going. You know how much she's missed him.'

Yes, Hannah knew all about the depth of her mother's love for her husband, and about how deeply she had mourned him. Charlotte Winthrop had been left a widow at the age of nine-and-thirty; far too young for a woman who had loved her husband as much as she had. And while the ragged edges of her grief had dulled somewhat over the years, Hannah knew—as Sally did—that the pain had never completely gone away.

Sadly, this time, there seemed to be little the doctor could do. Standing by the bed watching his efforts,

Hannah knew they were losing the battle. Her mother was barely breathing. She had slipped into a semi-consciousness state only moments after she and Sally had entered the room, and had shown no signs of recovering ever since.

At half past three, Hannah sat on the edge of the bed, holding her mother's hands, trying to infuse the frail little body with some of her own strength. But it was no use. There was nothing anyone could do.

And when, finally, the Viscountess slipped peacefully into God's care, Hannah closed her eyes and let the tears fall silently on her mother's chest. She could hear Sally weeping in the background, and the sounds of the doctor closing his bag, but all that mattered was her mother, and these last precious moments she had with her.

'Be at peace, dearest,' Hannah whispered, tracing the line of her mother's cheek with her fingers. 'Be at peace, and know that you have left behind people who love you...so very much.'

Hannah's voice broke as she bent to press a kiss to her mother's forehead. She'd known this was coming. Known there could be no outcome other than death. But even so, she hadn't been prepared for the devastating feeling of loss. This terrible sense of finality.

She hadn't been ready to say goodbye.

Some time later, Hannah felt the touch of the doctor's hands on her shoulders, and reluctantly got to her feet. She took one last look at her mother, and then slowly walked across the room to enfold Sally in her arms. She said nothing as the elderly woman wept, knowing there was little she *could* say that would relieve the woman's suffering. Instead, she waited until Sally's sobs had eased before putting her arm around her shoulder and taking her back to her room. Grief, like any strong emotion, was always tiring, and with luck, Sally would fall asleep quickly once the initial shock had passed.

After that, Hannah slipped back downstairs to the music-room where, only hours before, she and her mother had passed the hours in pleasant conversation. Where she had played the pianoforte for her, and where the two of them had laughed and talked as though they'd had all the time in the world.

But they hadn't had that much time. They'd had only a few precious hours before God had come to claim her mother, and Hannah had been left alone, broken-hearted, and sure in the fact that one part of her life was over, and that nothing was ever going to be the same again.

Robert received his sister's letter late the following day. Alone in his study, he read it over, regret etching deep lines into his face as he digested the fact that both of his parents were now dead. But he did not cry. He had not allowed himself the luxury of tears in nearly twenty-one years, and he didn't intend to start now. But in his own way, he grieved. Grieved for a woman he had once loved in the way a son *should* love his mother.

A love that had dried up when his mother had lain with another man and become pregnant by him.

Robert pushed the letter away and restlessly got to his feet. It was years since he'd let himself think about this. Years since he'd had to. But time notwithstanding, he knew it to be the truth. The simple, accidental overhearing of a whispered conversation between his mother and her maid when he'd been just thirteen years of age had told him all he'd needed to know.

Hannah was not his father's child.

It had been an appalling discovery for a young boy still innocent as to the ways of the world. He'd heard, of course, that gentlemen took mistresses and that married women took lovers, but it had never occurred to him that his own mother might do such a wicked thing.

Still, even had he not learned of his mother's treachery in such a way, Robert knew that he would have eventually discovered the truth about Hannah. He'd only had to look at her to know she wasn't truly his sister. She bore not the slightest physical resemblance to him, or to anyone else in the family. And in a line where likenesses were so striking as to be uncanny, any deviation from the norm was easily discernible.

Unfortunately, it wasn't so much his mother's indiscretion that had hardened him against her, but the fact that she had never told him the truth. Even the last time Robert had visited his mother at Gillingdon Park, when he had been a young man of five-and-twenty and well versed in the ways of the world, she had still not confessed her sin to him. And that had made him angry. As had the fact that the man involved had never had the decency to step forward and claim responsibility for his actions.

Robert had often wondered who the man was. It had been impossible to tell, given that his mother had never shown any partiality for one gentleman over another. Nor had anyone else in the family been inclined to question the fact that Charlotte Winthrop might have been involved with another man. Why would they? She had told everyone that she was carrying

John's child, so they had all accepted as natural the fact that she had given birth to a daughter within nine months of her husband's death.

But Robert had known it wasn't true. And, knowing that, was it any wonder he'd stopped going home and pretending that everything was all right? How could he be expected to take part in the family celebrations his mother and half-sister had been so determined to put on? What should he have done in light of his mother's continued silence? How would it have looked if he had openly questioned her story?

What would that have said about him? About his father?

Robert already knew the answer to that. It was the reason he'd never forced the issue with his mother. He hadn't been prepared to listen to the lies he knew she would try to tell him. But he suspected it was the reason she hadn't brought Hannah to London and launched her into Society, as she should have done.

After all, his sister *was* the Honourable Hannah Winthrop, a young lady entitled to a court presentation like all of the other well-bred society chits. She should have been paraded in front of a select group of hand-some, eligible gentlemen and then been allowed to take her pick from amongst them in the hopes of achieving an illustrious match.

But she hadn't. Instead, she'd been kept at home. Closeted in the rolling Sussex countryside. Protected by a mother who was afraid that others might finally see and discover the truth.

But would they have cared, even had they seen it?

Robert swore softly under his breath. He thought it unlikely, because it seemed that everyone who met Hannah soon came to love her. They were all quick to say what a delightful child she was, and how sweet and good-natured she appeared. They all told him how lucky he was to have her for a sister.

But would they have been as accepting of her had they known she'd been the result of his mother's lying with another man—even as her own husband had been suffering through his final weeks of life?

He thought not.

Still, when it came right down to it, what did it matter what anybody thought? *He* knew what his mother had done. And it had been reason enough for him to sever any kind of relationship he might have had with her.

It was also the reason he'd shut himself off from Hannah. He had been unable to see in her anything but the evidence of his mother's treachery.

Unfortunately, it wasn't only his mother and half-sister who had suffered from his hardening. In the years that followed, Robert had allowed very few people to penetrate the protective shell he built around himself. James Stanford was one of the few, but certainly no woman had ever laid claim to his heart. He'd had affairs, of course, but only because they satiated the physical cravings of his body. His partners were usually older women content to indulge in passions of the flesh. They were not looking for emotional commitment. Or perhaps they knew better than to expect it, since it was well known that Robert Winthrop did not give away his heart.

But now, as he stood alone in the silence of his study, Robert did experience a brief sense of loss for the woman who had done her best to love him, in spite of his refusal to open his arms to her. He was not made of stone, and on some deeply buried level, he realised that he was truly sorry he had not been able to show her more affection. But he also realised it was too late to do anything now but pick up the pieces of his life and move on.

He had become Viscount Winthrop on his father's death, and now, on his mother's, he became master of Gillingdon Park. But with that responsibility came a situation he had no idea how to handle.

How did he tell a young woman who had grown up believing that she was a full-blooded Winthrop that she was not his full sister, and that he had absolutely no idea who her father really was?

Before the carriage came to a halt at the porticoed entrance to Gillingdon Park, Robert opened the door and jumped down. For a moment, he just stood there, ignoring the noise of stable boys and prancing horses, to concentrate on the unexpected beauty of the old house, shown to such perfection in the mellow light of the waning day.

From a purely structural sense, Gillingdon was an impressive house. Built of honey coloured stone, it was gracious in its age. Stately, like a grand old lady; elegant in its surroundings of lush rolling pastures and densely wooded forests. It was not an ungainly house, nor a sprawling one, but a comfortable home with rooms enough to accommodate a large number of guests. The stables and outbuildings were neatly arranged at some distance behind it, while the ornamental gardens, complete with lakes and fountains, stretched out before him.

Robert closed his eyes and took a deep breath of fresh, country air. Truly he had forgotten how lovely, and how peaceful, Gillingdon Park was.

'Welcome home, Robert.'

Robert turned, startled by the clear, bell-like quality of the voice, and wondering to whom it belonged. But when he saw the uncommonly lovely young woman dressed all in black standing on the uppermost step, he could only stare at her, speechless with shock and disbelief.

Good God, was this Hannah? Surely a mere seven years had not wrought such a startling change. Where was the awkwardness of youth he remembered? Where were the shy and downcast glances so typical of their previous meetings?

'Hannah?' he asked softly. 'Is that you?'

He was totally unprepared for the smile she gave him. 'Of course it's me. Have I changed so much that you do not even recognise your own sister?'

In truth, Robert recognised nothing about her. When had her voice changed and taken on such a sweetly seductive pitch? When had the youthful ruddiness of her complexion smoothed into this alabaster perfection?

'I have been listening for the sounds of your carriage,' Hannah said. 'I wanted to be here when you arrived.'

As he started towards her, Robert could only stare in astonishment, aware that it wasn't only Hannah's voice and smile that had changed, but every other aspect of her appearance as well. She had always struck him as being somewhat tall for a woman, yet now the gawkiness of youth was gone. She stood poised and elegant on the top step, her hips gently curved, her waist slender beneath the gown of black crape. Her breasts, barely noticeable when he had left, now rose in gentle swells beneath the dark bodice.

Surprisingly, her head was bare, revealing a cluster of dark gleaming curls that were somehow all the more striking against the creamy perfection of her skin. Her eyes were the clear, sparkling blue of the sky on a summer's day, and her lashes were long.

Ridiculously long, Robert thought uncharitably, as he looked up at her. The damn things all but cast shadows on her cheeks.

'Did you have…a good journey?' Hannah enquired, stumbling a little in the face of his unwelcoming silence.

'Yes, thank you, I did.' He slowly climbed the stairs and, glancing past her, saw Mrs Jenkins, the housekeeper, and Mr Mudd, the butler, awaiting him just inside the door. 'But it was unnecessary for you to wait upon my arrival.'

'Nevertheless, it was something I wished to do. It has been a long time, Robert.'

There was no recrimination in her voice, and Robert found himself in the unfamiliar position of having nothing to say. Hannah, mistaking his silence for impatience, turned and walked into the house. Robert followed her, feeling uncomfortably as if he'd just kicked a puppy.

On the threshold, he hesitated again, glancing around at the spacious contours of the hall. How strange his being here felt. For years, he had come to this house as a visitor. Now, he was master of it. Where was the pleasure he had expected to feel? The pleasure he surely ought to feel upon walking into his own home?

He took off his hat and handed it to the butler. 'Mr Mudd.'

'Welcome home, my lord. And on behalf of all the

staff, may I say how deeply sorry we are for your loss. The Viscountess was a fine lady, and we all miss her very much.'

'Thank you.' Robert pulled off his soft leather gloves. 'Have the necessary preparations been made for the funeral?'

It was a question that should have been addressed to Hannah, but if the butler was surprised at hearing it directed towards him, he was too well trained to show it. 'They have, my lord.'

'I hope you don't mind, Robert, but I took the liberty of placing Mama's casket in the blue salon,' Hannah said, her tone again indicating no awareness of a slight. 'It was always her favourite room and I thought it would be more appropriate than the formal parlour.'

'I have no objection at all,' Robert said, turning to look at her. 'I'm not about to pretend a greater knowledge of my mother's likes and dislikes than you, Hannah, therefore, it is only right that you be the one to make such decisions.'

Robert hadn't intended his voice to sound so stiff. Indeed, he wished he might have softened it so that it came out sounding natural and at ease, but it was more than he was able to do. Master of Gillingdon Park he might be, but intruder was more the role he saw himself in. Or was it simply the presence of Hannah in this new and unexpected guise that was throwing him so completely off stride?

'Have my usual rooms been prepared?' he asked brusquely. At his sister's nod, he finally managed a smile. 'Good. I would like a few minutes to freshen up. Then perhaps you could have Cook send up a tray—'

'Actually, I was hoping you might like to join me for dinner in the small dining-room,' Hannah said hesitantly. 'I thought it might give us an opportunity to talk.'

Robert stared at her in surprise. 'You have not yet dined? But it is nearly six.'

'Yes, but we do not keep country hours here. Mama preferred to dine at the later time, and I saw no reason to change that, especially today. I thought you would be hungry after your journey, and might wish for something more substantial than a light repast.'

Her unexpected consideration shouldn't have surprised him, but it did. 'Thank you. Yes, I will join you. There is, as you say, much we need to talk about.'

Hannah did not seem daunted by the prospect, but merely bowed her head. 'Then I shall see you at dinner.' With that, she turned and walked slowly towards the stairs.

Robert followed her with his eyes, struck as much by his sister's new-found air of maturity as he was by her physical appearance. There had been no clumsiness in her speech, no uncertainty in her manner when she had addressed him. She had conducted herself with all the grace and refinement of a well-bred young lady. But then, she *was* a well-bred young lady, Robert reminded himself. She had been raised at his mother's knee to be exactly what she appeared. She had simply not been exposed to society—though he could well imagine what would happen when she was. Hannah might be his sister, but there was no denying that she was also a remarkably beautiful woman.

Suddenly realising that the butler was waiting for his instructions, Robert abruptly turned his attention back to the matters at hand. There would be time enough to deal with his sister over the next few days. Hannah wasn't going anywhere. Yet.

Sitting in the green drawing-room in the aftermath of her meeting with Robert, Hannah tried to make some sense of what had just taken place. To say that she was disheartened would have been putting it mildly.

Older, and even more reserved than he'd been on his last visit, Robert had been cold, distant, and abrupt, almost to the point of rudeness. There had been no shared condolences on their loss, no expressions of sympathy or concern as to how she was bearing up. He hadn't even had the courtesy to address a question regarding the funeral arrangements to her, as he should have done.

Unfortunately, it wasn't only Robert's manners and attitude that bothered her, Hannah admitted now. There was something else, something she couldn't quite put her finger on. She suspected it might have had something to do with his physical appearance, though she was at a loss to understand why.

After all, he was a gentleman in every other way. His clothes bore the stamp of London's finest tailors, and his boots the mark of a discerning valet. But for all his outward appearance of respectability, there was a darker side to Robert. A smouldering passionate side that would have been indiscernible to a girl of thirteen.

A side a woman of nearly one-and-twenty couldn't help but notice.

Hannah quickly gave herself a shake. No, it wasn't seemly to be thinking about her brother in such a manner. And perhaps had she been more like a sister to him, she wouldn't have viewed his appearance in quite that way. But the reality of their situation made him *seem* more like a stranger than a well-loved brother, and there was no denying that the wavy black hair, the dark, intensely probing eyes, and the full-lipped, sensual mouth would have generated feelings of breathlessness in *any* woman.

Still, stranger or not, Robert *was* her brother, and now that she was over the initial shock of seeing him, Hannah knew she would be able to deal with him on those terms. And in light of his brisk, impersonal manner, she was very glad she had made sure that his rooms were prepared, and that Gillingdon Park was looking its best. She didn't want him thinking she was incapable of looking after the house. It was one of the reasons she had asked the staff to give the place an extra dust and polish. It hadn't needed it, but the servants had been grateful for something to do. Everyone was feeling the loss of the Viscountess, particularly the older servants who had been with her for such a long time.

As for herself, Hannah could scarce believe that her mother was really gone. She kept expecting to look up and see her walking down the stairs, her familiar laughter preceding her into the room. Perhaps it was always that way when a child lost a parent, but theirs had been such a special relationship, Hannah reflected, and she was feeling the loss most keenly. While most girls her age were married and raising children of their own, she was still living at home.

Her social world too was very narrow, confined to assemblies at the local hall, and to soirées held at neighbouring houses. It was certainly a far narrower world than the one in which her brother moved. And yet, Hannah had never been unhappy in it. She knew that her mother had loved her, and there had been so many wonderful moments in their lives, so much laughter, and joy, that she could not find anything in her heart to be regretful for.

Except that it had all come to such an abrupt end.

And now, she had no idea *what* to expect. The house she had lived in her whole life now belonged to Robert. If he wished to turn her out, he was perfectly within his rights to do so. If he wished to marry and bring his wife here, no one had the right to tell him he could not. The fact that Gillingdon Park had been *her* home for the past twenty years would have no legal bearing on the situation. Only time would tell if it had a moral one.

Breathing a heavy sigh, Hannah glanced up at a painting on the wall, a portrait of her brother at the age of eight. It had long been one of her mother's favourites. She had refused to hang it in the long gallery with the rest of the family portraits, but had brought it down here where she might see it every day. She'd said it reminded her of Robert at a time when he had laughed often and loved easily.

Hannah's mouth curved in a sad smile. It was hard to associate that bright, beautiful boy with the cold-eyed man she had just left. They might have been two entirely different people. But it gave her some comfort to know that if she had been uneasy at seeing him, Robert had been just as startled by his first sight of her. The look of astonishment on his face, fleeting as it had been, had appeared entirely genuine.

He had not been expecting an elegant young lady to greet him at the door. He had been expecting the thirteen-year-old girl he'd left behind.

But why would he be so surprised by the change? Hannah wondered. It was only natural she would have grown up. Perhaps he simply hadn't been prepared for the ways in which she had grown, Hannah reflected as she got up and moved slowly around the room. After all, even she knew that she bore little resemblance to the awkward girl she'd been the last time Robert had visited Gillingdon. That reality had come home to her a few months ago, when she and her mother had attended a soirée at the home of Mrs Branksmuir.

Hannah had been wearing one of her new gowns, a lovely concoction of buttery yellow muslin trimmed with deep bands of lace, and she'd had her hair dressed in a completely different style. Something more becoming to her age, her mother had said as Sarah had swept the dark tresses up and skilfully arranged them with a jewelled comb.

Certainly the young men in attendance had been startled by Hannah's new appearance. They had stumbled over themselves, blushing and stuttering when they had asked her to dance, falling all over each other in an attempt to bring her refreshments. Even poor Mr Twickenham, who had just announced his engagement to Miss Branksmuir, had seemed awkward and ill at ease.

Her mother, however, had only smiled at their confusion, telling Hannah that for the first time in their lives they were seeing her as an elegant young lady rather than the gauche and inexperienced girl with whom they had grown up.

Hannah had simply put it down to their being silly. After all, she really hadn't changed all that much. Yes, the dancing and deportment lessons had lent her movements an added grace and fluidity, and certainly her new gown and hairstyle were most becoming to her features, but she was still the same person underneath. She really did not think there was *that* much of a difference—until she'd caught sight of her reflection in a glass later that evening and barely recognised herself! Even to her own eyes, she'd no longer looked like a blushing schoolroom miss.

Hannah breathed another sigh as she stared up at her brother's portrait. *That* was the change Robert had seen when he had arrived tonight, and was no doubt the reason he'd been so stiff and formal. And while she wished she could say that she was flattered by his regard, it was pointless to deceive herself in such a way.

After all, how could she be flattered when she knew he didn't like her any better now than he had in the past?

It might be a strange feeling for a sister to have about her brother, but Hannah knew it was the truth. Robert had never said so in as many words, but she knew he held her in dislike. There was a distance between them, a coldness, as though he disapproved of her in some way. Indeed, they were more like strangers than they were siblings.

But perhaps that was only to be expected. After all, what had they in common? She was twelve years his junior, and had grown up in an entirely different world. They had not even seen each other more than a dozen times in their lives.

Still, he *was* her brother. Surely he owed her some small degree of affection and respect, if for no other reason than that!

In the elegant blue salon, Robert approached the coffin where his mother lay and steeled himself for the feelings of anger and disdain his first sight of her would surely engender. To his surprise, all he felt upon looking at her was sorrow and regret.

When had she become this tiny, withered person? She had always seemed so strong to him. So resilient. When he'd been a child, she had played with him, swinging him up in her arms, or throwing a ball for him to catch. Now, as he brushed her face with his fingers, feeling it cold and lifeless to his touch, he wondered when she had become this fragile shell with white skin and closed eyes.

Still, she looked peaceful in death, Robert acknowledged. Was she happy at finally being released from this mortal prison? Was she up in heaven with his father? Or had her soul been sent to hell for deceiving the man she'd once loved, and for breaking her marriage vows?

Looking down at her, Robert did not wish to think of her suffering in such a way. He knew as well as any man how weak were the ways of the flesh. Perhaps he had been wrong to castigate her for her conduct. Perhaps, in his father's dying days, he had encouraged his beautiful wife to seek a lover. Perhaps in loving her as much as he had, his father had not wished to be selfish, but had turned a blind eye to anything she might have done, if it allowed her a brief moment of happiness. If that was the case, who was he to condemn her?

'Goodbye, Mama,' Robert whispered. 'May you find in heaven the happiness you did not find on earth. And may God forgive you for your sins, whatever they might have been.'

Robert bent down and pressed his lips to her forehead. Then, with one last look, he turned and walked from the room.

Dinner that evening was a dismal affair. Hannah called upon every skill at her disposal to keep the conversation light and entertaining, but as the evening dragged on and nothing she said seemed to make any difference, she began to despair that anything would. Robert was polite but distant, the silences between them growing more uncomfortable as the evening wore on. Nor did they speak of any important matters, as he had led her to believe they would.

Finally, when the last removes had been cleared, Hannah got up to leave. 'I think I shall retire, Robert. It has been a long day and tomorrow will not be any easier.'

Something in her tone must have penetrated his mood of preoccupation, for he roused himself to look up at her. 'Hmm? Oh, yes, of course. Goodnight, Hannah.'

She was almost at the door when he stopped her. 'Hannah?'

She turned. 'Yes?'

'Forgive me. I fear I have been…less than agreeable company this evening.' He hesitated for a moment, as though struggling for words. 'You have been trying to entertain me and have earned little response for your efforts.'

Hannah smoothed down her skirts, glad that he had at least acknowledged her attempts, but still too hurt to so easily forgive. 'I'm sure you have much on your mind, Robert. Besides, we do not know each other well. In some ways, we are more like strangers than family, and strangers are never easy upon first meeting.'

'Nevertheless, it does not excuse rudeness.' He offered her a half-hearted smile. 'Pray forgive me.'

It was an apology, Hannah realised, but one offered out of duty rather than remorse. He was a gentleman offering a lady an apology for unbecoming behaviour. It had nothing to do with feelings of regret for the lack of closeness between them. Still, it was an apology.

'Of course,' she said, answering his brief smile with one of her own, 'but it is not necessary. You may behave in whatever manner you wish in your own home.'

'My home.' He laughed, but the sound rang empty and somehow hollow. 'Yes, every now and then I remember that Gillingdon Park is mine, and that I am no longer a guest in my mother's home. Or in yours,' he said, gazing at her over the rim of his glass.

The veiled insinuation brought a flush to Hannah's cheeks. 'I am well aware of my position here, Robert. Though I cannot think of Gillingdon Park as anything *but* my home, I would not presume to consider myself mistress of it in light of our mother's passing. That position rests with your wife, and with her alone. Well, there is much to be done before the funeral tomorrow. I expect the family will start arriving early. Did Mr Haberford tell you when we could expect him?'

'Some time tomorrow, I believe. Why?' Robert looked at her, his expression veiled. 'Are you anxious for the lawyer's arrival?'

Intent on her own thoughts, Hannah missed the note of enquiry in her brother's voice. 'No, but his note said only that he would be posting down directly, so

I had Ned secure a room for him at the Angel. I suppose I had thought to see him arrive today.'

'Perhaps he was delayed leaving London,' Robert said. 'Speaking of matters legal, are you acquainted with the contents of Mama's will?'

Hannah's dark brows drew together in surprise. 'No. Why should I be?'

'I simply thought the two of you might have spoken of it in recent days.'

The implication of what he was saying—or of what she *thought* he was saying—caused Hannah to stiffen. 'There was no reason for us to discuss it. I knew Mama was failing, but I did not expect her to...' She broke off, the constriction in her throat making it impossible for her to finish.

'Of course. And I apologise for sounding callous,' Robert said, though his voice, like his face, was impassive. 'But you did tell me that Mama had been suffering with a cough for some time, and that the doctor himself had remarked on her failing health. Knowing what I do of my mother, I cannot believe she did not know she was dying.'

It was a blatantly unfeeling remark, and hearing it caused Hannah to wince. However, drawing on years of training, she kept her voice, and her anger, admirably restrained. 'I know you and Mama were not close, Robert, but I would thank you to remember that she and I were, and that I loved her very much. If I have any interest in the will at all, it is only to see what provisions have been made for the servants. I know they are your servants now, but it is only natural that they will be wondering about their futures. Especially the older servants, like Sally, who effectively *has* no position any more. She will no doubt be hoping that Mama has made some provision for her.'

'And I'm quite sure Mama did,' Robert said, putting his glass down on the table. 'Just as I'm sure she will have made adequate provisions for you.'

Eyebrows raised, Hannah shook her head. 'I have no reason to expect anything apart from a few sentimental objects. You are the heir, Robert, and entitled to it all. But in truth, if she'd left me her entire estate, I would give it all back if I thought doing so would return her to me.' She stared at her brother, looking for some crack in the marble façade. 'Why do you not love her, Robert? What did she do to earn such antipathy from you? You were her only son. Was it asking too much that you gave her the respect and the love she so deserved?'

A nerve jumped in his cheek. 'I had no need to give her love, Hannah. She had you. Remember?'

The words were spoken quietly and without force, yet Hannah flinched as though he had shouted them at her. 'Yes, and all I can say is thank goodness she did.'

Then, without so much as a backward glance, Hannah turned and left the room, consigning her brother and his uncharitable thoughts to a place far warmer than this.

CHAPTER THREE

THE funeral of Charlotte Emily, Viscountess Winthrop, was well attended. The stone chapel was filled to overflowing with family and friends, and as Mr Howard read the moving words of the sermon, the sounds of ladies weeping softly could be heard throughout the old building.

Hannah sat in her usual pew at the front, with Robert on her right, and Sir Roger and Lady Montgomery, her mother's sister and brother-in-law, on her left. Lady MacInnes, the Viscountess's first cousin, had sent word that she would travel down from Scotland as soon as she could, but that she was unable to leave immediately due to the precarious state of her husband's health. Other nieces, nephews, cousins, as well as most of the servants from Gillingdon Park, occupied the pews behind.

It was a moving and dignified service, just as her mother would have wished, and for the first time since her death Hannah began to experience a feeling of peace. A small bouquet of white roses—her mother's favourites—lay atop the casket, along with a prayer Hannah had written for her.

It was comforting to know that at long last her mother and father would finally be reunited. That they would lie side by side in the Winthrop vault, her mother's coffin placed there by Robert and the five other gentlemen who had volunteered to carry it.

The church bell heralded her passing, a sad, mournful tolling in the quiet of the afternoon.

The wake was a quiet affair. The ladies of the village had kindly provided refreshments, but Hannah partook of very little. In truth, she knew herself to be in something of a daze. She heard people speaking to her, some offering condolences, others just making polite conversation, and she knew that she gave the appropriate replies, though afterwards she could scarce remember what she'd said.

What she did remember was Robert standing at the edge of the room watching her. She could feel his gaze following her as she moved, talking to people and trying to make them feel welcome. But why did he study her so intently? Was he afraid she was in fear of collapsing? It hardly seemed likely, given that he didn't like her well enough to harbour any such concerns about her health.

'Oh, my dear niece,' Lady Montgomery said, coming up and throwing her arms around Hannah. 'What a sad day this is for us all. And for you especially, my dear. You will miss her very much, I think.'

'I shall indeed, Aunt.' Hannah said with a tremulous smile. 'But I am glad she is no longer suffering.'

'Yes, that is true. Poor Lottie. So very frail at the end. Indeed, it broke my heart to see her like that when I remember how beautiful she was as a young woman. But then, we were all young and beautiful once,' she said in a wistful voice. 'Ah, Robert, there you are. I dare say this has come as a terrible shock.'

Robert, formally dressed and surprisingly sombre, inclined his head. 'It has indeed, Aunt. Hannah wrote to tell me that Mama was suffering from coughing spells, but I had not expected them to be so serious.'

'But that is often the way of it, is it not, my dears? One minute here, the next gone.'

'How is Alice, Aunt?' Hannah asked, endeavouring to move the conversation to a more cheerful topic. Her aunt was a kindly soul, but at times she could be dreadfully maudlin. 'I was sorry not to see her here with you.'

'Alas, when I left, the poor child was abed with a most dreadful megrim. I vow, I have never seen anyone suffer with such pain. When she is having a spell, I must go about in complete silence, for even the slightest noise causes her poor head to ache.'

'How unfortunate,' Hannah murmured.

'It is to be hoped she recovers quickly,' Robert put in, 'for I have heard that she is a popular young lady about Town.'

'Oh, indeed she is, Robert, indeed she is. In fact, she has any number of young gentlemen calling upon her,' Lady Montgomery said, brightening a little. 'Sir Roger and I are hopeful that we will see her advantageously settled before the end of the year.'

'You must be very pleased,' Hannah said, genuinely happy for her cousin's good fortune.

'I confess we are, my dear, but what about you? Surely you will not wish to continue living here. Why don't you come to London and stay with us for a while?'

Hannah felt Robert's eyes on her and raised her chin. 'To be truthful, I am not sure what I shall be doing for the next while, Aunt. There has been so little time to think of it.'

'But I'm sure my sister is grateful for the invitation, and will give it her due consideration.'

Hannah caught her breath as she turned to stare at

her brother. What could have prompted him to speak for her in such a way? He might be the master of this house but that did not give him control over her.

Lady Montgomery, however, only took her hand and patted it reassuringly.

'Of course she will. And I only offer because I think it is what dear Lottie would have wished. But there is no need for you to rush into a decision, Hannah. You are welcome to come and stay with us for as long as you like. Our social activities will, of course, be somewhat curtailed over the next few months, but we can enjoy the pleasure of each other's company and make ourselves as merry as possible. Dear Alice has always enjoyed your company, and I know she will welcome the opportunity of spending time with you now.'

'It is very kind of you, Aunt,' Hannah said, carefully concealing her displeasure at her brother's offhand remark. 'And I *will* give it some thought, but I'm sure you can understand that there are things I must attend to here first.'

Lady Montgomery seemed to find that perfectly understandable, and did not press Hannah for an answer. Instead, she moved away to speak to Mrs Branksmuir and her daughter, who were clearly delighted at being addressed by a lady of such distinction. Robert also turned away to speak to a neighbour, leaving Hannah alone to enjoy a few minutes of solitude. But even that did not last long.

'Good afternoon, Miss Winthrop,' Philip Twickenham said, appearing at her side. Then, in a voice that only she might hear, added, 'How are you bearing up, old girl?'

In spite of her feelings of annoyance, Hannah found a smile for her childhood friend. Dear Philip. So uncomplicated and likeable. He had matured considerably over the last few years, and was now a handsome young man with a thick head of curly blond hair and the warmest green eyes Hannah had ever seen. He was amiable in nature, quick to smile, and seldom displayed the flashes of temper that had so characterised his youth. Hannah could understand why most of the young ladies in the village found him so appealing.

Unfortunately, his good looks and easy manners had never succeeded in capturing her deeper sentiments. To her, he would always be Philip—the freckle-faced boy who'd dared her to climb the old elm tree in front of the house, and who had put her on the back of his pony when she'd been little more than six years old.

'Reasonably well, Philip, thank you,' Hannah said now, 'though I shall be glad when all of this is over and I am left to myself once more.'

'Yes, I'm sure it must be tedious dealing with all of these people at such a time.' Philip looked up, and his glance rested for a moment on her brother. 'I see Lord Winthrop managed to make it home in time for the funeral. How are things between the two of you?'

'Well enough, I suppose, though we've not had much opportunity to talk.' Hannah did not look at her brother. 'He arrived late yesterday afternoon, and today has been rather hectic.'

'Yes, I'm sure it has. Do you think he means to take up residence here?'

'I've no idea. I suspect he'll prefer to remain in Town, at least until he is married. But Gillingdon Park is his now, so it is entirely his decision to make.'

'And what of your plans, Hannah? Have you given any thought to whether or not you'll stay on here?'

The familiar form of address did not surprise

Hannah. She and Philip had long since agreed to call each other by their Christian names, at least when they were alone. Nor was she surprised at finding herself more at ease in his company than she was in her brother's.

'To tell the truth, Philip, I really haven't given it any thought. The last thing I expected a week ago was that I would be wondering what my future held in store for me today.'

'Well, I shouldn't worry about it. I dare say your mother will have seen to your welfare.'

'Robert seems to think she has left me a considerable inheritance,' Hannah said quietly.

'And I sincerely hope she has,' Philip said, surprising her with the remark. 'After all, she's seen a great deal more of you than she has of him these last years.'

As if becoming aware that he was the topic of conversation, Robert drifted back towards them. 'Afternoon, Twickenham.'

'Lord Winthrop.' Philip bowed perfunctorily. 'Please accept my deepest sympathies on your loss.'

'Thank you. It is a sad time for all of us. On a happier note, I understand that congratulations are in order.'

'Hmm?'

'Your engagement to Miss Branksmuir.'

'Oh yes, of course.' Philip coloured at his lack of recollection. 'Thank you.'

'I must say it came as something of a surprise.' Robert smiled as he glanced from Hannah's face to Twickenham's. 'I always thought you and my sister would end up marrying.'

Hannah stared at her brother in horror. 'Robert! You are embarrassing poor Mr Twickenham.'

'Not in the least,' Philip assured her. 'But you're quite right, my lord. I might well have proposed to your sister had I thought there was the slightest chance of her accepting me. But I suspect she has always looked upon me more as a thorn in her side than as a potential husband. Isn't that right, Miss Winthrop?'

Hannah looked at him and hardly knew what to say. He *might* have proposed to her…?

'Is that what you thought, Hannah?' Robert softly repeated.

'Well, yes…I suppose I did.' *Did she?* 'After all, Mr Twickenham and I were children together, and I certainly had no reason to think he would wish to marry someone who had pushed him into a smelly duckpond.'

There was a brief silence. 'You pushed Mr Twickenham into a duckpond?' Robert said.

'Yes. Farmer Brownley's, to be precise,' Philip said in all good humour. 'Possibly the foulest, most ill-smelling pool in the area. It was a very long time before I forgave her for it.'

'There, you see,' Hannah said, relief lightening her voice. 'The adventures of our youth put paid to the chances of our ever enjoying a life together. Mr Twickenham saw what a troublesome minx I was and obviously decided to marry an amiable young lady who was less inclined to such hoydenish pastimes.'

'Hoydenish they might have been, but no one could have been more amiable,' Philip assured her. 'In fact, had you given me *any* indication—'

'Philip, what are you saying to Miss Winthrop?' Frances Branksmuir demanded, suddenly appearing at his side. 'I vow, she has gone quite pink.'

Hannah was indeed aware of the heat stealing into

her cheeks, but she couldn't help it given the unexpected turn the conversation had just taken. Heavens, what had Philip been about to say? Surely he'd not been about to admit that he'd been harbouring a *tendre* for her all these years…?

'Actually, my sister was being reminded of the time she pushed your fiancé into the duckpond,' Robert said smoothly. 'Isn't that right, Hannah?'

Hannah blinked, aware that they were all looking at her, aware of the jealous glint in the other girl's eyes. 'Yes, that's…right. And I do admit to being somewhat…embarrassed at having my conduct brought up for discussion all these years later.'

In a gesture that could only be called smug, Miss Branksmuir slipped her hand into the crook of Mr Twickenham's arm. 'Come to think of it, I do remember Mama talking about that particular event. She said it was quite the most appalling display of behaviour she had ever seen. Tell me, Lord Winthrop, what did you think of your sister's antics? I cannot imagine you approving of such conduct.'

'As a matter of fact, this is the first I've heard of it,' Robert admitted with a smile. 'But I shall make sure I hear the rest of the details in the very near future,' he said, sliding an amiable glance in Hannah's direction.

Having obviously held out hopes of a more censorious reply, Miss Branksmuir pouted. 'I do hope you'll not leave out any of the details when you recount the story, Miss Winthrop. Well, come along, Philip, I see Mama waving to us. Good afternoon, Miss Winthrop, Lord Winthrop.'

Robert executed a polite bow. 'Miss Branksmuir, Twickenham.'

Hannah felt the warmth linger in her cheeks as the two moved away.

'You pushed him into a duckpond?' Robert said under his breath.

'It was a childish impulse, I admit, but one that seemed entirely appropriate at the time,' Hannah murmured, watching them go. 'However, I dare say it will prevent me from ever taking Mr Twickenham or his new bride too seriously.'

Robert glanced at his sister in surprise. It was hard to imagine the poised young woman beside him resorting to such tactics, or to believe that she would take seriously the conduct of such a prissy miss as Frances Branksmuir. The thirteen-year-old girl he remembered might have, but not this considerably more mature and composed Hannah.

It was only later, as Robert watched Hannah in conversation with the vicar and his wife, that he realised he was already starting to forget what that thirteen-year-old girl had looked like.

The reading of the will took place in the library. Mr Haberford, having arrived that morning, gathered all of the family members and staff together, and once they were seated, proceeded to outline what the Viscountess's final wishes had been. As expected, each of the servants had been given a generous financial bequest. Sally had received the largest amount, in the form of an annual annuity, as well as a small piece of jewellery as a token of Lady Winthrop's affection and gratitude.

Hannah smiled at her across the room, seeing the tears rising in the old woman's eyes. Now, no matter what Robert did, the woman who had served her mother so long and so well would be able to live comfortably into her old age. She would never have to worry about finding work again.

After that, the servants were dismissed so that only the family members remained.

Lady Winthrop had again been generous, dispensing gifts of money and personal effects to almost every member of the family. Her sister, Prudence, received several pieces of very fine jewellery, and her first cousin, Lady MacInnes, was left a particularly beautiful fan that had been given to Lady Winthrop by the King.

'Lastly, I come to my son, Robert, and my daughter, Hannah,' Mr Haberford read in a suitably solemn voice. 'I shall not go into Robert's portion, as the terms of his inheritance are set out by law and by the right of succession. However, I do wish to make provision for my daughter, which I have set out as follows. To Hannah, I leave my sapphire necklace, ring, and bracelet, as well as the Winthrop emeralds, the diamonds having already gone to Robert.' The lawyer stopped to glance at Robert, but receiving only a brief nod, continued. 'I further bequeath to her the sum of thirty thousand pounds, to be put immediately into her possession, and with no stipulations whatsoever as to its use.'

A soft gasp echoed around the room. Hannah merely stared; stunned by the fortune she had just been left.

'Furthermore,' the lawyer went on, 'it is my wish that Gillingdon Park continue to be her home until either she or Robert marry. This may engender some discussion between my children, but knowing them both to be of sensible mind and completely lacking in avarice, I foresee no problems arising from it. If, however, Hannah wishes to leave Gillingdon Park and to use some of her inheritance to purchase an establishment of her own, she is entirely free to do so.'

It was a most unusual bequest, and Hannah couldn't help risking a sideways glance at Robert, wondering what he would have to say about it. But his face gave nothing away. He might have been carved of granite for all the emotion he displayed.

'My final request,' Mr Haberford went on, 'is that Robert be held accountable for Hannah's welfare until she is safely married. It will soon become known that she is an heiress and while I have no concerns about Hannah's common sense, I do have doubts about the scruples of some of the gentlemen who will wish to court her. This is not a formal guardianship as I do not believe either would welcome it, but I feel that protection of some kind is required for a young lady possessed of both beauty and fortune. And that,' Mr Haberford said, closing his file, 'concludes the reading of the final will of the late Viscountess Winthrop.'

Hannah heard the murmur of conversation as her family began to get up and move around, but for some reason, she was unable to do the same. Her legs seemed totally incapable of movement, and even had they been capable, she was not sure they would have been strong enough to support her.

Dear heavens, what was she to make of it all? She had just been granted not only a small fortune in money and jewels, but also the right to remain at Gillingdon Park until either she or Robert married. And given that neither of them seemed anxious to settle, it could be a stay of some duration.

But what would her brother have to say about it? It

was an unusual stipulation to say the least, and one she had no doubt he would be most unhappy about, given his position in life and his relationship to her.

'Oh, my dear, I am so *very* pleased for you,' Lady Montgomery said, obviously suffering no such qualms. 'Thirty thousand pounds *and* the Winthrop emeralds! La, you will be quite the independent young lady now!'

Hannah finally did manage to stand, but she quickly placed her hands on the back of the chair for support. 'I will indeed, Aunt, but I must say, I am completely taken aback by it all. I never expected Mama to be so generous.'

'But why would she not be, child? She loved you dearly, and in reality, all she has done is assure you of your dowry. After all, had Lottie not made provision for it, your brother would have been forced to do so from his own funds. This way, there is no need for him to be involved.'

'Except that he must approve whomever I wish to marry,' Hannah said, unable to keep a trace of resentment from her voice.

'Now, Hannah, your mother did not say that Robert *had* to approve your choice of husband. She merely said he was to look out for your welfare, and how onerous a task can that be? You are both sensible adults. I doubt Robert will be called upon to correct any errors in judgement on your part. The gentlemen who court you will do so for any number of reasons, but you are intelligent enough to recognise a fortune hunter when you see one. Personally, I think my dear sister was merely trying to ensure that the two of you do not lose touch.'

Hannah sighed. It might have been an altruistic

thought on her mother's part, but it was hardly an encouraging prospect for her or her brother. She was quite sure Robert would have preferred to see as little of her as possible once all of this was over. And she certainly didn't believe he would be happy about being made responsible for her welfare until the time of her marriage.

She wished she knew what his feelings about the matter really were, but it seemed she was not destined to find out. Robert did not approach her after the reading of the will. Instead, he walked across to the lawyer and engaged him in what looked to be a very serious conversation. She saw Mr Haberford nod, and then glance across the room at her. But he did not signal her to join them, and moments later, he and Robert left the room.

Hannah couldn't help wondering what that brief look had been about. Or what the two gentlemen had felt it necessary to go off to another room to discuss.

The day's surprises were not over. At the conclusion of dinner that evening, Hannah was enjoying some quiet conversation with her aunt and uncle in the parlour—her brother having once again returned to the library—when there came a knock at the door and Mr Mudd walked in. He hesitated for a moment on the threshold, the expression on his face prompting Hannah to get up and move towards him. 'Yes, Mr Mudd?'

'Pardon the interruption, Miss Hannah, but Lady MacInnes has arrived.'

'Oh, splendid. Would you be so good as to show her in?' Hannah said, genuinely looking forward to seeing her mother's first cousin.

'I already have, miss.'

'I beg your pardon?'

The butler looked uncomfortable. 'Lady MacInnes asked me to give you her regards, and then to take her to see Lord Winthrop.'

Having spent years learning the proper way to behave, Hannah knew how to control her features. She was grateful for that training now. 'Of course. Then I would be happy if you would bring Lady MacInnes here upon the conclusion of her meeting with my brother, Mr Mudd.'

'Very good, miss.'

As the butler left, Hannah rejoined her aunt and uncle, but she could not help but wonder at her cousin's behaviour. Lady MacInnes had not remained close to either her or Robert, and indeed, Hannah doubted Robert had seen any more of Lady MacInnes than she had over the last twenty years. And yet her cousin had asked to see her brother in private before paying her respects to her dear departed cousin, her surviving daughter and to the rest of the family.

Well, Robert was the head of the household now, and Hannah supposed it was only natural that people would look to him first. There was no point in feeling miffed. She was just going to have to get used to the fact that this *was* Robert's house, and that no matter what the lawyer said, she was only a guest in it. Which meant there was nothing she could do but wait until her brother summoned her, or bide her time until Lady MacInnes was ready to see her.

What a pity, Hannah reflected, that she hadn't learned patience as well as she had some of her other lessons.

* * *

In the library, Robert greeted with genuine warmth the elegantly dressed lady whom Mr Mudd had just brought to the room. 'Cousin Margaret,' he said, crossing to take her hand. 'It is a pleasure to see you again after all these years. And looking very well, I might add.'

The tall, regal-looking lady inclined her head, though her lips pulled into a rueful smile. 'It has been years, Robert, though I fear time has not been as kind to me as it has been to you. I have grown old, while you have only grown more handsome.'

Robert's mouth curved upwards in a smile. 'I've always held beauty to be in the eye of the beholder, Cousin. I'm sure that what I see in you is seen by everyone else too.'

She did indeed look well, Robert reflected, though he couldn't deny that she had changed. The last time he'd seen his mother's first cousin, her hair had been as dark as Hannah's. Now it was almost white. Surprisingly, however, it only added to the elegance of her appearance. He suspected that she was somewhere in her late fifties, but her gown of black bombazine was of the first stare, and her straw bonnet tied with black lace was extremely becoming.

Robert knew that his mother and Lady MacInnes had once been very close. Indeed, it was to Burgley Hall in Scotland that his mother had retired after his father's death. It was there too, that she had given birth to Hannah. But something had happened in the weeks following his sister's birth. For some reason, the two women had suffered a falling out. At least, Robert had always assumed that that was what had happened. He knew from his Aunt Prudence that Lady MacInnes had stopped coming to Gillingdon Park, and that his mother had never paid a return visit to Burgley Hall.

He, of course, not being close to his mother, and not inclined to write to his cousin, had never learned the reasons why. Nor did it matter now. Lady MacInnes had come to pay her final respects to his mother, and hopefully, to put aside whatever manner of argument had caused them to distance themselves from one another in the first place.

'How is Lord MacInnes?' Robert enquired. 'I recall Hannah saying that he was not well.'

'He is much recovered now, thank you, Robert. We were all quite concerned at the time, but the doctor has assured me that the worst is over, and that with rest, he will be fine.'

'Was he well enough for you to leave him un-attended while you came to see us?'

Lady MacInnes smiled. 'He is not unattended. My daughter, Fiona, is looking after him, and I trust her to do whatever is necessary. But I had to come, Robert. And I had to come now. Not only to pay my last respects to your mother, but to see you.'

Something in her voice caught Robert's attention. 'Is everything all right?'

'I wish I could say that it was, but what I have come to say will not be easy for you to hear, and it will come as a tremendous shock. But I have wrestled long and hard with my conscience and feel I cannot remain silent any longer.'

Wondering what manner of news could be so alarming, Robert leaned back against the edge of the desk. 'Then tell me what you came to say, Cousin. And pray, do it quickly, for I have found that suspense is only effective when employed upon the stage.'

'Do not mock, Robert,' Lady MacInnes scolded. 'This is not a matter to be taken lightly. What I am about to say will have far-reaching consequences on your life and on the lives of many others. And you may trust me when I say it is nothing you are expecting to hear.'

Robert could see that Lady MacInnes was indeed uncomfortable with the news she was about to impart, and for the first time, felt a frisson of alarm. 'Has this anything to do with you personally?'

'Mercifully, no.'

'Then, with some other member of your family? Cedric is not in any kind of trouble? Or Fiona?'

'Thank God, they are both fine. No, this has nothing to do with my immediate family, but rather with yours.'

'*Mine?*' And then, Robert knew. 'Hannah.'

Lady MacInnes stared at him. 'How did you know?'

'Process of elimination, I suppose. My mother and father are dead and I am well, so that only leaves Hannah.'

'Well, I fear you are right. It does concern your sister,' Lady MacInnes told him. 'Or rather, with she whom you have always *believed* to be your sister.'

Robert strove to ignore the sudden pounding of his heart. *Believed to be?* Surely that telling remark meant he was about to receive confirmation of what he had always suspected.

'Would it help you to know, Margaret,' he said slowly, 'that what you are about to tell me may not be as much of a shock as you think?'

'It may help me in the telling of it, but I cannot believe it would come as any less of a shock to you, especially given what you know of your mother.'

'Perhaps it is *because* of what I know of her that the shock will not be so great,' Robert said, in a voice that was barely above a whisper. He pushed himself away from the desk, but rather than look at his cousin, he turned towards the fireplace and stared down into the grate. 'If you are about to tell me that Hannah is not who my mother has always led us to believe, pray do not trouble yourself. I already know that Hannah…is not my sister.'

Lady MacInnes caught her breath. '*Dear heavens!* How could you ever have guessed such a thing?'

'Guessing had nothing to do with it. I learned of my mother's infidelity when I was quite young.'

There was a brief, but weighty pause. 'Your mother's *infidelity*?'

'Yes. But even had I not discovered the degree to which she betrayed my father, I would eventually have found out the truth about Hannah.' Robert turned to look at his cousin—and was astonished to see her looking even more stricken than before. 'What's the matter? Have I not the right of it?'

'You are right in believing that Hannah is not your sister, but not that your mother was unfaithful to your father.' Lady MacInnes slowly stood up. 'Oh, my dear boy, wherever did you get such a dreadful idea?'

Robert stared back at her, aware of a rushing sound in his ears. *His mother had not been unfaithful?* 'I overheard Mama talking to her maid. It was…many years ago now, but I remember it as clearly as though it were yesterday. They said that…Hannah was not my father's child.'

'And they were telling the truth. She is not.'

Robert frowned. 'Then I was right. My mother *was* unfaithful to him.'

'Dear Robert, I fear the truth is much worse than that.' Lady MacInnes moved to his side and put her hand gently upon his shoulder. 'You were right when you said that Hannah was not your father's child. But the tragic part is…she is not your mother's either.'

CHAPTER FOUR

IF THE moon had suddenly dropped from the sky to land at Robert's feet he could not have been more dumbfounded. He stared at Lady MacInnes, his gut twisting in a paroxysm of shock and disbelief.

Hannah was not his mother's child? But…what the hell did that mean? If his father hadn't sired her, and his mother hadn't given birth to her—

'What are you saying, Margaret?' Robert demanded. 'If Hannah isn't my sister, who the hell is she?'

'I have no idea,' Lady MacInnes told him. 'As hard as this is for me to say, I really have no choice. We don't know who Hannah is. Your mother found her when she was but a few weeks old.'

'*Found* her?'

'Yes. She'd been left abandoned in your mother's carriage. And Charlotte had absolutely no idea who her parents were or where she'd been born.'

Robert stared at his cousin as though she had suddenly sprouted two heads. 'You surely don't expect me to believe that my mother found a baby in her carriage—and that she actually brought it home? Dear God, what kind of lunacy is this!'

'It is neither lunacy nor nonsense,' Lady MacInnes assured him. 'Indeed, I wish I could tell you it was, but I cannot. The very day your mother left Burgley Hall, she stopped for the night at an inn. The next morning, she came down to find that a baby had been left in her carriage. That baby was Hannah.'

Robert's brows snapped together in an angry line. 'I can't *believe* this! Why the devil didn't anyone tell me about this before?'

'Because I was the only one who knew—'

'Then why didn't *you* tell me? You knew where to reach me.'

'Yes, and I wanted to tell you years ago, but I promised your mother that I wouldn't breathe a word of this to anyone.'

'I am hardly anyone, madam!' Robert cried, feeling anger and betrayal burning like twin fires in his soul. 'I am my mother's only son and the legitimate heir!'

'Yes, and as such, I knew there was nothing that could be done to usurp your position. Especially by a woman.'

'The fact that the child was female has no bearing on the issue!' Robert snapped. 'I had a right to know that a child brought up in my mother's house, and who was foisted upon me as a sibling, was not related to me by blood.' Robert stalked across the room, fighting to control his temper. 'Why are you breaking your confidence now?'

'Because on your mother's death I saw no reason to continue to honour the promise I gave her,' Lady MacInnes said. 'Besides, as Viscount Winthrop, I felt it was your right to know.'

'A feeling my mother obviously did not share,' Robert said bitterly.

'I cannot make any comment on your mother's choice not to tell you, Robert. I only knew that *I* could no longer remain silent.'

Robert took a long, deep breath and then slowly let

it out. Lady MacInnes was right. He certainly hadn't been expecting anything like this. Smugly confident that the matter had been one of betrayal, he now found himself struggling to come to grips with a new and entirely unthinkable scenario.

'I think you'd best tell me the whole story,' he said, torn by a jumble of conflicting emotions. 'And I would ask you to start at the beginning and not leave anything out.'

'Of course. That is only fair. But do not reproach me, Robert, for I did warn you that what I had to say would come as a tremendous shock.' Lady MacInnes picked up her skirts and walked back to her chair. 'Well, as you know, your mother came to stay with us at Burgley Hall after your father died. Poor Charlotte. She was so terribly grief-stricken over John's death. Indeed, I had serious concerns for her health when she first arrived. She was so lacklustre in spirit, and she had lost so much weight. But I never thought she would do anything so foolish—'

'Pray keep to the story, madam.'

'Yes, of course. Well, your mother left us after eight months to return home and she spent her first night at a small inn called the Golden Thistle near Bonnyrigg. To be honest, I was surprised when she told me she had stayed there.'

'Why, is this…Golden Thistle a disreputable place?'

'Not at all. The rooms are clean and the fare is good, but I had expected her to book a room at one of the larger inns along the road to Edinburgh.'

'I see. And when Mama went to leave the next morning, you say she found…a baby in her carriage.'

'That's right.'

'Which begs the question, why did she not just leave it with the innkeeper?'

'That would, of course, have been the logical course of action, but it was not what your mother chose to do.'

'Why not?' Robert abruptly halted his pacing. 'What in God's name was she thinking? What could have possessed her to take a baby home and pretend it was hers? It is beyond all things conceivable, not to mention incredibly stupid and irresponsible.'

'Your mother thought it was anything but irresponsible at the time,' Lady MacInnes told him. 'Indeed, I think Charlotte felt the irresponsible person was the one who had left the baby in her carriage in the first place.'

'Undoubtedly. But the logical remedy for that would have been to take the baby back into the inn and leave it there!' Silent for a moment, Robert struggled to sort through the chaotic whirl of thoughts and emotions clogging his mind. 'How did you find out what my mother had done?'

'She wrote to me about a week after she got home.'

'What did she say?'

'That she had found an abandoned child in her carriage and that she intended to keep it.'

Robert stared at her. 'You must have been flabbergasted. Both at what she'd done, and that she'd had the courage to admit it to you.'

'I was shocked that she wanted to keep the child, but not that she'd wanted to tell me.' Lady MacInnes sighed. 'Your mother and I were very close, Robert. In fact, I looked upon her more as a sister than as a cousin, and when she came to stay with me rather than go to London to be with Prudence after your father's death, I was absolutely delighted. But she stayed with me for eight months, and it was obvious she wasn't with child at any time during her stay, so she could hardly have pretended that the child was John's. A deceit like that could only be perpetrated on people who didn't know any better. I did, so she *had* to tell me.'

'She could have pretended it was another man's, even to you.'

'Oh, my dear, she would never have done that. Charlotte loved your father with all her heart. The last thing she would have done was claim that the child was another man's. She would never have disgraced John's memory in such a way.'

Robert swallowed, abruptly feeling the guilt for having thought exactly that—and for having held it against his mother his entire adult life. 'Go on,' he said harshly.

'Well, after she wrote to tell me about the child, I immediately came here to see her,' Lady MacInnes continued. 'I thought perhaps I might be able to talk some sense into Charlotte, and to convince her to see reason. But I soon realised that there would be no changing her mind. Your mother told me, without emotion or histrionics, how she had found the baby in her carriage, and how, after a great deal of consideration, she had decided to keep it. Then she showed me the letter.'

Robert froze. 'There was a letter?'

'Yes. Tucked down inside the shawl the baby came wrapped in.'

'What did it say?'

'Only that the child's mother was dead, and that the father knew nothing of its existence. Charlotte even showed me the shawl in the hopes it would convince me that Hannah had not come from the depths of poverty and degradation.'

'And did it?'

Lady MacInnes shook her head. 'Hannah could have been wrapped in gold for all the difference it would have made to me. She was still a foundling as far as I was concerned. But the shawl was a lovely piece of work, and your mother was right, it could have been worn by a lady of quality or a gentleman's daughter.'

'What did you say? About the baby, I mean.'

'Well, naturally, I was appalled. I accused your mother of having lost her senses. I told her that to take an unknown child home and raise it as her own was not only a contradiction of society's laws, but of God's. But she wouldn't listen. She told me she understood my feelings but that she had no intention of giving the child up, or of denying that Hannah was her own. Instead, she tried to appeal to my sense of compassion. She begged me to think what could have happened to the infant had she simply abandoned it at that inn.'

'But surely *someone* must have missed the child,' Robert said, needing to think through, with as much logic as possible, all aspects of this incredible tale.

'Perhaps, but you must remember that the note said the baby's mother was dead and that the father was unaware of its existence. Your mother certainly believed that to be the case.'

'Did you?'

'It didn't matter what I believed. The fact was, *someone* left a baby in your mother's carriage and obviously had no intention of retrieving it.'

'Did it not occur to my mother that the letter might have been a complete sham? That she might inadvertently have been involved in a kidnapping attempt?'

'Gracious, Robert, I'm sure no such thought ever crossed her mind. She saw no reason to question what the letter said, nor to be honest, did I. Such things happen in the lower orders. But Charlotte did what she did *because* she believed that the child would come to harm if she abandoned it.'

'But my mother was always such a sensible woman,' Robert said, more to himself than to her. 'Why wouldn't she have tried to find out more about the child's parents at the time?'

'Because you are looking at the situation without emotion or sentiment. It is easy to be rational when you are not intimately involved, or when you have the luxury of time and distance to see the state of affairs as they really are.'

'But you were as close to my mother as anyone, Margaret, yet even you could see that what she wanted to do was insane.'

'Yes, but I was not mourning the loss of my husband. You must remember, Robert, your mother was deeply grief-stricken over your father's death. She loved him passionately. Indeed, in a way I believe few women are ever fortunate enough to know. And she certainly hadn't expected to find herself a widow at the age of nine-and-thirty. She was lonely, and she was alone. That's why she came to stay with me. She'd also been praying for another child. Oh, yes. Your mother desperately wanted more children,' Lady MacInnes said in response to his look of surprise. 'So did your father. And it broke her heart that she wasn't able to conceive a second time.'

Robert nodded, beginning to see how the ground-work for this most extraordinary event had been laid. 'So she woke up one morning to find a baby abandoned in her carriage, with the mother supposedly dead and the father blissfully ignorant of its birth, and decided it was the answer to her prayers. A most convenient arrangement, when you think about it.'

'Convenient indeed. Some would even go so far as to say it was fate. But make no mistake, your mother was furious that the child had been abandoned in such a callous manner. She believed that Hannah was the result of some thoughtless nobleman's dalliance with a local girl, and she knew that with the mother dead, there would be no one left to see to her welfare. The father certainly wouldn't, even had he known of its existence. You know as well as I do that children born on the wrong side of the blanket are sometimes recognised by their fathers, but they are seldom accepted by their fathers' legitimate wives or families.'

'So she brought the...' Robert stopped, then forced himself to say it. 'She brought Hannah home and raised her as her own.'

'Yes. Charlotte told me that finding Hannah was like being given a second chance. Indeed, she christened her Hannah Jean, because in Scottish Jean means gift from God.'

'I had no idea Hannah even *had* a second name,' Robert muttered.

'More importantly, in finding Hannah, Charlotte had found a reason to go on living. Then she asked me to promise that I wouldn't say anything to anyone about Hannah, unless it was absolutely necessary.'

'And you agreed.'

'Well, what else was I to do?' Lady MacInnes cried.

'I loved your mother, Robert, and even I could see how much the child meant to her. And in truth, I did not see that any harm could come of it. After all, you were the rightful heir. You did not stand to lose anything by your mother bringing home a female child. It would have been different had the baby been a boy, but it wasn't. And if you could only have seen the difference it made to her—'

'It might have made a difference, but it does not excuse what she did!' Robert snapped, wishing he could find it in his heart to be more forgiving of the heinous deceit his mother had perpetrated on their family. 'She brought a Scottish bastard home and let everyone think it was a legitimate member of our family!'

Lady MacInnes met his gaze without flinching. 'Yes, she did. And I cannot deny that what she did was wrong. But neither could I find it in my heart to condemn her, nor to expose her for what she had done. Not when she was so desperately lonely and heart-sick.'

Struggling to regain control of his temper, Robert turned away. *Damn it!* His cousin might be calmly accepting of what his mother had done, but she'd had twenty years to come to terms with it. He had just learned of it, and there was still a hell of a lot he needed to know and to understand. But how was he to learn any of it now? With his mother gone, what hope had he of finding out what was truth, and what was not?

He didn't know whether to be furious with his mother, or to feel wretchedly sorry for her.

'I suppose this explains why the two of you saw so little of each other over the years,' he said stiffly. 'I often wondered, knowing what good friends you once were.'

For the first time, Robert saw colour rise to Lady MacInnes's cheeks. 'My husband has always had…strong convictions about morality,' she admitted. 'When I told him—as I had to—what Charlotte had done, and what she had asked of me, he said that he could not, in all good conscience, see his way clear to receiving her in our home, or to recognising the child as her legitimate daughter. Nor could he feel comfortable about allowing me to socialise with her in public.'

'And you knew what that would mean?' Robert turned back to face her. 'You both knew what it would mean?'

Lady MacInnes nodded, and the sadness returned to her eyes. 'We knew. And it hurt us both deeply to know that our friendship would have to come to an end. But I could not go against the wishes of my husband. And for what it's worth, Charlotte believed that if the forfeit of our friendship was what was necessary to ensure my silence, it was a price she was willing to pay. We never spoke of Hannah's origins again. Nor did I see your mother in private after that. If we met at family or society functions, we were cordial but that was all. I regret that such was the outcome of the event, but I had no choice. I felt I had done enough in making her the promise I had.'

Robert locked his hands behind his back and turned to face the window again. He was silent for a very long time.

'I hardly know what to say,' he finally said in a voice devoid of all emotion. 'For years I suspected my mother of having had an affair with another man. I came to hate her for it. You cannot imagine how I feel now upon learning the truth.' He lapsed into silence again, thinking through not only the situation as it stood but also the ramifications that could result from it. 'Who else knows about this?'

'Very few people, to my knowledge. My husband, of course, but he agreed to keep silent.'

'And your children, Cedric and Fiona, do they know?'

'No, they were too young. Cedric was just four and Fiona barely two when your mother came to stay with us, and since there was very little talk of Charlotte after she left, there were no awkward questions raised. But I imagine some of the servants here must know. The coachman who brought your mother north, and the outriders. And certainly Sally.'

'Sally?'

'Your mother's companion. Or maid, as she was at the time. She accompanied Charlotte on that trip so she would certainly have been there the morning Hannah was found.'

Robert eased out his breath on a long, expressive sigh. 'Well, given that I haven't heard so much as a whisper about it, either here or in London, I can only assume that whichever servants knew *chose* not to say anything, or that they were asked not to.'

'I believe they chose not to,' Lady MacInnes told him. 'Your mother was well liked by her staff, Robert. And though it comforts us to think that servants know far less than they do, I think every one of them knew how much your mother wanted another child. And as long as the Viscountess was happy, what need was there to expose her secret? Or to risk sacrificing their positions by exposing theirs?'

Robert fixed his attention on a small miniature on the shelf behind his desk. Ironically, it was a likeness of Hannah, painted when she had been no more than eight or nine years old. 'And you have no idea who Hannah's real parents are?'

'None. The letter left with her asked only that she be taken care of.'

Robert nodded. It was worse than he'd expected. As incredible as it seemed, his sister—or rather, the woman he'd been led to *believe* was his sister—was actually a motherless waif who had been abandoned in his family's carriage twenty years ago. She had been taken up by his mother and given a name, and then raised to be a beautiful and elegant young woman.

But who was she really? Where had she come from, and who were her people?

Sadly, Robert knew there was very little chance of discovering the truth now. Hannah's mother might have been a tavern wench and her father a stable hand, for all he knew. Or worse.

The only good thing to have come out of his cousin's revelation was the knowledge that he had been completely wrong in his belief of his mother's infidelity. She had *not* engaged in a sordid affair with another man. She had held fast to his father's memory, and had spent the rest of her life honouring the love that existed between them.

Robert wished he could apologise to her for that, if nothing else.

'What will you do now, Robert?' Lady MacInnes asked, breaking into his thoughts.

He turned away from the window and stared at the wide mahogany desk, as if to find answers carved in the deeply polished surface. 'I wish I knew. It never occurred to me that *this* might be the outcome of my suspicions. I always believed Hannah to be my half-sister, even though we shared no physical characteristics.'

'It would have been a miracle if you had.'

Her remark elicited a small smile. 'Yes, I dare say it would. But why did no one else think to question Hannah's parentage, Cousin Margaret? Surely someone else must have noticed that she bore not the slightest resemblance to me, or to my parents.'

'They may have noticed it, but no one had any reason to doubt that what your mother told them was true,' Lady MacInnes said quietly. 'Charlotte returned to Sussex ten months after your father died, with a baby that was no more than a few weeks old. There was no reason to suspect it was not John's, especially since Charlotte made sure everyone thought it was. Indeed, had she not spent as much time with us as she did, I doubt I would have questioned it myself. Certainly I would have had no reason to.'

It made sense, Robert admitted. The timing was perfect. And because no one had had any reason to doubt his mother's word, no one had.

'I should think this would change things between you and Hannah,' Lady MacInnes said.

'Hmm?' Robert glanced up. 'Oh yes, I suppose it will. It must. But she will be devastated,' he said, recalling what Hannah had said to him earlier of her feelings for his mother.

'Yes, and you must remember that it is not Hannah who did anything wrong. She has no reason to believe she is anyone but the person she was raised to be. It's quite obvious your mother never told her the truth.'

'Are you so sure about that?' Robert said, doubt making his voice sharp.

Lady MacInnes stared at him. 'What are you saying?'

'I'm saying that perhaps Hannah does know, and has decided to say nothing.'

'But…surely you do not think she would maintain this…charade if she knew it to be false? I do not know her well, Robert, but I cannot believe her capable of such deceit.'

'As you say, you do not know her well, Cousin. Nor, for all her being my sister, do I. Who can say what she is capable of? This is a fine house and Hannah has had the benefit of a privileged upbringing in it. Do you honestly believe she would throw all that away if she did not have to?'

'It is not Hannah's nature to be false-hearted,' Lady MacInnes repeated stubbornly.

'You just said you hardly knew her.'

'I do not, but what I have heard about her from Prudence and other members of the family has led me to believe she is honourable above all.'

'Then what would you have me do, Cousin?' Robert enquired. 'How do you suggest I go about resolving the predicament I now find myself in?'

On the heels of his last words, the library door swung open. Robert turned to see the object of the conversation standing in the doorway. 'Hannah!'

'Good evening, Robert, Cousin Margaret. Pray forgive my interrupting, but I was anxious to greet you before the hour grew too late.'

There was a split second's silence before Lady MacInnes rose gracefully to her feet. 'Hannah, my dear, I am so very sorry about your mama.' She gently embraced the younger woman. 'I regret I was not able to be here in time for the service, but I could not leave my husband.'

'You owe me no apologies,' Hannah assured her with a warm smile. 'Is Lord MacInnes improving?'

'He is, thank you, my dear. The doctor has been in constant attendance, and he has predicted a full recovery.'

'I'm so very glad to hear it. But it was good of you to travel all the way down to see us when you were so fully occupied at home.'

'On the contrary, I would not have missed paying my final respects to dear Charlotte.' Lady MacInnes glanced quickly at Robert, and then turned to address Hannah again. 'Well, you must tell me what has been happening here at Gillingdon. And perhaps I might prevail upon you for a cup of tea. It has been a very long and tiring journey.'

'Of course. My aunt and uncle are here as well and longing to see you.' Hannah paused then, and looked uncertainly at her brother. 'Will you join us, Robert?'

He glanced at her, but shook his head. 'Not immediately. I have...a few things to look after here first.'

'Very well. We shall be in the parlour when you are ready.'

The rustle of silk skirts was a hushed whisper as Hannah and Lady MacInnes left, but as soon as the door closed behind them, Robert turned and walked back towards the window, staring with blank eyes into the darkness.

What in God's name was he to do? What, in the name of all that was holy, was he to make of this bizarre happenstance? His sister, the Honourable

Hannah Winthrop, was nothing more than a nameless child; one of the hundreds that were abandoned in London every year.

Except Hannah hadn't been abandoned in London. She'd been left in a carriage no more than fifty miles from his cousin's home in Scotland. She'd been put there with nothing more than a shawl to keep her warm and a note to explain her circumstances. And his mother, rather than do the sensible thing and leave the child with the innkeeper, had brought her back to Gillingdon Park. She'd told no one—other than Lady MacInnes—the conditions of Hannah's birth, but had convinced everyone that she had given birth to the child whilst in Scotland. She'd then spent the rest of her life building upon that lie. She hadn't even told her own son the truth.

But then, why would she tell him? Robert thought bitterly. What had he done to earn her trust, or to encourage her to take him into her confidence? He had been too young to understand the truth when she'd first brought Hannah home, and by the time he *had* been old enough, it had been too late. He had already severed their relationship.

What choice had his mother had *but* to treat him the same way she'd treated everyone else?

Was that what hurt so much now, Robert wondered. The fact that she had lied to him about Hannah, the same way she'd lied to everyone else? Had being her son not made enough of a difference to her? Was that what was cutting into his chest as deeply as a steel blade plunged into his heart?

But with the discovery of the truth came an even more urgent and terrible question.

What was he to do now? How did he treat Hannah?

What did he *say* to a woman who, until a few moments ago, had been his sister, regardless of who he'd believed her father to be? What were the social implications of such a discovery? Worse, what were the legal ramifications? Who was Hannah in the eyes of the law, and what was she entitled to? She was *not* his sister, nor even his *half sister*, yet she was living in this house as though she had every right to. And what of the will?

Robert blinked. Dear God, what indeed was to be done about the will? His mother had left Hannah a small fortune in money and jewels. Jewels that had been in his family for generations! What the devil was he to do until answers to his questions could be found? He might now know the truth of Hannah's birth, but she didn't. She had absolutely no reason to suspect she wasn't exactly who she'd grown up believing herself to be, so how could he threaten to take anything back from her without explaining his reasons why? Was he ready to take on that onerous responsibility?

Was he ready to bring an innocent young woman's world crashing down around her shoulders?

In the parlour, Hannah's relatives were clearly enjoying the opportunity of getting reacquainted. Lady MacInnes seldom travelled down from Scotland, and the chance for her to do so now, despite the sadness of the occasion, was clearly a welcome one.

'Well, Margaret, you are looking very fit for a woman your age,' Lady Montgomery said as the two of them sat together on the sofa. 'I vow, taking care of an ailing husband can be an onerous chore, but you seem to have borne it remarkably well.'

'Actually, I have my eldest daughter to thank for

getting me through this,' Lady MacInnes said. 'Fiona has been a treasure, offering to take over so that I might get some much-needed rest, and ministering to her father's needs as attentive as you please. Without her, I doubt I would be looking as rested as I do.'

'I've not seen Fiona in years,' Hannah said, thinking back to the last time she had seen her cousin. 'Is she well?'

'She is, Hannah. And she has grown into such a lovely girl I can scarce credit that she is my daughter.'

'Tosh, you were always one of the beauties in the family, Margaret,' Lady Montgomery said. 'Along with my dear sister, of course.'

'And Cedric?' Sir Roger piped up. 'How is the lad?'

'He's a fine young man, Sir Roger, I'm pleased to say.' Lady MacInnes's lips curved in a proud smile. 'I see very little of him, given that he is staying with friends in Edinburgh, but he is as handsome as Fiona is beautiful, and for that reason, I consider myself well blessed.'

Hannah sipped her drink in silence. She had little recollection of her two Scottish cousins, having seen them only a few times during her life, but she remembered her mother saying that Fiona MacInnes was a bright, outgoing girl who loved to ride and that Cedric was a sturdy young lad who was always game for an adventure.

Hannah often wished she might have seen more of her cousins, being that they were all so close in age, but Lady MacInnes had had little inclination to travel to London, and she'd not come to Gillingdon Park at all. Nor had Hannah been back to Burgley Hall, though she would have dearly loved to. It was, after all, the house where she had been born. Fortunately, her mother had spoken of it so often that she almost felt as though she knew the place.

Hannah had once asked her mother why they saw so little of their Scottish cousins, but the Viscountess had gone very quiet, and Hannah was sure she'd seen tears shimmering in her eyes. But then she had said something amusing, they had both laughed, and the moment had passed. It was only afterwards as Hannah lay in bed going over the conversation that she'd realised her mother had never answered her question.

'Has Fiona entered society yet?' Lady Montgomery enquired. 'She is older than Hannah, I believe.'

'Yes, by two years.' Lady MacInnes took a sip of her tea. 'She has been formally presented, and she does go about in society, but she has not formed any serious attachments. We are not so richly blessed with company as you are in London.'

'Well, it is not to be expected, living as far north as you do.'

'We are hardly in the wilds of Scotland, Prudence,' Lady MacInnes drawled. 'After all, we are less than seventy-five miles from Edinburgh.'

'Wait, I have just had the most splendid idea,' Lady Montgomery said. 'Why do you and Fiona not come and spend some time with us in London? I'm sure you would both enjoy it. And there is no need to go to the expense of taking a house when there is room enough in ours. Would that find favour with you, my dear?' she asked of her husband.

'I suppose it would,' Sir Roger said in a dry tone. 'It might be good for Alice to have other young ladies to compete with for a change.'

'Now, my dear, you know there is no need for Alice to compete,' Lady Montgomery said. 'With any luck, she will be engaged before the end of the Season. But I know she would be happy for the company. Indeed, I have been trying to persuade Hannah to come and stay with us for a while.'

'Really?' Lady MacInnes glanced at her sharply. 'Have you given any thought to what you will do now, Hannah? I assume Robert will wish to move in here.'

'As a matter of fact, I haven't decided what I intend to do,' Robert said, suddenly appearing in the doorway. 'Hannah is in agreement, there is much that needs to be considered before any definite plans are put in place.'

Hannah glanced up at her brother and was dismayed to see him watching her again. But not with the resolute stare he had given her all afternoon. This look was different. More thoughtful. And if possible, even more disconcerting.

'My dear sister made a stipulation in her will that Hannah be allowed to remain at Gillingdon Park until either she or Robert marry,' Lady Montgomery said for the edification of Lady MacInnes. 'So there is really no need for her to depart in haste. And since she was left a most generous inheritance, she certainly need have no concerns about her future.'

'Oh?' Hannah saw Lady MacInnes glance quickly at Robert, before turning thoughtful eyes towards her again. 'How fortunate that your mother wished you to be so well taken care of, Hannah.'

'And why would she not?' Lady Montgomery demanded. 'Hannah has been a good and loving daughter all the years of her life. Indeed, I have seldom seen so close a relationship. Except, of course, for my own relationship with dear Alice. And perhaps yours with Fiona, cousin,' she added belatedly.

Hannah sipped thoughtfully at her tea. She had no idea why she couldn't shake the feeling that an awkward moment had just been passed over, but she couldn't shake the feeling that one had. Had it something to do, perhaps, with the fact that the smile on her cousin's lips had seemed forced after hearing that Hannah had been left a sizeable inheritance?

Hannah glanced at her brother, only to see him engaged in conversation with their uncle. And with her aunt and cousin now occupied in a conversation about the trials and tribulations of raising daughters, the atmosphere in the room had turned decidedly convivial.

But just for a moment, there had been a feeling of tension in the air; an undercurrent of stress running through the conversation. And she was sure it had originated with her brother's arrival—and with Lady Montgomery's innocent comment about Hannah having been left a considerable heiress.

The question was, what possible objection could anyone in the family have to that?

CHAPTER FIVE

IN SPITE of the sad events of the previous day, the sun shone gloriously bright the next, and the air was scented with the fragrance of the flowers that grew in such abundance. In the gardens behind the house, Hannah moved slowly up and down the rows, her sombre black gown clashing with the brilliant colours of the blooms.

The house would be busy today. Her aunt and uncle had decided to head back to London, given that Lady Montgomery was anxious to see how her dear Alice was faring, and that Sir Roger was anxious to get back to his paperwork. Lady MacInnes had decided to stay on until the day after, saying that she was in no hurry to get back on the road after having spent so much time on it on the trip down. She also had no reason to worry about her husband's welfare, given that Fiona was there to look after him.

'Hannah?'

Hannah stopped and turned around. She raised her hand to shade her eyes, and saw the tall, broad figure of her brother silhouetted against the sun. He was still in riding attire, which likely explained why he had not been at breakfast. 'Good morning,' she called, surprised that he had gone to the trouble of finding her. 'Did you enjoy your ride?'

'I did, thank you. You have some prime cattle in the stables. I'm surprised, since I cannot recall Mama being overly fond of the creatures.'

'She wasn't, but Papa was and that was reason enough for her to keep them. And she knew I loved to ride, of course.'

Robert awarded her a keen glance. 'You do?'

'Oh yes. My mare is not the powerful brute Balthazar is, but we get along very well.'

A dark eyebrow arched in silent enquiry. 'How did you know I rode Balthazar?'

'Because he is the finest blood-horse in the stable, and the only one I thought you would deem worthy of consideration. Your reputation as a crack-whip and Corinthian is known even here, brother.'

Robert's mouth twisted. 'I assure you, reputations can be grossly exaggerated. Which one is your mare?'

'The dapple grey in the stall one up from the end.'

Robert nodded. 'A good mount for you, I should think.'

Hannah inclined her head. 'I find her to be pleasing in all ways.'

To her surprise, Robert joined her, and for a few minutes, they strolled in silence, content to enjoy the freshness of the morning. Nevertheless, Hannah couldn't help but wonder what was really on her brother's mind. She didn't believe that he had come out here to talk about the quality of the horseflesh stabled at Gillingdon Park.

'You never did tell me what predicament you and Cousin Margaret were discussing last evening,' Hannah said, boldly taking the lead.

She was surprised to see a flush darken his cheeks. 'You heard me say that?'

'Yes, but I did not hear what went before. I hope it is nothing serious.'

He sighed and looked away from her. 'I wish I

could say that it was not, but it is, in fact, of considerable import.'

'Then I'm surprised you would be discussing it with Cousin Margaret.'

'Why would you say that?'

'Because I doubt you are any closer to her than I am, and for you to be discussing a problem of considerable consequence with her seems to me somewhat unusual.'

'Not really.' Robert glanced out over the distance fields, squinting his eyes against the sun. 'It was Cousin Margaret who brought the problem to my attention.'

'Really?' How strange, Hannah reflected silently. What manner of problem could Lady MacInnes have had that would warrant Robert's intervention? Perhaps she had particular concerns about her husband or children that she was reluctant to share with anyone else.

'Hannah,' Robert said presently. 'Have you given any thought to what you will do now that Mama is gone?'

Surprised by the sudden change in subject, Hannah didn't answer at once. Instead, she turned her attention to the blooms in her basket, wondering whether or not she had enough to fill the crystal vase. In truth, all she really wanted was a moment to think. She felt quite sure that Robert had a good reason for asking what she was going to do. Just as she was quite sure that the answer she gave him would be equally important.

'In all honesty, I haven't given it much thought,' Hannah said finally, deciding to tell him the truth. 'There is much you and I need to talk about before I feel ready to make any decisions. For one thing, I have no idea how you feel about the conditions Mama set forth in her will. In particular, the one granting me the right to remain at Gillingdon Park until either you marry, or I do. I cannot pretend there is a great deal of affection between us—'

'That is not true.'

Her smile was pragmatic. 'Let us not cavil, Robert. We have spent too much time apart. We are not like brother and sister. Indeed, Mr Twickenham is more in the way of a brother to me than you are.'

Robert paused. 'I would advise you to be cautious as regards Mr Twickenham, Hannah. *You* may like to think of him as a brother, but I can assure you, his feelings for you are hardly platonic.'

'What his feelings are for me have no bearing on the situation. He is engaged to Miss Branksmuir and happy to be so, judging by what he says.'

'Yes, but what a man says is not always a true indication of what he feels.'

Refusing to comment on what she feared might be the truth, Hannah said instead, 'Nevertheless, I cannot help but feel that you would prefer to have as little to do with me as possible. And if we continue as Mama wishes us to, we will be forced into association whether we desire it or not. However, since it is naïve of me to presume that you will not be married before me, and since you will wish to bring your bride to Gillingdon Park, I think it would be best if I were to take some of the money Mama left me and try to secure alternate accommodation as soon as possible.'

It was the first time Hannah had put her thoughts into words, and for a moment, she was as surprised at hearing them as Robert so obviously was. Indeed, she hadn't thought she *would* be leaving Gillingdon Park until she'd heard herself say the words out loud.

But the more she thought about it, the more she realised it was the only logical resolution to their situation. After all, she was quickly approaching her twenty-first birthday, and Robert was nearing his thirty-third. It was only a matter of time before he took a wife. It was his duty, after all.

But in acknowledging that, Hannah also knew that it would be impractical for her to continue living at Gillingdon Park. If she did, her life would be in a constant state of uncertainty. She would never know how long it might be before a letter arrived, telling her that Robert was getting married and that he and his new wife were taking up residence at Gillingdon Park. And in such a case, Hannah would be forced to move quickly, and perhaps to do something that was not in her best interests.

Of course, she could always go and stay with her aunt and uncle in London, but it was hard to accept that Gillingdon would not always be her home. She loved this house so much. She loved the graciousness of its rooms, and the beauty of the lands that surrounded it. She knew every tree, every hedgerow, every small river and brook that ran through it.

Of course, when she married, it was quite possible she would become mistress of a grand house, perhaps even one similar to Gillingdon Park, but it would never be the same. She would never feel the same kind of attachment to a house as she did to this one.

It was a few moments before Hannah realised that Robert was no longer walking beside her. She stopped and looked back, aware that he was standing about ten feet behind her. She'd been so intent on her thoughts that everything else had momentarily faded away.

'Forgive me,' she said in embarrassment as she walked back to join him. 'I fear I was wool-gathering.'

'That's all right.' His eyes were shuttered, but at least his mouth wasn't pulled into the hard line she'd seen so often since his arrival. 'Hannah, there are things we must talk about. Important matters that need to be discussed before you set out on *any* course of action. For that reason, I would like to assure you that there is no need for you to make plans to leave Gillingdon Park in haste. I am not involved with anyone at present, so the likelihood of my marrying in the near future is remote. But there are issues that must be dealt with. Issues that will have a considerable bearing on your life—' He broke off, frowning. 'Why do you smile?'

'Because Mama said much the same thing to me the night before she died. We were sitting in the music room, and she told me…it was time we talked about matters of considerable importance.'

'She said that?'

'Mmm.' Hannah looked down at the flowers so she wouldn't have to look at him. 'I thought she was referring to my going up to London, but when I told her that, she said that what she wanted to talk to me about was far more important than whether or not I spent a Season in London. She said it was something she should have told me, *and* you, years ago, but that she'd never found the right time to do so. I have to admit, I've been wondering about it ever since.' Hannah finally did look up, expecting to see Robert regarding her with an expression of either amusement or disdain. She saw neither.

'I have to go out this afternoon,' he told her quietly,

'but I shall be back in time for dinner. Perhaps we can talk about it then. Unless you have other plans?'

Hannah shook her head. 'I have no plans. And if you are of a mind to talk, I shall be happy enough to listen.' She sighed. 'Perhaps you would like to discuss the other condition in Mama's will too.'

'The other condition?'

'Yes. The one that sets forth your responsibility to look after me and to approve whomever I wish to marry. I can't imagine your being pleased at the prospect of having to look after your little sister in such a way.'

A nerve jumped in his cheek, but a grudging smile accompanied it. 'I admit I was somewhat taken aback by that particular provision. Especially since you appear to be a young woman who has both the intelligence and the maturity to deal quite capably with her own life.'

The compliment surprised her, but at the same time, Hannah was glad of her brother's approval. 'Thank you. Aunt Prudence seems to think Mama only made the stipulation so that you and I would be forced to remain in contact with one another.'

His look of astonishment was genuine. 'Really?'

'She seems to think you wouldn't choose to see me unless you were forced to. Unfortunately, I tend to believe she's right.'

His gaze held hers momentarily. 'Unfortunately?'

'Well, you are my brother, Robert. And while I know that might not mean much to you, it means a great deal to me. I'd like to get to know you better, I always have. I don't understand why you turned away from us, or why you chose not to keep in touch with Mama.' When he said nothing, Hannah took a deep breath. 'Well, I suppose I had best return to the house. Are you coming?'

He seemed about to say yes, and then shook his head. 'I think I'll take a walk.'

'Of course. You will no doubt wish to become reacquainted with Gillingdon Park. It has been…many years since you spent time here.'

'Yes.' His expression grew suddenly remote, his eyes shadowed, as though in pain. 'I'd forgotten how lovely it was, and how much I enjoyed being a boy here.'

Hannah looked out over the fields, seeing the majestic stand of trees away in the distance, and the clear blue lake in the foreground. 'It is the most beautiful place I know,' she whispered. 'Strange, though I was born in Scotland, it is here I feel the most at home. Perhaps because this is where I was first conceived.'

She heard Robert's sharply indrawn breath and knew that she had surprised him. But then, it was only to be expected. Ladies seldom talked about conception or birth, and certainly not in the presence of gentlemen. But Robert was her brother, after all, and if she could not speak plainly to him, to whom could she speak?

Besides, she rather liked saying things that shocked him—since she doubted there was very much that could.

Robert watched his sister—or Hannah, as he must now think of her—walk back up the path to the house, and marvelled at the conversation they had just had. She was a surprising young woman to be sure.

But in spite of his reservations, he found himself coming to like her. He appreciated her predilection for speaking her mind. She didn't dither as did so many pampered society chits. She spoke clearly and without artifice. She'd told him they weren't close, because she believed it to be true, but she made no apology to him for it. Nor had she expected him to deny it.

And yet, for all that, she *wanted* to be close to him. Her words and expressions had convinced him of that. She wanted there to exist between them the kind of love and respect that was normally to be found between a brother and sister.

But what she'd said about his mother's comments to her on the night of her death had definitely struck a nerve, Robert admitted. It seemed that his mother had indeed been about to tell Hannah that she was not her daughter. What else could she have said that would have had more effect on Hannah's life than whether or not she spent a Season in London?

But where did that leave him? Should he now be the one to tell Hannah the facts of life? If he did, what did he do *after* he'd made her aware of the situation, because there was no doubt in his mind that that's when their problems would really begin. Hannah *would* be devastated. She would be left feeling as though her very world had been turned upside down, because Hannah *believed* she was the Honourable Hannah Winthrop. Just like she believed that Lady Winthrop had been her mother, and that she'd had every right to grow up at Gillingdon Park. Which made it all the more difficult to gauge how she would react when she learned the truth.

What would she say in response to his words, Robert wondered. Would she claim it was all lies? Would she accuse him of doing this to be purposely cruel to her? Or would she accept the shocking realisation that she had no more right to live at Gillingdon than did a pauper in a king's court?

Lady MacInnes sought him out shortly after he returned to the house.

'Robert, I was hoping to speak to you,' she said, drawing him aside. 'I saw you and Hannah walking in the garden. Have you decided what you are going to do?'

Robert ran his hand through his hair, hopelessly dishevelling it. 'I haven't. But Hannah did tell me that Mama had been about to tell her something of great import the night she died.'

Lady MacInnes gasped. 'Do you think she planned on telling Hannah the truth?'

'I think it likely. Apparently, Mama said it was something she should have told Hannah *and* myself years ago, but that she hadn't because she'd never found the right time.'

Lady MacInnes nodded. 'I can understand her feeling that way. Who can say when the time would be right for such a difficult disclosure.'

'Indeed. But given that Mama knew her health was failing, I'm sure she wanted Hannah to hear it from her, rather than risk anyone else telling her.'

'I suppose,' Lady MacInnes reluctantly agreed, 'though I am not convinced Hannah would ever have found out had I not said anything to you about it.'

Robert eased his breath out on a long, weary sigh. 'Well, the fact is, I *do* know, and in an effort to protect the family, I don't see that I have any choice but to tell Hannah. Lord knows, I've no desire to hurt the girl, but Mama left her a considerable inheritance. And while I'm not as concerned about the money, I do feel the emeralds should remain in the family.'

'Perhaps it would be kinder if I told her, Robert,' Lady MacInnes offered. 'After all, I'm little more than a stranger to her.'

'You're no more a stranger to her than I am,' Robert said, grimacing. 'I've not exactly gone out of my way to further our relationship. No, thank you for the offer, Cousin Margaret, but I think it only right that I be the one to do it.'

'When will you tell her?'

Robert thought for a moment. There could be no good time for such a disclosure. The question was when would it hurt the least?

'I told her we would talk after dinner tonight, but perhaps it would be better if I waited until you returned to Scotland. Hannah will no doubt be grievously hurt and embarrassed, and I think the fewer people who are around to witness her discomfort, the better. She does not deserve what is about to happen to her, but she cannot go on living a lie. None of us can.'

As he turned to walk away, Lady MacInnes put her hand on his arm, gently staying him. 'You have much of your father in you, Robert. You may choose to hide it under a gruff exterior, but you are every bit as kind and as compassionate as he was.'

Robert sighed. 'I only wonder if Hannah will think as kindly of me as you do, Cousin. After all, I am about to destroy her world. How compassionate can that be deemed by anyone, I wonder.'

Dinner that evening was a far more convivial occasion than it had been on the previous nights. The presence of Lady MacInnes seemed to mitigate some of the lingering stiffness between Robert and Hannah, and though he was still a little subdued, Hannah felt considerably more relaxed in his company than she had at any time since his arrival. If anything, *she* was the quiet one, knowing that they were to talk after dinner, and wondering what the nature of the conversation was to be.

'Hannah?' Lady MacInnes said.

Glancing up, Hannah smiled. 'Forgive me, Cousin, my mind was wandering.'

'That's all right, my dear. I only said that you are to be commended on the quality of the meals served at Gillingdon Park. That was as fine a dinner as any I have enjoyed.'

'Thank you. Mrs Broughton is an excellent cook,' Hannah said, quick to give credit where it was due. 'She has been with Mama for as long as I can remember.'

Lady MacInnes smiled. 'As I recall, a number of the servants have been here quite some time.'

'Oh, yes. Mama believed in treating them well. I doubt they saw anything to gain by going elsewhere.'

'So they were loyal to her,' Robert said, his attention seemingly fixed on the glass in his hand.

'Indeed. They respected her, you see, Robert. And I truly believe some of them loved her. Sally certainly did. But then, Mama was such a warm and caring lady…' Hannah broke off, her voice thickening. 'Forgive me, it is still…so recent.'

To her surprise, she saw moisture gathering in Lady MacInnes's warm brown eyes. 'Time will make it easier, my dear. But right now, as you say, it is still so new, and the pain is so fresh.'

Hannah nodded, not wishing to break down in front of them but knowing she was perilously close to doing so. 'Well, perhaps we should retire and leave Robert to his port,' she said. 'Mr Mudd, would you have coffee brought to the green drawing-room for Lady MacInnes and myself.'

The butler bowed. 'Very good, miss.'

'I shall not be long,' Robert told them.

Hannah wanted to tell him to take all the time he liked, indeed, to take all night if he desired, but she knew there was no point. It would only put off the inevitable.

As it turned out, however, the inevitable came sooner than expected. After only a brief time together in the drawing-room, Lady MacInnes begged leave to return to her room, complaining of a megrime that she feared would only worsen as the hour grew late. Hannah assured her that she was not in any way offended, and wished her a good night.

Then, she sat in silence, quietly sipping her coffee as she waited for her brother to arrive and the revelations to begin.

In the dining-room, Robert mulled over the situation as he stared down into the depths of his glass. He went over everything Lady MacInnes had told him, reviewing the events in his mind, desperately trying to find some way of softening the blow he had to deliver. But he knew there was none. There was simply no easy way of saying what he knew he must.

But at least he did not have to tell her tonight. He would wait until tomorrow, after Lady MacInnes had left and there were only the two of them in the house.

It was better that way. Kinder. With that in mind, Robert got up and made his way to the drawing-room.

The door was open, and for a moment he just stood in the shadows of the hall, looking into the room, watching Hannah. He was surprised to see that his cousin had already left, but in truth, he wasn't disappointed. It would give him an opportunity to spend a little time alone with Hannah.

At the moment, she was seated in a high-backed chair next to the window. Her dark mourning clothes served as a stark contrast to the light green silk of the chair, and to the dainty ornaments sprinkled throughout the room. She was turned slightly away from him, and seemed to be lost in thought. Her eyes were fixed on a painting on the wall, but somehow, Robert doubted it was the focus of her thoughts.

For the first time, he found himself looking at her through the eyes of a man, rather than through those of a brother. Funny how the simple knowledge that she wasn't his sister had changed his attitude towards her. Where before he would have given only cursory interest to her appearance, now he found himself openly admiring of it. The soft curve of her cheek, the graceful line of her neck and shoulders. In the flickering candlelight, her dark hair glowed with shadows of deep gold and rich copper. And still, those long dark lashes cast shadows on her cheeks.

She would be well received in London, Robert found himself thinking. Not only for her outward beauty but for her inner serenity. He had watched her closely these last few days. Indeed, at times he had scrutinised her almost to the point of cruelty. And yet he had seen nothing in her that was not to be admired. Her consideration to even the most inconsequential of guests, her attitude towards the servants, and her general good nature were qualities to be admired, and they would attract rich and poor alike.

Yes, she would make some man an excellent wife, Robert thought of a sudden, surprised to find his thoughts drifting in that direction. Even more surprising was the realisation that he was rethinking his plan with regard to introducing her to his good friend, James. In the fullness of time, Stanford would assume his father's title, and become the master of a vast and profitable estate. Not a bad match for a young lady of questionable birth.

Funny that the thought did not make him happier.

'Are you going to stand in the shadows all night, Robert, or will you come in and join me?'

Startled, Robert smiled. Feeling a little sheepish, he walked into the room. 'Forgive me. I had not thought you aware of my presence.'

For the first time, she turned her head to look at him, and he saw the sparkle in her deep blue eyes. 'I always seem to know when you are near. It must be the connection between us. It makes us seem closer than most.'

He walked towards her, glancing at the furnishings in the room as he did so. He had forgotten so much about this house. But then, why would he remember? As a boy, he would hardly have been interested in the exquisite perfection of a Meissen vase, or in the delicacy of a porcelain shepherdess. He would have paid scant attention to the Gainsboroughs and Rembrandts hanging on the walls, or to the quality of the centuries old furnishings. But as a man, he appreciated it all, recognising how it worked together to make the room stylish, yet comfortable.

And as a man, he noticed how Hannah Winthrop, sitting quietly in the green silk chair, only added to the beauty and elegance of the room.

'I have not complimented you on your composure over the last few days, Hannah,' Robert said now as he crossed to stand by the fireplace. 'You are as gracious a hostess as I ever remember my mother being.'

Her cheeks flushed pink at the compliment. 'To be compared to Mama in such a way is flattering indeed, Robert, thank you. May I pour you some coffee?'

He shook his head. 'I am content to savour the lingering taste of brandy. Perhaps later.'

She nodded, and the silence resumed. Strange how such a large house could be so quiet, Robert marvelled. They might have been the only two people in it.

'Hannah—'

'Robert—'

They laughed, both feeling the tension, perhaps both anxious to set the other at ease. 'After you,' he offered.

'No, please, I fear I interrupted.'

He glanced down at the floor, then removed his arm from the mantle. He took a few steps towards her, hoping to look at ease as he locked his hands behind his back. 'Hannah, I said earlier that we would talk this evening, but I think perhaps it is better that we wait until tomorrow.'

He saw her alarm, then her confusion. 'Why? Have you changed your mind about what you wish to tell me?'

'No,' he said in a regretful tone. 'I simply thought it might be better for you if we discussed it tomorrow.'

'You mean, after Lady MacInnes leaves?'

Her perceptiveness surprised him. 'What makes you say that?'

'I'm not sure. Perhaps because I have no idea what you are going to say, but because I expect it to be unpleasant. And if that is the case, you're probably feeling I would not be inclined to entertain company after I hear it.'

'*I'm* company,' he pointed out. 'At least, you have repeatedly told me that we are more like strangers than we are brother and sister. Perhaps you will not wish to see me either.'

'Ah, but you are the bearer of the bad news, so you have no choice but to stay.'

Robert winced. 'You are sure, then, that it is bad news I bring?'

'Oh, yes. After all, Mama said it was something that would change my life, and you have said nothing to make me think differently. I have racked my brain trying to think what it might be, but I cannot conceive that it is anything but bad. So, to be honest, Robert— if you are going to tell me something like that, I would just as soon you say it now and get it over with.'

'It is not something that will be easy for you to hear, Hannah.'

'Nevertheless, it is something that I *must* hear, yes?'

'I'm afraid it is.'

'Then whether you tell me tonight or tomorrow really makes no difference.' Hannah slowly got to her feet. 'Am I to understand this *is* what Mama wished to tell me before she died?'

'I believe so.'

'You're not sure?'

'I cannot be sure under the circumstances. But even if it were not, it is something you must know.'

She straightened her shoulders and then turned to face him. 'Then I beg you, say it as quickly as possible. For I know I should not be able to sleep if I knew I had to go through another day of waiting.'

'You may wish to be seated.'

The tensing of her jaw betrayed her anxiety, but her features remained composed. 'If it is truly so bad, I would rather be on my feet so that I may run from the room to hide my dismay.' Her words were accompanied by a smile, but he could see by the way her lips trembled that she was not as serene as she appeared. 'Say what you must, Robert.'

Where did he start? There was both delicacy and strength to Hannah's face, but what kind of strength would it take to withstand the terrible blow she was about to receive?

'Hannah, you know that…my mother went to stay with Cousin Margaret in Scotland shortly after Father died,' he began slowly. 'And you know that she stayed with her for approximately ten months.'

Hannah nodded, obviously seeing nothing frightening in the remark. 'Yes.'

'You may also know, that on the trip back from Scotland, she was required to break her journey and to spend a few nights at various inns along the way.'

'Of course.'

'Well, what you do not know is that at one of the places she stayed something of a rather…extraordinary nature occurred.'

'Oh? How extraordinary?'

'She came out one morning to find that someone had left…something in her carriage.'

'Something?'

'A package, if you will.'

Hannah smiled. 'Am I supposed to guess what was in this package?' The amusement in her voice indicated an attempt to lighten the mood, but the look on his face must have assured her it wasn't possible. 'Forgive me,' she said, instantly contrite.

'That's all right,' Robert said. 'I'm not doing a very good job of this. As I said, Mama found this…bundle in her carriage, and was at a loss to know what to do with it. Apparently, no one was seen leaving it there, nor did anyone return to collect it. But it was something that would change the course of my mother's life, and indeed all of our lives, for ever.'

'Robert, I beg you, do not keep me in suspense any longer,' Hannah cried. 'What was the nature of this package?'

He took another long, deep breath, and then turned to face her. 'A baby.'

Had he told her the Regent himself had been left in the carriage, Hannah could not have appeared any more astonished. He watched the colour drain from her face. 'Dear God.' She put a hand to her mouth, and her fingers were trembling. 'Someone left…a *baby* in Mama's carriage? But who would do such a thing? Whose baby was it?'

'Mama had no idea. There was…a letter tucked inside the baby's blanket, but it made no mention of who the infant's parents were or where it had been born. It said only that…the mother was dead, and that the father knew nothing of its existence.'

'The mother was dead—' Contrary to her resolve, Hannah sank weakly into the nearest chair. 'Oh, Robert, this is not at all what I had been expecting you to say.'

'No, I'm sure it isn't,' Robert murmured. He noticed

the whiteness around her mouth and took a step towards her. 'Are you all right? Can I pour you a brandy?'

'No, no, I'm...fine. I'm just horrified that Mama would have been put in such a terrible position. But who would have done such a thing?' She looked up at him with eyes that spoke eloquently of her sadness. 'How could anyone with a heart or a conscience abandon an innocent baby in such a way?'

'Apparently, those were my mother's sentiments too. And because she was still so deeply grief-stricken over my father's death, she did what most people would have considered unthinkable. She brought the baby back to Sussex with her.'

Hannah drew a quick breath of utter astonishment. 'Oh, poor Mama. What anguish she must have suffered in making such a decision. But I cannot say I am surprised. It would be just like her to try to help the poor creature. She must have taken it to the orphanage. Mr Howard and his sister have always been so good with the children—'

'She did not take the child to the orphanage, Hannah.'

'She didn't?'

'No. Because what I didn't know was that my mother was desperate to have another child. She and my father both were. But she could not conceive a second time. So she brought the child...here.'

Hannah stared at him in confusion. 'But I don't understand. Mama *did* conceive a second time. She gave birth to me only a month before we left Scotland. And there's never been any other child here. There's only ever been you and me.'

'That's right, Hannah.' Robert took a step towards

her. 'There has only ever been you and me. But you weren't conceived before my father died.' He looked at her, needing to see her eyes when he told her. 'In fact, *my* father had nothing to do with your conception.'

She gazed at him, struggling to comprehend what he was saying. 'Nothing to do with—' Then, horrified, she gasped. '*Oh, dear God!* Oh, Robert, please don't tell me…' Her cheeks turned a bright, flaming red. 'Surely you don't mean to say that Mama…that my father…' She gulped hard and closed her eyes. 'That Mama was with…*another man*?'

Had the situation not been so grave, Robert might have laughed at hearing Hannah whisper aloud the dark suspicion he'd harboured most of his life. But now, in light of the shocking truth, it seemed anything but humorous. 'No, Hannah. Mama was not involved with another man. She loved my father deeply, and she remained faithful to his memory until the day she died.'

'Then what…?'

'The baby she found, the baby she raised here, as her own child—was you.'

She stared up at him for what seemed like an eternity. Then, as the harsh reality of what he was saying finally sunk in, Hannah's face went deathly pale. '*No!* It isn't *possible*—'

'It is possible. In fact, I'm afraid it's more than possible.' Robert dropped to the floor at her feet and took her ice-cold hands in his. 'Mama let everyone think you were her daughter, and the timing of it led everyone to believe that you were. But the sad truth is, you're not her daughter by birth.'

'This isn't true!' she gasped.

'I wish to God it wasn't, Hannah, but I can't keep the truth from you any longer. You *were* the baby left in my mother's carriage. You were the child whose mother died.'

'No—'

'I'm so sorry. I wish I could tell you it was all a lie—'

'But it is a lie!' Hannah's eyes widened in shock and disbelief. 'I wasn't abandoned. Mama gave birth to me...in Scotland. My father...was your father! Why are you telling me these terrible lies?'

Robert could hardly bear to look at her. He had never seen another human being in such anguish and pain. 'Hannah, I swear to you, I'm not lying—'

'You *are* lying! You must be!' She jerked her hands free and got to her feet. 'What proof have you of this? What...justification have you for telling me such a contemptible story?'

'I have no physical proof. I only know what Cousin Margaret told me—'

'Cousin Margaret!' Hannah's eyes flashed blue fire. 'You heard about this from her? Is that why she wanted to see you first? To tell you these abominable lies?'

Robert slowly got to his feet, but he did not attempt to approach her. 'They're not lies, Hannah. Lady MacInnes is my mother's first cousin. She would have no reason to lie to me or to you.'

'She must have, otherwise she wouldn't have said these things! None of it's true! I don't care what Margaret told you! She's making it all up!'

'No, she isn't, Hannah. Nor am I saying this to hurt you.' Robert kept his voice low, knowing it was imperative that he remain calm. Hannah was hurling words at him, lashing out in pain. If he responded in kind, God only knew what kind of damage they would inflict upon one another, upon their relationship. 'I truly wish I could tell you this was a mistake—'

'It *is* a mistake! Mama would *never* do this to me. She loved me.' Hannah gazed up at him as tears filled her eyes and then spilled down over her cheeks. 'She wouldn't have lied to me. She *loved* me! She loved…'

Robert caught her as she fell, scooping her up in his arms and gently cradling her head against his shoulder. She was a delicate wisp in his arms, and the scent of her filled his head like sweet, heady perfume. But as he carried her up to her room, he couldn't help but think how ironic it was that the very first time he had *ever* put his arms around his sister was the very day he had found out she was not.

CHAPTER SIX

HANNAH opened her eyes and stared at the ceiling. *Where was she?*

For a moment, she had no recollection of that, or of what had happened to her. Then, blinking, she looked around and realised she was in her bedroom. But how had she come to be here? The last thing she remembered was standing in the drawing-room talking to her brother—

Robert...

Hannah gasped as memory returned. *Oh God.* Yes, *now* she remembered. And with the memory, came pain. Terrible debilitating pain that left her gasping for air as she recalled the horrible lies Robert had told her. Because they had to be lies, she thought feverishly. They couldn't be true. They couldn't possibly be true!

Hannah slowly sat up in bed, groggy and lethargic, as though she'd had one glass of wine too many. Someone had left a candle burning at her bedside but the rest of the room was in darkness. She pressed her fingers to her throbbing temples and tried to shut out the memory.

Why had Robert said such horrid things to her? Why would he claim that she wasn't his sister? Granted, there was little enough affection between them, but surely he did not hate her so much that he would speak to her this way. Surely there was no justification for lying to her in such a vile, contemptible way!

Hannah dropped her head into her hands, aware of feeling as sick at heart as she did in body. For a moment, she feared she would be physically ill, but she took a few deep breaths and the nausea passed. Unfortunately, the trembling in her body did not, nor did the memory of his cruelty.

She was not Hannah Winthrop. She had not been born at Burgley Hall to the Viscountess Winthrop. She had been born in an unidentified place, to a nameless stranger who hadn't wanted her. A woman who had abandoned her when she'd been only a few weeks old.

And Robert was not her brother. He was just…a man. Someone she had spent the last twenty years *believing* to be her brother, but who was, in fact, no more related to her than…Philip Twickenham or any other gentleman of her acquaintance.

But what did that make *her*? Who was she? Who were her parents? And why, dear God, why had she been tossed aside?

Sally!

Hannah caught her breath. Sally would be able to tell her the truth. Sally had been with her mother since the early days of her marriage. She had gone with her to Scotland following her husband's death. She would know what had happened on that fateful day.

Sally would know if she was the Viscountess's legitimate daughter or not!

It took some doing, but eventually, Sally opened her door. She stared at Hannah in bewilderment, looking sleepy and dishevelled in her mobcap and gown. 'Miss Hannah?'

'Sally, I *have* to talk to you,' Hannah said in a low, urgent whisper. 'It's of the utmost importance. I'm sorry to have woken you, but it can't wait until the morning.'

'Well, bless your heart, miss, I can see you're in a tizzy, but whatever is this all about?'

'I have to ask you something, Sally, and I beg you to be honest with me. You *have* to be honest, no matter what.'

For the first time, Hannah saw a flicker of doubt—of alarm—in the older woman's eyes. 'What question are you wanting to ask, miss?'

'I need to know what happened twenty years ago, when Mama went to Scotland to stay with Lady MacInnes.' Hannah swallowed hard and, glancing up and down the hall, lowered her voice even further. 'I need to know...what she found in her carriage.'

Sally gasped, and in the dim light of the candle, Hannah saw her face go white. 'Oh, miss, I can't. I darn't—'

'Sally, *please*. I'm begging you! I *must* know!'

She could see that the woman was struggling—and as soon as she did, Hannah felt the walls begin to close in around her. For Sally to be this uneasy, there had to be some truth to the events.

'Come inside, miss,' the older woman said abruptly. 'It won't do to be talking about things like this out in the hall.'

'Then...it's true?' Hannah said as the door closed behind them.

'I didn't say whether it was or it wasn't.' Sally bustled across to the table, and taking up a candle, lit it from the one in Hannah's hand. 'What have you heard, and who told you?'

Briefly, Hannah relayed the information Robert had given her, but when she mentioned Lady MacInnes's name, Sally put her hand to her heart and uttered a soft cry.

'Are you all right?' Hannah asked, alarmed to see tears form in the old woman's eyes.

'Oh, miss—' Sally pulled a handkerchief from her sleeve and dabbed at her eyes. 'I always feared it would come out. It just didn't seem right you not knowing, but I always wondered where it would come from. If it was one of the servants, I might have thought to deny it, but if her ladyship herself told Lord Winthrop what she knew, then there's no point in trying to.'

'You mean…it *is* true? I'm not—' Hannah closed her eyes and swallowed hard. 'I am not…Hannah Winthrop.'

'You *are* Hannah Winthrop, as sure as I'm Sally Taylor,' the woman said fiercely. 'And don't you ever think otherwise. It's just that…' She stopped and took a deep breath. 'It's just that you weren't born in the usual way. That is to say, her ladyship wasn't the one who—'

'Gave birth to me,' Hannah said in a hollow voice. 'Which means the same thing. I'm not Hannah Winthrop.'

Hannah stared down at the floor. She was aware of Sally saying something but she had no idea what it was. Because until this moment, she hadn't been willing to believe that what Robert had told her was the truth. She'd harboured a tiny hope, clung to it in fact, that for whatever reason, Robert had concocted this wild story to discredit or embarrass her. But now, hearing the story confirmed by Sally, when she knew the woman had no reason to lie, or any grudge to bear, Hannah knew there was nothing she could do but accept it as fact.

'I can't believe this is happening to me,' she whispered in a hoarse voice. 'I can't believe Mama would do this to me. That she would *lie* to me all those years.'

'She never meant to deceive you, Miss Hannah. Indeed, she didn't,' Sally said, as fresh tears pooled in her eyes. 'And don't you ever think that she didn't love you as fierce as any daughter born of her own body. But she was just so lonely after her husband died, and she wanted so desperately to have another child. But try as they might, she wasn't able to conceive a second time.'

'How did it happen, Sally?' Hannah hesitated, trying to find the words. 'How did I…come into her life? I need to know.'

'Yes, I suppose it's only right you do. Indeed, my dear lady was planning on telling you the very night she died.'

Hannah stilled. 'Did she say that?'

'Oh, yes.' Sally wiped her eyes with the handkerchief again. 'When I took her up to bed that night, she told me she was going to tell you the truth the very next morning. She said it was time you knew, and that you were old enough to make your own decisions as to what you did with the information. But then, she took that turn and…'

'Start at the beginning, Sally,' Hannah said quietly. 'Please. I must know it all.'

And so, reluctantly, Sally told her. She told her how Lady Winthrop had gone to stay with Lady MacInnes in Scotland after her husband's death, and how, upon returning to her carriage that fateful morning eight months later, she had discovered a tiny baby left in her carriage. A baby she had brought home and raised as her own.

'So I wasn't conceived by the Viscountess before she went to Scotland,' Hannah said, needing to say it out loud. 'And she was not…with child, at any time during her stay.'

Sally hung her head. 'No, miss.'

The nausea hit again, bringing a dappling of perspiration to Hannah's forehead and lip. She closed her eyes and willed it to pass. Her body was continuing in its normal functions. Her heart was still beating, her chest still rising in concert with her breath. But inwardly, it was as though everything had stopped.

She had become a different person. She wasn't Charlotte Winthrop's daughter any more.

'Dear God,' she said, aware that the pain in her chest was far too deep to be assuaged by tears.

'Aye, that's much what I said at the time and all,' Sally murmured.

'But who could have done such a thing? Who would have left me there like that?'

'I wish I knew, miss.' Sally's sigh was filled with remorse. 'The baby was wrapped in a shawl as soft as thistledown but it gave us no clue as to where the babe had come from.'

'So no one saw…anything, or anyone, the night I was left in her carriage?'

'No, miss. Her ladyship did ask the coachman, but he said he hadn't seen a soul about. And it was just after I found the letter.'

Hannah stiffened. 'So there *was* a letter.'

'Yes, miss. Tucked down inside the blanket. Unfortunately, it still didn't tell us who the baby was.'

'You mean, who *I* was,' Hannah said dully. She saw the look on Sally's face and sighed. 'Well, you may as well say it, Sally. There's no use pretending I don't know any more.'

The older woman's face fell. 'No, I don't suppose there is.'

'I still don't understand why Mama—' Hannah blushed furiously. 'Why Lady Winthrop didn't take me back into the inn.'

'She was going to,' Sally admitted. 'But then you made a sound, just the faintest little cry, and her ladyship pushed the shawl aside and looked into your sweet face. And that was it.'

Hannah sucked in her breath. 'It happened so quickly?'

'Oh, yes. Your Mama was fair entranced. But even then you had the most beautiful blue eyes, and when you smiled up at her she quite lost her heart. We both did.' Sally chuckled. 'I said you were smiling at her, but her ladyship said I was talking nonsense, that babies so young didn't smile at strangers. But then she held you close and smoothed her finger over your cheek, and told me it had been a long time since she'd held anything so small and precious. That's when she told me you were her little gift from God.'

'She said that?' Hannah asked, needing something positive to hold on to.

'Yes. And though I'd never known her ladyship to believe in fate before, she surely did that day. She told me that God had sent you to her in exchange for the husband He'd taken. In fact, did you know that your second name means a gift from God?'

Hannah shook her head in wonder. 'In truth, I didn't.'

'Well, it does. Your Mama firmly believed there was a reason we'd stopped at that particular inn on that particular night. Because it wasn't the type of place she normally frequented. But, stay there we did, and when your mother came down to find you in the carriage, she honestly believed that it was meant to be. She said it would have been wrong to ignore what God so obviously wanted her to have.'

'So she…took me with her.'

'Yes, miss, that's exactly what she did.'

From somewhere deep inside, Hannah found the courage to smile. 'You must have thought it all a little bizarre.'

'A *little* bizarre?' Sally gave a laugh. 'To be truthful, I said to her, Whatever will people say, m'lady? A widow can't be bringing a child back from some God-forsaken place and raising it as her own. To which she replied that nobody had to know the child wasn't hers, except me, of course, and she trusted me to keep silent about the matter. Then she went on to say that it was entirely possible she'd been with child at the time of his lordship's death, and given that she'd been away all that time, there would be nothing strange in her returning home with a baby a few weeks old.'

'But Lady MacInnes knew the child wasn't hers.'

Sally's expression changed, her smile fading. 'Aye, she knew. And that was the one thing that nearly made your Mama change her mind. She said it was one thing to try to deceive people who *didn't* know the truth, but it was another to try to deceive those who *did*. And since she had no intention of allowing Lady

MacInnes to think you were another man's child, your Mama wrote to her and told her what she'd done.'

'It must have come as a tremendous shock to my…to Lady MacInnes.'

'It did indeed. In fact, Lady MacInnes came down to see your Mama the very next week. And she tried everything she could to persuade her not to do what she was planning. But it made no difference. There was no talking your Mama out of it.'

'But if Lady MacInnes knew the truth, why didn't she tell anyone? Why did she wait until Mama died before telling Rob…Lord Winthrop what she knew?'

'Because your mother made Lady MacInnes promise that she wouldn't breathe a word of what she knew to anyone,' Sally said, 'unless it was absolutely necessary. That is, to prevent a personal slight, or a grave injustice being done.'

Was that why she had come down here now? Hannah wondered. To prevent a grave injustice being done? Was that how she—and the rest of society— viewed the leaving of thirty thousand pounds to the bastard child of a dead woman?

'Did my…arrival on the scene have anything to do with my…with Lady Winthrop and Lady MacInnes not seeing each other again?' Hannah asked in a choked voice.

'I'm afraid it did, miss. I know how much it hurt your mama, because she and Lady MacInnes had always been close. But keeping you safe meant more to her than anything else in the world. She said that whoever put you in her carriage wanted you to have a chance at a better life. And as God is my witness, she said, that was exactly what she was going to give you!'

Hannah drew another long, deep breath. Well, she

knew it all now. And it still seemed too incredible to believe.

Hannah wasn't aware of Sally getting up until she heard the sound of a drawer being opened behind her. She looked around to see the old woman take a small package from the chest, and held her breath as Sally handed it to her. 'Here, Miss Hannah. I think it's time you had this.'

It was a small bundle, wrapped in white silk and tied with a pink ribbon.

For a moment, Hannah just stared at it. She felt like Pandora, about to open something that would change the course of her life for ever. Because whatever lay within was undeniable proof of everything Sally had told her.

Still, if it was proof, wasn't it best she look at it now and get it over with?

With fingers that visibly shook, Hannah unfastened the ribbon and pushed back the silk to reveal a beautifully woven shawl. It was of the palest green, and felt as soft as a whisper against her fingers. It was also of good size, as she discovered when she shook it out. Then she saw the small piece of paper lying on the silk.

Hannah swallowed, her chest tight as she set the shawl aside. She could hardly breathe as she reached for the fragile piece of parchment. The handwriting was barely legible, but the letters were neat and looked as though they had been painstakingly copied.

The message was brief, and there was no signature, but Hannah was left in no doubt as to its meaning.

I beg you take care of this wee girl. Her mother is dead, and her father knows nothing of her birth.

She has no family here, and I canna take care of her. But she deserves better than she's been given.

Hannah bit her lip until it throbbed. Here, then, was the proof she had been seeking. This piece of paper was her birth announcement. This shawl, her christening-gown. Together they formed the only tie to her past that existed.

A past that indicated without a shadow of a doubt that she was not now, nor ever had been, the Honourable Hannah Winthrop.

Robert was convinced he must have passed as poor a night as Hannah. Why else would he feel like hell this morning? After he'd taken her up to her room last night, he'd stayed with her until she'd fallen asleep. Then he'd gone back down to the library and poured himself a large brandy. He'd tossed it back, poured himself another, then tossed that one back too. But even the potent liquid hadn't been strong enough to eradicate the memory of the pain in Hannah's face, and the stunned disbelief that such a wretched thing could happen to her.

He wondered if a hundred years would be long enough. Certainly, if he'd harboured any doubts that Hannah knew the truth and was hiding it, he didn't now. Not even the greatest actor or actress could have feigned such grief and shock at hearing that they were not the person they'd spent their entire life believing themselves to be.

But that was last night. How would Hannah feel upon waking this morning, Robert wondered as he sat alone at the breakfast table. What would she do? Would she continue to believe he had lied to her? That he had...made it all up in an attempt to...what? To disinherit her? To humiliate her?

The servant refilled his cup with fresh coffee, and as Robert raised it to his lips, he tried to put himself in the position Hannah had been in last night. But it was more than even he could manage. How would *he* have felt upon hearing from someone who was little more than a stranger to him, that he was not the person he'd grown up believing himself to be? That he was, in fact, a nameless child who had been abandoned by his mother in the carriage of a complete stranger.

What did that say about the depth of affection his mother had felt for him, or about the feelings of her family that they had not even been willing to give him a home and to raise him amongst them?

Robert didn't like what it said any better than Hannah would. But he had no doubt it was exactly what she was thinking right now. She was probably lying upstairs, believing she'd been abandoned by everyone she'd ever known. She would be thinking that no one had cared enough about the welfare of a tiny baby to look after her and that she had been completely unwanted. Unloved.

That was, *if* she believed any of what he'd told her last night, Robert reminded himself. If she didn't, she was likely going through emotional acrobatics of an entirely different sort—with the uppermost one in her mind being that he'd done this to hurt her. She might be thinking he had told her this terrible lie to get back at her for accusing him of not caring about their mother. Or maybe, because he didn't care for *her*, as she so obviously believed to be the case. But surely she did not think him so contemptible that he would shatter a young girl's life in such a way? Surely she did not believe him such a monster...

'Good morning, Lord Winthrop.'

Lost in the tangle of his thoughts, Hannah's voice caused Robert to start. He jerked his hand, spilling coffee. Swearing softly, he got to his feet and turned to look at her.

She was standing in the doorway; hesitating, as though uncertain of her welcome. There was very little colour in her face, and there were purple shadows under her eyes. The rims were red and swollen. Obviously, she'd spent a good part of the night awake, and crying.

Robert's first instinct was to go to her, but something in her posture warned him against it. 'Hannah. How are you feeling this morning?'

'I am...tolerably well, thank you.'

She stayed where she was, prompting him to say with a faint smile, 'Are you going to come in and join me for breakfast?'

'I wasn't sure I should. I thought perhaps I might not be welcome. Besides, I fear I have...little appetite for food this morning.'

'A cup of tea, perhaps,' he suggested.

She seemed to think about it for a moment, and then inclined her head. 'Yes, tea would be most welcome.'

Robert dismissed the waiting servant and then moved to assist Hannah to her chair. She walked stiffly, as though her legs were made of wood. 'Are you sure I cannot fetch you something from the sideboard?' he offered gently.

'Thank you, no.' She slid into the chair he held for her. 'Tea will be fine.'

Because he was attentive to detail, Robert already

knew how she liked it. He prepared it for her now with a drop of milk, and a small spoonful of sugar. He was tempted to tip in a measure of brandy, but Lord only knew what that would do to her so early in the day. Then he set the fine china cup down in front of her and eased himself into the chair beside her. Where did he start?

'Hannah, you must believe me when I say that I didn't tell you what I did last night to hurt you.'

She raised the cup to her lips. 'I know.'

Her hand was shaking so badly that Robert was surprised she didn't spill tea all over the table. 'Nor did I make it up. I would never concoct such a cruel and hurtful story.'

Hannah took a few sips of her tea, closing her eyes to savour the hot, sweet liquid, before carefully putting the cup back down in the saucer. 'I know that too. There may not be a great deal of affection between us, Lord Winthrop, but I do not believe you capable of such cruelty. But because it all came as such…a shock, and because I had so much trouble accepting that…something like that could have happened, I went to see Sally.'

He started. 'Sally?'

'Yes. I had to know it all, you see,' Hannah told him quietly, 'and Sally was the only one who could tell me. She was there. She knew exactly what had happened twenty years ago. So I asked her, because I knew she would have no reason to lie to me.'

'But you thought I did.'

Hannah closed her eyes. 'Let us not go back over that again, my lord. I have told you I do not hold you culpable for anything that happened. I know that…what you told me last night was the truth, and after speaking to Sally, I know it is what my...what the Viscountess wanted to tell me the night before she died.'

Robert hadn't missed the change in reference to both his mother and himself. Hannah knew that the woman who had raised her was not truly her mother, nor was he her brother, and clearly, she felt she had no right to address them as such. But he could see from the anguish on her face the tremendous emotional toll this was taking.

'There is still much we must talk about, Hannah,' he said, wishing only to set her mind at ease. At least as much as he could under the circumstances. 'But it is imperative you realise that nothing has changed.'

'Everything has changed, my lord. Even a blind man could see that.'

'But not to the outside world. Nothing has changed in the eyes of the people who've known you all your life. The servants will still look to you as mistress of the house, and your friends and family will treat you exactly as they always have.'

'But *I* know I'm not the same person,' Hannah said in a voice quivering with emotion. 'I know I'm not Hannah Winthrop and so do you. And, knowing that, how can I possibly go on pretending that everything's all right, and that nothing has changed? I don't know who I am any more. Do you have any idea how it feels to wake up one morning and suddenly have no identity?'

'No, I do not,' Robert said, not even attempting to try to make her think he could understand that extent of her pain. It would serve nothing to try to console her with empty platitudes. 'But I have no wish to make this any harder for you than it already is. I will not expose you, Hannah. What has happened to you is not your fault. If anything, it is anger towards my mother I should be feeling for having allowed this subterfuge to go on. She should have told you the truth long before now.'

Hannah stared at the table. 'Yes, she should. And I have been trying to figure out ever since I spoke to Sally why she did not. Other people obviously knew I was not...her daughter. Lady MacInnes, her husband. Some of the servants here. Perhaps all of them. Why would she let me go on believing I was someone I was not when she knew there were others who could expose me?'

She shivered convulsively, and it was all Robert could do not to pull her into his arms and hold her until the trembling passed. He had never seen any person so emotionally raw. It was as though her wounds were open and bleeding, and no one was doing anything to heal them.

'I wish I could say I knew, Hannah, but I can't. Perhaps she was afraid of what you would say. Perhaps she thought you would be angry with her—'

'And she was right. I *am* angry with her,' Hannah cried. 'I'm angry that she spent the last twenty years convincing me that I had a right to be here. I'm angry that she let me feel...entitled to share her love, and that she encouraged me to love her as my rightful mother.'

'But she *was* your rightful mother. Oh, all right, perhaps not in the truest sense of the word, but she was your mother nonetheless. She brought you home and raised you as her daughter. She gave you every consideration, and loved you as her own. How can you say she was not your rightful mother?'

'Because she did not give me birth! Someone else did!'

'Yes, someone who obviously cared a great deal less for your welfare than my mother!'

The words, spoken in the heat of the moment, were out before Robert even realised what he was saying, and he knew at once how deeply they had hurt. He saw the stricken look on Hannah's face, and cursed himself for his clumsiness.

'Forgive me.' He pushed himself to his feet. 'I did not mean to sound so harsh.'

'No. You only spoke…the truth.' Hannah's voice was haunted. 'The woman who gave me birth…didn't love me. She couldn't have. Otherwise she wouldn't have abandoned me the way she did.'

'Hannah, the note said your mother was dead.' He turned back to face her. 'If that was the case, there was no choice—'

'There is always a choice, my lord. If my mother knew she was dying…if she even had reason to suspect that she was, she could have asked someone else to look after me. Or she could have given me to an orphanage.' She looked up at him with eyes filled with the pain of betrayal. 'Is that not what most mothers would do, Lord Winthrop? Would they not take the trouble to ensure their child's welfare, if they could not see to it themselves?'

'Perhaps your mother *did* charge someone to look after you,' Robert said softly. 'But perhaps that person was not able to see to your welfare either, and felt this was the only way to give you a chance at a better life.'

'By leaving me in the carriage of a complete stranger?' Hannah shook her head. 'I'm afraid I cannot see it in such a noble light as you, my lord.'

'Hannah, you told me that the night Mama died she wanted to tell you the truth about your origins. Why didn't she?'

A soft sweep of colour brushed Hannah's cheeks. 'Because I…discouraged her from doing so. She was tired. She'd spent…long hours at her needlework, and I didn't want her getting into any kind of emotional discussions. I told her that we would talk about it in the morning. But how was I to know what she wanted to say?' Hannah pushed her cup aside in agitation. 'How was I to know that what she was about to tell me would affect the rest of my life?'

'I believe she told you it would have a great deal more impact on your life than a Season in London,' he reminded her gently. 'And I should think the fact that she'd never been able to find the right time to tell you should have indicated that the matter was of considerable consequence.'

'Forgive me, but it did not,' Hannah answered, her voice stiff. 'I'm not a mind-reader, Lord Winthrop. I am not able to divine people's thoughts, or to assess the degree of importance attached to something they *might* wish to tell me. Your mother should have told me the truth as soon as I was old enough to understand the ramifications behind it.'

'True,' Robert said slowly. 'But I think the reason she did not was because she was afraid of what *you* would do when you heard it. I think she was terrified of inflicting the kind of pain she knew such an admission would cause. The kind of pain you're suffering now. She wanted to protect you from that for as long as she could. What loving mother would ever wish to see her child suffer so?'

Hannah pressed her lips together. 'So she did not

tell me, but left me instead to hear it from the mouths of strangers. She left me to deal with it, without giving me the benefit of being able to ask her *why* she did it.' Hannah slowly got to her feet, leaving her tea unfinished. 'Now I must draw my own conclusions, and I will never know if they are right.'

'Where are you going?' Robert asked.

'To my room. I have...much to think about.' She finally turned to him, and Robert saw the torment in her eyes. 'I appreciate your offer of silence in the matter, Lord Winthrop. It is difficult enough to know what I do, without fearing that everyone else is aware of it too.' She hesitated again. 'Was this why...Lady MacInnes was so anxious to see you?'

Robert thought to deny it, then realised there was little point. 'Yes.'

'So this *was* the predicament you were referring to in the library.'

There was nothing he could say to excuse his rather tactless use of words. 'Forgive me. You heard emotion speaking when you walked into the room. But you must remember that Lady MacInnes's recounting of the story was the first *I'd* heard of it. And while I was not as devastated as you, the news still came as a considerable shock.'

Hannah nodded. 'Yes, I'm sure it did. And now that you know, is Lady MacInnes intending to publicise the information?'

'She is not. She only told me because she felt I had a right to know, and because she had no idea whether I would hear it from anyone else. But the rest of the family genuinely believe you to be my sister in every sense of the word, Hannah. That is why I think it would be best for all concerned that we say nothing about this for the moment. No one else need know.'

'You and I know, my lord,' Hannah said quietly. 'Lady MacInnes and her family know. Most likely, all of the servants here know. People always have the best of intentions when it comes to matters like this, but it is human nature to wish to make others aware of things they do not know. I doubt it will be very long before word of this gets out.'

'I think you may be surprised to find that it does not.'

'Then it would be a pleasurable surprise indeed.' Hannah glanced down at her attire, fingering the black silk of her skirts. 'I realise there is no need for me to wear full mourning for a woman I was not related to—'

'Hannah—'

'However, with your permission, I would like to remain in half-mourning for at least three months. If I am asked by anyone why I have gone so quickly into colours, I shall simply say that…Mama did not wish me to grieve, but to…carry on with my life.'

When the tears started, Robert didn't stop to consider what was right. He just walked across the room and drew Hannah into his arms. He felt her stiffen, sensing her resistance to his embrace, but within seconds felt her body go limp, as though she hadn't the strength to object. His hand smoothed over her hair, lowering to the back of her neck, feeling her skin dewy soft and warm to his touch. It had been a long time since he'd held a woman in his arms, but as he drew her closer, Robert knew there was nothing sexual in the embrace. He simply felt a desire to protect and to offer comfort.

He held Hannah there until her sobs eased and she eventually regained control of her emotions. Only then did he gently put her away from him. But with his hands still resting on her shoulders, he looked straight into her eyes. 'You must do as you see fit, Hannah, but you should remember that she is the only mother you will ever know, and she loved you as dearly as though you were her own. I would not expect you to forget that, nor to dishonour her memory by allowing everything that has passed between the two of you to be forgotten. But you may mourn her as you think appropriate, and I shall support you.'

'Thank you, my lord.'

He grimaced. 'Must you call me that? Until last night I was Robert.'

'Until last night, we were both very different people,' Hannah said sadly. 'But in the cold light of day, I cannot pretend to be someone I am not.' She closed her eyes, and fresh tears rolled down her cheeks. 'Forgive me. Perhaps when I am a little more composed, we can talk again.'

'Of course.' Robert let his hands fall back to his sides. 'I am at your service.'

'Have you seen…Lady MacInnes this morning?'

'No. I suspect she is taking breakfast in her room.'

Hannah nodded. 'Then, perhaps you would be so kind as to…say goodbye to her for me. I know she is planning on leaving today, and I suspect it would be better if I did not see her.'

'I think she would like to say goodbye to *you*.'

Hannah smiled, but it held both a trace of wistfulness and pragmatism. 'I doubt that is the case, my lord. Lady MacInnes knows, as she has all along, that I am not a blood relation. Indeed, it was my appearance on the scene that caused her to disassociate herself from a beloved family member.'

'Yes, but she has treated you with respect and courtesy at all times,' Robert reminded her. 'She has not shunned you, as she might have done.'

'No, but there was a great deal of love between your mother and her cousin, and I shall always carry the guilt for having been the one to come between them. It was love for your mother, not loyalty to me, that kept Lady MacInnes silent. Now, there is no need for her to continue with the pretence. I do not expect it of her, nor, I'm sure, will she expect it of me. Perhaps the less said by either of us, the better.' She turned to go, and then hesitated again. 'Have you plans for returning immediately to London?'

'No. I think it best I stay here until we decide what we are going to do, and what is best for all concerned.'

She inclined her head. 'You need have no fear that I will make things difficult for you, my lord.'

Robert watched a shaft of morning sunlight fall upon her head, caressing the dark, glowing curls, and burnishing them an even deeper, richer hue. He wondered if he had ever seen such a glorious colour before. 'I never expected you would.'

With dignity apparent in every step, Hannah left the room. She seemed to float rather than walk, her carriage erect, her head held high as she moved towards the stairs. Robert watched her in silent admiration. Truly, his mother's lessons had been well learned. And not for the first time since he'd learned of this whole sorry mess, he found himself wishing that Lady MacInnes had kept her own counsel, and left them to their happiness, such as it was.

CHAPTER SEVEN

CONTRARY to Hannah's expectations, Lady MacInnes did seek her out before she left for Scotland. Hannah was in her room, staring down at the gardens, when she heard the knock upon her door. Expecting it to be Sarah, or perhaps Sally, she was astonished to look around and see Lady MacInnes standing in the doorway.

'Oh!' Hannah quickly dropped a curtsey. 'I had not thought to see you before you left. And I certainly had not expected you to come here.'

In an instant, she knew that she had misjudged Lady MacInnes. Regret hovered in the woman's soft brown eyes, and lingering sadness marred the tranquillity of her features. 'Surely you did not expect me to ignore you and just leave without saying goodbye, Hannah.'

'Yes, I think perhaps I did.'

In a rustle of skirts, Lady MacInnes walked into the room. 'Robert told me that he spoke to you last night, and that you in turn, spoke to your mother's maid. Why? Did you not believe what he told you?'

Overcome with embarrassment, Hannah glanced away. 'In truth, I did not wish to. I could not understand why Rob—why Lord Winthrop would say such terrible things to me. So I went to Sally. I knew she had been with...Lady Winthrop the entire time she was in Scotland. Which meant she knew exactly what had happened, and how I came to be here.'

'And did she tell you what you needed to know?'

Hannah caught her lower lip between her teeth. 'Yes.'

Silence filled the room, and for a moment, Hannah thought Lady MacInnes would leave. But again, the older woman surprised her. 'I know there is nothing I can say that will help ease your pain, Hannah. But I would ask you to remember one thing. Your mother— and I refer to my cousin, rather than the woman who gave you birth—loved you very much. I have seldom seen such selfless devotion, and you should be thankful for that, for true devotion is a rare gift, and one all too often overlooked.'

Hannah felt the ever-present tears begin to gather, and blinked hard, not wishing to disgrace herself in front of this woman. 'I loved her…as much as it was possible for any daughter to love her mother, Lady MacInnes. Indeed, I believed her to *be* my mother in every sense of the word. But to discover now that she was not…that it was not she who gave me birth…' She pressed her lips together and turned towards the window. 'It has shaken the very foundation of my belief, both in myself, and in those around me.' She let her gaze fall on the tranquillity of the gardens, and upon the lush paradise she would soon be leaving for ever. 'You cannot know what it is to have your identity so thoroughly destroyed. I look at my life now through the eyes of a stranger.'

'Yes, but you would have done that even had Charlotte lived,' Lady MacInnes reminded her.

Hannah nodded. 'I know. But at least I would have had her here by my side to help me deal with the truth. I would have been able to look into her eyes and see that she loved me when she told me that I was not her daughter. I would have been able to ask her all the

questions I have here—' Hannah touched her heart
'—but am now unable to ask. All I can do now is
imagine what she might have said. And it is not nearly
so comforting as hearing the words spoken aloud. For
our imaginations are so often wrong when it comes to
matters of the heart.'

Lady MacInnes nodded. 'Your mother would not
have disappointed you, my dear. She loved you very
much, and she would have done everything she could
to ease this most terrible blow. She was the most gentle, compassionate woman I have ever known.'

'You must hate me for having come between you,'
Hannah whispered.

Lady MacInnes sighed. 'I do not hate you, child. In
truth, I barely know you. But I would be lying if I
said I am not relieved that both you and Robert now
know the truth. I never believed it was right for
Charlotte to keep it from you. As to what you will do
with the information, only you can say. After all, in
the eyes of society, you *are* the Honourable Hannah
Winthrop.'

'But not in the eyes of God,' Hannah whispered.

'True. But God does not rule the world in which we
live. If He did there would be no murders or poverty.
We would harbour no feelings of ill will towards our
fellow man. God lives in our hearts and in our souls.
His existence in our life is reflected in the ways we
conduct our relationships with others.'

'But by pretending to be Lady Winthrop's legitimate daughter, I *am* being deceitful in my relationships.'

'Perhaps, but I cannot believe that even He would
wish to see you suffer for the mistakes of another,'
Lady MacInnes said with a rueful smile. 'However, I

will not attempt to change your mind. Only you can say how you wish to live your life. But I would caution you to think very carefully before setting out on any course of action. For once the first stone is cast, there can be no turning back.'

Lady MacInnes departed shortly thereafter.

Hannah did not accompany her to her carriage. She had no wish for the servants to see her in such an emotional state. Deciding, however, that it was best she spend some time alone, she changed into her riding habit and sent instructions that her mare be saddled and brought around. She always thought best when in the freedom of the outdoors. Riding alone over the fields, she would be better able to think what she must do. To figure out, as Lord Winthrop had said, exactly what was best for all concerned. And in particular, what was best for her.

One thing Hannah did know. She had no intention of accepting the money Lady Winthrop had bequeathed to her. She doubted Lord Winthrop would allow such a transfer to take place regardless, but even had he encouraged her to take a portion of the money, she would not accept. And she would certainly not take the exquisite sapphire pendant and brooch, or the beautiful Winthrop emeralds with her when she left.

Because she would be leaving. That conclusion was now settled firmly in her mind. As soon as she could make suitable arrangements, she would leave Gillingdon Park and travel to London. She felt sure she could prevail upon Lord Winthrop to take her as far as that. What she would live on once she arrived was as yet undetermined, but she would deal with that in her own way, and at the appropriate time.

After all, she was not without skills. She could apply for a position as governess to a family of quality. She could speak French and Italian. She could play the pianoforte and the harp. She could certainly educate young ladies in the manners expected of those about to enter society. But she would take nothing from *this* family.

She had no right to any more.

A short while later, Hannah pulled her mare to a halt. She had ridden non-stop, wishing to put the house as far behind her as possible, as if by doing so, she might escape the nightmare her life had suddenly become. But as she gazed out over the undulating hills, she knew she would never be able to run far enough to escape the torment.

How could she bear to leave Gillingdon Park? How could she leave this beautiful place, knowing she would never have occasion to see it again? Everything she had grown up believing in was here. And yet, on this pristine morning, it was nothing more than an illusion. Nothing she'd believed in was true any more. She had no right to live here. For all intents and purposes, she was trespassing.

No, surely that was silly, Hannah chided herself. She might not have been born into the family, but she had certainly been brought into it.

Hannah clung to that fact. As she did to Sally's and Lady MacInnes's assurances that the Viscountess had loved her as deeply as though she had been her own daughter. Perhaps because somewhere deep down inside, Hannah knew it to be the truth. There had been nothing false in Lady Winthrop's affections towards her.

But someone else had given her birth. Someone else had carried her through nine long months, and then, at the moment of her birth or shortly after, abandoned her to her fate. Was that when her mother had died? Hannah wondered. Had she abandoned her *because* she'd known she was dying? Or had she simply not wanted the encumbrance of a child? Perhaps she had been too young or too stupid to accept responsibility for what she had done. Perhaps her father had cast her out in disgrace when he had learned of her sin.

And what of the man who had sired her? Who was he, and why had he taken no interest in her? Was he a labourer or a man of noble birth? Had he been unable to marry her mother or not desirous of doing so? If what the faded parchment note said was true, her mother was not living, but her father likely was. The question was how did she go about finding out who he was?

Was it possible to?

Did she want to?

Hannah heard the sound of another rider long before she saw him. And when she recognised the horse, she knew at once that it was Rob…Lord Winthrop, approaching.

Hannah silently cursed her absent-mindedness. Would she ever get used to calling the man by his proper title? Because in spite of what he'd said, it was the only way she *should* be addressing him.

Lord Winthrop appeared over the ridge a few minutes later. Hannah stayed where she was, safely tucked into a small grove of trees. He was riding parallel to her, so she didn't think it likely he would have noticed her. But she watched him regardless, admiring how tall and straight he sat in the saddle. He was a superb equestrian, controlling the powerful animal as though he were no more than a pony. And having been on Balthazar's back a few times herself, Hannah knew that was no small feat.

Suddenly, like the shifting wind, stallion and rider changed direction. Now they were coming directly towards her.

Hannah caught her breath. She had no hope of slipping away now. Any movement would immediately be spotted, and she had no wish to make Lord Winthrop think she was avoiding him. For that reason, she waited, attempting to calm her fidgety mare as the stallion drew closer.

'What's this, Aphrodite?' Hannah murmured as the mare did a funny little sidestep. 'Never say that you are anxious for the company of the mighty Balthazar?'

The thought made her smile, a smile that was still on her lips when Lord Winthrop drew his mount to a prancing halt in front of them. 'So this is where you've been hiding. You look well pleased with yourself at having dragged me to the ends of the earth to find you.'

Hannah started. 'I did not know you were looking for me, my lord.'

'I went up to your room to see if you might like to join me for a ride. When there was no answer, I sent for Sarah, who informed me that you had already gone out. But I hadn't expected to find you all the way up here.'

'No doubt you thought I would have stayed to the lower path.'

'As a matter of fact, I did.' Lord Winthrop's smile flashed again, his teeth appearing very white against his lightly tanned skin. 'The road closer to the house offers a much less challenging road than the one you have chosen.'

'Ah, but it was not a less challenging road I wished to follow. When I need to think, I find a full out gallop far more stimulating than a sedate trot.'

'My sentiments exactly—whoa, Balthazar!' The stallion shied to one side, forcing Lord Winthrop to tighten his grip on the reins. He closed his gloved fingers around them and held the animal with a firm but steady grip.

'He is not amiable when forced to remain standing, my lord,' Hannah said. 'Especially in the presence of a lady.'

'Then perhaps I should allow him to run a little. If I can wind the beast, you and I may be able to enjoy some civil conversation. What do you say, shall we both take the air?'

Hannah needed no further encouragement. Pressing her heel into the mare's side, she flicked the crop lightly against her withers and set Aphrodite to an easy canter. The mare would not be able to sustain a gallop for the same length of time as the stallion, but the fields were wide open, and even if Balthazar took his master into the distance, they would still be visible and easy to catch.

Surprisingly, however, Lord Winthrop did not attempt to pull ahead. He kept his mount to a rolling gait, not allowing him to extend himself, until in the end, the great creature was in the way of getting quite unruly. 'Do you mind if I let him out for a bit?' he called to her.

'Not at all. He needs it.'

With that, Lord Winthrop gave the stallion his head and the two of them took off across the field.

Hannah held her breath. Dear heavens, they were all but flying over the grass. Lord Winthrop's dark head was low over the black stallion's neck, the reins held taut in his strong hands. The mighty horse's legs flew, his powerful hooves pounding over the turf, his mane and tail flying in the wind.

Hannah shivered at the sight, but it wasn't with fear. Watching Lord Winthrop control the great horse was exhilarating. She'd never seen any man ride like that before. Never felt as breathless in her admiration of his form and figure.

Then, suddenly, as she realised *who* she was looking at, she gasped in dismay.

Had she lost her senses?

The stallion's energy was spent by the brief burst of speed, and Robert cantered him in small circles until Hannah eventually reached his side. He was quite confident that Balthazar would be far more content to walk sedately at the mare's side now, and was about to suggest they ride on to the top pasture, when Hannah suddenly begged leave to return to Gillingdon Park. She seemed reluctant to meet his eyes, and not wishing to appear churlish, Robert agreed, though in truth, he was equally reluctant to bring the ride to a close. For here, well away from the house, it was as though their problems didn't exist.

And he certainly wasn't about to say he did not enjoy the sight of Hannah mounted on her pretty dapple-grey mare. Her beautifully tailored habit of dark blue Georgian cloth trimmed with black piping was extremely becoming. The styling was quite severe, but given Hannah's height, it looked striking rather than mannish. A frothy white spill of lace at cuffs and neckline served to soften the appearance even more. Her riding hat, an elegant concoction with a single curling feather and a flowing black ribbon, sat at a decidedly rakish angle on her head. The colour seemed to accentuate the blue of her eyes. Eyes made even more alluring by the frivolous bit of net she had pulled down over the brim...

'My lord—'

'Robert,' he corrected automatically.

Hannah sighed in frustration. 'It is not appropriate that I address you in such a manner.'

'I don't give a damn whether it's appropriate or not. You've called me Robert all your life. Why should you start addressing me by my title now?'

'Because our altered circumstances demand it.'

'In your eyes, perhaps, but not in mine. I refuse to be hobbled by such altered circumstances, as you call them. My name is Robert. Be so good as to call me that. At least when we are alone together.'

Hannah gave him a reproving look. 'It is not the accepted thing.'

'It is not the accepted thing to call Philip Twickenham by his first name either, but you do that when you are alone.' He sent her a teasing glance. 'Why should I not receive the same consideration?'

Hannah caught her breath. 'How did you know that?'

'You would be surprised at the things I know.'

The colour deepened in her cheeks. 'You should be willing to divulge your sources so that I may reprimand them for being indiscreet.'

'Oh, come, Hannah, surely you do not expect me to start calling you Miss Winthrop?'

'As a matter of fact, I do. Unfortunately,' Hannah

said in a quieter voice, 'I do not know that I am even *entitled* to be called Miss Winthrop any more. Perhaps I should start calling myself Miss MacDonald, or Miss MacLean.'

'Those are highland names. You'd more likely be a Miss Douglas or a Miss Gordon, coming from the area you did.'

She glanced at him—surprised by his impertinence—then realised he was still smiling. 'Odious man, you are teasing me.'

'Of course I am. A childish impulse, I admit, but one which seemed entirely appropriate at the time.'

Because she couldn't help herself, Hannah started to laugh. Whether it was hearing him repeat something she'd said herself only a few days ago, or the strain of the past few weeks catching up with her, she really didn't care. She needed to laugh. And she was delighted to hear him laughing right along with her.

'You do have the most annoying memory, my lord,' Hannah said when her laughter faded away. 'And you are shameless for encouraging me to behave in a manner that is not at all appropriate.'

'Ah, Hannah. We spend so much of our lives behaving in an appropriate manner. Do you not find it refreshing to be able to say what you really think, or to do what you really wish?'

'I imagine it would be liberating indeed, but we are not always free to give in to the wishes of our heart. Nor is it easy to change the patterns which have been so deeply ingrained in us.'

'Really?' He glanced at her in amusement. 'I do not find it difficult at all. In fact, I welcome the opportunity. For example, the flow of conversation and the conduct between a brother and sister should be natural and easy, yes?'

'Of course.'

'And yet, that same ease is noticeably lacking between a man and a woman, is it not?'

'It is.'

'So are you saying that you and I must forfeit one because we have suddenly become the other?'

'I suppose I am.'

'All right. Then what about Mr Twickenham?'

Hannah turned her head and met his eyes. 'What about Mr Twickenham?'

'By your own admission, you've made an exception in the way you speak to him, and he is no more a brother to you than I. Can you not make an exception in my case, if you can make one in his? After all, at one time we did *believe* ourselves to be brother and sister, whereas he has *never* been able to claim such an association with you.'

Hannah made a little moue of frustration. 'Are you so persuasive in all of your arguments?'

'Only in the ones that matter. Come, Hannah. Let us continue to behave in the manner we always have.'

Hannah thought about it for a moment, and then, deciding that no harm could come of it, agreed. 'Very well. When we are alone, I shall continue to talk to you, or try to, in a manner befitting that of a sister talking to her brother.'

'Good. We are making progress. That does, of course, beget the next question.'

'Which is?'

'If you start addressing me as Lord Winthrop when we are in company, it will generate some very quizzical looks.'

'Oh! I hadn't thought of that.'

'Perhaps you should. Because if you start treating me differently in public, people are bound to know that something has happened between us.'

'Perhaps they will think we have quarrelled.'

'They might. But curiosity being what it is, they will most certainly ask what we have quarrelled about. And when you continue to address me in such a way, yet remain civil in every other, they will begin to wonder even more.'

He was making a very good point, and Hannah was surprised she hadn't thought of it before. But it all came down to what she intended to do about her problem. Once she let it be known that she was not the Honourable Hannah Winthrop, she would certainly have to treat others—and expect others to treat her—in a completely different way.

'It is a dilemma which warrants further consideration,' Hannah said at length. 'But perhaps, as you say, in the interim it would be best if I continue to address you as Robert, in all situations.'

'That's my girl.'

'And now that we have overcome that little hurdle, I suggest we move on to the next.'

'Which is?'

'How am I to go about finding out who I really am?'

She couldn't have surprised him more had she told him she wanted to go to America and live with the Indians. 'You want to do *what*!'

'Well, surely you did not think I would leave matters as they are?'

'As a matter of fact, I did. Why on earth would you wish to dredge up the details of your past? They can have no bearing on your present life.'

'No bearing? How can you say that? My past life has *everything* to do with my present one. Without my past, I have no idea who I am, or who my parents are.'

'True. But who's to say that if you *did* know, you would be happier than you are now? Chances are you'd feel a damn sight worse.'

Hannah bit her lip. 'I have to do this, Robert. I have to at least *try* to find out where I came from. You've already said you can't imagine what it would be like to wake up one morning and discover you're not who you thought you were.'

He looked at her then, and his expression was grim. 'No, I can't. But you may never find out.'

'I know. But at least I will have tried. Please say you understand my need to do that much, if nothing else.'

Robert didn't answer for a while, because he knew that whatever he said wasn't going to make any difference. Hannah was going to try to find out who she was and where she'd come from, even though he knew for a fact that she had absolutely no idea how difficult the task would be. Tracing her roots back to a place where no one knew her, or even of her existence, would be like trying to trace a wild creature back to its place of birth.

'How do you intend to do this?' he asked, deciding to see if she had given it any thought at all.

'I suspect it would be best if I returned to Scotland,' Hannah said promptly. 'Perhaps I could stay with Lady MacInnes. After all, she knows of my circumstances, and does not seem to hold me in dislike.'

'She may not, but I have a feeling her husband may not share her sentiments,' Robert warned. 'It was

Lord MacInnes who told Margaret that he didn't want her to see my mother any more.'

'It was?'

'I'm afraid so.'

Hannah bit her lip. 'Ah. I suppose that also explains why I was never invited to stay at Burgley Hall. Which means there is very little chance of my staying there now.'

'Never mind. I have a better idea,' Robert said. 'Why don't we go to London? You can stay with Aunt Prudence while I start making enquiries.'

'*You?* But…why would you make enquiries rather than me?'

'Because I'll have a much better chance of getting answers than you will. Doors which will most certainly remain closed to you will be opened for me.'

Robert's confidence in his ability to get answers might have made Hannah angry, had she not been as familiar as she was with the ways of the world. Men and women were not equal in any way, and certainly not when it came to matters pertaining to the law. 'You really think we should go to London?'

'I do. I think we should also agree to strike a bargain before we set off.'

'What kind of bargain?'

'I propose we say nothing to anyone of what we have learned,' Robert said, 'and that we carry on completely as normal. That means you will go to London and stay with my aunt and uncle until such time as your period of mourning comes to an end and you start going about in society again.'

'But I am not entitled to move in society any more!'

'You are as the Honourable Hannah Winthrop,'

Robert reminded her. 'And if you agree to the bargain, that is precisely who you will continue to be.'

'But—'

'The other reason I suggest it is because it will help keep your mind off your worries. If your time is occupied with fending off all manner of eligible young gentlemen, you will hardly have time to worry about who you really are,' he said in a teasing manner.

Her smile faded and her eyes darkened to the colour of sapphires. 'Please do not lessen the importance of this, Robert. Who I am is the only thing that matters in my life right now.'

'Forgive me. I did not mean to make it sound any less significant than it is, Hannah. But you must be prepared to face facts. It may take a very long time to find out who your parents were, if it is possible to find out anything at all. Remember what the letter said. Your father has no knowledge that you exist, and the woman who bore you is dead. The trail back to either one of them may have been lost a very long time ago.'

They were hard words to say, but Hannah knew she had to hear them. 'Everything you say is true, Robert, but I must try regardless. If I do not, I shall always wonder if someone out there knows who I am and is trying to find me. I know the chances are slight, but before I abandon the idea altogether, I must try to discover my roots. And to that end, I agree to your bargain.' Hannah took a deep breath, and lifted her chin. 'I shall go to London and do my best to carry on as I always have. But I will not make you a promise as to what I shall do at the end of the time, because until I am forced to *make* that decision, I cannot say what I shall do.' She drew the mare to a halt, and then turned to face him. 'Have I your agreement on that…Robert?' she asked, slowly extending her hand.

He likewise drew the stallion to a halt and clasped her hand in his. 'You have my agreement on it…Miss Winthrop.'

CHAPTER EIGHT

IT WAS amazing how quickly one could make things happen when one put one's mind to it, Hannah reflected. Because not more than a week after she and Robert talked about their removing to London, that was exactly what they did.

Thankfully, Robert saw to all the pertinent details before they left Gillingdon Park. He advised the staff of their intention to go to London, and assured them that they would all be kept on. Then he wrote to his aunt and told her they were coming, advising her that Hannah would be staying with her for an unspecified length of time.

'Thank goodness I keep only bachelor quarters in Town,' Robert had said as the two of them had enjoyed a last leisurely stroll through the gardens at Gillingdon. 'Had I a large house, people might have expected you to stay with me, and while I would have no objection, I doubt *you* would take kindly to staying alone in the house of an unmarried gentleman who was no longer your brother.'

It was the first time they had talked about the nature of their relationship in such terms, and seeing the wicked look in his eyes, Hannah had felt her cheeks glow. 'I suppose it would be inappropriate,' she'd agreed. 'But you are right, it is just as well we have no need to worry about it. I confess, I still feel exceedingly ill at ease, knowing that Lady Montgomery is not really my aunt, and that I am planning on staying with her as though I had every right—'

'You do have every right. We agreed we would maintain our positions, and you cannot back out of the bargain now. There are penalties to be incurred for the breaking of contracts in such a manner.'

In spite of her concerns, Hannah had smiled. 'You are harsh indeed to threaten penalties merely for the talk of dissension.'

'Ah, but what better time to threaten than when the chance of transgression is so slight? I would far rather warn you of retribution, than be forced to administer it.' Robert had raised his hand and brushed it lightly against her cheek. 'I should hate to be the one to inflict such cruel punishment on one so lovely.'

Hannah thought about his remarks now as she sat in the morning-room at Sir Roger and Lady Montgomery's comfortable house in Cavendish Square, remembering how startled she had been upon hearing them. She had never expected Robert to be so sympathetic, especially given the distance that had always existed between them. It had been strange to hear him so attentive and thoughtful. Almost as though he had become a different person.

But then, why would that seem strange? He *was* a different person—and so was she.

'Cousin Hannah, are you ready to set off? Mama said the carriage is waiting.'

Hannah glanced up to see her cousin, Miss Alice Montgomery, fairly dancing with impatience, and carefully bit back a smile. Alice was always in a hurry to go somewhere, whether it was to the modiste's for a new gown, or simply out for an afternoon walk. It was a peculiarity Hannah had noticed almost from the moment of her arrival in London some four months ago. And while it was not necessarily a negative trait, Hannah felt sure it must be tiring on the girl. Certainly it was on anyone who found themselves in her company for any length of time.

Overall, however, Alice was very pleasant company. She was bright and cheery, flitting about the house like a little sparrow, so that at times Hannah was inclined to think of her in such a way. She was slim and dainty, barely reaching Hannah's shoulder, and had light brown hair and warm brown eyes. And she was clearly in great spirits tonight as a result of their being off to enjoy Hannah's first foray into society since Lady Winthrop's death.

Hannah had spent most of her time in London in tranquillity, not accepting invitations or seeing visitors, but content to pass her days quietly at home. Sometimes she read, or wrote in her diary. Other times she played Lady Montgomery's pianoforte, or browsed through Sir Roger's extensive collection of books, which he had kindly made available to her.

Lady Montgomery and Alice, of course, were now finished with their mourning, and free to accept whatever manner of invitations they wished. And clearly Alice was delighted to be back in colours again.

For her own part, Hannah agreed to have a few new outfits made, and for the dinner tonight at Lord and Lady Donaldson's home, she wore a most becoming gown of lilac silk. The occasion was not a grand one, but it would be the first time Hannah had ventured into society of any kind since arriving in London. The first time she would take her place as the daughter of the late Viscountess Winthrop.

Hannah might have been daunted by the prospect

had Lady Winthrop's lessons not been so well learned. She had spent too much of her life *believing* she was a lady to act as anything but one now. Besides, Alice was convinced that her elegant country cousin would most surely attract the attention of every single gentleman who happened to be in attendance.

Thankfully, there was no malice in Alice's enthusiasm, for she did not seem to harbour jealousy. She was pretty enough that she seldom lacked for admirers, and though she did tell Hannah there was one particular gentleman she liked above all others, she could not be persuaded to say who he was.

Hannah was content to wait. She knew that sooner or later, Alice would tell her who he was. It was virtually impossible for the girl to keep a secret longer than two days. It might even be that the gentleman would be there tonight, which would make their attendance even more interesting.

And Robert would be there too, of course.

Hannah drew a deep breath and released it slowly. It was difficult to comprehend the degree to which her relationship with Robert had changed. Not only was he more compassionate towards her, but he had also become an invaluable source of support over the last four months. Indeed, they were more like brother and sister now than they had ever been. And as the comfort level between them grew, Hannah was more inclined to let down her guard, and to be even more natural with him, thereby allowing him to see a side of her—and her of him—that neither of them even knew existed.

Tonight, for example, as Robert escorted her from the carriage into Lord and Lady Donaldson's elegant Eaton Place townhouse, he leaned in close to make a comment about her gown. Hannah turned to find her face only inches from his, and caught her breath, seeing his eyes rest briefly on her lips, and his smile broaden wickedly.

'Never say that I am responsible for that delightful blush,' he whispered. 'Lady Donaldson will certainly be wondering what I have said to you.'

'Odious creature!' Hannah hissed, hiding her embarrassment in a scold. 'I merely thought I had stepped on your foot. I hadn't realised you were standing so close behind me.'

'Ah, but it provides such a lovely view. Has anyone ever told you you have lovely shoulders, Miss Winthrop?'

Heat suffused her face, as though the temperature had suddenly risen twenty degrees.

'No, I thought not.' Robert chuckled as they walked into the house.

Deciding it was best to keep a still tongue, Hannah said nothing. But it was becoming painfully clear to her that the one area of her education in which Lady Winthrop had not spent as much time as she should was in the receiving of flattery. And yet, to be fair, she seldom blushed when other gentlemen paid her compliments. And she'd never felt any kind of embarrassment when Philip Twickenham had told her how lovely she was.

Why, then, was everything so different with Robert?

Lady Donaldson had already greeted Sir Roger and Lady Montgomery, and now turned to welcome Robert and Hannah. 'Ah, Lord Winthrop,' she said warmly. 'How very good to see you again.'

Robert bowed over her hand, and smiled. 'Lady Donaldson, you are looking very well. Have you met my sister?'

'Not officially, but I am very pleased to do so,' the lady said. 'And please accept my condolences on the loss of your dear mother. She will be greatly missed by all who knew her.'

Hannah dropped a curtsey. The reference to being Robert's sister still sat awkwardly on her ears, but she smiled nevertheless, knowing it was expected. 'Thank you, Lady Donaldson.'

'Well, Lord Winthrop, I vow all of the ladies in attendance will be pleased indeed at finding you back in London,' the older woman said with a twinkle in her eye. She leaned in closer to Hannah. 'I must tell you, Miss Winthrop, that your brother is one of the most eligible gentlemen in London.'

'Is he, indeed?' Hannah forced herself to say.

'Oh yes. In fact, I once held out hopes that he might have offered for my own dear Kitty,' the lady confessed, 'but then she fell head over heels in love with Lord Peckford, and well, that was the end of that. Still, I dare say your brother will have the pick of the crop.'

'Do not tell her too much, Lady Donaldson,' Robert warned, 'lest she try to persuade me to favour one over another.'

'Nonsense. As your sister, she has every right to try to affect your decision. After all, she will be sister-in-law to your wife, and, given the closeness of such a relationship, why should she not tell you which lady she likes best?'

Hannah kept the smile on her lips, but was aware of feeling strangely hollow inside. *Why* she should feel that way, she had no idea. After all, there was certainly no reason for her to feel any kind of disappointment at the thought of Robert marrying someone else.

'I am quite sure my brother will choose the lady most suitable to being his wife,' Hannah said quietly. 'As to my liking her, I dare say it won't matter. I shall not have that much to do with her.'

'Ah, but perhaps that is because you will be busy setting up your own establishment,' Lady Donaldson said knowingly. 'Now that you have finally come to London, and being as lovely as you are, I dare say your name will soon be on the lips of every eligible gentleman in Town. But now, come in, my dears, and meet the rest of the company.'

There were twenty people to dinner that evening. Four of the couples were married, two were engaged, and there were five other singles besides Alice, Robert and herself. Not surprisingly, Robert seemed to know them all quite well. He identified the single ladies as Miss Caroline Thorpe and Lady Jane Merriweather, and the gentlemen as Lord Rutherford, Sir Geoffrey Turnbull and Mr James Stanford.

Mr Stanford, it seemed, was a particularly good friend.

'Hannah,' Robert said, bringing that gentleman towards her. 'I would like to introduce my good friend, Mr James Stanford. James, this is my sister, Hannah.'

Hannah gracefully inclined her head. 'Mr Stanford.'

He bowed. 'Miss Winthrop. I am delighted to make your acquaintance. And please accept my condolences on the loss of your mother. The news came as a great shock.'

His voice was all that was polite, yet Hannah could

have sworn there was something in his manner that indicated surprise at meeting her. 'Thank you, Mr Stanford. It came as a shock to…all of us.'

The mention of the lady she had so long believed to be her mother still brought a lump to Hannah's throat. It was hard to accept that the Viscountess passed away four months ago. At times, it seemed like only yesterday…

'Are you enjoying your stay in London?' Mr Stanford asked. 'I know you've not been here long, but I was wondering if you've had an opportunity to see the city?'

'I have not seen a great deal of it,' Hannah admitted. 'My aunt and uncle have been most kind, but we have been leading a somewhat restricted life these past few months.'

'Of course.' Mr Stanford's expression softened. 'And knowing that, I'm very glad you decided to favour us with your company this evening.'

'Hannah, will you excuse us for a moment?' Robert interjected. 'There is someone to whom I promised Mr Stanford an introduction. Will you be all right on your own?'

'Yes, of course. I shall go and speak to Alice. She is looking a little out of sorts at the moment.'

Robert glanced over towards his younger cousin, who was indeed looking a little perturbed, and grinned. 'I shall rejoin you directly.'

'Miss Winthrop,' Stanford said, again with a most amiable smile.

Hannah dipped a curtsey and then set off in her cousin's direction. To her surprise, Alice did seem unusually anxious to talk to her.

'Cousin Hannah,' she said in a voice that was perhaps a touch overly bright. 'Are you having a good time?'

'I am, thank you, Alice. And you?'

'Oh, yes, delightful. Lady Donaldson has invited an interesting assortment of people, do you not think?'

Hannah glanced over the assembly and nodded. 'From what I can gather, they are all very nice.'

'I saw you talking to Mr Stanford.' Alice fluttered her fan in front of her face. 'Did you find him pleasant company?'

Hannah glanced at the girl, hearing something in her voice that suggested more than a passing interest in the gentleman, but she only smiled. 'Yes, very pleasant. Robert introduced us. Are you acquainted with the gentleman?'

The fan fluttered a little faster. 'We were introduced earlier in the Season. And we did dance, once or twice. He's quite handsome, don't you think?'

Hannah looked at Alice again, her suspicions confirmed by the colour in the girl's cheeks. 'Yes, though to be honest, he does not appeal to me in that way.'

Alice all but gasped. 'He doesn't?'

Hannah wished she'd thought to bring her own fan so she might hide her amusement. Clearly, Alice found it difficult to credit that not *all* ladies found Mr Stanford as dashing as she. 'No. I have always preferred gentlemen with dark hair, rather than fair.'

'Oh. You mean, like Robert.'

Alice's relief almost made Hannah laugh. 'Yes, I suppose I mean like—'

She stopped, unable to finish the sentence. She had been about to say that men *like* Robert were attractive

to her, until she realised that she wasn't talking about
men *like* Robert.

She was talking *about* Robert.

At the other side of the room, Robert was undergoing
an interrogation of his own.

'I say, Winthrop, you're a devil for keeping secrets.'
Stanford muttered in tones of obvious exasperation. 'If
I didn't know better, I'd almost be tempted to call you
conniving.'

'Conniving? What on earth are you talking about?'

'I'm talking about the fact that you've been having
me on as regards your sister,' Stanford accused. 'Why
didn't you tell me she was a diamond?'

Wishing to make light of it, Robert smiled. 'I didn't
think you would be interested.'

'Not interested? In a lady who will undoubtedly set
London on its ear? You'll have to do better than that,
my friend.'

'On the contrary, I had no reason to believe you
would look at Hannah with any degree of interest,
since you've already told me you were madly in love
with Miss Blazel.'

'Well, of course I did. And I am,' Stanford blustered. 'But *you* were the one who told me that Miss
Blazel wasn't good enough for me. You were the one
who said I should look elsewhere for a bride.' The
younger man's eyes narrowed. 'I say, Winthrop, this
isn't all part of some grand scheme, is it?'

'A scheme?'

'Yes. To make me forget Miss Blazel.'

'Rest assured, I am guilty of no such ploy.'

'Then what was all that nonsense about introducing
me to a young lady of quality? Someone with impec-

cable breeding who was coming up from the country? You were referring to your sister all along, weren't you?'

'Gudgeon.' Robert abruptly pulled his friend into the shadow of a large potted plant. 'I was referring to the young lady I was just on my way to introduce you to.'

Stanford looked blank. 'What lady?'

'The one standing over there by the Chinese screen. Miss Caroline Thorpe.'

Stanford glanced towards the screen, where an exquisite young lady was indeed engaged in conversation with Lord Rutherford. '*That* is the lady you wished me to meet?'

'It is. As you can see, she is exceptionally beautiful, and her breeding is all that any parent could wish. Her father is Lord Thorpe, and her mother was the eldest daughter of the Earl of Trowbridge.'

Stanford glanced at Miss Thorpe again, and then slid his gaze back across the room to where Hannah and Alice were chatting. 'I think if you don't mind, I should rather become better acquainted with your sister.'

Surprised at the guilt he felt over having to keep a secret from his friend, Robert sighed. 'James, you don't understand. Hannah isn't ready to form any serious attachments yet. She told me so herself.'

'She may not be ready, but I'll wager there'll be plenty of gentlemen willing to give it a try. Oh, come along, Winthrop, you must see your sister's a beauty. When you said she was ungainly, I thought you meant it.'

'I did. And she was.'

'Well, she isn't now. And if you weren't her brother, I'd accuse you of having kept her in the country for your own evil purposes.'

'Thank you for that small concession,' Robert muttered, finding his friend's remark a little too close to the truth for comfort. Much as he wanted to tell Stanford the truth, he knew he couldn't. Not after *he* had been the one to convince Hannah of the need for secrecy. What would she say if she were to learn that he had broken his promise to her by telling one of his closest friends the truth the first chance he'd got?

'Still, you may as well get used to the fact that she's not going to be your sister much longer,' Stanford said, cutting into his thoughts.

'I beg your pardon?'

'Well, look at her. Apart from the fact that she's beautiful, there's something about her that makes a man want to be with her. Dashed if I'm not tempted to run back to her side this very instant.'

Robert bit back the sharp retort he'd been about to make, because he knew there was no justification for him to make it. Despite the need for secrecy, he had no reason to be annoyed that Stanford wished to further an acquaintance with Hannah. On the contrary, he should have been happy that his friend was so taken with her, because it proved there was absolutely no reason for Hannah to be concerned about her future. Even if she didn't find out who her real parents were, she could still look forward to the prospect of a successful marriage. And James Stanford would be an excellent match, Robert told himself. And that was what he wanted for Hannah.

Wasn't it?

Hannah was agreeably surprised to find herself enjoying the evening. Perhaps because the company was comprised of such a wide variety of ages and backgrounds, the conversation did not become boring and predictable as it so often could. Indeed, they discussed everything from politics to agriculture, before switching to a lively discussion of literature and the finer points of Shakespeare's plays.

Alice was a little out of her depth, Hannah noticed, but she was wise enough not to draw attention to herself over it. She did not offer opinions on topics she knew nothing about, and pretended a believable interest in the subjects that were being discussed. For her own part, Hannah thoroughly enjoyed the opportunity of being able to exchange ideas with people of like mind and interests.

At the conclusion of dinner, Lady Donaldson led the ladies to the drawing-room so that the gentlemen might enjoy more masculine conversation over port and cigars. Hannah chatted for a while with Lady Donaldson and her good friend, Mrs Benbrook-Hyde, before making her way to a comfortable looking loveseat located next to the window.

Moments later, she looked up to see Miss Caroline Thorpe standing in front of her.

'Good evening, Miss Winthrop,' the elegant young woman greeted her.

Hannah inclined her head. 'Miss Thorpe.' She could see why Caroline Thorpe had been deemed an Incomparable by the *ton*, for everything about her was pleasing to the eye. Slim of build and dainty of form, she nevertheless possessed enough feminine curves to attract the attention of even the most discerning gentleman in the room. And it was only to be expected that her attire would be of the first stare. Her gown of

pink gros de Naples was striking, cut low over the
bodice and draped with a folded gauze of pale pink
that only accentuated the dusty rose in her cheeks.

'I hope you don't mind,' the young lady said now,
'but I wonder if I might sit with you for a while? I
have been longing to speak to you, but this is the first
opportunity I've had to do so all evening.'

Surprised that the acknowledged beauty should be
so anxious to sit down for a coz, Hannah nevertheless
smiled and moved over on the bench. 'Of course.'

'Oh, good.' Miss Thorpe's smile was open and
warm. 'Lord Winthrop has spoken of you in the past,
of course, but never in any great detail. And I must
admit, I have long been curious to meet you. But first,
let me say how very sorry I was to hear about your
loss of your mother, Miss Winthrop. Lord Winthrop
said the two of you were very close.'

'Thank you,' Hannah replied, surprised to learn that
Robert had spoken of her at all. 'Yes, we were.'

'You are fortunate that your family has rallied
around you.'

'Y-yes. My…aunt and uncle have been most kind
in having me to stay with them, and they do try to
keep me occupied.' Hannah hoped the girl would put
her stumbling hesitation down to emotion. 'And
Robert has been most attentive, of course.'

'Yes. I should think he is a most wonderful brother.'

Hannah glanced at the girl sharply. Was that adoration she'd heard in her voice? 'Do you know my
brother well, Miss Thorpe?'

A tell tale sweep of colour rose to the lady's cheeks.
'I cannot say I know him well, but I do admit to think-
ing most highly of him. He and my eldest brother,
Jeremy, were at Oxford together, and Lord Winthrop

often used to come stay with us during the summers. But he has not been to see us for some time, so I was very pleased when he paid a call upon us in London a few weeks ago. He is not like the other gentlemen I've met. But then, you would know that better than anyone.'

Hannah smiled, gleaning more from the lady's heightened colour than she did from her carefully phrased words. 'Actually, I've had very little to do with my brother or with any other gentlemen, Miss Thorpe, so the comparison is a difficult one for me to make.'

'Oh, but the other gentlemen are all quite gay and charming, and prone to saying the most flattering things. Your brother isn't like that at all. I mean, he does say nice things,' the lady added hastily, 'but not in such ridiculous ways. He does not compare my beauty to the radiance of a flower, or the colour of my hair to spun gold. Rather, he is quiet and thoughtful. He doesn't speak until he has given careful consideration to what he wishes to say, and when he does speak, it is with intelligence and wit.'

Hannah bit her lip, wondering how far the lady's revelations would go, surprised to discover she had no wish to encourage them.

'He has said nothing to me, of course,' the lady carried on, 'because it is widely known that he is not looking to bestow his favours on anyone. But I do hold out hope that, when the time is right, he may look kindly in my direction.' Miss Thorpe turned to gaze at Hannah with what could only be called an expression of hopeful expectation. 'You do understand what I'm saying, don't you, Miss Winthrop?'

'I'm not sure I do, Miss Thorpe.'

The young lady bit her lip. 'I've noticed the closeness between you and your brother, and I simply thought that perhaps you might consider telling him, should the chance ever arise, that I think of him with the utmost respect and…affection.'

'Ah, I think I do begin to see now,' Hannah said slowly. 'You wish me to speak favourably of you to my brother, should the opportunity present itself.'

The girl's lashes dropped down, hiding the expression in her magnificent violet eyes. 'I would never wish to be so forward, Miss Winthrop. I only thought that, if you knew of my…affection for your brother, you might be able to assure him, should he ever enquire, that he would be very welcome to call upon me. I know my father would also be most accepting of his visits.'

Finding herself at something of a loss, Hannah merely looked at the girl and smiled. Thankfully, Lady Donaldson chose that moment to approach with a request of her own. 'Ah, Miss Winthrop, forgive me for interrupting your little coz, but I wonder if I might prevail upon you to entertain us. Your aunt has been most generous in her compliments, and I should dearly love to hear you play whilst we await the return of the gentlemen.'

Grateful for the reprieve, Hannah nodded. 'Thank you, Lady Donaldson, I should be happy to play for you.' Then, after giving Miss Thorpe another smile, and assuring her that she would do whatever she could to further her case with her brother, Hannah made quickly for the pianoforte in the far corner of the room.

Faith, but the evening was growing stranger by the minute. First, her cousin Alice had quizzed her about her feelings for Mr Stanford, and now the lovely Miss

Thorpe had sought her out to ask her if she might be willing to help further an amorous acquaintance with Robert. How had she suddenly become the centre of all this romantic upheaval?

More to the point, why was she feeling so irritated about it? There was certainly no reason for her to feel out of sorts because Miss Thorpe liked Robert and wished to share her feelings about him with her. Or because she had asked Hannah to speak to him in a helpful way, should he happen to mention her in conversation. After all, was not such honesty expected between a sister and her brother?

Hannah sat down on the bench and began flipping through the music. Of course it was, and as Robert's *sister*, she would likely have done all she could to facilitate a match between him and the lady of his choosing. As his sister, she would have done her best to ensure that the woman who married him did so because she loved him, and not simply because she was looking for a title or a comfortable living. As his sister, she would have done all those things.

But she wasn't his sister, which made her present mood of disgruntlement all the more difficult to comprehend. After all, why should she resent being involved in Robert's love life?

Coward, a tiny voice murmured in the back of her mind. *You know why you don't wish to be involved.*

Hannah placed her fingers on the keys and began to play. The voice was right, of course. As ridiculous as it seemed, she didn't wish to know which young ladies might be in love with him.

Because she also didn't want to know which young ladies Robert might be in love with in return!

CHAPTER NINE

THE following morning Hannah awoke feeling strangely out of sorts, though what the cause of her malaise might be, she was reluctant to say. She suspected it had something to do with the conversations she'd had the night before, but she preferred not to delve too deeply into the matter for fear of what she might discover. Suffice it to say that the dinner at Lady Donaldson's had been enlightening.

But it had been enjoyable too, Hannah admitted. She had carried out her subterfuge with little or no difficulty, and had been complimented both on her appearance and on her resilience in dealing with her recent loss. She had also made the acquaintance of several very pleasant people, including Mr James Stanford, the gentleman with whom she now knew Alice to be enamoured. The fact that Mr Stanford had seemed more interested in *her* than in Alice had robbed Hannah of some of the pleasure she might have taken in the introduction, but she had done her best to downplay the significance of the event.

As for the lovely Miss Caroline Thorpe's willingness to share her intimate feelings for Lord Winthrop with her, Hannah wasn't quite sure what to make of that. It was the first time her standing as Robert's sister had truly been called into play, and while there was no doubt in her mind that Miss Thorpe had spoken to her with her own interests in mind, she had to admire the girl for having had the courage to do so. After all,

Miss Thorpe had taken a chance in admitting her affection for one of society's most eligible bachelors to a lady who might or might not be willing to help her. If, for example, Hannah had taken an instant dislike to Miss Thorpe, she could have influenced Robert's opinion away from her and thereby ruined any chance she might have had of becoming the next Lady Winthrop. Yes, Miss Thorpe was sure to have recognised that she did not run the same risks in speaking to Hannah as she would in speaking to another rival for Lord Winthrop's affections, but there was still a chance that Hannah might have been of a mind to sabotage her efforts.

What would Miss Thorpe have said, Hannah wondered, if she'd known that she was no more in a position to influence Robert's opinion than Caroline herself? Would the confessions have flowed so easily from her lips? Hannah doubted it, because at that point, she would simply have become one more rival for Robert's affections. After all, had Miss Thorpe not already made note of the fact that the two of them seemed particularly…close?

The remark had given Hannah pause at the time, and she thought about it again now as she sat down to breakfast. Not because she was willing to attach any emotional significance to the remark. She didn't deceive herself into believing that Robert had any romantic feelings for her. He had been more attentive to her these last few months than he had at any time during their past, but that was only because he felt sorry for her.

Oh, yes, Hannah knew sympathy when she saw it. A less than flattering reality, perhaps, but a fact of life nonetheless. Lord Winthrop knew that he had turned her world upside down, and perhaps as a result of some deeply rooted sense of obligation, he now felt compelled to try to make things better for her—at least until she decided what she was going to do with her life.

But dealing with her life was one thing. What was she to do about her growing feelings of affection for Robert? She wasn't even sure when her feelings had begun to change. Perhaps when she had started seeing him as a man rather than the self-centred brother she'd always believed him to be. Yes, he was reserved, but that was only because he preferred to keep his thoughts to himself rather than share them with the world. Nor was he as selfish as she had been inclined to think. Certainly, he had demonstrated his compassion to her by not forcing her to reveal her secret to the world when he could quite easily have done so. She could not be absolutely sure what his motivation for such conduct had been, but she suspected it had a lot to do with pride—his *and* hers.

Whatever the case, the awareness of considerably warmer feelings towards him had crept up on Hannah like a thief in the night, threatening to steal her heart as surely as a pickpocket stole her purse. Perhaps it would have been better had her feelings towards him *been* more in the nature of what a sister might feel for a brother, because at least then she would be able to *miss* him in such a way when she left Gillingdon Park. But what she felt for him now had little to do with such obligation.

Still, whatever her feelings, it did not alter the fact that her association with Robert would come to an end once she left Gillingdon Park. And since she intended to do that in the very near future, Hannah knew their time together was drawing to a close. She had no wish to leave her home, but doing so now was more necessary than ever. She couldn't risk exposing her heart, and there was no question in her mind that that's what would happen if she stayed. The more time she spent with Robert, the more time she would want to spend with him. And that was not only a foolish dream but an unattainable one.

Better to walk away now when she still had a choice, than be forced to leave when the situation became intolerable.

As it turned out, Hannah was not the only one feeling a little blue that morning. Alice too, appeared rather subdued as they sat together in the drawing-room. Suspecting her cousin's mood of preoccupation had to do with Mr Stanford's conduct the previous evening, Hannah tactfully put the question to her. She was surprised at finding her cousin grudgingly accepting of the situation.

'Well, why would he not be taken with you? You are so lovely, Cousin Hannah, and you have such a sweet personality that I do not see how any gentleman could fail to be charmed.'

'Nonsense. You are reading far too much into his attentions,' Hannah said briskly. 'Mr Stanford seems a jovial man by nature, and I am sure he tries to make everyone he meets feel special.'

'Oh, yes, he does have a gift for making a lady feel special. Is that not so, Mama?'

'It most certainly is, my dear.' Lady Montgomery was perusing a selection of fashion magazines. 'Mr Stanford is a very fine gentleman to be sure, and while he does seem to smile kindly upon all the ladies he meets, I do not believe he is the type to dangle after one lady, if he is interested in another.'

'I wouldn't be so sure about that,' Robert said upon entering the room. 'Stanford changes his mind as frequently as the breeze changes direction.' He cast a sharp glance in Alice's direction. 'I wouldn't pin all my hopes on his coming up to scratch in the near future, cousin.'

Alice flushed. 'I haven't pinned any hopes on him at all. I was merely telling Cousin Hannah that Mr Stanford seemed to show a marked interest in her last evening, and that she should be pleased to have his affection. After all, he is your best friend, Cousin Robert. Do *you* not think Hannah is fortunate to have been singled out for his attention?'

'If I thought she *had* been singled out for his attention, I might be more willing to comment,' came Robert's somewhat dry retort. 'But I happen to know that James's affections are engaged elsewhere at the moment.'

Hannah flicked a quick glance at Alice, fearing that the casually uttered remark would serve to depress her even further. She was not wrong. Alice went pale, and then quickly looked down at her embroidery, pretending an intense concentration on the French knots she was endeavouring to tie.

'Sister,' Robert said suddenly. 'Would you care to accompany me to Hatchard's? I've a mind to pick up some new reading material, and thought you might appreciate the opportunity to do the same.'

Hannah looked up and seeing a gleam of purpose in Robert's eyes, hastily put aside her hoop. 'Yes, of course.'

'Oh, please, may I come too?' Alice said, her own expression brightening.

Hannah's gaze slid towards Robert, wondering how he would gracefully extricate himself from the problem, when Lady Montgomery unexpectedly solved it for them.

'Now, Alice, have you forgotten that we are expected at Mrs Pendleton's? And given that we have already cancelled the outing once, I suggest we do not do so again for fear of not being invited back at all.'

Alice's face fell. 'Oh, bother. Yes, I had forgotten. Well, never mind. I shall go with you next time, Cousin Hannah.'

Relieved that they had achieved a painless resolution to what might have been an awkward situation, Hannah gave her cousin a reassuring smile. 'Of course you will. I'll just go and fetch my bonnet, Robert.'

It was a beautiful morning, and upon stepping out Hannah tipped her face up to the sky, thinking how lovely it was to see the sun after all the rain they had endured over the last few weeks. 'I vow, if I must be in one place or the other, I should far rather find myself in the country than in Town when it comes to the bearing of inclement weather,' she said. 'Everything smells so fresh and clean there after a rain, whereas here, everything just seems muddier and more hopelessly soiled.'

'Never say that you are actually missing rural life?' Robert teased as he handed her up into the carriage. 'I thought you might have enjoyed the conveniences of living in Town for a change.'

'Well, yes, I suppose I do, in some ways, but it is not where I would wish to spend my life.'

'So you would prefer to live in the country?'

I would prefer to live at Gillingdon, Hannah wanted to tell him. But she did not, because there really wasn't any point. It wasn't her decision to make any more.

Perhaps because of her own heightened awareness of Robert, Hannah felt somewhat strange at being alone in the carriage with him. She knew, of course, that society would not expect a brother and sister to go out in the company of a chaperone, but because *she* knew the truth, Hannah felt the breach of decorum keenly. Unfortunately, Robert would not expect anyone to join them, and given that they were going to the library, it was hardly necessary that she ask her maid to accompany her.

But was it only the lack of suitable chaperonage that was causing her such distress?

Hatchard's on Piccadilly was particularly crowded that afternoon, but as Hannah soon found out, it was not merely a bookshop and circulating library. It was a popular meeting place for the *ton*. Ladies turned out in all their finery to chat with well-dressed gentlemen who were there ostensibly to acquire new editions for their libraries but who were actually more intent on furthering their acquaintances with said ladies, while older matrons gathered to exchange the latest news and scandal broth.

Strictly there for intellectual pursuits, Hannah's eyes widened in delight at the selection of books stretching out before her, everything from gothic romances to tomes of a more improving nature. There were volumes in the original Latin and Greek, or more recent translations for those not skilled in the ancient languages, as well as an excellent selection of novels by the current authors of the day.

Skimming over the shelves, Hannah took a few

minutes to look for something to take back to Alice. She couldn't help but feel sorry for the girl, both for having had to miss the outing, and for being forced to face the fact that her dear Mr Stanford was enamoured of someone else. As such, Hannah was delighted to come upon a collection of beautifully bound Shakespearean sonnets. She also discovered a copy of *Essays on Various Subjects, Principally Designed for Young Ladies*, but knowing that her cousin was more romantically inclined than intellectually so, she quickly decided on the sonnets.

Lord Winthrop too, found what he was looking for, and with a copy of *The Memoirs of Signor Gaudentio di Lucca* tucked under his arm, the two prepared to leave. They were stayed by a cry of 'I say!' echoing across the floor, and turned to see a grinning James Stanford striding across the shop towards them.

'Winthrop, what a pleasant surprise. And Miss Winthrop, how delightful you look this morning.' The warmth in his eyes was as bright as the smile on his face. 'Did you enjoy yourself last evening?'

Hannah smiled too, for it was difficult not to respond to Mr Stanford's amiability. 'I did indeed, sir, thank you.'

'Yes, excellent company, I thought. Quite... excellent,' he said, fixing his gaze intently upon her face.

Beside Hannah, Robert cleared his throat. 'I was thinking of taking Hannah over to Gunter's for some refreshments, James. Would you care to join us?'

'Gunter's? I say, what a splendid idea! Haven't been there this age.'

'Fine. Have you a carriage outside? If so, we can meet you there.'

'Oh. Well, yes, all right, that would probably be best. I'll just take care of these books and see you there.'

Having already made their purchases, Robert and Hannah headed back outside to their carriage.

'I hope you did not mind my inviting him,' Robert said in a quiet aside, 'but I feared that unless I suggested some other diversion, you were quite likely to spend the next half-hour engaged in conversation with him, and in a place where his attentions to you would most surely not go unnoticed.'

Hannah laughed, but her cheeks grew warm. 'I have no objection to your inviting him to join us, Robert. He seems a very pleasant young man.'

'You think him young?'

Hannah shrugged. 'He appears that way to me, but perhaps that is because his expression is so open and guileless, and because I have always associated youth with such freedom from care.' She risked a hesitant glance in his direction. 'You know, of course, that Alice is very fond of him.'

Robert briefly inclined his head. 'I gathered as much from the conversation earlier. Which is why I let it be known that his feelings are engaged elsewhere.'

'Did you say that in an attempt to make Alice feel better, or to convince her that I was not a rival for his affections?'

Robert turned to her in amusement. 'You think me so noble?'

'I think you would not wish to see her hurt if it was within your power to prevent it.'

'You credit me with far more integrity than I possess,' Robert muttered as he helped her climb into the carriage. 'In truth, it was *your* feelings I was trying to spare.'

'*Mine?* Good heavens, there is little chance of my feelings entering into this.'

'Why? Alice was right in saying that you've caught Stanford's eye. Are you not curious to know him better?'

Coming from him, the question caught at her heart. 'I'm not curious to know *any* gentleman better. I have nothing to offer, remember?'

'What kind of nonsense is that? You have a great deal to offer.'

'Except the truth of who I am,' Hannah said as she waited for Robert to climb up beside her. 'Or have you forgotten that we are fabricating a charade? I am supposedly the daughter of the late Viscount and Viscountess Winthrop, but you and I both know that I could be…well, anyone's daughter. And knowing that, how can I enter into a relationship with a gentleman where I can tell him nothing of my family or myself? Truly, I have very little to offer.'

Robert's face darkened. 'You can offer him all that you are, and I think that a considerable gift.'

Hannah was silent for a moment, struck by the tone of his voice. *Oh, that you might find it such a gift*, she thought sadly. But she only shook her head and said, 'Anyone I marry will have to know the truth, Robert. If there is not trust and openness in a marriage, I cannot help but feel that it is doomed from the start.'

'I do not question or disagree with the need for honesty, but when a man falls in love with a woman, he forgives much.'

'Yes, but he will be less likely to do so if the woman goes *into* the relationship knowing the truth, as I do.'

'On the contrary, you don't know what the truth is.'

'But I know what it is *not*, Lord Winthrop.' Hannah addressed him as such on purpose, and looking at him, knew that he had understood.

They made the rest of the short trip in silence.

In spite of her resolve not to, Hannah found herself coming to like James Stanford. He was utterly charming, endearingly modest, and had an ability to laugh at himself that Hannah found most refreshing. She could see why Alice was smitten by him.

'Miss Winthrop, I fear I must profess myself totally charmed by you,' that gentleman said as they lingered over tea and cakes at Gunter's. 'Indeed, I intend to take your brother to task for not having encouraged you to come to London sooner.'

'It is not Robert who should be taken to task, Mr Stanford.' Touching the napkin to her lips, Hannah gave him a rueful smile. '*I* am the one who has been reluctant to come.'

'There, did I not tell you?' Robert said. 'Not all young ladies are anxious to spend their days traipsing about London, James.'

'Then I can only say that Miss Winthrop's preference to stay in the country has been London's loss,' came Stanford's gallant reply. 'But since you have seen so little of the city, perhaps I might prevail upon you to join me for a drive in the park tomorrow afternoon, Miss Winthrop? It is a pleasant way to pass an hour or two, and I dare say it will afford you your first good look at society.'

Hannah's smile wavered. 'Tomorrow?' Instinctively, she glanced at Robert, who said without faltering, 'Ah, I'm afraid that won't do, James. I promised

Hannah that I would take her and Alice driving to-morrow. But if you would care to join us, you are more than welcome. We can take the landau.'

Mr Stanford's disappointment was evident. 'Oh. Well, if you've already made plans—'

'Oh, do say you will join us, Mr Stanford.' Hannah placed her hand lightly upon his arm. 'Robert made the invitation because he knows that I have been…desirous of a drive in the park. But there is no reason not to include you. In fact, I'm sure the four of us would have a splendid time.'

Mr Stanford seemed to mull over her words, for while it was obvious that he would have liked to spend some time with her, it was also clear that the only way he was going to do so was by joining the prearranged excursion. For that reason, he reluctantly agreed. 'Very well. Since the outing has already been ar-ranged, I should be happy to accept your invitation. Thank you, Miss Winthrop, for encouraging me to come along. Certainly, it would take a stronger man than I to resist such an eloquent plea. But now, I fear I must take my leave of you,' he said, rising. 'Other engagements demand my attention. I look forward to seeing you on the morrow, Miss Winthrop. Winthrop.'

Robert inclined his head. 'James.' He waited until the younger man left before leaning in closer to Hannah and saying, 'Well, was my intervention in the proceedings satisfactory?'

'Perfectly,' Hannah said, trying not to sound as re-lieved as she felt. 'But I do admit to feeling very bad for having deceived him like that.'

'Take heart, my dear, *you* did not deceive him. *I* did. And it was not such a grievous lie.' A devilish look came into Robert's eyes. 'I had every intention of asking you and Alice to go driving in the park with me as I told James. I simply hadn't got round to it.'

'Well, you did it so well I'm sure poor Mr Stanford had no idea it was the first time *I'd* heard of it too. But thank you for stepping into the breach, Robert.'

He looked at her in that way he had, his eyes glinting like dark jewels in the sunlight. 'You're welcome. Only remember that I won't always be around to prevent the two of you being alone together. James is a determined young man, and he *is* looking for a wife.'

Hannah paled. 'Then he must look elsewhere. You must convince him to look elsewhere for I do not wish to cause him any pain. I will not encourage him, Robert, nor any other gentleman of your acquaintance. I cannot do so until I know who I am.'

Troubled by her own thoughts, Hannah did not see the pensive look Robert sent her. But it was likely just as well. It would have only added to the conundrum she was already finding herself in.

That evening, in an attempt to take Hannah's mind off her troubles, Robert took her and Alice to a performance of *A Midsummer Night's Dream*. It was a most enjoyable production, and for a short time, Hannah actually seemed to forget about her problems as she concentrated on the excellent portrayals of the characters by the talented band of actors on stage.

During the performance, Robert was not surprised to see a number of curious glances being sent their way from the boxes around them, and not all of them for his cousin. Alice was a lovely young woman, and as the only daughter of Sir Roger and Lady Montgomery she was considered an excellent catch, but Robert had a sneaking suspicion that at least half the glances being sent in their direction were for the *other* young lady sitting quietly in his box.

And why would people not gaze at Hannah with admiration? Robert thought to himself. She was in exceptional looks this evening. Her stylish gown of dove-grey silk became her very well, setting off her fair skin and dark hair to perfection. Her eyes were bright, and her enchanting mouth was a pleasure to watch, moving frequently to smiles and laughter at the antics on the stage. But his true enjoyment came in watching her observe the performance, for he truly believed that in watching the actors Hannah was able to forget, if only for a short time, the role she herself was being forced to play.

'Are you enjoying the play?' he leaned over to ask as the intermission approached.

'Oh, yes, very much.' Hannah glanced at him briefly, and her smile was open and completely without guile. 'Thank you so much for bringing me, Robert, this is a lovely treat.'

Somewhat bemused, Robert sat back in his chair. He wouldn't have thought it possible to derive such satisfaction from the simple act of pleasing someone else, and yet that was precisely what he was feeling. But perhaps that had something to do with the fact that Hannah *was* so very easy to please. It was obvious that she took great pleasure in watching the story unfold, and in becoming involved with characters' lives, unlike Alice, who was far more interested in the audience than she was in the actors on stage.

Fascinated, Robert looked at Hannah again, and indeed, there was much pleasing in her appearance. Dark curls danced against the porcelain perfection of her skin, while her slender neck and throat reminded him of the colour of new cream. She had a dainty build, yet her breasts were high and full, rising sensually above the fashionably low neckline of her gown. Shadows coloured the cleft between them, inviting touch.

Robert glanced away, aware of muscles tightening in a most uncomfortable way, evidence of the physical effect she was beginning to have upon him.

When intermission arrived, the three of them leisurely made their way downstairs. No sooner had they done so, however, than they found themselves surrounded by a crowd of people—many of whom were gentlemen anxious to know and be made known to the lovely Miss Winthrop.

Suddenly finding himself cast in the role of the devoted brother, Robert stood back and watched with a keen eye, the men clustered around Hannah. He assured himself he had every right to do so. After all, had his mother not charged him with the responsibility of looking after her, and to ensuring that she was not set upon by every wastrel and fortune hunter in London? But if that was the case, why was he looking with jaundiced eye upon *any* gentleman who approached her?

'Lord Winthrop, what an unexpected pleasure. I had not thought to see you here this evening.'

The deep female voice belonged to the redoubtable Lady Thorpe, society maven, and mother of the lovely Miss Caroline Thorpe. Robert had known the family for years, indeed, long before Caroline had become London's reigning beauty, and he had a genuine fondness for them all. 'On the contrary, Lady Thorpe, I like to enjoy a bit of theatre every now and then. Especially when the calibre of the performance is as good as it is this evening.'

'Never mind all that, tell me about the young lady I saw sitting in your box.'

Robert feigned a look of bewilderment. 'Miss Montgomery, you mean?'

'Imp! I am well acquainted with your cousin. It is the *other* young lady with whom I am *not* that I express curiosity.'

'Ah, yes, of course.' Robert's mouth twitched. 'I keep forgetting that Hannah is not well known in society.'

'Hannah?' Lady Thorpe's eyes opened wide. 'Are you already on first-name terms with the lady?'

'Most certainly, since the lady happens to be my sister.'

It was the first time Robert had been called upon to lie about Hannah's identity since he'd been made aware of the truth, yet he was surprised at how easily the falsehood came to his lips. But clearly, he was not the only one who was surprised.

'Your *sister*? Good Lord!'

'Why so surprised? Surely you knew I *had* a sister.'

'Of course, but I had not expected her to be so lovely,' Lady Thorpe admitted. 'In fact, I often wondered why your mother did not bring her to London when she was of an age to make her bows. I thought perhaps to find her plain of face or ungainly of form, but the young woman I see before me is neither.' She glanced at Robert in bewilderment. 'Why did Charlotte not introduce her to society, as she should have?'

'I'm afraid I cannot answer that, Lady Thorpe. As you know, I did not spend a great deal of time at

Gillingdon before my mother's death, and though that is something I now regret, there is nothing I can do to change it. As such, I have no idea why Mama did not bring Hannah to Town. I suspect it had more to do with her not wishing to come, than with any reluctance on my mother's part.'

'A young lady of such beauty *not* wish to be acclaimed by society? How singular. Pray, introduce me to this most unusual sister of yours, Robert.'

The introductions were duly made, with Hannah sinking into a curtsey that would have done a duchess proud. 'Lady Thorpe.'

'My dear Miss Winthrop, how very pleased I am to make your acquaintance. But may I also say how sorry I was to hear of your dear mother's passing. I hadn't seen Charlotte in years, but I remember her as being the kindest of ladies. How are you bearing up, child? The loss of a mother is never easy.'

Hannah's smile flickered. 'No, it is not, my lady, but I am doing…the best I can.'

'She is indeed,' Robert said, hearing the slight catch in Hannah's voice. 'And your expressions of sympathy are most appreciated, Lady Thorpe.'

The older woman's eyes softened. 'Oh, my poor dears. It will get easier in time, you know. And I'm sure being here tonight is helping to take your mind off your sadness. Are you enjoying the performance, Miss Winthrop?'

'Oh, yes, very much,' Hannah said, glad to have something else upon which to concentrate. 'Other than the occasional band of travelling players, we had little opportunity of seeing performances like this in our local village.'

Lady Thorpe nodded. 'I have long believed that one

of the great pleasures of living in Town is the opportunity it provides for enjoying a wide variety of cultural entertainments. Are you planning on staying long in London, Miss Winthrop?'

'I cannot say. I am presently residing with my aunt and uncle, and they have been exceedingly kind, but I would not wish to trespass too long upon their good nature.'

'Nonsense, I'm sure they are as delighted to have you as you are to be staying with them. And I'm sure Alice is enjoying having someone her own age to go about with.'

'My aunt tells me she is, though I fear Alice is somewhat preoccupied at the moment,' Hannah said carefully.

'Oh?'

'My cousin has developed a fondness for a certain young gentleman,' Robert said. 'As a result, she seems to spend little time thinking of anything else.'

'Well, I suppose that is hardly surprising.' Lady Thorpe chuckled. 'It is the way of the world, is it not? But I shouldn't be at all surprised to hear that *you* are soon in a similar position, Miss Winthrop.'

'I beg your pardon?'

'Now, my dear, there is no need to be modest. Looking as you do, you will surely attract a great deal of attention. Indeed, Robert, I wouldn't be surprised to hear that a number of your friends have been asking for an introduction.'

'A few,' Robert agreed, 'but most are aware that Hannah is still in mourning, and that it is not an appropriate time to approach her.'

'Yes, of course. And I myself know that you are not socialising much, but I would be honoured if you and your family would dine with us on Wednesday next. It will be a very quiet affair, but I suspect it will make a pleasant change from staying at home.'

Hannah looked to Robert, who once again handled the situation with aplomb. 'I shall check with my aunt and uncle to make sure they are not engaged, Lady Thorpe. If they are not we should be pleased to accept your invitation.'

'Splendid. Send word of your intentions at your convenience, Lord Winthrop. Well, I suppose I should be heading back. It was a pleasure meeting you, Miss Winthrop, and I look forward to seeing you again in the near future.'

Hannah dipped a gracious curtsey. 'Thank you, Lady Thorpe.'

'My lord, a word before you go,' Lady Thorpe said.

Robert glanced at Hannah, who only smiled and said, 'Take your time, Robert. Alice and I will wait for you in the box.'

He watched her go, affection softening his gaze. He was careful to adjust his expression before turning back to Lady Thorpe. 'You wished to speak to me, Lady Thorpe?'

'Yes, but only to say that if your aunt and uncle are engaged, and your sister is reluctant to venture out without them, the invitation for you to join us still stands. I know my husband would enjoy the opportunity of a conversation, and of course, Caroline is always pleased to receive you.'

Robert might have taken Lady Thorpe's last remark as a blatant bit of matchmaking, had he not known that she would never resort to such tactics. And knew him well enough to know that if he did have an interest in Caroline, he would be the one to further it.

'Thank you, Lady Thorpe, I shall bear that in mind, and send you a reply at my earliest convenience.'

'Your sister is a lovely young woman, Robert,' Lady Thorpe said thoughtfully. 'So elegant and refined. Indeed, it is easy to see your mother's influence in her. But I must admit to some surprise upon first seeing her.'

'Oh?'

'Well, had you not introduced her as such, I would never have taken her for your sister. There is not so much as a hint of resemblance between the two of you.'

The remark gave him a moment's pause, but again, Robert schooled his expression to one of resigned amusement. 'You are not the first to comment upon it, Lady Thorpe. Hannah and I have oft remarked upon how unlike we are.'

'No doubt. And yet, do you know, when I first saw her, she reminded me most forcefully of someone else.'

'Oh?' This time, Robert found it harder to maintain his air of indifference. 'And who might that be?'

'Dashed if I can remember. I've been racking my brain trying to think of it ever since I saw her, but it just won't come.' Lady Thorpe admitted with a laugh. 'I can't even remember if it was a man or a woman. But then, there are many people who resemble others more closely than they do their own families. Is that not so, my dear?'

Robert made some manner of suitable reply before bidding Lady Thorpe a good evening and then leisurely heading back to his box. But he wasn't so easily able to forget what she had said. *Hannah reminded her of someone?* Who? Obviously someone to whom the resemblance was so strong that the lady had felt inclined to remark upon it.

But how did he go about finding out who it was without arousing the lady's suspicions? Lady Thorpe was no fool, and she would surely begin to wonder if he pressed her into remembering the name of someone simply because they chanced to resemble his sister.

After all, what possible concern could it be to him if his sister looked like someone else?

CHAPTER TEN

THE following afternoon, Mr Stanford arrived at Cavendish Square at the agreed upon time for the drive that Robert had promised them the previous day. Unfortunately, the event did not get off to an auspicious start. Hannah, having met Alice coming out of her room, could see at once that the girl was nervous, and she soon discovered that Alice had, in fact, been at sixes and sevens all morning. The girl had changed her outfit three times, and had spent more than an hour in front of the glass, fussing over an appearance that Hannah was inclined to think a little overdone for a simple drive in the park. She, on the other hand, had dressed simply and worn little in the way of adornment, expecting little in the way of compliments on her appearance. As a result, when they went downstairs to hear Mr Stanford pay his most gallant compliments to *her* rather than to Alice, it was easy to see why a look of disappointment appeared on the younger girl's face. Unfortunately, Hannah could do naught but accept his compliments, and then try to direct his attention towards Alice whenever possible.

Thankfully, Robert was his usual, unruffled self. He had the carriage brought around, and as if sensing the potential for disaster, calmly suggested that he and Mr Stanford sit across from the ladies so that they might have the advantage of gazing at both of the ladies at once. Hannah silently blessed him for his foresight.

She could only imagine how dreadful Alice would have felt, had she been forced to sit beside her own cousin while Hannah ended up sitting beside her precious Mr Stanford!

Fortunately, emotional dramas notwithstanding, it was a perfect day for a drive. The park was crowded but that did not detract from their enjoyment of the outing. Robert simply directed the coachman to avoid the most congested areas and to take them where the horses might be able to trot briskly and thereby generate a pleasant breeze.

Whether it was the fineness of the day, or the pleasure of being in the midst of company, Alice's spirits rose, and she was soon chatting away in her usual animated fashion. For her own part, Hannah was happy to let her, for it was at times like these that she felt most sharply the deception she was perpetrating. Here, in the company of a viscount, a gentleman who would one day be a viscount, and a young lady who might very well end up marrying a viscount, Hannah felt most keenly her own lack of identity. As she did the fear that she had no right to be here at all.

After all, had Lady Winthrop not brought her home, what might she be doing? Scrubbing floors in a great house? Waiting on a fine lady? Serving behind a counter as a barmaid or shop clerk? Whatever it was, Hannah was hard pressed to believe it would have been anything remotely resembling what she was doing now.

'You're very quiet, Miss Winthrop,' Mr Stanford remarked of a sudden. 'Are you deep in thought or simply enjoying the pleasures of this lovely afternoon?'

Hannah looked up to find all eyes focused on her, and blushed deeply. 'Forgive me, sir, I did not mean to appear rude, though I admit my thoughts were elsewhere.'

'I hope it is not lack of interest in the company which forces your mind to wander,' Mr Stanford said.

'On the contrary, it is matters of family which weigh upon my mind, sir.'

It was a truthful answer, Hannah reflected, but one so innocuous as to risk little chance of exposure. No doubt they all assumed it was Lady Winthrop who occupied her thoughts. 'However, it was rude of me to appear so inattentive, and I apologise for my behaviour. From this moment on I shall endeavour to be the very best of guests.'

'But you are not a guest,' Alice said in confusion. 'You are a member of the family.'

'Indeed, it is *I* who am the guest,' Mr Stanford pointed out.

'I think what my sister means is that *all* of you are my guests,' Robert said, once again coming to her rescue. 'Isn't that right, Hannah?'

Hannah looked up to find Robert's eyes on her, and was immediately warmed by the expression of concern she saw in them. But she saw something else too. Something that tugged at her heart, and made her throat constrict in a most painful way.

'That is…precisely what I meant,' she stammered, looking away. *What had she seen in Robert's eyes just now? Surely it was not…?*

No, it couldn't have been, Hannah told herself. Robert had no special feelings for her. He was merely concerned that everyone have a good time. And by the time the carriage arrived home, Hannah was reasonably sure that everyone had. There had been no more awkward moments, though whether that was as a result of Robert more or less controlling the direction of the conversation, Hannah wasn't sure. All she knew was that no one person had seemed to receive any more attention than anyone else. And while such an arrangement was obviously of disappointment to Alice, it had certainly made matters a great deal easier for her.

It wasn't until later that afternoon, when she and Hannah were alone, that Alice reaffirmed her opinion that Mr Stanford was definitely more interested in Hannah than he was in her.

'Nonsense,' Hannah felt obliged to say. 'Mr Stanford is a very nice man but he is not enamoured of me.'

'Of course he is. Did you not see the way he looked at you all during the drive?' Alice stared down at the embroidery hoop in her lap, her face a picture of dejection. 'It was obvious from his expression that he is taken with you. And why would he not be? You are so elegant and well spoken, while I fall all over myself in an attempt to say the right thing.' Her eyes were bleak. 'I'm sure Mr Stanford saw that this afternoon too.'

'I think what Mr Stanford saw,' Hannah said, placing a reassuring hand on her cousin's arm, 'was a lovely young lady who was perhaps a little *too* obvious in her affections for him.'

Alice looked up, her big brown eyes as soft as a spaniel's. 'Really?'

'Yes. I think he also saw a lady who, *because* she had no interest in him, presented him with something of a challenge. And since it is well known that gentlemen cannot resist a challenge, Mr Stanford rose to meet it.'

'You mean…because you showed no partiality towards Mr Stanford, his interest in you increased?'

'More or less.'

'So you're suggesting that…a lady has a better chance of attracting a gentleman's attention, if she pretends she really doesn't want it?'

Hannah smiled as she cut a length of silk. 'A little intrigue goes a long way towards heightening attraction. You tend to lessen that intrigue by being a little obvious in your affections.'

The girl's shoulders sagged. 'Yes, I do, don't I? But I honestly cannot help myself. Mr Stanford is such a handsome gentleman, and he is so eminently likeable.'

'Yes. But he has a forgiving nature, and I think we can use that to our advantage in having you try again.'

'Truly?' Alice sat up, the animation coming back to her face. 'Do you mean that, if I were to become more…unattainable, Mr Stanford might like me better?'

'He might. And I only say might, Alice, for the heart is a fickle thing. Sometimes it is impossible to say who it will find pleasing, or in which direction it will take us,' Hannah cautioned. 'Sometimes, people have no idea they are being led towards the right person until—'

It happened as simply as that. Hannah stared at Alice, shocked by the realisation she had just come to.

Or by the one she suspected she had been coming to for the past four months.

'Cousin Hannah, are you all right?' Alice asked in some concern. 'You've gone a trifle pale.'

'Have I? No, I'm...fine. Really.'

No you're not! the voice inside her head shouted. *How can you be fine, when you've just admitted to yourself that you're hopelessly in love with Robert Winthrop!*

Hannah sat in her chair for a long time after Alice went up to her room. She put aside her needlework, finding she had neither the desire nor the patience for it, and sat with her hands folded in her lap, her eyes on the floor, thinking about the startling truth she had so recently discovered.

She was in love with Robert Winthrop.

Was she mad?

She must be. How had such a thing happened? He was a peer of the realm. She was a woman with no identity. It had to be madness.

Yes, she'd known that her feelings were changing towards him, but she'd comforted herself with the knowledge that they were feelings of friendship and respect. For surely it was wrong, or at best immoral, to think such a way of a man who until a few months ago had been her brother?

'Ah, there you are, Hannah.'

She jumped at the sound of his voice, then blushed at seeing him standing in the doorway. 'Robert!'

'Forgive me, I didn't mean to startle you.' Seemingly unaware of her heightened colour, he walked into the room and sank wearily into a chair. 'It has been an interesting day, has it not?'

Interesting indeed, Hannah thought, but said only, 'Did you enjoy the drive in the park?'

'Not particularly. I felt I was standing in the midst of a battlefield and stumbling over hidden perils as I tried to navigate the safest way out.'

Robert's analogy made her smile. 'I know the feeling. I've just travelled a similar path with Alice.'

'Oh? What has the little minx said now?'

'Only that she is firmly convinced Mr Stanford is not as enamoured of her as she would like him to be.'

'I dare say she's right,' Robert agreed. 'Alice could do with a lesson in the art of subtlety. The changes in her mood in response to anything James said or didn't say were excruciatingly obvious.'

Hannah looked down at her skirt, painfully aware of Robert sitting beside her. Painfully aware of loving him, and of how exposed it left her feeling. 'Do you think Mr Stanford has *any* feelings of affection for her?'

Robert glanced at her. 'You sound as though you're hopeful he has.'

'Well, of course I am. In truth, I wish he would declare himself totally smitten by her.'

'Instead of being smitten by you?'

Hannah blushed furiously. 'Why would you say that?'

'Because it's quite obvious that he is. And why would he not be?' Robert added softly. 'Lady Thorpe was right. Any man would be a fool not to wish to know you better. But take heart, my dear. It is not the first time Stanford has professed himself in love with a lady.'

Taken aback by his first remark, Hannah found herself struggling to recover from his second. *'In love!'* she gasped. 'Pray do not tell me he has professed such feelings to you in regards to *me*!'

'Not in so many words, but I know James well enough to recognise the signs. Still, I suppose I should be thankful to you for one thing.'

'And what is that?'

'That you have succeeded in making him forget Miss Blazel.'

'Miss Blazel?'

'Yes. A rather exquisite little dancer he's fancied himself in love with these many months.'

For some reason, the knowledge that Mr Stanford could so quickly transfer his affections from one woman to another lessened some of Hannah's concern. Obviously he was a man who did not commit his heart too deeply. But if that was the case, was Alice not better off without him?

'You're frowning,' Robert said suddenly. 'Was it something I said?'

Hannah sighed. 'I was only thinking that if Mr Stanford is capable of bestowing his affections so freely, and of changing them so frequently, there can be no great depth to his feelings.'

'I dare say you're right. James tends to attach himself to a pretty face rather than to the qualities in a lady he should attach himself to.'

'Is Miss Blazel pretty?'

'Uncommonly so. But it goes without saying that she is entirely unsuitable for him. That was one of the reasons I endeavoured to introduce him to Miss Thorpe the other night. Caroline has been deemed an Incomparable by society, but she also comes from a very good family.'

'Is that of import to Mr Stanford?'

'No, but it is of considerable import to his parents. I've simply tried to impress upon James the importance of knowing what is right and what isn't when considering a wife.'

'Gracious, never say that Mr Stanford truly considered *marrying* Miss Blazel.'

'Oh, he considered it. Though I do think perhaps I—or you—have discouraged him from acting upon it.'

Hannah's face grew warm with embarrassment. 'I am not sure I wish to save a man from his mistakes in such a way.'

'Don't worry, Hannah. I honestly believe that James would have come to the conclusion that he and Miss Blazel should not have suited. I told him any number of times that he would have been a fool to leg-shackle himself to a woman he knew nothing about. Marriage is a risky enough business as it is, without increasing the odds in such a way.'

Hannah went very still. 'So you told him it was…important that he know who his bride's people were and what her background was.'

'Of course. As to his feelings for Alice,' Robert continued as he got to his feet, 'I do not hold out hopes of anything developing there. Alice is young and foolish, and for all his own immaturity, James actually looks for wisdom and sensibility in a lady, which is no doubt part of the reason he is so attracted to you.'

Something in his voice made Hannah look up. Something in his eyes made her look away again. 'Well, he will have no success with me, and you may tell him so if he asks.'

'I know. That is why I intend to continue in my efforts to further his acquaintance with Miss Thorpe.'

Hannah too got to her feet, but only to pick up her book and start towards the door. 'I would not put my hopes too much in that direction if I were you, Robert.'

'Why? Do you not think he finds her attractive?'

'I think *any* man would find her attractive, but it matters little if her affections are engaged elsewhere.'

'I wasn't aware that her feelings *were* engaged.'

'They are, and I'm afraid that Mr Stanford, as pleasant as he is, offers the gentleman little in the way of competition.'

Robert didn't so much as blink. 'How do you know of the lady's affections when you are so recently come to London?'

'Because ladies like to talk, and for whatever reason, Miss Thorpe decided to talk to me. Now if you will excuse me, I think I shall retire to my room. I'll see you at dinner.'

Hannah closed the door and walked out. Strangely enough, she was quite sure Robert had no idea what she was talking about, but even so, she could not bring herself to be the one to reveal the truth of Miss Thorpe's affections. If the lady was so inclined, Robert would learn of them soon enough.

Later that same evening, Hannah again found herself alone in Robert's company. Her aunt and uncle had been invited to an elegant function, and once Hannah had assured them that she was quite happy to remain at home, they had gone merrily on their way, thankfully taking Alice with them.

In truth, Hannah had not wished to go to Lady Mackleby's ball. It would have been far too grand an occasion for her to attend while still in mourning. Instead, she had retired to the music-room and lost herself in practice for a few hours. As a result, she did not notice Robert standing in the doorway until she brought her fingers down on the final notes on the sonata, prompting him to say, 'That was beautiful, Hannah.'

She lifted her head with a gasp. 'Robert! Forgive me, I did not see you there.'

'I had no wish to interrupt. You were totally engrossed in your piece, and indeed, you played it exceptionally well. I had no idea you were so skilled.'

'Thank you. I have always enjoyed playing, and Lady Montgomery's instrument is a very fine one.' Her voice was more breathless than it should have been, but that was what Robert's presence did to her now. The mere sight of him caused such a flurry of emotions in her heart that at times they threatened to block out everything else.

'You are alone this evening?' he asked, advancing a few steps into the room.

'I...yes.' The air suddenly felt thick around her. 'The family have gone to...Lady Mackleby's ball.' Hannah looked up at him and struggled for composure. He was dressed formally in an elegant black coat over cream satin breeches, making her wonder if he planned on going to a party, or whether he'd just come from one. Certainly, his appearance would have allowed him access to any gathering, however formal. 'You are dressed for a grand ball yourself.'

Robert glanced down at his attire and shrugged. 'I had thought to stop in at a few places, but once in the carriage found myself strangely reluctant to do so. So I decided to come here and see how my dear sister was passing the time.'

My dear sister. The remark was casually uttered yet caused such a sharp pain in Hannah's heart that she actually flinched. *Oh, that she might be so light-hearted and flippant with him.*

'As a matter of fact, your *sister* is thinking it is well past time she started doing something of value,' Hannah told him, needing to take charge of her emotions. 'In particular, with regard to finding out who she is.'

Robert approached the pianoforte and, after a moment's perusal of the music scattered across the top, pulled out a sheet and placed it before her. 'Have you given any thought as to how you intend to go about doing that?'

'A little.' Hannah glanced at the piece, swallowing a smile when she realised it was one of her favourites. 'But it occurs to me it would be foolish to think I can do it from here.'

'From this house?'

'From London. After all, I was abandoned in Scotland.'

Hannah saw him wince a little as he sat down in a chair, but he merely closed his eyes and said, 'Play for me, Hannah.'

It was spoken as a command yet in a tone so gentle

Hannah couldn't possibly take offence. As such, she placed her fingers upon the keys and began to play. For a few minutes, neither of them spoke, content to listen to the richness of the instrument, and to the delightful sounds of the Beethoven sonata. At its conclusion, Robert, eyes still closed, inclined his head. 'Thank you. You truly do the instrument proud.'

Hannah sighed, abandoning all attempts at indifference. 'I'm not sure that I do. There are only so many hours in the day available to practise one's skills.'

'Then I would venture to say you have made excellent use of the time you have.'

'Robert,' Hannah pushed herself away from the instrument. 'May I ask you something?'

'Of course.'

'What would be involved in my travelling to Scotland?'

He opened his eyes and looked at her. 'More than is worth considering.'

'But—'

'What do you expect to find there, Hannah? Where would you go?'

'Well, I thought I would start by returning to the village where I was abandoned. I believe Bonnyrigg was the name.'

'All right. And where would you stay?'

'At the inn where your mother found me.'

'Do you intend to take your maid?'

'I hadn't thought to.' Hannah hesitated. 'I would prefer that no one be aware of my intentions.'

'Very well. So as a single, gently bred young woman, you are going to stay at a coaching inn in

Scotland with no other family or maid to attend you, and…do what?'

'Ask questions.'

'Of whom?'

'The innkeeper, for a start.'

'And when the innkeeper tells you he has no knowledge of a baby who was abandoned in a lady's carriage some twenty-one years ago, what are you going to do then?'

Hannah knew that Robert was trying to make this difficult for her, but she supposed it was for the best. What she was thinking of doing wasn't easy. 'I know there are any number of problems inherent in my plan, Robert, but I *have* to make some effort to discover who I am, or I will never know peace in my life.'

'Is it not enough that you are, to all who know you, the daughter of the late Viscountess Winthrop?'

'No. Because I know I am not.'

'Not by birth, perhaps, but in every other way.'

'Robert, please. I know it's difficult for you to understand, but I have to know. Not knowing who I am affects every part of my life, including whom I marry and what happens when I have children.'

He studied her in silence for a moment. 'Very well. I will set out on this quest for your identity, as I said I would, now that I see you are still intent on pursuing it.'

Her surprise was unconcealed. 'Did you think I would change my mind?'

'To be truthful, I'd hoped you might. You have no idea what a mammoth undertaking this is, or how potentially upsetting the results may be. But, because you are set on your course, I shall do whatever I can to assist you.'

'This isn't your concern,' Hannah said softly. 'It isn't your battle.'

'No, but it is a battle you were thrust into because of something my mother did.' Getting to his feet, Robert walked towards her, his eyes lingering on hers, his gaze softening as it rested on her mouth. 'It seems to me that as her only son, the least I can do is take up the cause.'

True to his word, Robert began making enquiries into Hannah's background the very next day. He knew before he started, however, that it would be a waste of time. His questions had to be so carefully worded, so protective of the person for whom the questions were being asked, that it was impossible to give anyone enough information to formulate intelligent answers in response.

Not that he'd expected any. For who in London would be likely to know anything about a man who had fathered a child in Scotland twenty-one years ago—when it was very likely the man himself didn't know of the child's existence? Certainly, that was what the letter had indicated. In which case, it was only to be expected that no one would have raised a hue and cry when the child disappeared.

But even had the father known, would he have made any attempt to locate her? If he was a man of consequence, she was probably just one more bastard he need not concern himself with. Still, Robert did what he could because he'd told Hannah he would. And for some reason, keeping his word to Hannah had become very important to him. He was willing to risk a great deal to make her happy, because she'd come to mean a great deal to him.

Robert thought about that as he walked back to his house later that evening. It was ironic, really, that he should feel this closeness to her when he had all but ignored her the rest of her life. But to be fair, he hadn't known Hannah then. And he'd certainly had no knowledge of the woman she had become. He hadn't expected her to be so gracious and refined, or to possess such a delightful sense of humour. He hadn't known that honour and integrity would be the cornerstones of her character, or that for all her outer beauty, she would be so refreshingly unaffected. Instead, believing her to be someone and something she was not, he had purposely stayed away.

Yes, he'd been a fool, Robert admitted now. He could have been enjoying Hannah's companionship and laughter all of those years instead of shunning her *and* his mother, robbing himself of the pleasure of their company. He had made strangers of them both when they should have been the two most important people in his life. He would carry the guilt for that until the day he died.

'Will you ever forgive me, Mama?' he whispered some time later into the darkness of the library, where he sat nursing a glass of brandy. 'For truly, I have been the most stupid of men. Stupid to hold you guilty for something you did *not* do, when I should have been trying to help you with something you *did*.'

No answer came back to him from the heavens, nor did he expect one, but somehow it comforted Robert to know that he had made the confession out loud.

On his second glass of brandy, he started thinking about Hannah again, and about the strange quest for truth he now found himself on. What would he tell her if he was unable to discover anything about her past? She'd said she could no longer accept who she was or who she thought she'd been her entire life, but if he found out nothing, what choice would she have *but* to accept it?

And how would she react when she found out that she was never going to know the truth? Would she run away? Would she take leave of everything she knew and disappear into some isolated backwoods village? She'd told him that the discovery of her past would have an effect on her future, including whom she married and any children she might bear. But surely she did not intend to avoid marriage all together in order to avoid having to lie to them?

Robert swirled the amber liquid in his glass. It would not have surprised him if she had, because she was honourable enough not to wish to discredit the man she married. But he also acknowledged that it would be a terrible waste. Hannah *should* be married. She was meant to be loved, and to give love in return. She was an incredibly warm and caring woman, and she was certainly beautiful enough to take her place in any man's home.

Even his.

The thought jerked Robert upright, causing brandy to slop over the edges of his glass. *Hannah take her place in* his *house?* What in God's name was he thinking? What was he saying? That he was...

No, it wasn't possible. He didn't have *those* kinds of feelings for Hannah. She'd been his sister too long—or his sister in mind—for him to think of her as anything else now. But if that was the case, why did the idea of her wanting to go to Scotland to seek the truth sit so ill with him? Was it only concern for her welfare that had him wishing her to stay home? Was it a desire to spare her the hurt he knew she would suffer when she got there and found no answers to satisfy her that had him standing in her way?

Or was it something more basic than that? Was it simply that he *wanted* her to stay here, where he could see her whenever he wished. Somewhere safe, where he could be assured of her protection, and where he could make sure she came to no harm. If it was, surely all that demonstrated was the depth of concern he had for a woman who had been a part of his life since he'd been twelve years old.

Surely that was all this feeling could be.

CHAPTER ELEVEN

AS PROMISED, the gathering at the home of Lord and Lady Thorpe was a quiet family affair. Lord Thorpe and his wife were a few years older than Sir Roger and Lady Montgomery, but they shared many similar interests. The ladies spoke about fashion and the best assemblies for their daughters to attend, while Lord Thorpe and Sir Roger discovered a mutual passion for fishing.

That, of course, left Miss Thorpe to entertain the three younger people, but since it was really only Robert in whom Caroline had any interest, Hannah soon found herself in charge of keeping Alice entertained. Which was fine, since she truly did not find the younger girl tiresome in any way. She simply asked Miss Thorpe for a deck of cards so that they might amuse themselves for a while.

So occupied, the group passed a pleasant hour or so. But it soon came to Hannah's attention that her cousin's attention was not focused solely on her cards.

'I do not think Miss Thorpe is doing a very good job of being subtle,' Alice whispered as Hannah dealt a new hand. 'Or of keeping your brother in suspense. If you ask me, she is being very obvious in her affections for him.'

Hannah dutifully picked up her cards. 'I believe the friendship between Miss Thorpe and my brother goes back a long way. She probably feels she has no need to be guarded in her actions or speech.'

'But it is so obvious that she likes him,' Alice insisted, 'and she is not making any attempts to conceal it. Look at the way she flutters her eyelashes at him, and then so prettily blushes.'

Hannah turned her head and did indeed catch the lovely Miss Thorpe in the midst of a most becoming blush. But given that Robert's head was only a few inches from hers, Hannah could well understand why. Had Robert smiled at her like that, she likely would have melted in a puddle at his feet.

She quickly returned her attention to her cards, finding it difficult to look on the happiness of others when it was obvious she would be denied such happiness herself.

'You are not paying attention to your cards, Cousin Hannah,' Alice complained a few minutes later. 'You have just thrown down your Queen.'

Abruptly recalled to the game, Hannah saw that she had indeed made a tactical error, but when a silvery peal of laughter erupted from Miss Thorpe, it was all she could do not to fling the entire deck across the room.

'Forgive me, Cousin Alice, but I think I shall take a walk outside.'

'But we have not yet finished the game!'

'Perhaps you could persuade your mother to take my place.' Hannah abruptly got to her feet. 'I fear I have not the head for cards tonight.'

Not waiting for her cousin's reply, Hannah picked up her skirts and headed for the terrace. Thankfully, it was a beautiful night, but she knew she would have sought escape outside even had it been frigid.

Oh, come along, Hannah, you can do better than this. You must learn to accept that Robert will pay attention to other young women.

Hannah sighed. Yes, she must, but oh, dear, it was becoming harder and harder to do. When she had looked up to see him laughing with Caroline, it had taken all the will-power she'd possessed not to cry out loud. Indeed, the tightness in her chest had been akin to pain. *Would that he might laugh with me like that*, she'd thought longingly.

But he never would, of course, because he'd said it himself when speaking of his good friend, Mr Stanford. *A gentleman could not afford to involve himself with a woman whose background he knew nothing about.* It was important to know where a lady came from and who her people were before committing to a relationship with her. What did he know of her background, or people?

What did she know of it?

'Hannah, are you well?'

His voice caught her unawares, bringing her thoughts tumbling back to the present. 'I'm fine, Robert, thank you. I was simply a little warm and thought to take some air.' She looked at him quickly, and then away. 'Miss Thorpe does not join you?'

'No. She is engaged at cards with Alice.'

'With Alice?' A startled laugh sprang from her lips. 'Dear me. I wondered who she would find to replace me. I did not think it would be Miss Thorpe.'

'Why? Do you not think Caroline enjoys a game of cards?'

'Perhaps, but not when you are in the room.'

The unconscious slip caused Robert's eyes to widen in surprise, then to narrow in thought. 'What do you mean by that?'

'Nothing.' *Fool!* She must be careful not to expose herself in such a way. Robert was far too astute. 'Forgive me, it was a silly remark. I should not have made it.'

'But you did, which means your mind is intent upon such thoughts.' With unhurried grace, he took a step towards her, closing the distance between them. 'Have you taken a dislike to Miss Thorpe?'

Flustered by his nearness, Hannah blushed. 'There is no reason why I should dislike her.'

'Perhaps not, but you do. Your face is most expressive of your feelings, my dear. Your eyes tell me what your words do not.'

Hannah glanced away, cursing her body's inadvertent betrayal. 'I fear you are misreading what you see.'

'Am I?' He took another step closer, and, reaching out his hand, cupped her chin in his fingers and forced her to look at him. 'Why do I get the feeling there's something you're not telling me, Hannah? Why do I feel that something neither of us suspected of happening *is* happening even as we stand here trying to deny it?'

The touch of his hand was unbearable in its tenderness, and Hannah closed her eyes, frightened of revealing what was in her heart. There were no words to describe the thoughts whirling madly about in her head. His breath was warm on her cheek, his body so close as to almost be touching, but it did not give her comfort. Indeed, it only left her aching for what she could not have. 'Go back inside, Robert. They will be looking for you.'

'Perhaps,' he said on a silky breath, 'but I have no wish to leave you.'

'Robert, *please*—'

'If you would beg me for anything, let it be that I should stay, Hannah. I'll not spare you now. Not when there's so much that needs to be said between us!'

'There's nothing to be said—'

'There is, and you know it,' he said quietly. 'We're not brother and sister any more. You're as aware of me as I am of you, and we must talk about it.' Robert slid his other arm around her waist, pulling her so close that she could scarcely breathe. 'The mere sight of you makes me feel like a man who's gone too long without water. A man who's been lost in the desert, struggling to find his way out. But I'm not the only one who's suffering, am I, Hannah? Even now, I can feel you trembling. I can see it in your eyes. In your—'

'Ah, there you are, Lord Winthrop. I thought—*oh*!'

The visitor's words came to an abrupt halt, but it was the surprise in her voice that made Hannah look up in horror. Miss Thorpe was standing frozen in the doorway. Her eyes were wide, her expression was a mixture of shock, embarrassment and utter confusion. And why would she not look confused? Hannah thought, drowning in guilt. The lady had come on to the terrace to find Robert standing only inches away from his sister, with one arm wrapped firmly around her waist and his other hand holding her face in a manner that could only be called intimate. What was she supposed to think?

Cheeks flaming, Hannah wrenched free. 'Miss Thorpe!'

'Miss...Winthrop.' Miss Thorpe stared at her, then glanced away, unwilling to meet her eyes. 'Forgive me, I fear I may have...intruded on a private moment—'

'Don't be silly, Caroline, you haven't intruded on anything,' Robert said in a voice intended to make her objection sound ridiculous. 'I was merely teasing Hannah about a secret I might or might not divulge, and she was threatening to expose me. Hence, I decided to whisper the secret in her ear.'

The explanation sounded plausible, as did the tone in which it was offered, but it was a few moments before Miss Thorpe's expression of dismay lightened. 'Oh. Well, yes, of course.' She laughed, but the sound was still uncertain. 'I apologise for...interrupting your game, but I wanted to tell you that Mama is putting together a foursome for whist. I wondered if you might like to partner me in the game.'

'I should be delighted,' Robert said without hesitation.

Miss Thorpe turned and finally, met Hannah's eyes. 'I believe your...aunt and uncle are hoping you will also return to the drawing-room, and make a foursome with Miss Montgomery.'

Striving to be as cool as Robert—and failing miserably—Hannah inclined her head. 'Of course.'

Thankfully, Miss Thorpe said nothing more, and Hannah returned to the drawing-room with an unconcerned smile upon her face. But it came as no surprise to her that once the games commenced, she lost every hand she played.

* * *

The rest of the evening passed in a relatively uneventful manner. Hannah did not seek the seclusion of the terrace again, and there were no more whispered messages between her and Robert. Fortunately, Miss Thorpe seemed to have accepted his explanation for their behaviour on the terrace, and Hannah heard her familiar bell-like laughter ring clearly throughout the evening. But she couldn't help but notice, as they were preparing to leave, that Miss Thorpe looked at her quizzically once more.

Hannah thought about that look now as she lay in bed, trying without success to find oblivion in sleep. How had it looked to Miss Thorpe, coming out on to the terrace, to find Robert standing so close to her? What had she thought upon seeing him cupping her chin so tenderly in his hand? Yes, Robert's explanation had suggested something entirely logical, but had his expression—or hers—suggested something else?

Hannah feared it quite likely that her own face had given something away, because she knew what she'd been thinking as Robert had moved closer to her. And she certainly remembered what she'd been feeling as the distance between their bodies—and their lips—had narrowed.

Was that what Miss Thorpe had seen on her face tonight?

Robert too, found himself wondering what truths Miss Thorpe had gleaned from Hannah's face. He knew he need have no concerns about his own expression, for experience had taught him to control his features so that not even the most perceptive of onlookers might discern his thoughts. But Hannah was not so adept at deceiving others. She might be able to pretend a convincing interest in a boring conversation, or hide her dismay at a blatant social gaff, but she would never be as proficient as him at masking the depth of her personal feelings.

Which was why he had reacted so quickly to Caroline Thorpe's question. He had taken pains to assure her that his conduct with Hannah had been all that was natural—because he'd known damn well it wasn't. It was all well and good to say that siblings enjoyed a certain familiarity, but he and Hannah weren't siblings any more.

He found himself looking forward to spending time with her as a woman. He welcomed the opportunity of talking to her, and of learning how she really felt about matters that were of interest to them both. And in that regard she constantly amazed him. Used to the empty-headed chatter of society ladies, Robert had been delighted to discover not only that Hannah was well educated, but that she had a sharp and remarkably agile mind. She was quick to pick up on new ideas, and she would only argue a subject if she knew it well enough to do so intelligently. Conversely, when confronted with a subject she wasn't familiar with, she was willing to ask for information and had more than once sought Robert's opinion, instead of being resigned to her own ignorance on the matter.

All in all, she was a remarkable woman, and one whose company Robert found himself enjoying more every day. But if he was being honest with himself, he knew his feelings towards her were not in the least brotherly, or even that of one friend for another. But where did that leave him, more importantly, where did it leave *them*? Was she as drawn to him as he was to her? She seemed to blush a lot more now than she had in the past, but did that signify the existence of any romantic feelings for him? Did it account for the wistful look in her eyes this evening when he'd tipped back her head and forced her to look at him?

Was it regret he'd seen in those beautiful sapphire eyes when she'd made that telling remark about Miss Thorpe—or something more?

Robert slowly sat up. Was it possible that Hannah had been *jealous* of Caroline tonight? Was that why she'd fled the drawing-room? Because if it was, it meant she wasn't indifferent to him at all. Jealousy signified the existence of strong emotions. If you didn't care about someone, you didn't care if they looked at someone else.

He cared if Hannah looked at other men. In fact, for the first time, Robert realised that the only reason he'd been able to tease Hannah about Stanford's feelings for her was because he'd known that she didn't have any feelings for the man. But what if that was to change? What if he were to discover, through his quest for her identity, that she was someone with whom James could associate? And if that knowledge allowed her to permit the acquaintance, how would he feel? Would he be able to watch Hannah walk into James Stanford's arms, knowing that he would be the one to teach her all that love could be between a man and a woman?

Was he truly willing to let Hannah walk out of his life and pretend there was nothing going on?

Hannah eventually managed to fall asleep, but she woke feeling far from refreshed. Her mind was still in a whirl over everything Robert had said to her. What had he meant when he'd said that something was happening between them—something that neither of them had expected? Was that his way of telling her that he was developing feelings for her? For surely he must have guessed that she was in love with him.

But if he had guessed, and by some miracle he returned her feelings, what good would it do them? They could not entertain thoughts of a relationship. Society would never condone such a liaison, nor could she, knowing of the social disparity that existed between them. But how was she to convince Robert of that? If he was truly falling in love with her, what could she say that would dissuade him?

Hannah was still on edge when Robert paid her an unexpected visit later that morning. Lady Montgomery and Alice had gone out, desirous of ordering new gowns and bonnets, while Sir Roger was closeted in his study, which meant Hannah had no choice but to see Robert alone. As her brother, he didn't have to seek permission to see her, nor was it expected that a chaperone or servant be present during their meetings, but this morning, Hannah wished she might have had that option. She felt as defenceless as a lamb; her emotions too fragile in her new-found awareness of her love.

And yet, when Robert walked into the room, it was as though she suddenly came alive. Every feeling was heightened, every sensation magnified. As she rose to greet him, the sight of him was like sunlight pouring straight into her heart. Everything about him was perfect.

Everything—except the way he made her feel.

'I hope I've not come too early,' Robert said, closing the door behind him.

Hannah glanced at it briefly. 'Not at all. I've long been up and about. But to what do I owe the pleasure of your visit?' Suddenly, her heart skipped a beat. 'Have you news to give me? Have you learned something?'

'I have learned something, but not in regard to the news you were seeking,' he said quietly. 'I'm sorry.'

Hope quickly born, died a fluttering death. 'Oh. Well, I suppose it is too early to hope for such things,' she admitted with a smile. 'You have only just begun to make enquiries.' She moved away from her desk, pressing her hand to her stomach, trying to quell the butterflies that danced within. 'Will you sit down?'

Robert shook his head. 'I should prefer to stand. There is something I wish to ask you. Or perhaps, to have you clarify for me.'

Hannah looked at him quickly. 'What is it?'

'It concerns Miss Thorpe.'

Her heart began to pound. 'What about her?'

'Am I the gentleman upon whom her affections are fixed?'

Hannah blinked, momentarily at a loss. It wasn't the question she'd been expecting. 'Why would you think—?'

'Pray do not dissemble, Hannah. We have been honest with each other, and I am asking you to be honest with me now. Are you aware of Miss Thorpe's affection for me?'

Hannah stared at him in dismay. She did not wish to lie to him, but surely she had no right to divulge the lady's secret? 'It is not my place to tell you of another's sentiments.'

'It is if they concern me.'

'But surely you have more insight into Miss Thorpe's feelings than I.'

'Unfortunately, any insight I might have is somewhat coloured.' Robert's mouth pulled into a tight smile. 'The nature of my relationship with Caroline is not unlike yours with Mr Twickenham.'

Surprise elicited a gasp from her. 'It is?'

'I've known Caroline since she was eleven years old. The first time I saw her, she was even more awkward than you.'

That remark had the unwelcome effect of bringing the colour to Hannah's cheeks. 'Thank you, Lord Winthrop. You cannot imagine how flattered I feel upon hearing *that*.'

'Forgive me, it was not my intention to criticise or to wound.' Robert's smile warmed. 'I only said it so you would know that my feelings for Miss Thorpe are not what they should be, or, perhaps, what you think they are.'

Risking a quick glance in his direction, Hannah saw that he was watching her, and her pulse skittered in alarm. 'Rest assured, I have no thoughts on the matter. It can be of no concern to me what your feelings are for Miss Thorpe. Or any other young lady, for that matter.'

'Are you sure?'

'Of course. Why would you think otherwise?'

'I suppose because I was hoping to hear that you were interested in whom I might profess myself to be in love with.'

Hannah blanched. *Robert was in love?*

She put her hand on the back of the sofa, thankful she was close enough to it to do so. 'I am…delighted to know you are not intending to spend the rest of your life as a bachelor.' *Oh, God, how was she to bear it?* 'Are you planning on telling me the name of this most fortunate young lady?'

'I think it best I do.' Robert moved towards her slowly, never taking his eyes from her face. 'You may wish to have time to come to terms with the news.'

Hannah glanced away, desperately trying to think of the name that would so shortly be on his lips. There were so few people in London she knew. So few whose names would mean anything to her…

'There is nothing for me to…come to terms with.' It had to be someone she knew, otherwise he wouldn't have made the comment, but who could it be? *Please God, let it be someone worthy of him.*

'Will you not ask me to say her name?' Robert asked softly. 'Or have you no interest in the lady's identity?'

'Of course I'm interested,' Hannah said. 'Just as I'm…delighted that you have finally made your choice.'

'Yet you do not sound as though you are happy for me. There is a hesitation in your voice and a shadow in your eyes that tells me otherwise.'

Robert had moved closer as he'd been speaking, until he was standing so close Hannah could scarcely breathe. Her body felt heavy, as though the weight of the world rested upon her shoulders. 'You are mistaken, Robert. I am most…anxious to share in your happiness.'

'Are you?' He touched her face, gently, asking questions without asking. 'Because what I'm about to say will change things between us, Hannah.'

She closed her eyes. *Then tell me quickly, Robert. Tell me now and get it over with.*

Hannah hadn't realised she'd said the words aloud until he smiled down at her and said, 'With pleasure, my dear. The lady I'm in love with…is you.'

For a moment, Hannah was quite sure the world must have stopped turning. Because it wasn't possible that she'd heard him correctly. He couldn't have said that he was *in love* with her…

'Have you nothing to say?'

Hannah shook her head. 'I've no idea…what to say.' How could she tell him that what he'd said was everything she'd ever wanted to hear—and the last thing she needed to? 'It never occurred to me that you…that I…' Her words trailed off, silenced by the prickling in her eyes and the burning in her throat. She swallowed hard, willing herself not to cry. *If you cry now, he'll know everything…*

Fortunately, Robert didn't attempt to draw her any closer. He only stood gazing down at her, his own eyes dark with emotion. 'You could say that you have feelings for me in return. If you don't, it's probably best you tell me now before I make a complete fool of myself.'

Hannah looked at him in silence. *He couldn't be in love with her.* It was all so terribly wrong. Just as it was wrong that she was in love with him. And yet, how could she help herself, or keep hidden all that she felt? This was not some passing infatuation. She was in love with Robert Winthrop. Every moment she spent in his company, knowing there could be nothing between them, was its own sweet kind of torture. 'What I feel cannot have any bearing on this, my lord,' she whispered finally.

'My name is Robert.'

'But that is not what I may call you!' Heartsick and trembling, Hannah turned her back to him. 'It was one thing when we thought we were brother and sister. It was…another when we agreed to be friends. But now, it is not appropriate…in any way.'

'I've just told you I love you. How much more appropriate can it be? What would you have a man call the woman he loves?'

He spoke quietly, yet Hannah heard every word. *He loved her*. He truly *loved* her. Yet the knowledge of how wrong it was caused misery to wrap like a chain around her heart. 'This is not seemly, Lord Winthrop. You cannot feel—'

'I can feel whatever I want. It's *you* who've not told me how you feel.' He took a step towards her. 'You've not told me if you return my love.'

'It is not for me to say—'

'It *is* for you to say, damn it! How am I to know where I stand if you do not?' He reached for her and turned her around to face him. 'I love you, Hannah. I didn't ask for it to happen. Indeed, I never expected that it would, but I do love you and I'm not ashamed to say it out loud. All I'm asking is that you tell me the truth. Do you love me or not?'

It was within her power to end it. With one word, she could resolve it here and now, with no one any the wiser for what had happened. Here, in this room, she could bring matters to a close. Because if Robert knew that she did not love him, he would go away and leave her in peace. One word was all it would take. One word.

And as the seconds ticked by, she knew she couldn't say it.

With a muffled cry, Robert pulled her into his arms. 'Oh, my sweet love.'

And then he kissed her. Kissed her with all the passion, all the longing he must surely have been holding in check. His mouth was warm on hers, his lips insistent, teasing hers apart. His tongue devoured, dipping in to explore the velvety sweetness of her mouth.

Lost to all reason, Hannah let him. Her own breath quickened, and heat spread through her body, leaving her feeling weak and light-headed. Her body felt fragile, as if it might explode at the slightest touch. And yet, as his arms tightened around her, Hannah knew this was where she wanted to be. She clung to him because it felt right. But knowing it was anything but, she finally broke away.

'Hannah?' Robert's voice was thick and unsteady, his emotions fully engaged.

Hannah too, struggled to bring her breathing back under control. *This was too powerful, the feeling too potent.* For the first time in her life, she truly understood the incredible power love wielded. 'We cannot, Robert. It is wrong!'

'It is not wrong if we love each other!'

'But don't you understand? Love has nothing to do with this. You must remember your position. You are Viscount Winthrop. You have…an obligation to continue the line.'

'If it makes you feel any better, that's exactly what

I was thinking about doing,' he said, a devilish light suddenly appearing in his eyes.

'Do not tease, Robert,' Hannah pleaded, nevertheless blushing all the way down to her toes. 'You know as well as I do that what we are doing is wrong.'

'The only thing that's wrong is allowing what we feel for each other to be ignored. The passion I feel for you, the love and the respect—'

'Are all sadly misplaced,' Hannah interrupted before he had a chance to finish. 'You don't know who I am, Robert. I don't know who I am. And until I do, I can't allow you to continue in this. You said yourself, a gentleman must know all there is to know about his intended.'

'Damn it, Hannah, I was talking about Stanford!'

'But the circumstances are no different because we're talking about you. Don't you understand? You have as much right to know everything there is to know about the woman you would marry as any man. More, in fact. Because you *believe* in the importance of such knowledge. Mr Stanford was willing to marry his dancer because he believed himself in love with her! You would never allow your heart to be so sadly compromised.'

'And yet, what have I just done if not that?' Robert said. 'Have I not just shown you that I am capable of being every bit as reckless as James?'

Hannah bit her lip. 'You have. And it is as wrong for you as it was for him.'

Robert stared at her, watching her, searching for any cracks in the armour she was building around herself. But he saw nothing. No breaks. No tiny openings. No answers.

'I won't sacrifice this, Hannah,' he said quietly. 'I've never felt this way about a woman before, and I'm damned if I'll let you push me away now.'

'You have no choice. Stop to see how impossible the situation is, Robert. Society will never allow it. By your own admission, we are brother and sister in everyone's eyes. How will you justify *that* to the people who see you professing love for me?'

'I shall tell them the truth.'

'So you will admit to everyone that the woman you grew up believing to be your sister was actually a bastard child who was abandoned in your mother's carriage. You would reveal my secret in such a way?'

'I would, if it meant that you and I could be open about our feelings for one another.'

'Then you would be ridiculed by all who know you for being stupid enough to have feelings for someone who is not worthy of your affections,' Hannah said sadly. 'They will look upon you as a fool, and me as an intruder. I am no longer one of your class, Robert, don't you understand? I am not deserving of your love.'

'Don't you *ever* say that to me again!' Furious, Robert closed the distance between them and drew her back into his arms. 'I have yet to meet a woman more worthy of my love. You are the most remarkable, the most courageous, the most admirable woman I've ever met, Hannah Winthrop. And I love everything about you. Your sense of humour, your compassion, your joy. There is no other I wish to have beside me.'

'Nevertheless, you must find another.' Hannah felt tears well in her eyes. 'I will not allow you to dishonour yourself and your name like this!'

'Do you love me, Hannah?' he asked in a low, urgent whisper.

'Robert, *please!*'

'Do you *love* me? Answer me, damn it, for I'll not let you go until you do.'

Hannah shook her head. 'Robert, I beg you, do not ask me this now.'

But he would not give in. 'All I want to know is the truth. Either you love me or you don't. All I'm asking, is that you tell me the truth.'

Hannah choked back a sob. She couldn't fight him. Not now. She was too weak. She might have been able to lie about it before and sound convincing, but not now. 'I love you. May God forgive me, but, yes, I love you.'

Robert pulled her into his arms and pressed his lips to her hair. 'Then there is nothing more we need say. Whatever it takes, whatever we have to endure, we will. Because I shall not let you go. I can't, beloved. Whatever it takes, I will make this happen. And woe betide any man who tries to stand in my way!'

He left her soon after, but as Robert climbed into his carriage, there was but one thought on his mind. *He had to find out who Hannah was.* That was now the single most important thing in his life. Because he knew it was the only hope he had of convincing her to marry him.

Hannah loved him. She could have hated him, and probably should have, given the callous way he'd treated her over the years. But she didn't hate him. Her passionate response to his kisses had assured him that she loved him as deeply as he loved her. But he was not so foolish as to believe that she would marry him.

Hannah didn't know who she was and because of that, she wouldn't risk sullying his name or his title. She might be the daughter of an aristocrat. Or she might be the child of a whore. But until she knew for sure, she wouldn't marry him or anyone else.

'Reynolds,' he called to his driver. 'Take me to Grosvenor Square.'

'Yes, my lord.'

It was a gamble, Robert admitted, and a risk, but at the moment it was the only hope he had. It was the only lead he'd stumbled upon and as slight as it was, it was worth following up. Consequently, a short time later, he stood in the drawing-room of an imposing house in Grosvenor Square, bowing over the hand of the one person he prayed might be able to help him.

'Good afternoon, Lady Thorpe. I hope you don't mind my stopping by, but there is something of great import I need to ask you.'

CHAPTER TWELVE

'ROBERT, whatever is the matter?' Lady Thorpe asked. 'You seem unusually disturbed about something.'

'I am, and in truth, the matter I've come to speak to you about is highly unusual,' he admitted. 'It is also distressful in that there are facts about certain people you'll be very surprised to hear. But before I begin, I must have your word that what I am about to tell you will go no further than this room.'

'Of course, Robert, if that is what you wish. But what in the world is this mystery about?'

'It concerns Hannah.'

'Oh, dear.' Lady Thorpe's surprise quickly gave way to concern. 'Nothing's happened to the sweet child, I hope?'

'No, nothing at all. Hannah's fine.'

'Then, what is it?'

Robert took a deep breath, hoping he wasn't about to make the biggest mistake of his life. 'There's really no easy way to say this, Lady Thorpe, so I may as well just say it straight out. Hannah is not my sister.'

'I beg your pardon?' The older woman stared at him in bewilderment. 'How can she not be your sister?'

'I know this is going to be difficult for you to believe but—' he took another deep breath '—my mother only pretended that Hannah was her natural born daughter. In fact, Hannah was abandoned in my mother's carriage when she was only a few weeks old.'

'Good God!'

'Yes, I thought you would be surprised.'

'Surprised!' Lady Thorpe sank weakly into a chair. 'That does not even *begin* to describe it. Hannah was left in your mother's carriage, and your mother actually brought her home and raised her?'

'Incredible as it seems, yes, that is exactly what happened.'

'But why? And how did you come to learn of this most bizarre happenstance?'

'It was told to me by my mother's first cousin, Lady MacInnes, when she came down from Scotland for Mama's funeral.'

'And you'd had no inkling prior to that?'

'I'd held a few beliefs of my own, but as it turned out, they were only partially correct.' Robert then proceeded to tell Lady Thorpe, in whatever detail he felt necessary, the incredible story of how Hannah had come to live at Gillingdon Park. He did not tell her about his feelings for Hannah, fearing she would have enough to come to terms with as it was.

At the conclusion of the tale, Lady Thorpe was silent for a long time. Robert held his breath, wondering what form her reaction would take. When it came, it was almost anticlimactic. 'Dear me, Robert,' Lady Thorpe said. 'This *would* set Society on its ear.'

'Yes, I dare say it would. Which is why I have asked for your complete silence in the matter.'

'And you shall have it, of course. I'm not sure I would even *wish* to be the one to make the news known.' Lady Thorpe glanced at him again. 'And you say that your sis…that is, that Hannah is determined to find out who she is and where she came from?'

'I'm afraid so. She says she can have no life as things are now.'

'Well, in all honesty, I can see why the poor girl would feel that way. Imagine finding out after all these years that Lady Winthrop wasn't really her mother. At least not in the truest sense.' Lady Thorpe sighed, and shook her head again. 'Dear me, Robert, I think it would be best for all concerned if you just encouraged her to continue the charade. You must know what her life will be if this gets out. The *ton* can be merciless in their condemnation, and if they do not take her to heart, she will be subjected to the most hurtful gossip and recrimination.'

Robert nodded. 'I know. But it is *her* life, Lady Thorpe. I can only suggest what I think would be appropriate. But I do know that every day Hannah is forced to continue the charade, the harder for her it becomes.'

'Have you any leads at all?'

'None. That is why when you told me that Hannah reminded you of someone, I felt I had to take a chance on following it up.'

'Yes, I can see why you would. And there's no question that she does remind me of someone. I only wish I could remember who it was, now that I am fully aware of the circumstances.'

'Lady Thorpe, I am asking you with all my heart to try to remember,' Robert said. 'I know it may be nothing, but in the absence of any other leads, it is imperative that I follow up on this one.'

'Have you made any mention of this to Hannah?'

'No. I refuse to raise her hopes unnecessarily. If anything, I have been rather blunt in telling her that I believe it highly unlikely we will find any links to her past in existence.'

Lady Thorpe nodded. 'That's probably for the best. Better she be prepared for the worst than wait in hopeful anticipation of good news. Because for the life of me, I cannot imagine how you would go about discovering the truth of her origins now.'

'Unless it is through a link to this person you say she resembles,' Robert said. 'But if, as I suspect, the trail dies with no leads, I do intend to try to convince Hannah to continue with her existing identity.'

'In which case, you will tell no one else the truth?'

'I believe the less people who know, the better. The few who do know can be trusted to keep silent, but the more people *outside* our immediate circle who learn of it, the greater the risk of exposure.'

'Well, I shall certainly keep the matter to myself. I shall not even breathe a word of it to my husband,' Lady Thorpe promised as she walked Robert to the door. 'I can be mindful of what my own tongue says, but I cannot say the same for anyone else's!'

The meeting with Lady Thorpe had gone better than he'd hoped, but it had been difficult nonetheless. Robert found sharing news like this with people outside the family extremely discomforting, because he'd meant what he'd said about every additional person who knew increasing the risk.

Unfortunately, it seemed his day was not destined to improve. When he arrived back home, it was to find James Stanford waiting for him in his study. 'Afternoon, Winthrop.'

Robert stared at him in surprise. 'James, what brings you here?'

'Your absent-mindedness.'

'I beg your pardon?'

'Did you forget that we were to be at Monsieur Rochefort's an hour ago?'

'Damn and *blast*! Yes, I had, and that is most unlike me.'

'Exactly. So what's at the heart of it, my friend? A business matter or a romantic one?'

For some reason, hearing his forgetfulness broken down into such simple terms made Robert smile. 'What makes you think it is one or the other?'

'Intuition. A woman makes a man forget all things by virtue of her sweetness. A business problem makes him forget everything out of fear of ruination.'

Robert thought carefully for a moment, reluctant to disclose too much. 'If you must know, I went to see Lady Thorpe on a matter of some urgency.'

'Lady Thorpe?' Stanford's brow puckered. 'Shouldn't it have been Lord Thorpe you went to see if you were enquiring after his daughter's hand?'

'Had it been his daughter's hand I was enquiring after, I suppose it should have,' Robert said dryly. 'But as it happens, my discussions with Lady Thorpe had nothing to do with Caroline.'

'Then what urgent matters were they about?'

'Regretfully, nothing I can discuss with you at the moment, but I shall go round to Monsieur Rochefort and extend my most sincere apologies.'

'I shouldn't worry about it,' Stanford assured him. 'I took advantage of your absence to have a private lesson with him. I dare say you will see some improvement in my parries the next time we are so engaged.'

Picking up the salver upon which his valet had deposited a number of cards and invitations, Robert smiled. 'I sincerely hope so. Well, thank you for coming to remind me of my tardiness, James.'

'Actually, there was another reason for my call.'

'Oh?' Robert glanced at his friend and was astonished to see a dark sweep of colour in his cheeks. 'All right, out with it. What manner of trouble have you landed yourself in now?'

'It's nothing like that, I can assure you,' Stanford said hastily. 'But…well, there was something I wanted to speak to you about.'

'Very well. Speak.'

'It's not that easy to put into words.'

'Try.'

'Ah. Well, you see, Winthrop, it's like this.' Stanford cleared his throat. 'I've taken rather a fancy to your sister, and I'd like to have your permission to pay my addresses to her.'

Robert froze. 'I beg your pardon?'

'You needn't sound like that,' Stanford said, misinterpreting the tone. 'I've only the most honourable of intentions in mind. In fact, if it meets with your approval, I'd like to…ask if I might have your permission to speak to Hannah in private.'

'*What?*'

'Well, you did say I should marry a woman of impeccable breeding, and your sister certainly fits the bill in that regard. And she is so incredibly lovely—'

'James, you barely know her. How many times have you seen her?'

'No more than three, I admit.'

'And on the strength of three visits, you feel you know her well enough to propose marriage to her?'

'Why not? I know how I *feel* about her.'

'Really.' Robert's tone was withering. 'Not so long ago, you were telling me how you *felt* about Miss Blazel, and how you wanted to spend the rest of your life with her!'

'Yes, but you made me see the error of my ways, and you were absolutely right,' Stanford said. 'As lovely as Miss Blazel is, she would never have made me a suitable bride. But your sister, well, I cannot think of any lady whom it would please me more to gift with my name and my title.'

Robert slowly put down the silver salver and tried to marshal his thoughts. *Damn it.* A few months ago he would have been delighted to hear of his friend's change of heart. Now he was anything but. It was Caroline Thorpe he'd hoped to encourage his friend to fall in love with, not Hannah. But how was he to discourage it? What could he say that would convince Stanford to keep his distance from her without making it sound as if he had reasons of his own for keeping them apart? He certainly couldn't admit his own affections for Hannah. James still believed her to be his sister. Nor could he admit that Hannah was in love with him, for the very same reasons.

He could claim that Hannah was in love with someone else. But then it would be only natural that Stanford would want to know who the man was. And it would no doubt seem very strange if he, as her brother, was not willing to say.

Still, that route might buy him a little time, Robert thought, well aware that he was grasping at straws. At least it would give him time enough to warn Hannah of James's intentions.

'Very well, you may speak to Hannah if you wish,

but I feel I should warn you that you may already be too late.'

'Too late! Do you mean to tell me that someone has stolen a march on me?' Stanford cried in dismay.

'I'm afraid so.'

'But who? I wasn't aware your sister was seeing anyone here—oh, good Lord. Is it someone from the country?'

Silently thanking James for giving him the answer, Robert nodded. 'Hannah didn't wish to say anything, of course, what with Mama's death, but I do believe she has felt an attachment to the gentleman for some time.'

'What is the fellow's name?'

'His name?' Robert went blank for a moment. Then, from heaven knew where, the answer came. 'Philip Twickenham.' Robert held his breath, praying that Stanford wasn't familiar with Twickenham's name, or with the lady to whom he had recently become engaged. Fortunately, it seemed that he was not.

'Can't say I know the chap,' Stanford said slowly. 'But you say Miss Winthrop is enamoured of him?'

'I've heard her refer to him on more than one occasion as Philip.'

'Damn!' Stanford's face fell. 'Has he made her an offer, then?'

Robert turned away. 'I don't believe so, but that's not to say one won't be coming soon.'

Stanford was silent, clearly dismayed by what he'd learned. 'Winthrop? Have I your permission to speak to your sister alone?'

Alarmed, Robert turned back to his friend. 'You would speak to her even though you knew she had feelings for someone else?'

'Yes. Because sometimes ladies pretend affection where they feel none, and hide affections where they are concerned about showing them.'

'And you think Hannah is…afraid to show you how she really feels about you?'

Stanford blushed. 'Well, I wouldn't say that precisely, but I'd rather know for certain. And it was damned good of you to tell me, Robert.'

Not sure whether he'd made the situation better or worse, Robert simply shrugged. 'Of course. I just wanted to warn you beforehand not to get your hopes up.'

'I know. As a friend, I would do the same for you,' Stanford said as he got up to leave. 'Who knows? Perhaps I will meet with success. All I can do is try. With luck, I'll do a better job of turning your sister up sweet than this Twickenham fellow ever could!'

Believing it likely that Stanford would pay Hannah a visit in the very near future, Robert set off for his aunt's house the next morning. He knew how impetuous James could be. If he was anxious to speak his peace before his so-called 'rival' in the country did, he would likely do so at the earliest opportunity. Which meant that *he* had to warn Hannah early enough for her to prepare a reasonable excuse—and to make sure their stories were in accord.

'Robert,' Hannah said when he was shown into the music-room where she was practising. 'What a delightful surprise.'

For a moment, Robert allowed himself the simple pleasure of looking at her. She was getting close to the end of her mourning, and this morning was wearing a charming gown of sprigged muslin with a delicate fichu tucked into the bodice. Her dark hair was caught up in a casual cluster of curls, and a few wispy tendrils lay against her temple and throat. Robert thought she had never looked more beautiful.

'Forgive me interrupting you like this, my dear, but I thought it wise that I come as soon as possible.'

It must have been the tone of his voice, for she immediately rose and walked towards him. 'Why? Has something happened?'

'Not yet, but I fear something is about to. James Stanford came to see me yesterday.'

'And?'

'And it seems he is of a mind to pay his addresses to you.'

Hannah pressed her hand to her heart. 'But he must not. I cannot accept him. You know that, Robert.'

'Of course I know it, but *he* doesn't.' Robert glanced towards the open door, his senses alert for the sound of anyone approaching as he reached for her hands. 'He has no idea I love you so desperately.'

Hannah blushed. 'Nor must he learn of it. And you must stop saying these things. You know that nothing can come of it.'

'Only because *you* say it cannot. But I love you, Hannah. And I don't intend to stop telling you.'

'Please, Robert, do not put me through this again. I will not change my mind. But tell me quickly what has happened with Mr Stanford.'

He let go of her hands then, frustrated at being forced to put aside his feelings. 'I told James, when he came to see me, that you were enamoured of someone else.'

Her eyes went wide with shock. 'You didn't say—'

'Of course not! I could hardly tell him you were in

love with me when he still believes you to be my sister.'

'Then what do you tell him?'

'That you were harbouring a *tendre* for…Philip Twickenham.'

'Philip!' Hannah gasped. 'Oh, Robert, how *could* you?'

'It was the only name that came to mind.'

'But Philip is engaged!'

'Yes, but only you and I know that. And the only reason I'm telling you this now is because James will be coming to see you. I wanted to give you time to prepare yourself. I was afraid that if he caught you off guard, you wouldn't know what to say.'

'I dare say you'd also prefer that I didn't make a liar out of *you* by admitting I have no feelings for Philip,' she said ruefully.

His smile appeared briefly. 'Truly?'

'Of course not. How could you even be so foolish as to think I had?'

'Because a man is always foolish when it comes to the woman he loves. Surely I have no need to tell you that?'

'I'm not sure what I need to be told any more,' Hannah said weakly. 'This is all…so confusing. I'd convinced myself I was the most stupid of creatures for allowing myself to fall in love with you. I told myself I had to leave Gillingdon because nothing could ever come of it, and because I couldn't bear to see you fall in love with someone else. But when you told me how you felt…' She looked up at him with wonder in her eyes. 'I didn't know what to do. I couldn't believe this was really happening to me. I never thought it could be like this. Never thought I could feel something so incredibly strong and pure.'

'Nor did I, sweetness,' Robert whispered. 'Nor did I.' He drew her into his arms and pressed his lips to the softness of her hair. The stirring in his loins was familiar to him, but he hadn't expected the yearnings of his heart to be so much stronger. He wanted to love Hannah in every sense of the word. To tell her, with the most beautiful words he knew, how deeply he felt about her. Yes, he yearned to take her to his bed, but his desire to explore the magic between them went far deeper than the physical. He kissed her forehead, drowning in her sweetness, and then, tilting her face up to his, bent his mouth to hers. 'Never in my wildest dreams did I think it was possible to feel like this. To love like—'

'I say, Winthrop!' came the shocked exclamation from the doorway. 'What the *hell* do you think you're doing?'

The voice was one she knew well, yet at the moment Hannah barely recognised it. Ringing with anger and condemnation, it was a far cry from the bantering, easy-going tones of the James Stanford she'd come to know. Unfortunately, Mr Stanford wasn't the only witness to their embrace. Alice, dear Alice, was standing in the doorway, her face twisted in a mask of horror and disbelief.

Hannah's heart plummeted. 'Alice!'

She might as well have called out to the moon. Alice covered her mouth and fled, running down the hall as though the devil were on her heels. Unfortunately, Stanford did not. He stood exactly where he was, glaring at Robert as if he was some kind of fiend.

'Aren't you getting a little familiar with your sister, Lord Winthrop?' he enquired icily.

'Mr Stanford, it isn't what you think!' Hannah cried.

'Then perhaps you would be as good as to tell me what it is. Or do you and your brother make a habit of kissing in such a way when you are alone?'

'Hannah, go up to your room,' Robert said in a quiet voice. 'I'll talk to James.'

'I'm not sure I want to talk to you. Dear God, what kind of monster are you?' Stanford said in disgust. 'Talking of *love* to your sister.'

'Mr Stanford—'

'Hannah, please,' Robert said, in an even quieter voice.

'Do not worry, Miss Winthrop, I do not hold you responsible,' Stanford said gallantly. 'A woman and a sister will always be ruled by her brother.' He glanced at Robert, and his lip curled in distaste. 'There are numerous kinds of depravity in society, but I never thought to find them here.'

Robert flushed. 'That's enough, James.'

'On the contrary, it's not enough by a long shot! I'm not even sure I should leave you here with this poor woman. God only knows what you might attempt to do—'

'I said that's enough!'

Robert's voice reverberated like a crack of thunder, causing Hannah to jump, and Mr Stanford to take a step backwards. But he was far too angry to be cowed. 'Damn it, Winthrop, all these years and I never suspected anything like this. Is this why you've spent so little time in the country? Because you felt this...unhealthy attraction to your sister? And is it only your sister who suffers your perverted lusts? What about poor Miss Montgomery? Is she a target for them too?'

'How *dare* you!' Hannah cried, anger flaring at the hateful things Mr Stanford was saying. 'You, who call yourself his friend. How could you accuse him of such infamy?'

'I accuse him because I know what I saw!' Stanford shot back. 'He was *kissing* you! And not in a manner of a brother kissing his sister. I saw no chaste kiss on the hand, or an affectionate buss on the cheek. What I saw was the conduct of a man who was…dare I say it, in love!'

Robert clenched his hands into fists. 'Stanford, I suggest you take your leave now, before any further damage is done.'

'What—you think I am likely to inflict damage? God only knows the extent of damage you've already done to Miss Winthrop. Not to mention poor Miss Montgomery. What do you think she is going to make of you kissing your sister in such a manner—'

'She will make nothing of it because I am not his sister!'

'Hannah, don't!' Robert shouted.

'No. I'll not stand here and let him think such wickedness of you, Robert,' Hannah cried, unable to stand it any more. 'Lord Winthrop has done nothing wrong, Mr Stanford,' she said, turning to glare at the man. 'His conduct is not that of a brother to a sister because he is *not* my brother!'

'Damn it,' Robert muttered as he turned away. 'Now you've truly cast us into the briars.'

She might have cast them into the briars, but at least she'd set matters to rights. Or tried to. At the moment,

Hannah wasn't sure that poor Mr Stanford hadn't turned to stone.

'*Not your brother?*' He glanced in bewilderment from one to the other. 'But…what kind of a lark is this? Of course he's your brother. He's always been your brother.'

Robert sighed as he sank down on to the sofa. 'It's no lark, James. Hannah isn't telling you a lie. She isn't now, nor has she ever truly been, my sister.'

'But that's impossible. She was born into your family the same as you.'

'I'm afraid that's where you are wrong, Mr Stanford,' Hannah said, needing to be the one who told him. 'Forgive me, Robert, but I could not allow your friend to go on believing you're some kind of monster. I was not born to Lady Winthrop, Mr Stanford. And Lord Winthrop's father was not my father. It is shocking, I know. Indeed it was to me when I learned of it only a few months ago.'

'A few months ago?' Stanford's mouth dropped open. 'You mean…you didn't *know* you weren't his sister?'

'I hadn't a notion until Lord Winthrop told me a few days after the Viscountess's death.'

Stanford glanced at Robert but, seeing no change in expression, looked back at Hannah. 'My God. How? I mean, where…?'

'I was left in Lady Winthrop's carriage,' Hannah told him. 'I was only a few weeks old. Apparently, my real mother had…died and there was no one else to look after me. Whoever put me in Lady Winthrop's carriage hoped I would have a better chance at life than if I'd stayed in Scotland.'

Stanford's eyes grew wider still. 'You were born in *Scotland*?'

'So it would seem.'

'And you only just found out…you *both* just found out…that you're not really brother and sister?'

'That's right.'

'Damn.' Stanford abruptly sat down. 'Then…what I just saw between the two of you…?'

'Hannah, would you leave us for a moment?' Robert said softly. 'I think I'd like a moment alone with James, now that he's heard the worst of it.'

'Of course.' Hannah got up, and the gentlemen rose with her. 'I'm so sorry you had to find out the truth like this, Mr Stanford, but I could not allow you to go on harbouring such mistaken impressions about Lord Winthrop. It was imperative that you be made to understand the situation so that you could see he had done nothing wrong. Lord Winthrop has been a perfect gentleman to me the entire time.'

Then, with a tremulous smile in Robert's direction, Hannah left, wishing, even as she did so, that she might have been able to hear how Robert was going to extricate himself from *this* one.

CHAPTER THIRTEEN

FOR all her curiosity, Hannah did not stop to ask Robert how his conversation with Mr Stanford had gone. She was far more concerned with her cousin's well being, because Alice wouldn't talk to her. She'd shut herself in her room and steadfastly refused to come out. And nothing Hannah or Lady Montgomery had said was sufficient to persuade her to come downstairs.

'I don't understand,' Lady Montgomery said in some concern over dinner. 'I've never known Alice to miss meals before. She's always had an excellent constitution and a very healthy appetite.'

Hannah, who had done nothing more than pick at her own food, finally put down her fork. 'Perhaps it is a touch of the megrime, Aunt. You said yourself that Alice suffers terribly with them.'

'She does, but I don't think that's what it is this time.'

'It isn't,' Robert said suddenly, appearing in the doorway. 'Unfortunately, the real source of Alice's reluctance to join us is far more serious than a mere physical ailment.'

Lady Montgomery put a hand to her heart. 'Robert, my dear, whatever do you mean?'

Robert glanced at Hannah, and the expression on his face made her blanch. 'Oh, Robert, please…' she said, shaking her head.

'I have no choice,' he said bleakly. 'I did my best

to settle James down, but he left in a considerably agitated state, and I have no way of knowing what he might say or do. I can't risk my own family hearing something like this from the prattle-boxes.'

'Prattle-boxes? Robert, what on earth are you talking about?' Lady Montgomery cried. 'What are you afraid we'll hear?'

'Just a moment, my dear,' Sir Roger interrupted. 'Thank you, Belkins, that will be all.'

The butler bowed, and signalling to the footman, quietly left the room. Robert waited until the door closed behind the two before saying, 'I won't risk either of you hearing stories about Hannah from anyone outside this house, Sir Roger. But the fact is, we can't keep the truth to ourselves any longer.'

'And what truth would that be?'

'That I am not Lady Winthrop's daughter,' Hannah said quietly.

There was a moment's shocked silence. Then, laughing, Lady Montgomery said, 'Not her daughter! What nonsense, Hannah, of course you're Charlotte's daughter. Dear me, child, wherever did you get such a ridiculous notion?'

'It isn't ridiculous, Aunt,' Robert said quietly. 'Hannah isn't my sister. At least not by birth.' He glanced at Hannah and the look on his face made her want to cry. 'Hannah was abandoned in my mother's carriage when she was only a few weeks old.'

'W-what?'

'I'm sorry to have to be the one to tell you, Aunt Prudence, but the fact is, Mama deceived all of us,' Robert continued. 'She found a baby in her carriage and, heartsick over my father's death, took the child home and pretended it was her own.'

'I say, sir, if this is some kind of a joke, I suggest you desist at once!' Sir Roger said, clearly angry. 'It isn't in the least bit funny.'

'No, sir, it isn't,' Robert said, equally serious. 'But the fact is, Hannah is not my sister, and Mama knew that all along.'

'You mean...Charlotte *lied* to us?' Lady Montgomery went as white as a sheet. 'My own sister *lied* to me about such a thing?'

'Yes, Aunt, I'm afraid she did.'

'But how could she do such a thing? How could she deceive us in such a way?' Lady Montgomery looked at Hannah as though she'd never seen her before. 'Were you aware of this deception, Miss?'

Miss? Hannah went white. 'I...I—'

'Of course she didn't know,' Robert said, biting off the words. 'Hannah learned the truth only a day after I did. Mama gave her no indication at *any* time during her life that she was not exactly who she'd been brought up to be. If you're going to be angry with anyone, it's Mama you should—'

'How *dare* you!' Lady Montgomery interrupted. 'How dare you even *think* to point the finger of blame at my sister! She would never do something so outrageous! And she would *never* lie to me.'

'I'm sorry, Aunt Prudence, but that is exactly what she did. Until a few months ago, Mama and Lady MacInnes were the only ones who knew the truth.'

'*Margaret* knew?' Lady Montgomery blinked in dismay. 'Margaret knew and didn't tell me?'

'No, because Mama asked her not to. The only reason she told me was because she felt I had a right to know,' Robert said in the same calm voice. 'That's why I'm telling you now.'

'And I suppose you expect me to believe this...ridiculous pack of lies?'

'You may believe it or not, but it *is* the truth. As to Hannah's true identity, I have told her I will do all I can to help find out who her real parents were.'

A long painful silence followed, during which Lady Montgomery held her handkerchief to her mouth and looked anywhere but at Hannah. Sir Roger slowly got to his feet. 'Am I also to understand that your telling us the truth now has something to do with Mr Stanford being made aware of the information this afternoon?'

'Yes. Unfortunately, James came upon Hannah and myself as I was...kissing her.'

'*Kissing* her!' Lady Montgomery cried out in shock. 'You were *kissing your sister*?'

'She is *not* my sister!'

'Oh, I cannot bear it!' And with that hysterical exclamation, Lady Montgomery abruptly departed.

An uncomfortable silence descended on the room once more.

'Well, this is a fine bloody mess,' Sir Roger muttered. He locked his hands behind his back and began to pace, finally coming to an abrupt halt in front of Robert. 'Do you swear to me, sir, that what you have just told me is the truth in so far as you are privileged to know it?'

'I swear, sir, that I have repeated the story faithfully as Lady MacInnes recounted it to me,' Robert said. 'And as much as I might wish to, I have no reason to doubt that anything she has told me is false.'

Feeling it incumbent upon her to add something to the conversation, Hannah said, 'Sir Roger, if it helps at all, Lady Winthrop did tell me that there was...something she wished to discuss with me the very night she died. She said it was something she should have told me a long time ago and that it was extremely important. But she did not tell me that night, and…well…'

'Yes, yes, I understand.' Sir Roger gruffly cleared his throat. 'I imagine this has come as quite a shock to you, young lady.'

Young lady? Was he not even willing to address her by her name now?

Hannah purposely averted her gaze, seeing all too clearly what her situation had become. 'Yes, it has. But I fear there is one more thing you should know, Sir Roger. Your daughter was standing beside Mr Stanford when he happened upon Lord Winthrop and myself in the music-room. Miss Montgomery saw Lord Winthrop…kiss me. That's when she ran away and locked herself in her room.'

'Alice saw the two of you embracing!' Sir Roger's face reddened in a most alarming fashion. 'Bloody hell, no wonder she's staying in her room. I've never heard the like. A daughter who isn't a daughter, a brother kissing his sister—'

'She is not my sister,' Robert repeated calmly.

'But everyone *thinks* she is, sir! And that's what makes this all so damned awkward!' Sir Roger's bushy white eyebrows rose in suspicion. 'By the way, why were you kissing her? I say, what exactly is going on here?'

'There is nothing going on,' Hannah spoke up quickly. 'Lord Winthrop was merely trying to…comfort me.'

'*Comfort* you! Damned if I've ever heard it called *that* before.'

Robert's gaze turned stony. 'There's no need for that—'

'No, please, Lord Winthrop, it's all right.' Hannah's face was burning as she got shakily to her feet. 'But, if you will excuse me, I think I shall return to my room.'

Hannah picked up her skirts and left, wanting nothing more than the privacy of her room. She heard Robert call out her name, but she didn't stop to answer or to look around. She had no wish to see the look of pity on his face. She wanted to be alone with her shame.

The unpleasant scene in the drawing-room had just given Hannah her first taste of what her new life would be like once people learned the truth, and it was worse than she could have anticipated. She had not expected to feel so utterly humiliated. Mr Stanford believing that she and Robert were indulging in some kind of incestuous affair, Alice likely believing the same, and Sir Roger and his wife making it sound as though *she* was the guilty party. If it hadn't been so heartbreaking, Hannah might have laughed.

Certainly, it would have made excellent fodder for a tragedy!

Robert didn't come to see her before he left the house, and in a way, Hannah was glad. She didn't want to see the expression on his face, or to hear what further speculations Sir Roger had made after she'd left the room. She'd never thought that her own family could have been so cruel. Of course, they didn't think of her as family any more. Discovering that she had been abandoned as a baby in Lady Winthrop's carriage had changed everything. And whether she was to blame for it or not, she would be the one made to carry the burden of shame.

No, there was no question she would have to leave the house as soon as possible. And she would, Hannah decided, as soon as she could make arrangements to go elsewhere. Her presence here was clearly unwelcome, and staying on would only add to the strain everyone was already feeling. But where would she go?

The knock on the bedroom door made her jump. Heart beating, she got to her feet. 'Come in?' To her astonishment, it was Alice. '*Alice!* I mean, Miss Montgomery. What are you doing here?'

The girl held on to the doorknob as though for dear life. Her voice, when she spoke, was barely audible. 'Robert…told me about you, but…I didn't know whether or not to believe him. Is it true?'

Hannah swallowed hard. 'What did he say?'

'That you…weren't really Aunt Charlotte's daughter. And that you aren't really…his sister.'

'Yes, I'm afraid it is true.'

'But how could such a thing happen?' Alice finally took her hand from the door and advanced a few steps into the room. 'Why would anyone leave you in a stranger's carriage?'

Hannah glanced at Alice in amazement, surprised that she would be concerned by that aspect of her past, rather than with the one her parents had seemed so troubled by. 'I wish I knew. Perhaps because…my real mother died, and whoever she left me with couldn't take care of me.'

Alice frowned. 'But that's no excuse. There must have been someone who would have been able to look after you.'

'I wish there had been.' Hannah sank back down on to the bed. 'Then none of this would have happened.'

Alice took another step closer, and to Hannah's surprise, sat down on the bed beside her. 'I'm so sorry, Hannah. Really, I am.'

Hannah looked over at her, and suddenly felt the tears began to flow. She cried for the mother she'd never known, and for the one she had known but hadn't had a right to love. She cried for everything she'd grown up believing in, knowing that it had formed the basis upon which she'd modelled her life, only now to be revealed as a lie.

She cried because for the first time in her life, she didn't know what else to do.

Robert walked home in a towering fury. *Damn it! Everything was going so bloody wrong!* First he and Hannah had had the great misfortune to be caught embracing in the music-room, not only by his best friend but by his impressionable young cousin, then he'd had to tell James the truth about Hannah, before having to do it all over again to his aunt and uncle—with Hannah sitting right there.

Was it possible to think of anything more distasteful?

But he hadn't had any choice. James had to be told the truth, and Robert knew he couldn't have risked Sir Roger and Lady Montgomery hearing the news from someone else. But he had expected them to take the news calmly and rationally, as Lady Thorpe had.

Unfortunately, they had done anything but. To his astonishment, they had gone completely the other way, becoming angry and defensive. His aunt had turned cold, accusatory eyes towards Hannah—as though she herself was to blame for the predicament—while Sir Roger had gone so far as to address her as 'young lady'.

Young lady! Was it any wonder Hannah had fled the room in despair?

Then, to make matters worse, Robert had felt obliged to go and see Alice, who had clearly been overset by what she'd seen in the music-room, and to try to explain the situation to her in a way that would enable her to understand. He'd sat down beside her and, using the same rational tone he'd adopted with Lady Thorpe, he had relayed most of what he'd come to learn about Hannah's sad circumstances. He hadn't bothered telling her that Stanford had come to the house to propose to Hannah because he hadn't seen any point in hurting the girl any further. Besides, he had a sneaking suspicion she already knew.

Alice had been very quiet during the narration, and when at length Robert realised she wasn't going to burst into hysterics, or cast herself upon the floor, he'd left. Poor girl. She'd had to deal with two crushing disappointments that afternoon. The fact that Hannah was not truly her cousin—the second, that Mr Stanford's affections were definitely engaged elsewhere.

Or at least, they had been, Robert reminded himself. He very much doubted there would be any communication between Hannah and James now. The man might have been able to come to terms with the fact that she was not the natural born daughter of a viscount, but there was nothing he could say in light of the fact that Hannah was in love with his best friend— and he with her.

Robert had thought it only fair to tell James exactly

how he felt about Hannah. And he'd known from the look on Stanford's face exactly what he'd been thinking. Robert had warned him not to get involved with a woman whose background he knew nothing about—and now that was precisely what he'd done.

Robert sighed. It would have served him right if James had run back to Miss Blazel's arms and proposed that very night!

Still, what James did or didn't do really didn't matter now. It certainly wasn't what was uppermost in Robert's mind as he climbed the steps to his townhouse and went inside. He gave his beaver and gloves to his manservant and, waving aside dinner, headed to his study for a brandy. He doubted he was suffering as much as Hannah, but it gave him some comfort to know that she was not alone in her misery.

Robert had just taken the lid from the crystal decanter when his butler entered. 'I beg your pardon, my lord, but this came for you earlier. I was instructed to put it into your hands immediately upon your arrival.'

Robert glanced briefly at the letter, and nodded. 'Thank you. You may leave it on the desk.'

'Can I get you anything else, my lord?'

'Hmm? Oh, no, thank you, that will be all.'

The butler bowed and left, and Robert poured a generous measure of brandy into a glass. Taking a deep mouthful, he closed his eyes, letting the golden liquid burn a fiery path down his throat. He only hoped the numbing effect would soon follow.

Damn. What was he to do now? Where did he go from here? Hannah would certainly start looking for somewhere else to live. He'd seen the look on her face tonight when Sir Roger and Lady Montgomery had heard the truth. He'd known she wouldn't stay in their house a moment longer than she had to. But where could she go? Certainly not here. Society might not yet be aware of the true nature of their relationship, but Robert wasn't about to risk damaging what was left of Hannah's reputation with the handful of people who *did* know by inviting her to stay with him.

So what other options did they have? He supposed he could arrange for her to stay at a hotel, but he would have to be careful how he went about it. Why, people would ask, was the Honourable Miss Winthrop no longer staying at the home of her aunt and uncle, or even with her brother? Had the lady fallen out of favour with her family?

Damn.

Robert downed his brandy and poured himself another. As he did, his eye fell upon the letter on the desk. He picked it up and, breaking the seal, unfolded it. It looked to have been written by a man but the spidery signature was that of a woman. One Mary MacKinnon who lived at—

Robert felt ghostly fingers run up his spine. *Culstock Cottage, Bonnyrigg.*

The town in Scotland where Hannah had been abandoned.

Hannah was unable to get any sleep that night, but in the grey hours before dawn she reached a decision as to what she would do.

She would go back to Gillingdon Park. She was quite sure Robert wouldn't object to her staying there, at least until she found somewhere else to live. Perhaps he would even allow her to stay on until she found suitable employment. But she would not stay

here another day. Sir Roger and Lady Montgomery
had made their feelings quite clear.

She was no longer welcome.

Perhaps the only good thing to come out of this
wretched affair was Alice's startling reaction to the
news. Rather than being horrified, she had become an
ally, staying with Hannah throughout her tears, saying
nothing, only holding her hand and refusing to leave
her even when Hannah had begged her to go.

Afterwards, when the initial burst of tears and frustration had been spent, the two had sat quietly on the
bed and talked. Hannah had been astonished by the
sudden change in the girl. It was as though Alice had
grown up right in front of her eyes.

Still, Alice's sympathy did nothing to alter the
course of Hannah's plans. She would leave London as
soon as she could. Today, in fact. She would pack her
things and arrange for conveyance back to Gillingdon
Park. She doubted Sir Roger or Lady Montgomery
would try to dissuade her. She was quite sure neither
of them would ever wish to see her again.

So it was with considerable surprise that Hannah
found herself summoned to Sir Roger's study shortly
before half past ten that morning.

Drawing on every ounce of courage she possessed,
Hannah went downstairs. She wore again her pale
lavender silk and held her head high as she walked
into Sir Roger's study.

He was standing alone in front of the tall French
windows. When he turned, Hannah saw the emotion
on his face. His expression was not cold, but it was
reserved, as though he himself had no idea how to
handle this most unusual situation. But with that look,
the hopes Hannah had so briefly held of a hand of

friendship being extended to her, disappeared like seeds scattered on the wind.

'Good morning, Sir Roger,' she said quietly.

'Hannah.'

She curtsied out of respect, noting that he was, at least, willing to address her by name this morning.

'Well, that was quite a story your…er, Lord Winthrop told us last night,' Sir Roger said, clearly uncomfortable with the situation. 'Shocked us both, I don't mind telling you.'

'Yes, I'm sure it did,' Hannah murmured. 'It came as rather a surprise to me when I learned of it a few months ago.'

He glanced at her, as if to see defiance or disrespect on her face. When he saw only a grim acceptance of the facts, he bent his head and sighed. 'Yes, I dare say it did. Wasn't even sure whether to believe it or not until I realised Robert would have no reason to lie to us.'

'Sir Roger, I know this is extremely awkward for you, but I want you to know that I plan on returning to Gillingdon Park this very day,' Hannah said quickly. 'Under the circumstances, I think it best that I remove myself from your house as quickly as possible. I have no wish to cause anyone any further embarrassment or pain.'

She could tell that Sir Roger was surprised. Perhaps he hadn't expected her to be so accommodating. Perhaps the fact that she was accounted for the look of grudging admiration which suddenly softened his features. 'I think that's probably for the best, my dear. I wouldn't ask you to leave on my own account, but my wife is…well, she's quite beside herself over it all. Her sister not telling her the truth, discovering that you aren't really—who we thought you were. She just needs some time to come to terms with it.'

'Of course. I can hardly blame her for feeling that way. As I said, it's come as a great shock to everyone.'

Sir Roger looked at her for a long time. Then, he gruffly cleared his throat. 'Well, since you've already made up your mind to leave, I won't try to change it. But I did want to say that if you needed any help...'

Hannah looked at him quizzically. 'Help, Sir Roger?'

'Well, I don't know how you're set for money, but if you need a little something to get you by...you know, to carry you over until you're settled again, I'm sure I could see my way clear to advancing you some funds.'

The offer was so unexpected that Hannah didn't know what to say. 'Sir Roger, I am...truly honoured that you would make such a gesture. But pray do not trouble yourself. Lady Winthrop did provide me with an allowance, and, while it was not large, it will be enough to tide me over until I am able to find employment.'

'You intend to seek a position?'

'I do not see that I have any choice.'

'But what will you do?'

Hannah lifted her shoulders. 'I have skills which could be useful in the education of young ladies. I thought perhaps to look for a position as a governess or a teacher.'

Sir Roger considered her answer for a moment. 'You probably wouldn't have any trouble finding such a post in London. Perhaps I could make some enquiries on your behalf.'

Surprised by his offer, Hannah nevertheless shook

her head. 'Thank you, Sir Roger, but I do not think that would be wise. When news of this leaks out, I doubt there will be anyone willing to employ me. Perhaps in the country I will manage to find employment in the home of a local squire, or at a small school.'

'Your life will be very different from what it has been.'

The enormity of the remark made Hannah smile. 'Yes, but I shall endeavour to do my best.' She hesitated then, wondering how best to say what she had to without giving offence in any way. 'Sir Roger, I wonder if I could ask you to express my most sincere appreciation to Lady Montgomery for the hospitality she has shown me. I would tell her myself, but I think after last night it would be easier if you were to say goodbye for me.'

'Of course. My wife will come to terms with the news eventually, Hannah, but not, I suspect, in the next few hours.' Sir Roger walked back to his desk, opened the top drawer and pulled out a slip of paper. 'I know you said you're all right for funds, but if you ever find yourself in need, use this.' He walked over and handed it to her. 'Any bank will honour it.'

Hannah looked down at the slip of paper and gasped. 'I can't possibly take this. I could never repay you!'

'I'm not asking to be repaid. Do not think for one moment that I am insensitive to the grief this has caused you,' Sir Roger said slowly. 'Whatever anyone else may say, *you* are the one who must now suffer for the choices my sister-in-law made twenty years ago. I only want you to know that I will help you in any way I can. But I trust you will keep this between ourselves.'

Hannah knew what he was saying. Lady Montgomery obviously didn't know of her husband's generous offer of assistance, nor was she ever likely to. This was Sir Roger's idea and his alone.

'Thank you, Sir Roger. I shall never forget your kindness, but I shall use this only if I must.'

'As you will. Now, since it is your plan to return to Gillingdon Park, I shall make available the carriage to take you there.'

'Oh, no! I would not dream of imposing. You have already been more than kind—'

'Nevertheless, you shall have the carriage. I will not see you leave here in any less state than you arrived.' Sir Roger paused then and took a deep breath. 'I don't know what the future holds for you, Hannah. Nor can I speak for the conduct of others when they learn of your circumstances, but as far as I am concerned, no one need learn of it from me.'

Touched beyond words, Hannah reached up and pressed a gentle kiss to his cheek. 'Thank you, Sir Roger. I shall always think of you with kindness, and take great pleasure in knowing that whatever news gets out, it was not put about by you.'

'Be well, Hannah,' Sir Roger said gently.

Hannah smiled, and knowing that the interview was at an end, tucked the bank draft into her pocket and left Sir Roger for the last time.

CHAPTER FOURTEEN

HANNAH was in her room putting the final touches to her packing when Robert arrived and summoned her to join him. Leaving her maid to continue, Hannah hastily went downstairs. She found him in the drawing-room, staring into the blackness of the empty hearth. 'Robert?'

He turned at once, and the look on his face made her want to forget propriety altogether. Indeed, as he took a step towards her, it was all she could do not to fling herself into his arms, and to take the comfort he so willingly offered. But knowing it would do neither of them any good, she sat down in a chair instead.

'Are you all right?' he asked.

'I am…as well as can be expected, but it has been a very quiet morning. Lady Montgomery is still abed, as is Alice.'

'I spoke to Alice last night, you know.'

'Yes. She came to see me after you left. I was astonished at how well she took the news. She seemed to grow up even as I watched.'

Robert's mouth twisted. 'Sometimes shock can do that to a person.'

Hannah paused for a moment, carefully formulating her next words, knowing how important they would be. 'Robert, I have been giving a great deal of thought as to what I should do, and I can see only one alternative. If it's all right with you, I should very much like to return to Gillingdon Park. I know it is your home, and that I have no right to ask...'

'You may ask anything you wish of me, Hannah, surely you know that,' Robert said gently. 'And of course you may go back to Gillingdon Park. In fact, I want you to stay there until I return from Scotland.'

'From Scotland?' Hannah gasped. 'Have you learned something?'

'Nothing conclusive, but I'm going to follow up on some information I received last evening.'

'Oh, Robert, take me with you! Please!'

'I wish I could, dearest, but I'll not expose you to any more hurt or embarrassment. It could be nothing more than a wild goose chase, and until I know for sure, I refuse to raise your hopes needlessly.'

'But I have nothing *but* hope to sustain me now,' she said. 'Surely you see that? Why should I not cling to any hope you can give me, however small?'

'Because when you cling to something so flimsy, the fall, when it comes, is that much harder to survive.' He crossed to where she sat and took her hands in his. 'Go home, Hannah,' he urged. 'Wait for me at Gillingdon. Say nothing to anyone of what you have learned, and just pick up the pieces of your life. You will be out of mourning within a matter of weeks and free to resume your life. Not that I wish you to resume it without me,' he added huskily, 'for every moment I spend away from you will seem like an eternity. But it is the best thing you can do for yourself right now.'

Hannah drew a deep breath, moved by the emotion in his voice and by the sincerity in his eyes. 'Very well, Robert, I shall do as you ask. Though, like you, it will not make me happy. By the by, I spoke to Sir Roger this morning.'

'And?'

'He gave me a bank draft and told me I was to use it if ever I found myself in need. He also told me that he would not be the one to put the story about.'

Robert slowly began to smile. 'I always knew Sir Roger was an honourable man, for all his quiet ways. But you have no need of his money, Hannah. I shall provide you with anything you need.' He hesitated briefly. 'I take it there's been no word from my aunt?'

'No. But then, I hadn't expected there to be. It wasn't only the truth of my identity that disturbed her, but the fact that she had been lied to. She was hurt and embarrassed that her own sister hadn't told her the truth, and no doubt, she heartily resented having to find out the way she did.'

'She'll get over it.'

'Yes, but she will do so more quickly if I am not here to remind her of it. You know that as well as I do.'

Robert nodded. 'Yes. As always, you're right.' He reached for her hand, and turning it over, pressed an ardent kiss into her palm. 'I will come to you at Gillingdon, Hannah, and we will talk about what is to be done.'

Hannah closed her eyes, her heart thundering at the intimate touch of his mouth. When he touched her like this, it was all she could do to breathe. 'Perhaps you...will have news to give me when you return.'

'Perhaps. But you must promise that you won't be too devastated if I do not.'

'I shall try not to be devastated,' Hannah said, 'but now more than ever, I need to know who I am, Robert. I need something to hold on to.'

'You have me,' he whispered softly. 'You have only to say the word, Hannah, and we can be married.'

Her eyes widened in shock. 'You wish to…marry me?'

'Of course. I love you. Did you think I would be willing to settle for anything less?'

'I don't know. I never thought…'

'Then start thinking. I've already told you I don't intend to take no for an answer.'

'You will have to if you cannot find proof of my identity. I will not marry you as matters stand, Robert.' Hannah spoke in a quiet but resolute voice. 'You are Viscount Winthrop, which means you must marry, and marry well.'

'But I will not marry where I do not love,' he said with equal conviction. 'And I cannot love out of convenience, simply to fulfil other people's expectations of me.'

'It is your duty.'

Robert slowly shook his head. 'My duty is to you. That is the only responsibility I wish to honour, or for which I care.'

'You must forget about me. You must find a suitable young woman to marry, and start your life with—'

'Will you forget about me, Hannah?'

She stopped dead, aware of a trembling deep in the pit of her stomach. 'That is not for me to say—'

'Will you forget me, Hannah?'

Lie to him! You must! There is no other answer.

'I will love you until the day I die,' Hannah whispered, flinging discretion to the wind. 'But that makes no difference.'

'Ah, but that's where you're wrong, beloved,'

Robert said in a throaty whisper. 'Because as far as I'm concerned, it makes all the difference in the world.'

Hannah received one more visitor before setting off for Gillingdon Park. One that surprised her even more than had the summons to Sir Roger's study. James Stanford called and asked if she would be willing to give him a few moments of her time.

Shocked that he would wish to see her, Hannah nevertheless agreed and made her way to the parlour. She took no maid with her, since she intended to answer his questions with honesty and candour. She also doubted that anyone would object to her seeing a gentleman without chaperonage now. After all, she was not the eminently respectable Miss Hannah Winthrop any more.

'Good afternoon, Mr Stanford,' she said upon entering the parlour.

He looked, as ever, the dashing young gentleman, in a cutaway coat over a claret-coloured waistcoat and buff breeches. But as he rose from his chair and took a step towards her, Hannah saw that his face was a little red. 'Miss Winthrop. Thank you for agreeing to see me.'

'It is very good of you to call, sir. I would certainly not refuse to see you, though I am a little surprised you would wish to see *me*.'

A faint smile softened the corners of Stanford's mouth. 'Yes, I thought you might be. And I will not take up much of your time, but I did wish to speak to you before you left. I understand you are returning to Gillingdon this afternoon.'

Hannah inclined her head. 'Lord Winthrop has

kindly agreed to let me stay there until I am able to make alternate arrangements.'

'Have you any idea what those alternate arrangements will be?'

'Not really,' she admitted. 'My first job will be to find somewhere to live. My second will be to seek employment.'

He looked puzzled. 'If you are seeking employment, why would you not stay in London? Surely the opportunities are better here.'

'I'm sure they are, but I have a feeling that matters are going to become a little…difficult over the next few months. As such, I think I am probably better off residing in the country.'

'You mean *hiding* in the country, don't you?'

Hannah smiled, and felt the warmth of a blush rise to her cheeks. 'Yes, I suppose I do.'

'The country is no more impervious to rumour and strife than London, Miss Winthrop,' Mr Stanford said with surprising gentleness. 'The news may simply be a little slower in getting there.'

'I am well aware of that, but I am hoping that people looking to hire a governess or a schoolmistress will not be as concerned with her background as they might be with one of a young woman looking to make her way in society.'

'It really is not fair, you know,' he said suddenly. 'You are being most unfairly persecuted. What happened was not your fault.'

'It is kind of you to say so, sir. I must confess, I have felt that way more than once since finding out about all this. But I cannot change what has happened, nor can I alter the circumstances of my birth. I only regret I had to reach the age of twenty before finding out the truth of it.'

Mr Stanford watched her for a moment, and then, catching her completely off guard, dropped to the floor at her feet. 'Miss Winthrop, I am…heartily ashamed of my conduct yesterday, and of the way I spoke to you. It was cruel and unnecessarily harsh, and I beg that you will forgive me.'

'There is nothing to forgive,' Hannah assured him. 'You reacted in a way any normal person would have. Indeed, I'm sure it must have come as quite a shock to walk into a room and see Rob—Lord Winthrop and I behaving in such a manner. Especially when you thought we were related.'

'Yes, but you were absolutely right when you said I should have known better than to accuse him of such behaviour. Winthrop would *never* have conducted himself in such a manner, and I should have realised straight off that there was a logical explanation for his actions. I should have asked him for it, rather than exploding like a cannon and saying all manner of disgraceful things.'

Touched by his confession, Hannah smiled. 'You are forgiven, Mr Stanford. And I'm quite certain Lord Winthrop feels the same.'

'I only hope he does. But Miss Winthrop,' the gentleman said, again most earnestly, 'I think it is important that you know why I was coming to see you yesterday.'

Hannah flushed. 'There is really no need—'

'On the contrary, there is every need. I want you to know that I had only the most honourable of intentions in mind. And what I have learned about your past has done nothing to change the way I feel about you.'

Hannah felt a flicker of apprehension. 'Mr Stanford, I think it would be best if you said nothing—'

'Rest assured, I do not intend to embarrass you by the making of an unwelcome proposition, Miss Winthrop. But I think it only right that you know I came here yesterday to ask you to be my wife. And were it not for the fact that your affections are elsewhere engaged, and not to Mr Twickenham,' he added with a smile, 'I would ask you to marry me even now.'

Hannah gazed into his eyes, and experienced the most inexplicable feeling of sadness. Even knowing what he did of her, Mr Stanford would have been willing to offer her marriage, simply because that's what he had been going to do *before* he had learned the truth. Alice was indeed right to place her affections with such a man.

'I am more flattered than you can imagine, Mr Stanford,' Hannah said, her voice husky with emotion. 'To have earned the affection of such an admirable gentleman is more than I deserve.'

'On the contrary, you deserve all of that and more,' Mr Stanford said. 'And I admit, I might have been less inclined to accept your refusal had I not learned of Winthrop's affection for you, and of yours for him. Oh, no, please, do not be embarrassed, Miss Winthrop. Robert told me how things stood. He more or less had to when I accused him of such wicked behaviour. He also admitted that you were not involved with Mr Twickenham, as he had led me to believe.'

Not sure which admission caused her the greatest embarrassment, Hannah lowered her eyes. 'Dear me, it would seem that Lord Winthrop has indeed set the record straight.'

Mr Stanford smiled. 'He is the most honourable of

men, Miss Winthrop, and I consider myself most fortunate to be counted as one of his closest friends. For in receiving that distinction, it means he cannot be anything but honest with me.'

'And in the face of such honesty, it would be churlish of me to be less than candid in my reply. I do hold Lord Winthrop...in the very highest regard, Mr Stanford. And yes, he has made me aware of his feelings. But I have told him that nothing can come of it.'

'You mean...you haven't agreed to marry him?'

'How can I when I have no knowledge of who I am?'

Mr Stanford appeared genuinely shocked. 'But Robert doesn't care about that. Nor did I.'

'No, because you are both kind and decent men who put honour before obligation. But you and I both know it could never be. Lord Winthrop *believes* in the importance of knowing all there is to know about a lady before committing his life to her, and he is absolutely right. A gentleman in his position, and indeed in yours, cannot afford to be careless. I believe he told you that some time ago.'

Mr Stanford had the grace to look embarrassed. 'You mean when he took me to task for my supposed affection for Miss Blazel.'

'Just so. And in knowing that, how could I possibly entertain his suit, or yours, when the value of lineage and background is so important.'

'I admire your courage and resolve, Miss Winthrop, but I cannot believe such sentiments will bring you happiness.'

Hannah's smile turned wistful. 'They will not. But life does not always guarantee us happiness, sir, nor offer promises of a happy ending. I am practical by nature and accept what I must.'

'So you wouldn't have accepted me, even had you not been in love with Lord Winthrop?'

'I could no more have accepted you and subjected you to the scrutiny which would surely follow, than I could Lord Winthrop. You are a gentleman of title and wealth, Mr Stanford. It behooves you to select wisely the woman who will bear your children. But I am deeply honoured that you considered making me such an offer. And I am even more honoured to have been made aware of it today, knowing what you do of me now.'

'It is *because* of what I know that I would still have offered, Miss Winthrop,' Stanford said quietly. 'My admiration for you has only risen in light of what has happened, and of how graciously you have reacted to it.' Then, realising that he was still on his knees, he quickly rose. 'When do you leave for the country?'

'Within the hour. Sir Roger has kindly offered me the use of a carriage. I will—oh, hello, Alice. No, please, don't go.'

Alice hesitated in the doorway. She looked extremely pretty this morning in a pale blue gown tied with a deeper blue sash, and with a light blue shawl thrown over her shoulders. Her maid had dressed her hair in a different style as well, making her appear older, and more sophisticated.

'Forgive me, Mr Stanford, I did not mean to intrude,' she said softly. 'Indeed, I was not aware you had company, Hannah. I simply thought to ask if you might like to take a walk with me. I was hoping we might be able to spend some time together before you leave.'

'You are not interrupting, Alice,' Hannah assured her. 'Mr Stanford and I have been enjoying a few minutes' conversation, but he was just leaving.'

Mr Stanford bowed. 'Yes, I was.'

'As to a walk, I regret I will not be able to join you. I still have some packing to do.'

Hannah was genuinely touched by the disappointment in the girl's face, knowing that Alice, at least, was sorry to see her go.

'Perhaps I might step in and take Miss Winthrop's place,' Mr Stanford said unexpectedly. 'If that is all right with you, Miss Montgomery?'

Hannah held her breath, praying the girl wouldn't suddenly revert to childish mannerisms. But it seemed that Alice had learned her lesson well. She smiled prettily, and when she spoke, her voice contained just the right amount of diffidence. 'I should like that very much, Mr Stanford. If you're sure you can spare the time.'

'I would be delighted. In fact, my carriage is outside. Perhaps you would care to take a drive, rather than a walk.'

Alice's soft eyes glowed with pleasure. 'I shall fetch my bonnet.'

As the door closed behind her, Mr Stanford turned to Hannah with a somewhat bemused expression. 'What a charming young woman. I'm surprised I hadn't noticed *how* charming before.'

Hannah was careful to conceal her satisfaction. 'Perhaps the timing was not right, Mr Stanford. Alice is a delightful young woman, and she has shown remarkable courage and grace herself these last two days.'

'If she demonstrates half the grace you have, Miss

Winthrop, I shall think her admirable indeed,' Mr Stanford said kindly. 'For certainly, you are, without question, a diamond in every way!'

Robert also came to see Hannah safely off. But his farewell was considerably more intimate and personal than Mr Stanford's had been. In the privacy of the drawing-room, he drew her into his arms, after taking care to make sure the door was closed, and kissed her until they were both trembling.

'Oh, my darling Hannah, how am I going to survive these next few weeks without being able to hear your voice or see your smile?' he murmured against her hair.

Hannah closed her eyes, luxuriating in the comforting strength of his arms around her. 'I shall miss you too, Robert.'

'I won't give up, you know. I want to marry you, and I shan't take no for an answer.'

'But you must,' Hannah whispered. 'There can be no other response.'

'There can be, and there is, but I shall not press you for it now. But I did want to see you before we both set off on our respective journeys.'

Hannah smiled and reluctantly stepped out of his arms. Being near him made it so difficult to think or behave in a rational manner. 'When are you leaving?'

'In the morning. As it happens, the Thorpes are travelling north to spend Christmas in Cumberland. They have invited me to travel with them.'

Unbidden, an image of the beautiful Miss Thorpe came to her mind, as well as a memory of her clearly spoken desire to become the next Viscountess Winthrop. But as quickly as it came, Hannah put it aside. She really didn't feel she had any reason to be jealous. She believed Robert when he told her that he loved her. Indeed, it was more her duty to make *him* believe his affections were misplaced than it was his to persuade her he truly loved her. But if he should find that there was no future in their relationship, perhaps she would be grateful for the time he would be spending in the company of Miss Thorpe.

'I'm glad to hear it, Robert. The association of your good friends will surely make the journey more enjoyable for you.'

'Perhaps, but I am not looking for it to be enjoyable, my love. In truth, I fear their progress will hinder me, as they will surely not travel fast enough for my liking. But once I told Lady Thorpe of my plans, and she extended the invitation, there was little I could offer in the way of a gracious refusal.' He hesitated a moment, then said, 'I told Lady Thorpe about you, you know.'

Hannah paled. 'Oh, Robert, why ever would you do such a thing? Surely there was no reason for her to know.'

'I told her because she made comment to me that you bear a striking resemblance to someone she knows.'

Hannah went very still. 'Did she say who?'

'No, because she couldn't remember. But the likeness was strong enough for her to mention it to me. That's why I told her. I knew that if I didn't, my constant asking her to remember someone who was obviously little more than an acquaintance would sound very strange indeed.'

'Was she as horrified as your aunt by the news?'

Robert chuckled. 'As a matter of fact, she took it

exceptionally well. And she did say she would keep trying to remember.' He looked down at her, as if attempting to memorise her features. 'Will you be all right at Gillingdon until I return? It may be a few weeks.'

Hannah wanted to say that even a moment away from him would seem like time without end, but what was the point? She was likely going to be spending the rest of her life without him. What were a few weeks compared to that?

'I'll be fine,' she assured him. 'And I intend to keep busy looking for a new home and for suitable avenues of employment.'

'I wish you wouldn't do this, Hannah.'

'I must.'

'But why? It will only raise awkward questions. People will not understand why you are looking for work. As the daughter of Lady Winthrop, they will more likely be expecting you to return home with news of an illustrious engagement.'

'Then I fear they are destined to be disappointed.'

'They do not have to be,' Robert whispered. 'I could give up this search. Cancel my trip to Scotland, and come back to Gillingdon with you. We could tell everyone the truth, and then advise them of our engagement. We could be married by Christmas. Sooner, if you wished!'

Hannah pressed her fingers to his lips, sadly shaking her head. She had to, for she was sorely tempted to do as he suggested. To go along with him, and to let honour and responsibility fall by the wayside. But she could not. She loved him too much to see him sacrifice so much for her. Because who was to say that in time,

he would not come to resent her for who she was—
or for who she was not.

'It will not do, Robert. You must understand that.'

'What I understand is that we love each other, but
that *you* refuse to acknowledge your feelings.'

'Ah, but I do acknowledge them. I simply refuse to
indulge them,' Hannah told him. 'You do not choose
to see the difficulties inherent in such a relationship. I
do.'

'And if what I discover in Scotland proves that you
are worthy to be my wife?'

Hannah briefly closed her eyes against the surge of
anticipation the thought gave her. 'Then you have only
to come back and tell me, and I shall marry you as
soon as it can be arranged. But if it does not, I want
you to make me a promise. I want you to promise that
you will not seek me out, and that you will go on with
your life.'

His eyes darkened. 'I cannot make such a promise.
It is asking too much!'

'I am only asking you to do what is right,' she whispered. 'There is no point in dragging this on, dearest.
We both have our lives to live, and if we are not meant
to spend them together, it is best we know as quickly
as possible.'

'Hannah—'

'Have I your promise, Robert?'

It was some time before he agreed, but eventually,
Robert gave her the promise she'd asked for. But as
she watched him walk away, Hannah knew that *she*
would have to be the strong one. If what he found out
in Scotland proved that she was unworthy of him, it
would be up to her to make sure that they did not see

each other again. And with that in mind, Hannah made a promise to herself.

If she had not received word from Robert by Christmas Day, she would consider the matter resolved, and she would leave Gillingdon Park for ever.

CHAPTER FIFTEEN

THE journey to Cumberland should not have taken as long as it did, but given that Lady Thorpe was not inclined to travel great distances each day, the party took its own leisurely time. They broke their journey considerably earlier than Robert might have liked and set out each morning with no particular haste. Unfortunately, as a guest travelling with them, he did not feel it was his place to complain about the pace they were setting. Nevertheless, at times he found it difficult to curb his impatience when his reasons for travelling north were so important.

Miss Caroline Thorpe clearly had no such regrets. She did not complain about the length of time the journey was taking, but seemed to take great pleasure in having Robert to herself, making use of the opportunity to further their acquaintance, and conversing with him about all manner of things. In the end, she only confirmed Robert's opinion that she was both a lively and witty companion and that she would make some man an excellent wife. But she would never be his wife. For all her wit and charm, Robert knew she would never take the place of the woman he loved.

On the fourth day of their journey, the party finally arrived at Lady Thorpe's ancestral home, and because it was the polite thing to do, Robert accepted their invitation to dine with them that evening. He took care not to retire too early, lingering over a glass of port with Lord Thorpe and then joining the ladies for some quiet conversation. But as soon as he could, he retired to his room, anxious to make his preparations for the morning. Lord Thorpe had already offered him the use of one of his best horses, and first thing in the morning he intended to set off for Culstock Cottage. Home of Mary MacKinnon, the woman who'd sent him the letter.

A woman who, with any luck, would be able to tell him all that he needed to know.

But what would he hear from this unknown woman? Who was Mary MacKinnon? Robert wondered. Would she reveal herself as Hannah's mother? Or would she simply tell him who Hannah's mother had been and explain why she hadn't been able to raise Hannah as her own? More importantly, would she be able to tell him who Hannah's father was, and if he was still living?

Robert didn't know. Nor was he sure what he would do with the information once he had it. So much depended on *what* he heard, and on how it would affect Hannah. He had no intention of losing her, but he also didn't wish to inflict any more grief on her than she had already suffered. Love wasn't about inflicting pain. It was about helping one to heal. And loving her as he did, he would do everything he could to spare her—even if it meant telling her that there was nothing more to learn.

Robert reached the village of Bonnyrigg late in the afternoon, and, not long after, Culstock Cottage. It had taken three sets of directions to find the tiny thatched-roofed dwelling, and at first glance Robert assumed it to be empty. But when he saw a thin trail of smoke rising from the chimney, he breathed a sigh of relief and quickly dismounting, tethered his horse's reins to the gate. Then he made his way to the front door, where he knocked and held his breath as he waited for a reply.

The door opened a crack to reveal a woman considerably older than he'd expected, and who, judging from the sallow complexion and sunken cheeks, was not in the best of health. And she was tiny. Even standing on the raised step, she barely reached his shoulder.

'Miss Mary MacKinnon?' Robert asked.

'Aye, MacKinnon it be, though it's nae Mary.' The woman's accent was broad, her eyes sharp as she peered up at him. 'We buried my sister two weeks ago. I'm Cora MacKinnon. Would you be the laird from London that replied to my sister's letter?'

Robert held his breath. The writer of the letter was dead? Surely he hadn't come all this way on a fool's errand? 'Yes, I am Lord Winthrop. But I'm so sorry to hear of your sister's passing, Mrs MacKinnon.'

'It's Miss. I've never been married, and I'm nae likely to be now. As to my poor sister, she's better off where she is. 'Tis not much of a life when you're confined to a bed. But Mary'd be glad to know you've come.' She opened the door and stood back to allow him entrance. 'She said the letter would bring you.'

Robert dipped his head as he walked through the doorway and into the shadowy interior of the building. Like most labourers' cottages, it was small and dark, containing only one main room in front and two in the back. The furnishings were humble, but at least the place was clean. He felt better about that. He'd been steeling himself for a hovel and an existence that matched. This at least, showed some degree of civility.

'Can I offer you tea, laird?' his tiny hostess asked.

Robert was about to say no when he noticed two good cups set out on an old sideboard, along with a few slices of crusty bread and a dish of rich, farm butter. He doubted the woman had enough to spare, but he also knew she had made the effort *because* of his visit, and that it would be rude to refuse. 'Thank you. Tea would be most welcome.'

Cora MacKinnon nodded, and then set about to prepare it. As she did, Robert took a moment to glance around the humble surroundings, trying to imagine Hannah coming from such a place. Was this where his beloved had first seen life? Had she been born in one of those back rooms, with only Cora MacKinnon and her sister Mary as witnesses to the birth?

Was it here in this tiny cottage that the plan to leave her in his mother's carriage had been devised?

'The bread's nae as good as I'd like,' Cora grumbled as she brought the tea things to the table, 'but Mary always saw to the baking. Had a way with bread, did Mary. The master was always asking her to make him her special oatcakes, the greedy old fool.'

Robert smiled. For all her appearance of ill health, there was obviously still spirit left in Cora MacKinnon. 'Your sister sent me a letter, Miss MacKinnon, saying that she had something to tell me about a baby that had been left in my mother's carriage a long time ago.'

'Aye, Mary wanted to do that before she died. She thought it was only right that you knew what she did, and why.' For a minute, Cora MacKinnon's pale blue eyes filled up with tears. 'The poor wee bairn. We would have kept her if we could, but Mary was right. We couldna take care of her. Not with both of us working up at the manor.' She looked at him then, and he could see the regret in her eyes. 'You ken that, don't ye, laird?'

Slowly, Robert nodded. 'Yes, I think I do, Miss MacKinnon.'

'Aye, I thought you would.' She sniffed suspiciously, then cleared her throat. 'But what can you tell me of her, laird? The child, I mean. Did she grow into a fine lady? Did your mother truly care for her?'

'My mother loved Hannah all the years of her life,' Robert said in a soft voice, 'and Hannah has grown into a beautiful young woman. I think you and your sister would be very proud. But tell me, how did Mary know who my mother was, or how to get in touch with me?'

Cora smiled then, and her wrinkled face took on an almost mischievous appearance. 'Aye, Mary said you'd be curious about that. But you see, Mary wasn't like me. She learned how to read and write, and she made good use of it. She found out who your mother was from one of the maids at the Thistle—'

'The Thistle? You mean, the place where my mother stayed?'

'Aye. Then she found out where she lived. But she had to ask for Mr Debenham's help when it came to finding you.'

'Mr Debenham?'

'Aye. He were a good friend of Mary's. He'd always been sweet on her, and he was very good at finding out things about people.' Miss MacKinnon winked at him. 'So it was no trouble at all to find out where you lived.'

Astonished to discover that he'd been the object of a clandestine search, Robert shook his head. Good thing the fellow hadn't been hired to do him in. 'Miss MacKinnon, what made your sister put Hannah into my mother's carriage in the first place, since I'm assuming it was her idea.'

'Och, aye, it was her idea. But she'd gone into the village late that afternoon, you see, and she'd seen the carriage standing in the yard, and a grand lady getting out. But Mary said she'd looked a kindly soul for all .her fine ways, and after she found out she was a titled lady from England she decided to take the bairn and leave her in her carriage.'

Robert's eyes narrowed. 'It was a daring plan. Did your sister not stop to consider that, rather than taking the baby home, my mother might simply have taken her back into the inn?'

'Aye, she considered that. But Mary said that if the bairn ended up back at the inn, she'd just go and bring her back here. Mary was like that, you see. She was always one for doin' what no one else would. It was her idea to let Ellen live with us, even when I told her she was crazy for doing it. After all, a gentleman's daughter canna just disappear, even if she is with child.'

Robert's hand stopped dead, the cup half-way to his lips. 'Ellen?'

'Aye. The wee bairn's mother. Ellen Chamberlain, she was. The name wouldna mean anything to you, but she was a bonnie lass, and as sweet as you'd wish to meet. But she was in love with him, you see, and when she found out she was carrying his child, well, she grew fearful of what the old laird would say.'

'The old laird?'

'Aye. Och, t'was a sad thing, poor Ellen dying like that.'

'How did she die?' Robert asked softly.

'Why, giving birth to the bairn. She was never a strong lass, and it was a hard labour she had. Mary did all she could, but it were no good. Ellen slipped away a few minutes after the child was born. Mary was so upset she threatened to take the bairn up to the big house and show it to her father then and there, but I warned her against it. I told her he'd nae thank her for giving him the knowledge of a child, when he was betrothed to another.'

Robert carefully put the cup back down in his saucer. 'Miss MacKinnon, is Hannah's father still alive?'

'Aye.'

'Would you be willing to tell me who he is?'

For the first time, a flicker of doubt crossed the old woman's face. 'I knew you'd ask. T'was the thing I feared most about your coming. All these years I've kept the secret to m'self.'

'But your sister must have planned on telling me.' Robert purposely kept his voice low and persuasive. 'Otherwise she wouldn't have written to me.'

'Aye, I suppose you're right.' Cora sighed. 'It's true. Mary must have wanted you to know. And I suppose you'll be wanting to tell Hannah who her father is.'

'Yes. Because you must understand, Miss MacKinnon, Hannah didn't know she wasn't my sister until some six months ago when my mother died.'

The woman's eyes widened in shock. 'Your mother never told her?'

Robert slowly shook his head. 'Consequently, I didn't discover that Hannah wasn't really my sister until that time either.'

'Och, it must have come as a terrible shock for you both.'

'It did. Particularly for Hannah. She'd had no idea she wasn't who my mother had always told her she was. When she found out she'd been abandoned, she kept wondering why.'

The old lady's mouth trembled a little. 'Och, the poor wee thing. She didna deserve what happened to her. And perhaps Mary was wrong to leave her in your mother's carriage. But Ellen was dead, ye see, and she said she'd risk the bairn's being returned to the inn, if leaving her in the carriage meant giving her a chance at being raised as a fine lady's daughter.'

'Miss MacKinnon, I can see how much love you and your sister had for Ellen's baby, but it would be a great gift if I could tell Hannah about the part of her life she has no knowledge of. You see, she's reluctant to move forward until she knows who she is. And right now she has no idea if her mother was a serving maid and her father a stable hand.'

'A stable hand?' To his surprise, Cora MacKinnon actually laughed. 'Nae, laird, the child's father is no stable hand. Mary would roll over in her grave if she'd thought her sweet Ellen had taken up with a servant. But the father doesn't know to this day that Ellen bore him a bairn. And after raising three of his own, I don't know that he'd acknowledge her, even if he did.'

Recognising that fear and uncertainty were keeping

the old woman from divulging the father's name, Robert carefully weighed his words. 'Miss MacKinnon, please believe me when I say that I have no intention of making trouble for Hannah's father. It would be stupid of me to pretend that things like this don't happen, because we both know that they do. But it would mean a great deal to Hannah if she could at least know the truth of her birth. She won't marry, you see, until she knows who her family is. She feels it wouldn't be fair to the gentleman who wanted to marry her. So by keeping that knowledge to yourself, you risk condemning her to a life without love. Because she is all that is honourable, and she would never knowingly deceive anyone.'

Miss MacKinnon looked at him for a long time, and Robert couldn't help but wonder how much those sharp old eyes saw. He had a feeling they were looking right down into his soul. Finally she got up and walked over to a cabinet that stood against the wall and, pulling open a drawer, took out a small book. 'Read this if ye've a mind to,' she said, handing it to him.

Robert stared down at the journal, noting the fine silk cord which held it closed. 'What is it?'

'Ellen's diary. It'll tell ye soon enough what ye want to know.'

Robert glanced at her in bewilderment. 'If I have the answer so close at hand, why won't *you* tell me?'

'Because I swore I'd never breathe his name to another living soul. I swore that to Mary as she lay dying, just as she swore it to Ellen as the poor lass drew her final breath. But I never said I wouldna give the book to the right person, if it meant helping the wee bairn in some way.'

Anxious as he was to read the journal, Robert made no move to do so. Instead, he tucked it into his pocket and reached for his cup. 'I am forever in your debt, Miss MacKinnon.'

She glanced at him, and sadly shook her head. 'I hope ye feel that way after ye've read the diary, laird. Because it surely didna help the two poor souls it was written about.'

The days approaching Christmas were difficult for Hannah. For one thing, it would be her first Christmas alone. The first one she would be spending without Lady Winthrop. And at such a festive time of year, it was hard not to remember all the wonderful Christmases they had enjoyed in the past.

Hannah thought about those times now as she decorated the mantel in the parlour with freshly cut pieces of greenery, and put new candles in the silver holders. She thought about the gatherings of friends and family that she and Lady Winthrop had enjoyed over the years. Being a widow had not stopped Lady Winthrop from entertaining. She had done so often and had earned a reputation for being a most gracious hostess, often arranging dinners for upwards of fifty or sixty people.

But it would be very quiet at Gillingdon Park this Christmas, Hannah reflected sadly. There would be no voices raised in song, no laughter filling the rooms. Children would not run up and down the corridors, and, while there would still be tasty mincemeat tarts and Mrs Broughton's Christmas pudding, there would be no lavish entertainments or joyous celebrations during which to enjoy them. Because Lady Winthrop was gone, and Robert had not come home. Both her mother and the man she loved had deserted her.

Had she truly been so bad that she deserved such a fate?

Everyone else in the village had been glad to see Hannah home, of course. Mrs Branksmuir and her daughter, now Mrs Twickenham, had come early to pay a call, and had said how pleased they were to see Hannah back at Gillingdon even if she'd missed the wedding. Mrs Branksmuir, of course, had quickly tried to determine whether or not Hannah had formed an attachment whilst in London, and had seemed pleased when Hannah had told her she had not.

Hannah couldn't help wondering why it was still of such importance, since Frances and Philip Twickenham were now safely wed.

Numerous other ladies from the surrounding houses had also taken the time to call, and most of them had extended invitations to Hannah for the various festivities taking place. Hannah had accepted some and declined others. She'd been free to accept them all now that she was out of mourning, but the deception she was engaged in still weighed heavily on her conscience. And as the days drew nearer to Christmas, with still no word from Robert, she knew there was even less chance of it being revealed as anything but a hoax. Honouring Robert's request, however, she did not tell anyone the truth, but she did spend hours with Sally talking about the past.

Not surprisingly, Sally had been deeply saddened to hear of Lady Montgomery's reaction to the news. But then, to be fair, she'd said she could understand why. After all, if a woman couldn't share a deep secret like that with her only sister, what did that say about the closeness of their relationship?

Hearing it put like that, Hannah could better understand Lady Montgomery's reaction to the news, but it still didn't make the memory of her resentment any easier to bear. She would never forget the expression on the woman's face, or the coldness in her voice when she had spoken to her after Robert had revealed the nature of what had happened all those years ago.

Still, Hannah took pleasure in remembering Sir Roger's kindness to her, and even greater pleasure in reading the letters that arrived regularly from Alice. She was particularly thrilled when one arrived telling her that Mr Stanford had asked her to marry him, and that she had accepted his proposal.

Naturally, Hannah had written back to offer her most sincere congratulations. She'd said how much she hoped this joyous occasion would help to alleviate some of Lady Montgomery's distress over the other matter, and while Alice had been mildly encouraging, she hadn't been able to say how long it might be before her mother made a full recovery.

Well, it was too much to hope that Lady Montgomery would forgive her so soon, Hannah reflected. But she was glad for all their sakes that they would have something joyful to look forward to.

Hannah had put down Alice's letter and sighed. Now if only she could start putting her *own* life back in order.

It was Sally who eventually provided Hannah with the name of a couple who were looking to engage the services of a governess. The couple had two daughters, aged eight and eleven, and were in need of a new governess given that the previous one had left to get married. Apparently, her hasty departure had left the family somewhat in the lurch, and they were now desperately seeking the services of a gently bred young woman who would be able to instruct their daughters in the areas of dancing and deportment, as well as in French, mathematics, and watercolours. They also lived in Dorset.

To Hannah, it seemed the ideal situation. Dorset was far enough away that she need have no fear of encountering anyone she knew, and since the couple were desperate to employ someone as quickly as possible, there might not be any need to go into detail about her background, other than to say that her situation had changed upon her mother's death. That would not raise any eyebrows. It was not unheard of for a woman's living conditions to change drastically upon a brother's inheritance of an estate.

With that in mind, Hannah sat down before she had time to change her mind and wrote out a letter of application. The position offered both room and wage, and would commence two days after Christmas. As Hannah folded and sealed the letter, she couldn't help but reflect that working as a governess in Dorset was a far cry from the way she had expected her life to turn out, but she would make the best of it regardless. At least being a governess was an honourable occupation. And Hannah felt sure she would be able to derive some pleasure from it, as long as her youthful charges were not horridly spoiled little girls.

From Robert, she heard nothing.

More than once, Hannah found herself lost in daydreams about him, wondering where he was and what he was doing. Had he found out anything about her mother and father? Or had the trail turned up one dead end after another, forcing him to admit that they truly had no future together? Was he back with Lord and Lady Thorpe even now, celebrating the Christmas holidays with them, and with their lovely daughter?

Certainly *that* did not make for pleasant speculation. But, once again, Hannah reminded herself that marriage to Robert had always been an impossible dream. As impossible as touching one of those bright, shining stars up there in the sky. For indeed, they were no more accessible to her than he was. But that did not stop her from remembering how wonderful his arms had felt around her.

Oh, how she wished he might kiss her again, the way he had that one time in London. She had never experienced anything like that before, and she knew in her heart that no other man would ever be able to stir such emotions in her—which was why it was wise that she leave here as soon as possible. Once she was safely employed as a governess with two young charges to keep her busy, she would be able to forget all about these lovely, whimsical dreams. But she would never forget Robert. Not if she lived to be a hundred.

Sitting for a moment on the window ledge, Hannah glanced up to the sky where thousands of stars twinkled and flashed. When one particularly bright star caught her eye, she closed her eyes and made a wish.

'Keep him safe,' she whispered to that shining light. 'Keep him safe, and make him happy, even if it means him finding his happiness without me.'

Hannah opened her eyes and breathed a sigh. Yes, that was what she wished for him. Peace, happiness, and love, even if it meant seeing him find it with another woman. For loving him as she did, how could she wish him anything else?

The twenty-fifth of December dawned clear and cold. A light dusting of snow had turned the countryside white, and transformed the grounds around Gillingdon Park into a mystical, fairy tale like place. For once, however, Hannah took no pleasure in its beauty. Christmas Day had come and there had been no word from Robert. She had to accept facts. He wasn't coming home.

Not wishing to spend the day alone, Hannah had accepted an invitation to attend a house party at the Branksmuirs'. She knew it would be difficult watching everyone else laugh and enjoy the day, but she was practical enough to know that it would be better than spending the day alone. After all, even poor company was better than none, and, given that this was her last day in Sussex, she knew it was best that she not spend it here. The letter from her future employers had arrived earlier in the week, accepting her application for the position of governess and confirming that her employment would commence two days after Christmas. Tomorrow she would set off.

There was no reason to stay any longer.

Because it was Christmas, Hannah dressed more elaborately than she might otherwise have done. Her mourning period was now at an end, and she took great pleasure in wearing colours again. Her gown of pale pink crape over pink satin, ornamented with silver

ribands and pearl beading, was one of her favourites.
Its short lacy sleeves necessitated the accompaniment
of an elegantly embroidered shawl, while pink silk
slippers and white kid gloves completed the ensemble.

Sarah had arranged Hannah's hair in a loose cluster
of ringlets, and wound an entwined band of pink and
white velvet through her hair. Her jewellery was simple. Pearl earrings and necklace, both gifts to her from
Lady Winthrop on the occasion of her sixteenth birthday.

Satisfied with her appearance, Hannah slowly made
her way downstairs. She had sent word to have the
carriage brought round, and now only awaited the arrival of Mr Mudd with her cape before setting off. But
as she stood in the great hall dressed in all her finery,
she couldn't help but compare what she was doing
now with what she would be doing at this same time
tomorrow.

How strange to think that she would be setting off
again, but with an entirely different destination in
mind. Today she went out as the Honourable Hannah
Winthrop, daughter of a viscountess and a welcome
guest in the home of any of her neighbours. Tomorrow
she would set off as plain Hannah Winthrop, a governess at a fine house in Dorset. She was starting a
new life; far from Gillingdon Park and from the wonderful memories it held. Far away from Robert, and
the sweet promise of a life as his wife…

The sound of a carriage approaching roused Hannah
from her thoughts, and with its arrival came a return
to sensibility. No, she mustn't think about that any
more. Her life as a fine lady was over. She would
make her way in the world as so many less fortunate

women had done. She would work hard and eke out what happiness she could. She would not allow herself to dwell on what was, or what might have been, for along that path lay only heartache and despair.

She glanced towards the stairs. Where was Mr Mudd with her cape?

It was the sound of carriage bells that drew her attention towards the front door, and their festive tinkling that caused her to smile. Obviously Briggs had fastened bells to the horses' harnesses in celebration of the day, and in spite of her sadness, she applauded his thoughtfulness. But moments later, when the sound of bells was joined by that of masculine laughter, Hannah's smile disappeared.

Was that Robert's voice she'd heard?

Tempted to fling open the door, she stopped when Mr Mudd made his belated entrance. 'Merry Christmas, Miss Winthrop,' he said, his face flushed as he hurried towards her.

Sure that her own colour was higher than it should have been, Hannah struggled for composure. 'Merry Christmas, Mr Mudd, but what is all the commotion? Have we company?'

'I don't know, miss. Young Ned rushed in to tell us that a very impressive coach and four was coming up the drive.'

Hardly daring to breathe, Hannah watched as the butler opened the door—and then, moments later, pressed her hands to her mouth. Robert had climbed out of the coach and was bounding up the stairs towards her.

He'd come home. Her darling Robert had come home!

'Hannah!' he cried, sweeping her into an embrace. 'Merry Christmas, my dear. Merry Christmas!'

Hannah was conscious of Mr Mudd standing by, but for once his presence was of no concern. She was conscious only of Robert, of his arms closing around her, drawing her close. 'Merry Christmas, dearest,' she whispered, her cheeks colouring under the intensity of his gaze.

Suddenly, a movement by the carriage alerted her to the fact that her brother was not alone. Another gentleman had emerged from the elegant equipage and was walking up the steps towards them. A man considerably older than Robert but whose beautifully tailored clothes left her in no doubt as to his status as a gentleman. But how unusual that Robert would bring a stranger to Gillingdon Park on Christmas Day, Hannah reflected. Stranger still, that he had not written to tell her of it.

'Robert…brother,' she said for the benefit of Mr Mudd and the other gentleman. 'How wonderful to have you home. And in time for Christmas. I had begun to despair of seeing you today.'

He drew back and smiled down at her. 'I wasn't sure of our arrival myself, hence my lack of correspondence. But as we drew nearer and I knew we should be here in time, I did not wish to waste any time by stopping.' He continued to gaze at her, the look in his eyes saying everything his words couldn't. 'You look…so beautiful.'

Hannah blushed deeply, the caress in his voice making her tremble. She had almost forgotten that it was the first time he'd seen her in anything but mourning attire.

By now, the other gentleman had made his way into the hall and Mr Mudd had taken his hat and cloak. Hannah's cheeks were glowing as she turned to look at him, hoping he had not detected the affection in Robert's greeting. She was relieved to see no hint of derision lurking in his incredibly blue eyes. 'Robert, will you do me the honour of introducing your guest?'

When Robert said nothing, she glanced at him in surprise. 'Robert?' To her amazement, he actually seemed at a loss for words.

'Forgive me, Hannah, but this is…one of the most important introductions I shall ever have the pleasure of making.' Robert glanced at the gentleman by his side, and slowly drew him forward. 'My dear, may I present the Earl of Kilkerran. My lord, this is Miss Hannah Winthrop.'

Hannah sent Robert a quick glance, wondering why he hadn't introduced her as his sister. 'I am very pleased to make your acquaintance, Lord Kilkerran.' She sank into a graceful curtsey, and then, rising, gave him her most welcoming smile. 'And may I wish you a very Merry Christmas.'

The gentleman stepped forward and bowed. 'Merry Christmas to you, Miss Winthrop. But I can assure you, the pleasure is all mine, for I see now that everything Lord Winthrop told me about you is true.'

His voice was deep, the Scottish lilt unmistakable, but something in his tone caused Hannah to glance at Robert in confusion. Both men were watching her, and there was a feeling in the air that Hannah couldn't describe. It was almost as though they were waiting.

Puzzled, Hannah looked at Lord Kilkerran again. Really looked at him.

And the moment she did, she knew.

'Oh, dear God!'

She took a step backwards, felt the room begin to spin as though a giant hand had suddenly picked it up and twirled it around. She was aware of Robert saying something to her, aware of his arm reaching out to support her, but beyond that, she could make no sense of what was going on around her. *Because she was looking at a ghost.* Or at someone she'd always *thought* of as a ghost. Until this moment, Hannah hadn't been able to give him any more substance than that. But now, standing here, she couldn't deny the evidence of her eyes.

She was face to face with the Earl of Kilkerran. A Scottish peer. A man who had haunted her dreams for the last six months.

A man who could not be mistaken for anyone but her father.

CHAPTER SIXTEEN

ROBERT suddenly appeared to have difficulty hiding his smile. 'Might I suggest we retire to the drawing-room?'

Infinitely grateful for the reassuring presence of his arm at her waist, Hannah nodded her agreement, her throat too tight to permit any kind of speech. She could only stare at the two men in astonishment, and in particular at the older man Robert had just introduced as a Scottish earl.

Was he truly just the Earl of Kilkerran? Or was he, as she suspected, so very much more?

Robert said something to Mr Mudd and then led the way to the drawing-room. Once there, he settled Hannah into a chair and then proceeded to pour them each a generous glass of brandy.

'Thank you, Lord Winthrop.' Lord Kilkerran smiled as he watched Robert hand a smaller glass to Hannah. 'I suggest you drink that down, Miss Winthrop. I've always found brandy to have a wonderfully restorative effect.'

Still at a loss for words, Hannah did as she was told. She didn't usually partake of strong spirits, but she was grateful for it now. As expected, the taste made her gasp, and the fiery heat brought tears to her eyes. But she had to admit it had a remarkably recuperative effect.

'I'm sure this has come as quite a shock,' Lord Kilkerran said gently. 'It certainly did to me when Lord Winthrop told me why he'd come.'

Hannah waited for her heart to stop pounding. When she realised it wasn't going to, she took a deep breath and did her best to talk over it. 'But…is it true? Or are my eyes deceiving me?'

'It's true,' the older man said. 'I am the Earl of Kilkerran. I am also the man who has the great honour of being your father.'

Hannah choked back a cry. He'd said it. There was no longer any need to wonder. The truth was out in the open. She had a father. And he was a member of the Scottish aristocracy.

'My lord, I hardly know…what to say,' Hannah whispered tremulously. 'I certainly didn't expect…anything like this.' She looked at Robert, not sure whether to be angry with him, or to get up and throw her arms around his neck. 'Why didn't you tell me? You must have known about this when you left here.'

'In truth, I had absolutely no idea,' he told her. 'I didn't know that Lord Kilkerran was your father until I arrived in Scotland.'

'But the information you told me you'd received…the letter…'

'The letter wasn't from Lord Kilkerran. It was from the woman who left you in Mama's carriage.'

Hannah's mouth fell open. '*What?* But how did she know…how did she find us?'

Recalled to Miss MacKinnon's interesting remark about her late sister's gentleman friend, Robert merely smiled. 'It doesn't matter how she found us, my dear, only that she did. As it turned out, however, Mary MacKinnon died a few weeks before I arrived. It was her sister who gave me the information I needed to uncover your father's identity.'

Your father. Hannah felt as though she was still awash in a sea of discovery. 'But why did you not write to tell me what you had discovered? I would gladly have come to Scotland and gone with you to meet Lord Kilkerran.'

'I know, and that is precisely why I did not write to you. Until I'd had a chance to speak to the earl myself, and to explain the situation, I had no way of knowing how your father would react. I didn't know how he would feel about revealing his identity to you, and it would have been the cruellest disappointment of all to have you travel all the way to Scotland, only to be denied an introduction to him. Lord Kilkerran,' Robert said to their guest, 'please make yourself at home. Mr Mudd will be here shortly with refreshments.'

'Oh, Robert, forgive me,' Hannah said, instantly contrite at having neglected her duties. 'I should have seen to that.'

'That's all right, my dear. Under the circumstances, I can understand your being somewhat preoccupied.'

The butler did arrive shortly with the promised tray of refreshments, and set them on the side table.

'Thank you, Mr Mudd,' Hannah said, moving to take her place beside it. 'I shall look after the gentlemen. Go and enjoy yourself with the others.'

'Thank you, Miss Hannah. But if you need anything further, you have only to ring.'

'Thank you, Mr Mudd,' Robert said. 'I'm sure we'll be able to manage.'

The elderly servant inclined his head. 'Thank you, my lord. And Merry Christmas to you all.'

Robert waited until the elderly servant had retired before telling Hannah that he and Lord Kilkerran had ridden through the night, hoping to reach Gillingdon in time for Christmas morning. They had been fortunate, and even the unexpected snowfall had not impeded their journey. Meanwhile, Hannah kept casting surreptitious glances at the Earl, hard pressed to believe that she was actually looking at her father.

'It must seem very strange, my sitting in your drawing-room like this,' the peer said as if reading her thoughts.

Hannah blushed deeply. 'Forgive me, Lord Kilkerran. I know that it is terribly rude of me to stare, but…I truly never expected to meet you. When I found out the truth, that…Lord Winthrop's father was not my father, I was horrified beyond belief. But I never truly thought, for all my assertions to the contrary, that I would one day meet the man who was.'

Hearing the wonder in her voice, Lord Kilkerran laughed. 'I am hardly any the less astonished at finding out that I have such a beautiful daughter, Miss Winthrop. When Lord Winthrop sent a note asking to see me, I had no idea it would be to tell me that I had a daughter I knew nothing about.'

Hannah glanced down at the floor. There was so much she wanted to ask him she hardly knew where to start. How did one go about asking one's father about his life?

'Ask what you will, Hannah,' Lord Kilkerran prompted quietly, again as though reading her mind. 'There is much, I suspect, you would like to know.'

'Perhaps the two of you would like to be alone for a while,' Robert said, getting up to leave.

'There is nothing I would say to Hannah that you cannot hear, Lord Winthrop,' the Earl assured him. 'In fact, given that you are likely to become my son-in-law, I think it probably best that you do hear it directly from me.'

A furious blush swept over Hannah's face. *Dear heavens, never say that Robert had told Lord Kilkerran how he felt about her?*

'Do not be embarrassed, Miss Winthrop,' the Earl said. 'Lord Winthrop's willingness to reveal his love for you made it much easier for us to say what needed to be said. The reason he'd come to see me was to set your mind at rest. Loving you as he does, he knew he risked losing you if he could not take back news of your birth. He told me that you were unwilling to compromise his future by agreeing to marry him when you knew nothing of your background.'

The admission eased Hannah's mind somewhat, but what of all the other things she needed to ask him? Some of them excruciatingly simple. 'What shall I call you?'

The eyes so much like hers twinkled with amusement. 'Father would seem to be the most appropriate, but I can understand why that might seem a little strange. My first name is Andrew. Perhaps you could begin by calling me that.'

Hannah smiled, liking the man's sense of humour. Liking *her father's* sense of humour.

'Perhaps until I get used to the idea of your *being* my father, that would be the best. Calling you Lord Kilkerran does seem rather inappropriate. I hope you will call me Hannah.'

The Earl inclined his head. 'I should be honoured to do so.'

'Does your—' Hannah swallowed hard '—your wife not accompany you?'

'My wife died four years ago,' Lord Kilkerran said.

'I live at home with my youngest daughter now. Kate is fifteen, and remarkably like you in appearance. But truly, the resemblance between you and your mother is the most striking. When I look at you, I see how Ellen must have looked at your age.'

There was something in his voice, a kind of reverence almost, that gave Hannah the courage she needed to ask him what she so desperately wanted to know. 'Tell me about…my mother.'

'Ah, my sweet Ellen.' Lord Kilkerran's face changed, his expression softening as his mind drifted back into the past. 'She was just sixteen years old when I met her, and so beautiful. Just as you are now. We met, at of all places, a local fair. She had come up from St Boswell's with her family. Her uncle had come to fish in the Tweed, and her aunt to visit her sister, who lived somewhere in the area.'

'She was not with her parents?' Hannah asked in surprise.

'Sadly, her parents had died several years earlier. Ellen went to live with her aunt and uncle immediately after, but she was not happy in their house. Her uncle was a dean, and he had hopes of Ellen making a good match with the local minister, whom she despised. I had ridden down from Edinburgh with some friends. We were a rather rowdy bunch, I'm afraid, as young men often are, but the moment I saw Ellen I knew that my wild days were over. But I had to be careful. Her uncle did not like his niece associating with the likes of me. I might have been the only son of an earl, but he did not care for the life of debauchery he felt I had been living.'

A shadow of alarm touched Hannah's face. 'And had you been leading such a life?'

'I'll not say I was an angel, but I was never as bad as he made me out to be. Still, in the end, his feelings had little bearing on the situation. Ellen fell in love with me in spite of his objections. But we were both young and foolish, and our behaviour was that of irresponsible children. Mine more than hers, no doubt, since I was older and supposedly wiser.' Lord Kilkerran's mouth twisted. 'But I wonder if any man is ever truly wise when it comes to the woman he loves.'

'Did you know she was...with child?' Hannah whispered.

Her father sighed again, and regret edged the sound. 'No. Had I known, I would never have let her go. It would have been difficult, of course. My father would not have approved of the match because of the disparity of our social positions. And her uncle would likely have fought it because I'd led Ellen into sin. But somehow I would have made it happen. Unfortunately, I completely misunderstood Ellen's feelings.'

'But...you just said she loved you.'

'Yes, but as I also said Ellen never told me that she was with child. I only saw her a few times after that fateful, though I might add blissful afternoon, and on the occasion of our last meeting she was very quiet. Distant, almost. Looking back now, I realise she must have known that she was with child and was afraid to tell me, though I had no idea at the time. With the naïveté of youth, I simply thought she regretted what had happened. I thought she no longer wished to see me. I did send her letters, addressed to her uncle's house, but they were all returned unopened. When my father chanced to read one of them, he absolutely forbade me to see Ellen again. He was appalled that I would associate with a woman so far beneath my own class. Shortly thereafter, he arranged for me to marry the eldest daughter of our closest neighbour. A lady he felt to be my social, if not emotional, equal.'

'How cruel,' Hannah cried.

'Perhaps, but in all fairness, I could not object,' Lord Kilkerran went on. 'After all, what did I care who I married? Ellen would not see me, and I had no way of knowing if she even loved me any more.'

'But did you not seek her out?' Hannah asked.

'I would have, had I known where to find her. But it was almost as though she'd vanished from the face of the earth.'

'Ellen ran away from her aunt and uncle's house and went to stay with the MacKinnon sisters,' Robert said, filling in the part of the story he'd learned from Cora. 'Apparently Mary MacKinnon had once worked for Ellen's parents, and she and Ellen had developed a close friendship, social positions notwithstanding. When Mary left to find work after the death of Mr and Mrs Chamberlain, Ellen secretly kept in touch with her. And when she discovered that she was with child, she ran away to Mary's house and begged her to let her stay there, at least until she gave birth, at which time she intended to go away and seek a position herself.'

'But surely her aunt and uncle searched for her?'

'Whether they did or not I cannot say,' Robert said. 'Suffice it to say, they never found her. For who would think to look for a gentleman's daughter in such a place?'

'Exactly,' Lord Kilkerran said in a grim voice. 'And because Ellen had become so difficult to find, and because I heard nothing more from her, I assumed, rightly or wrongly, that she did not *wish* to be found. At least, not by me.'

Hannah found herself blinking back tears. 'Then…you really did love her?'

'Oh, I loved her,' Lord Kilkerran admitted in a hushed voice. 'With all the misguided passion of youth and all of its attendant idiosyncrasies.' He sighed again, pausing for a moment to gather his thoughts. 'The lady I married was a good woman, and she loved me all the years of our life, but I cannot say that I loved her as I should. I was a faithful husband and a good father. I provided for my family well. But I was never able to give her what she deserved, for she was never able to take Ellen's place in my heart.'

'Did she know that?' Robert asked quietly.

'I suspect she did. She too, found one of my letters to Ellen. We never spoke of it, and I never gave her reason to doubt my fidelity once we were married, but I think she always knew that she was not my heart's first choice.'

'How terribly sad,' Hannah whispered. 'To live your whole life wishing you were with someone else.'

'It is sad indeed, Hannah,' Lord Kilkerran admitted. 'And it was a terrible waste. But I did what I had to do. I was my father's only heir, and not long after I married, he died and I ascended to the earldom. But with the title came responsibilities. I became a man of position, with lands and tenants to look after. I had no time to dwell on my own unhappiness when I had the lives of so many others to concern myself with.'

'Your children must bring you happiness.'

'My children *became* my happiness,' Lord Kilkerran admitted. 'My son, Sean, is to be wed in the spring, and my eldest daughter, Faith, has been married nigh on six months and is already expecting her first child. They are beautiful children, and I rejoice in their good fortune at having found mates whom they can truly love. Kate is presently in the care of a governess, but she will make her come-out next year.' He looked at Hannah and smiled. 'I'd thought myself a fortunate man to be blessed with three such fine children, Hannah. But today, having met you, I consider myself even more blessed. For in you I see my beloved Ellen. In you I see all that she was, and I rejoice that God has chosen to smile upon me again and bring us together.'

He got up then, and slowly walked towards her. 'I hope, in your heart, you can forgive the foolishness of two young people in love. For it was love as well as foolishness that resulted in your birth.' Stopping before her, he pulled something out of his coat pocket and put it into her hand. 'I sincerely regret that I was not there to watch you grow up. But I hope, on this blessed Christmas Day, that you will accept this as a token of my love, and see it as a special gift to you, my first and truly special daughter.'

Hannah looked down at the silver locket in her palm, holding her breath as he opened the clasp to reveal a tiny miniature of a woman inside. 'Oh, how lovely.'

'I had that portrait painted of Ellen shortly after we met. I've kept it with me all these years. Now, I wish you to have it.'

Hannah felt tears spring to her eyes. Here, finally, was her mother; the woman who had given her birth. She would never be any dearer to her than Lady Winthrop, but she was, by the simple fact of *being* her

mother, the person Hannah had so desperately wanted
to know.

'She's beautiful,' Hannah said, gazing at the picture.
'*This* is beautiful. But I couldn't possibly accept it. It
has far too great a sentimental value for you.'

'Your mother will always be with me, my dear,'
Lord Kilkerran said, gently closing Hannah's fingers
around the necklace. 'In my heart, and in my mind.
But you are here with me now. And even if I were to
forget how my darling Ellen looked, I have only to
look at you to see her image.'

Hannah opened her palm and looked at the locket
again. 'I regret I have nothing to give you in return.'

He smiled then, and looking up at him Hannah saw
the brightness of tears in his eyes. 'The greatest gift
you could give me is to say that you forgive me.'

Hannah saw the hope in his eyes, and when he put
out his hand, she couldn't help but put her own into
it. 'I can do nothing *but* forgive you, Papa,' she whispered. 'Nor could I help but love you, for you are, in
every sense of the word, my father.'

Robert left them then, aware of being an intruder on
a private moment. He was glad he'd been present for
Lord Kilkerran's confession, and he was deeply
moved by the man's graciousness in offering Hannah
a sincere and heartfelt apology. He was also relieved
that they had accepted one another. Because it meant,
quite simply, that Hannah had no excuse not to marry
him. She was now in effect Lady Hannah Kilkerran,
daughter of a Scottish earl. And there wasn't an argument in the world that was going to convince him
she wasn't good enough for him now!

He found her an hour later, still in the room where he'd left her talking to her father. But she was alone now, standing by the tall windows that gave view out over the snow-covered fields.

'Have you sent him away already?' Robert asked. 'I thought you might at least have offered him the hospitality of one night at Gillingdon Park.'

Hannah turned to him then, and the change in her appearance was astonishing. It was as though the doubts and worries that had plagued her over the last few months had disappeared, leaving her eyes bright and her expression clear. 'Actually, I did take the liberty of offering him a room for as long as he wished to stay. I didn't think you would mind me imposing on your generosity.'

'Well, given the extraordinary circumstances, I think I can overlook the breach of etiquette, *Lady* Hannah.'

The use of her new title caused the colour to rise prettily in Hannah's cheeks. 'Dear me, I'm not sure I'll ever get used to hearing *that*. But even more astonishing is finding out who my father is. And I have only you to thank for that, dearest Robert. I never truly believed you would find him. I never thought…I never dreamed, that one day he would walk into the room, and that we would sit down together and talk. I still have to pinch myself to believe it's really happened.'

'You have no reason to doubt it any more.' Robert strolled into the room, but rather than join her at the window, he stopped and warmed himself by the fire. 'By his own admission, Lord Kilkerran is your father, though there was never any doubt in my mind once I saw him. The resemblance between the two of you is striking. I can see now why Lady Thorpe was so taken by it.'

Abruptly reminded that Robert had travelled north with the Thorpes, Hannah said, 'Have you told Lady Thorpe of your discovery?'

'No. She was anxious for news, of course, and I was tempted to ask her if Lord Kilkerran was the man whose name she had been trying to remember, but I thought it best to wait. After all, it was only right that *you* be the first one to hear the news. But I am not surprised they knew one another. Living so close to the border, Lady Thorpe would have had occasion to see him at society functions in Edinburgh. With your permission, I shall write to her and tell her what has happened.'

'Yes, of course. As long as you do not think Lord Kilkerran will mind.'

'He will not mind at all. He is very proud to recognise you as his daughter.'

Hannah sighed. 'Do you know what the best part of all this has been?'

'What?'

'Hearing him say how much he loved my mother. I know I should feel sorry for the lady who became his wife, but I can't help but be happy knowing that he loved my mother with such passion. It makes everything so much better. So much more…forgivable.'

'And do you intend to forgive *me* for not writing to you the whole time I was away?'

'I'm not sure I should.' Hannah's eyes sparkled like polished sapphires. 'I thought you had decided to heed my advice, and to take up with the delightful Miss Thorpe.'

'Did you indeed?'

'Well, as the days went by with no word from you, what else was I to think?'

'You should have remembered what I said to you the day I left. Namely, that there could never be anyone else in my life but you.' Robert took a step closer, and his smile turned mischievous. 'However, I did find out that Miss Thorpe is a most accomplished young woman, knowledgeable in any number of subjects, some of which I have to admit I found rather surprising. She would make any man a good wife.'

'*Any* man? Hmm. Perhaps it is just as well, then, that I have accepted a position as governess to a young family in Dorset.'

Robert's joking mood vanished. 'You've done *what*?'

'Well, being that I had no intention of staying here, and that I had to secure some manner of employment in the event you discovered I was not the daughter of an earl—'

'Yes, yes, but in *Dorset*?'

'I've heard it's a very pretty place,' Hannah continued, avoiding his eye. 'The house is situated on the coast, and the two young ladies are supposedly very nice. I thought I would do quite well as their governess. After all, I have the skills required.'

'You have skills far beyond those required for employment in another man's house,' Robert growled. 'And being that you are now the Lady Hannah Kilkerran—'

'I'm not really.'

'Of course you are. The Earl told me he intends to introduce you to society as such.'

Hannah's eyes widened. 'Does that mean I shall also be required to live in Scotland?'

'Well, I suppose you might have to, at least until the wedding.'

A curious swooping sensation in the pit of her stomach caused Hannah to press her hands to it. 'Then…you have not…changed your mind?'

'I could never have a change of mind—or of heart—when it comes to you, my darling.' Robert came to her then, and taking her hand, led her away from the window. 'I love you, Hannah. I don't intend to spend the rest of my life without you. I've already wasted too many years as it is. I want us to be married as soon as possible. And you can't tell me you've any reason to object, unless it's to say that *I'm* not good enough for you.'

'*What?*'

'Well, as the Lady Hannah Kilkerran, you *are* the daughter of an earl. And one who owns, I might add, a vast estate in Scotland as well as a very nice townhouse in London. I, on the other hand, am a lowly viscount, in possession of a considerably smaller estate called Gillingdon Park. As such, I may be unworthy of *your* notice.'

'I suppose that must be taken into consideration,' Hannah said slowly, 'but since you've already secured my father's approval to the match, I don't see that I have any reason to object.'

'Then…' Robert dropped to one knee before her and took her hand in his. 'Will you marry me, Hannah? Will you agree to be my wife and become a Winthrop lady once more?'

Hannah gave him her most breathtaking smile. 'I should be honoured to be your wife, and a Winthrop lady, as you say. But I should warn you that our arrival at Mrs Branksmuir's dinner this evening as a newly engaged couple will likely raise quite a few eyebrows.'

He looked at her in surprise. 'We are going to Mrs Branksmuir's for dinner?'

'Well, I did accept her invitation, and it would be very bad manners to decline on such short notice. But then, I suppose it might be considered equally ill-mannered to arrive with uninvited guests, especially when one is my newly discovered father and the other my husband-to-be.'

'You make a good point.' Robert slowly stood up. 'Still, it is Christmas. A time when all slights are forgiven and good will is extended towards all men, even by Mrs Branksmuir.'

A smile of adoration lit up Hannah's face. 'I'm willing to take my chances if you are.'

'Oh, I most definitely am.' Robert smiled as he drew her into the circle of his arms. 'Because, as a delightful young lady once said to me, under the circumstances, it does seem the most appropriate thing to do.'

Snowbound
Sweetheart
by
Judy Christenberry

Dear Reader,

There's nothing I like better than holidays and family. What a terrific combination! But families don't come with instructions. They are an inexact science that some of us learn by trial and error. My heroine went so far as to leave home because she couldn't handle her family's teasing. Now, a year later, she wants to come home. Lindsay has grown up in the past year. She's learned she can't change her family, only her reaction to them. Sometimes she forgets that rule when she's really tested. But she works at it because families are worth the effort.

Time shared with family can sustain you and teach you about yourself. It also heightens the very meaning of holidays. So in this holiday season, may you and yours draw closer and celebrate with love.

Best wishes,

Judy Christenberry

CHAPTER ONE

LINDSAY Crawford was going home. True, it was only for the Thanksgiving holiday, but she was looking forward to presenting the new Lindsay to her family. She made the rounds of her apartment, watering her plants one last time, so that her neighbor would only have to water them once while she was gone.

She set her bags out into the hall and pulled the door behind her, locking it. Then she crossed the hall to the opposite door, knocked and waited for Kathy to answer.

Instead of her friend, though, a tall, handsome man opened the door. The biggest surprise of all, however, was his attire. Instead of Chicago chic, or city casual, as most of the men Lindsay met in the city wore, he was dressed in worn jeans, a flannel shirt and boots. Just like her brothers back home.

'Uh, is Kathy here?'

'Yeah. Just a sec.' He turned and called her neighbor's name over his shoulder. Then he opened the door wider. 'Come on in.'

Lindsay stepped inside the door just as Kathy came into the living area.

'Lindsay! You haven't left yet?'

'No, I thought I'd bring over my key. You said you wouldn't mind watering my plants. I just—'

'So your flight's still on?' Kathy interrupted.

Lindsay stared at her. 'Why wouldn't it be?'

'Well, Gil's flight was canceled,' Kathy replied.

'Oh, I haven't introduced you. This is my brother, Gil Daniels. Gil, my neighbor Lindsay Crawford.'

Lindsay nodded at the handsome man. 'I suppose I should've checked on my flight, but the bad weather's not supposed to hit until tonight, so I didn't think there'd be a problem.'

'That's what I thought, too,' the man said, his voice deep and rich. 'But the plane I'm on originated in Minneapolis. It's stuck there.'

Lindsay could sympathize, but she figured he'd just catch the next one out. 'Well, I hope you get out before the storm.' She turned to Kathy. 'Here's the key. And I just watered the plants, so probably watering them on Saturday will be enough.'

'Aren't you going to call and check on your plane?' Kathy asked. 'Maybe you and Gil were on the same flight.'

Both she and Gil spoke at once. 'I'm sure we're not.'

Then they stared at each other.

'But aren't you from Oklahoma?' Kathy asked.

'Yes, but—' Lindsay stopped and stared at the man. 'You were flying to Oklahoma?'

'Yeah, the three-thirty flight.'

'Oh, no! No, that can't—well, I'll find another flight.' She turned around to head for her apartment and the nearest phone.

'Won't do you any good,' his laconic voice informed her.

She spun around to stare at him.

Kathy answered her unspoken question. 'Gil's called every airline he could think of. They offered a flight tomorrow morning...if the storm hasn't closed the airport.'

The weather forecasters were expecting a huge snowstorm this evening, but Lindsay hadn't really been concerned. After all, they were usually alarmists. And it was early for a snowstorm, even in Chicago.

The panic filling her had no basis. Missing Thanksgiving with her family wasn't the end of the world.

Except that she was homesick.

Extremely homesick.

She instantly formed a new plan. Nothing was going to stop her from getting home. She smiled at the other two. 'Then I'll drive.'

'I already checked. There aren't any rental cars available. I guess because of the holiday,' Gil said, watching her.

Aha. She had him there. 'I have my own car. I can load up and be out of here in half an hour, long before the storm hits Chicago.' With a smile of triumph, she spun on her heel and was out in the hall when he called to her.

'Could I buy a seat in your car?'

Lindsay turned to stare at him. Her imagination immediately pictured the two of them enclosed in her tiny car, practically on top of each other. Heat pooled in her stomach. Which was ridiculous. He was Kathy's brother. The way her friend talked about him, he was a saint.

'Uh, my car is small.'

'I could spell you on the driving.'

That offer made her reconsider her decision. After all, she had at least fifteen hours of driving ahead of her. It was after one o'clock now. She'd need to drive straight through to get home by tomorrow morning.

Kathy spoke before Lindsay could, a disturbed look

on her face. 'Gil, I wish you'd stay. Brad and I would love to have you here for Thanksgiving.'

'Sorry, baby, but I promised Rafe I'd be back tonight.'

His calling his sister baby might have been thought endearing, but not to Lindsay. She'd grown up with five brothers and a father watching her every move, trying to direct every step. The phrase 'baby' always grated on her nerves.

The man turned back to Lindsay. 'I'll certainly be willing to pay all the expenses.'

She gave him a long look. He was a stranger. But she'd known Kathy a year and really liked her. And Kathy adored her brother. That should be reference enough. Her family certainly wouldn't object. They'd probably approve of her having a man to 'protect' her. How irritating!

Even so, she made her decision. 'All right, Mr. Daniels. But I'm leaving in half an hour.'

'I'm ready. Are you going dressed like that?'

She stiffened. Although she hadn't really thought about it, she probably would've changed.

Now she wouldn't do so for any amount of money.

Knee-jerk reaction, she knew. But she'd come all the way to Chicago to get away from men who thought they knew better than her.

'I don't think that's any of your business.' She didn't wait for his response. She crossed the hall, unlocked her door, entered and slammed it behind her.

'Men!' she exclaimed under her breath. She could do without them.

'Oh, dear. I hope she doesn't go without you, Gil. I think you upset her.'

'Good guess, baby,' he said with a rueful grin. 'City girls can be touchy, can't they?'

'But if she's from Oklahoma, she can't really be a city girl.'

'Oklahoma City's bigger than you think, Kathy. They've even got some decent restaurants there. You'll have to come see me in the spring.'

'Yes, of course, if Brad wants to.'

Gil pressed his lips tightly together. He'd flown up because his sister had called yesterday crying. When he'd arrived this morning, she'd assured him she was just a little blue. Everything was fine.

He didn't believe her.

'Listen, Kathy, I want you to take this.' He reached into his back pocket and pulled out his wallet. He took a plastic card from inside and gave it to her. 'Put it away, and don't mention it to Brad. If you ever need money or...want to get away...for a visit or something, you can use it.' Were his reasons tactful enough?

'Brad and I don't have secrets,' Kathy assured him, looking at the card doubtfully, her hand creeping across her stomach.

'Are you all right?' he asked, watching her.

'Yes. Lately my stomach's been a little unsettled. But I'm just not sure about—'

'Just for once, do what I ask. It won't hurt anything to have a resource Brad doesn't know about. If you don't ever use it, it won't matter. But I'll feel better. Do it for me.'

He breathed a sigh of relief when she finally took the charge card.

'Do you have a place to hide it?'

'I'll just put it in my billfold.'

'No! No, let's find another place.' He took her into her bedroom. 'How about taped to the bottom of this mirror thing,' he suggested, pointing to a mirror tray on her dresser.

'Okay.'

She got some tape and did as he requested. Then he asked to borrow a couple of pillows and several blankets. 'Just in case we run into bad weather. And maybe a jug of drinking water.'

He hoped distracting her from what she'd just done would make her forget her objections.

Half an hour later, Lindsay rapped on Kathy's door again. Because she wasn't an idiot, she'd exchanged her heels for loafers. But she carried her heels with her, in a tote bag, so she could put them on before she got out of the car when she got home.

Her suit, a fashionable teal green with gold buttons, didn't wrinkle, and though the skirt was narrow, it was short enough for her to maneuver stairs. She'd be fine in it.

The cowboy didn't know what he was talking about. Just like her brothers.

The door opened and the man in her thoughts stood there, his arms full of pillows, blankets and a thermos as well as a duffel bag. 'Ready?'

'Yes.' She'd already loaded everything she was taking into her car. Her trunk space was minimal. She wasn't even sure his duffel bag would fit.

'Aren't you taking any luggage?'

She sighed. 'I've already loaded my things.'

'I would've been glad to carry them for you.'

She wanted to go ballistic on him, letting him know that a woman could manage on her own. She didn't need a Neanderthal following her around, using his muscles on her behalf. But she realized he was just trying to be polite, even if stereotypical, and instead, she simply said, 'Not necessary.'

Kathy was just behind her brother. 'Gil, be careful, please, and call me after you've gotten home.'

'I will.' He hesitated, then said, 'Say hello to Brad for me. Sorry I couldn't stay to visit with him.'

Kathy turned a bright red. 'I—I'd rather not say you came. If I do, I'd have to tell him you came because I cried, and he'll be upset.'

Lindsay watched the interplay between brother and sister with curiosity. Kathy's words didn't please Gil, but he didn't argue with her. 'Your decision.'

'Thanks, Gil. Have a happy Thanksgiving.' Kathy hugged her brother's neck, almost dislodging everything he carried. He kissed her cheek and turned to Lindsay.

'Let's go.'

Like he was in charge.

'Bye, Kathy. Thanks for taking care of my plants.'

'I'll see you in a few days,' Kathy agreed with a smile, but the others noted the tears in her eyes.

Lindsay pressed the elevator button, hoping one would arrive quickly. Prolonged goodbyes were difficult, and Kathy seemed to be having problems with this one.

'Go on back in and get some rest, baby. We're on our way,' Gil insisted.

'No, I—'

The dinging of a bell signifying the arrival of an elevator stopped her. Lindsay waved and quickly stepped on, followed by Gil.

'Aren't you taking a coat? That jacket doesn't look heavy enough to keep you warm.'

Lindsay waited until they reached the lobby. Once she was out of the elevator, out of the confined space with the man, she turned around and faced him. 'Let's get something straight before we start. I am not your sister. Nor do I need a keeper. This is my car, my trip. You can come along, as long as you understand I'm in charge! Got it?'

Gil squared his jaw and considered walking away from this stubborn woman. He could take a hotel room and wait out the storm.

But he really wanted to get home.

Before he made up his mind, she spoke again. 'I'm sorry if that sounded rude, but I don't like someone hovering over me. If we're going to be in a car together for fifteen hours, I thought it would be better to clear the air now.'

In even tones, hiding his irritation, he said, 'Fair enough.' Then he stood there, waiting for her to lead the way.

It seemed to take a minute for her to realize he was waiting on her. Snapping her chin into the air, she turned and headed through the door that led to the parking garage.

Again he reconsidered his decision when he saw her car. A Miata. He was going to be trapped in a small car for fifteen hours with a feminist—a touchy feminist—which was like a cowboy being cornered by a bull with a hatred for humans. Unmanageable.

'The trunk is full,' she muttered. 'But I think all your things can go in the back seat.'

What back seat? There was a narrow ledge behind

the front two seats. But he wasn't about to argue. He stuffed everything where she said. Then he pulled off his denim, fleece-lined coat and laid it on top. It occurred to him again to ask where her coat was, and whether she shouldn't put it inside the car, too. But there was no way he was risking another pithy lecture.

Then he squeezed himself into the passenger seat. Damn, he was going to feel like a pretzel by the time they reached Oklahoma.

'Please fasten your seat belt,' she reminded him.

Oh, yeah, he didn't want to forget that little thing. A woman driver who had taken an instant dislike to him? No, he didn't want to take any *more* chances.

The minute they pulled out of the parking garage into city traffic, Gil knew the trip was going to take longer than expected. The roads were jammed, filled with impatient drivers using their horns to indicate their frustration.

'Crowded today,' he said, casually watching Lindsay out of the corner of his eye.

She was frowning, but as far as he could tell, she was in control. 'I've never seen it this crowded.'

'Well, with the snowstorm and the holiday, I suppose we should've expected it.'

'If it's too much for you, Mr. Daniels, you can get out now. It's only a short walk back to the apartment.' She made her statement without heat, as if it didn't matter to her either way.

'Hey, I wasn't trying to complain. I was only making a comment. An inoffensive comment.'

He watched her fingers tighten on the steering wheel before she released them. 'My apology. I guess I'm a little stressed today.'

'Understandable. A change of plans at the last minute can be hard to handle.'

She gave a hint of a smile that vanished quickly, and she concentrated on her driving.

Gil studied her. She was beautiful enough to satisfy any man. Her blond hair was swept up into some kind of twist, leaving him to wonder how long it was. Her makeup was discreet, enhancing her smooth features. Her hazel eyes were complemented by the color of her suit.

And she had killer legs.

He'd noticed them beneath the short skirt when he was following her to her car.

The rest of her seemed well-proportioned, too, though he couldn't tell much with the long, boxy jacket she wore.

Just the kind of woman he avoided.

Grimly, he pictured his ex-wife. She'd always been on the best-dressed list. Every hair had been in place. Nothing would do but the most expensive for her. Fashion was the most important thing in her life and came before everything else.

Including him. It was demoralizing to come in second to a cashmere sweater set. Ultimately, he just hadn't lived up to Amanda's expectations for a husband.

'Damn!' his companion muttered, catching him by surprise.

'What's wrong?'

They'd been edging their way along Lakeshore Drive. Now even edging had been eliminated. Long lines of traffic had come to a complete halt.

'I'd hoped we could reach Interstate 55 before it got

this bad. Surely once we get on that highway, things will move faster.'

'Interstate 55. That goes to St. Louis, doesn't it?'

'Yes. From there, we'll take Interstate 44. It goes to Oklahoma City.'

'You got a map?' he asked.

Her head snapped around. 'I know where I'm going!'

He heaved a sigh. Yep, an angry bull. 'I thought I might see if there was another way to get to 55. Lakeshore Drive is pretty famous.'

Her cheeks flushed. 'Sorry. I'm a little tense about— There's a map of Chicago in the glove compartment.'

Was she nervous about being alone with him? She wasn't fainthearted, like his sister, that was for sure. Without comment, he pulled out the map. He noted she had a map of the Midwest in there, also. She was well prepared.

After studying the map, he checked their location. 'Have we passed Madison Avenue yet?'

'Not yet. It's coming up.'

'We could exit on it. Then just about any road that crosses it will take us to 55.'

'You're sure? I've never—'

'We're not moving. Look for yourself.' He didn't point out that her doubting his word was as insulting as his telling her what to do.

She took the map from him and studied it. Then, with an apologetic smile, she said, 'You're right. Now, if the traffic will only move a little bit, we can get out of this maze.'

'Just don't be surprised if half of these drivers have the same idea,' he warned her.

'If half of them had the same idea, we'd at least be moving. I'm afraid the snowstorm will catch us before we can get out of town. Look at those clouds.'

She gestured over her shoulder and he realized she'd been watching the weather in the rearview mirror.

'Pretty ominous,' he agreed, 'but maybe it's lake effect clouds. I've heard it can increase the amount of snow. By the time it hits though, we should be out of Chicago.'

'I hope so. I think I'll try to catch the latest weather report.'

She fiddled with the radio for several minutes, finally settling on one playing music. 'I think this station gives a weather report on the hour.'

He checked his watch. They'd left at one-thirty and it was already almost two. They'd only gone a few blocks.

The weather report wasn't good. It seemed the storm predicted for that evening had strengthened even more and was picking up speed. Now its estimated time of arrival was three o'clock.

Lindsay moaned.

Gil's stomach clenched. He hadn't been with a woman in a long time, but his wife had made little moans in bed when they'd first married, when making love had been important to her.

He didn't want to be reminded.

'What's making you tense?' he said.

She turned startled eyes on him. 'I—what are you asking?'

'When I asked for a map, you said you were tense about something, but you stopped before you finished your sentence.'

'I really don't think that's any of your business,' she said stiffly.

'I guess not. But it made me curious.'

'I didn't offer to satisfy your curiosity. Just to drive you to Oklahoma.' She stared straight ahead.

'Fine.' He crossed his arms over his chest. He didn't need to listen to her problems anyway. He had some of his own.

'Where in Oklahoma do you live? Is it close to Interstate 44?'

'Yeah, pretty close, but if you get me to any major city, I can catch a flight out.'

'With the holiday traffic, that might not be true. What town do you live in?'

'You won't have heard of it. It's a little town south of Oklahoma City. Apache.'

'That explains it,' she said, a disgusted look on her face.

'Explains what?'

'You wanted to know what was making me tense? It's going home to my brothers.'

'You don't like your brothers?' he asked, even as he wondered why they were back on this subject.

'I love my brothers. But they're always bossing me around. Just like you. That's why I'm tense. And we live near Duncan, a few miles from Apache. I guess that's why you remind me of them.'

'Then we're even,' he replied, his voice tight. 'Because you remind me of my ex-wife, Amanda.'

She turned to gape at him, her eyes wide, just as the driver behind them sat down on his horn.

The traffic had begun to move.

Gil sighed. It was going to be a long ride home.

CHAPTER TWO

LINDSAY glared in her rearview mirror at the impatient driver behind her. Not that she could blame him, but she didn't like his rude reminder.

It made her think of the man sitting next to her.

She inched the car forward. 'Why did you say that?'

'Because it's the truth.'

'I didn't know you'd been married before. Kathy never mentioned it.' She reviewed their conversations about Gil. Kathy had raved about her wonderful brother, but a sister-in-law had never been mentioned.

'You and Kathy discuss me?' His question was abrupt, clipped, as if the idea of her discussing him offended him.

'No, *I* don't discuss you, but Kathy talks about you a lot.'

'Maybe the subject didn't come up because Kathy hated my ex. Especially after the divorce.' He stared out the window. 'Madison is just ahead.'

His reminder irritated her even more. 'I haven't forgotten.'

Nothing more was said until after she, along with a number of other cars, made the turn onto Madison, but their speed did pick up from a standstill to a slow crawl.

'Why do I remind you of your ex? Kathy and I get along just fine,' Lindsay said.

'You remind me of my ex because you're wearing

a dressy suit to make a fifteen hour drive in less-than-pleasant circumstances.'

Lindsay stared at him. 'Your ex-wife made a lot of long drives in suits?'

'You can go now,' he said, nodding to the road in front of them, not answering her question.

Lindsay kept her gaze on the road, determined not to be caught lagging again.

She was startled when he actually answered her question. She hadn't expected him to.

'My wife didn't make long drives. But she always insisted on being fashionably dressed no matter what the circumstances.'

Lindsay thought the man was being rather hard on his ex-wife. After all, there was nothing wrong with wanting to look one's best. But she wasn't going to argue with him about it.

'Look at the map and figure out which road it would be best to take to get to the highway,' she suggested, keeping her gaze on the traffic. 'The sooner we get on the interstate, the better off we'll be.'

'And you're willing to take my word for it?'

She ignored the temptation to glare at him. If she did, she'd get honked at again. Or barked at by her companion.

'Yes.'

He studied the map and suggested she take the next crossroad, Central Avenue. It only took a couple of minutes to reach the intersection and make the turn, but she gasped as she swung the car into the appropriate lane.

'What?' he asked sharply, staring at her.

'The snow's here,' she muttered, watching a large flake settle against the windshield.

After a moment of silence, he asked, 'Want to turn back? Have you changed your mind?'

'No! I'm going on, but you can change *your* mind, if you want.'

'Not me. I want to get home.'

'Why did you come to Chicago if you hate it here so much?' It wasn't that she didn't understand his attitude toward big cities. Her brothers all reacted the same way, even to Oklahoma City, which couldn't compare to Chicago for traffic jams and hordes of people.

Even she— But she shut that thought away. She couldn't afford to admit her annoyance of Chicago, even to herself.

'Do you know Brad, Kathy's husband?'

The non sequitur surprised her. 'Of course I do.'

'What do you think of him?'

She studied him out of the corner of her eye even as she paid attention to the traffic. 'Why?'

'It's a simple question.'

'Don't *you* know Brad?'

'Barely. I've met him a couple of times. Once at the wedding, and a couple of hours last Christmas.'

'And you don't like him.' She wasn't asking a question. The man's attitude toward his brother-in-law was evident.

'I don't know him.'

'And that's why you asked *my* opinion? A woman who reminds you of your ex?'

'Forget it.' He turned to stare out his window again.

But she couldn't. 'He seems nice enough. Devoted to Kathy.'

'Yeah?' he asked with a big frown. 'He hasn't—hit on you?'

'Me? You think he'd hit on me, living across from his wife?' She was astounded. Even if Brad had been the type to mess around, she wasn't. 'Even if he had, I would never—'

'Kathy called me yesterday. Crying.'

'And you thought—'

'I didn't know what to think. She wouldn't tell me what was wrong. I flew up this morning to see if there was anything I could do. She still wouldn't tell me. But you heard her. She didn't want to tell Brad I'd come.'

She should've known. He'd already reminded her of her brothers by his dress. Now he reminded her of her brothers with his protectiveness, his smothering of his sister.

'Look, all married couples go through some rough patches. They have to work things out themselves. You can't fix everything just because she's your little sister.' She tried to keep her voice calm, but she heard it tightening as she finished speaking.

'Thank you, Dr. Joyce Brothers.'

His sarcastic reply only irritated her more. If it had been left to her brothers, she would've sat upon a silken pillow all her days and never even learned to walk, much less fend for herself. That's why she'd been forced to leave home. She hadn't realized she and Kathy had that much in common.

Time to concentrate on her driving. This cowboy wouldn't appreciate her opinion any more than her brothers had.

'Have you ever heard them fighting?'

'No.' In fact, she'd been a little envious of Kathy. Not that she was attracted to Brad, but she was attracted to the devotion the two shared, the closeness.

Since she'd moved away from home, she'd sometimes longed for a relationship that could lead to marriage.

As long as the man understood she wouldn't be smothered.

She was glad she was concentrating on her driving when they got up on the interstate. As she increased her speed, her tires began to spin and the back end of the car skidded a little. She immediately eased up on the gas.

'Better keep your speed down,' her companion advised.

'Really? Are you sure I shouldn't go faster?'

His head snapped around to stare at her.

'I was being sarcastic,' she pointed out, as if speaking to a slow learner.

'Oh. Thanks for explaining.'

She shrugged her shoulders. Okay, so two could be sarcastic. Maybe she'd deserved that kind of answer. She turned her windshield wipers up to high speed as the snow began coming down faster. She'd be glad when the highway turned farther south. It was their only hope of outrunning the storm.

Gil didn't make any more attempts at conversation. It had been foolish to try to soothe his concerns about Kathy by asking Lindsay questions. Like he'd trust her evaluation anyway. A woman who dressed in a designer suit to drive in a snowstorm.

His ex-wife had been impressed with anyone with money. Their morals, or intelligence or even their warmth had no value compared to their bank account.

He knew Brad made a good living. But he wanted his sister to be happy, not well dressed. He wanted her husband to love her, not buy her things. Well, he wanted him to buy her things, too, but that wasn't the most important. He didn't want Kathy to wind up in the same kind of loveless marriage that he had.

As Lindsay carefully steered the car, Gil studied her hands. They looked smooth, soft, but he was surprised by her nails. While well tended, they weren't long, and the polish was clear. She only wore one ring, an opal with diamonds.

'Nice ring. A gift?'

'Yes.'

Aha. So she had some man on a string, willing to buy her expensive things. He remembered when he'd first fallen for Amanda. He'd prided himself on buying her what she wanted. Until he realized that was all she wanted. Real emotions—even love—meant nothing to her.

When Lindsay gasped again, he brought his attention back to the road. A car that had just passed by them went into a spin. It narrowly missed going over the side as it came to rest against the railing.

'You okay?' he asked, studying her to determine whether she would be able to continue driving.

'Yes,' she said with a sigh. 'Should we stop to help them?'

'There's not a lot we could do. Unless you want to call 911 for them.'

'My cell phone is in my purse. Could you call for me? I want to concentrate on my driving.'

He found the phone and called in the near accident. After hanging up, he said, 'They promised to send a cop to check on them.'

'Thank you.'

'They were going too fast,' he added.

She sent him a look that told him she got his less

than subtle message. But, in truth, she was keeping her speed down. In fact, she was doing a good job with her driving, though he hated to admit it.

He checked his watch. It was already after three. They'd been driving almost two hours and hadn't gotten out of Chicago yet.

She must've caught his movement out of the corner of her eye because she asked, 'What time is it?'

'Almost three-thirty.'

Though she frowned, she didn't say anything.

He settled more comfortably in his seat. 'If you get tired of driving, I can spell you.'

She didn't answer for a minute. Then she said, 'They don't get much snow in Oklahoma.'

So she doubted his skills? 'I lived in New York for almost ten years.'

'In New York City? I didn't think many people drove in the city.'

'We had a house in upstate New York, spent weekends there, particularly in the winter because of the skiing.' He'd enjoyed the skiing. But he hadn't enjoyed the collection of people his wife invited to join them. They'd been her friends, not his.

'I guess you don't get much skiing in Apache.'

'Nope. But I've made several trips to Colorado since I moved back.'

'What do you do for a living?'

'Ranching.'

'In New York City?' she asked, her voice rising in surprise.

'No, not in New York City. I was a stockbroker there.' And he'd been one of the best. Which had made it possible for him to come back to Oklahoma and buy his ranch, even after the divorce.

'Do you miss being a stockbroker?'

'Nope.' Which was the truth, but he didn't mention that he still bought and sold stocks, managing his personal fortune. He was also doing some investing for Rafe, his ranch manager, who had become a good friend and a mentor. Gil wanted to make it possible for Rafe to achieve his own dream.

Staring out the window, he realized the snow was getting thicker. 'Can you still see well enough to keep going? Maybe we should stop while we can still find a hotel and wait until morning.' He didn't want to do that, but he also didn't want to become a frozen Popsicle on the side of the road.

'No, I want to keep going. I have snow tires on my car.' She leaned forward to concentrate on her driving, and Gil figured she'd be sore before too long. The tension would make her ache.

He said nothing. She'd probably offer to dump him out on the closest sidewalk if he protested. And he had to admit they could still maneuver fairly well. But he wasn't sure how long that would be true.

An hour later, they were still struggling along, the snow several inches deep. He'd pulled his sheepskin-lined jacket into the front seat and draped it over himself. Lindsay, though occasionally shivering, said nothing.

He felt like a cur, sitting back and warm while she shivered and drove through the storm, but he'd offered to drive. And he'd asked her about her coat. And she'd responded to both those questions with a snarl.

So he kept quiet.

'I'm sure we'll be clear of the snow if we can just get to St. Louis,' she said suddenly.

'I won't argue with that,' he agreed, but he had his doubts about making it that far.

'Or even Springfield,' she added, sending him a hopeful look.

He stared straight ahead. Then they passed a sign showing an exit for a town named Pontiac. 'How far is Pontiac from Springfield?'

'I'm—I'm not sure.'

He opened the glove compartment and took out the larger map covering the Midwest. After a brief calculation, he looked at her. 'I believe it's over eighty miles.'

She pressed her lips tightly together and said nothing.

Neither did he, but he didn't think they'd make it eighty miles before midnight. Not when they were only going about fifteen miles an hour.

Finally, he said, 'I'm willing to pull over and find a place to stay to wait this out, whenever you're ready. You know we're not going to be able to drive straight through at this rate.'

She shook her head. 'We'll be able to go a lot faster as soon as we outrun the snowstorm.'

Stubborn woman. He couldn't argue with her statement. In fact, he totally agreed with her. The disagreement came in exactly when they'd outrun the snowstorm.

'Mind if I turn on the radio?' he asked. 'We might get some weather news.'

'No, of course not. That's a good idea.' She reached for the radio herself.

'I'll handle the radio, since you're driving.' He thought he'd put that tactfully, and her hand returned to the steering wheel, leaving it to him to find a station.

'This is a weather bulletin,' the announcer said. 'Forecasters say the storm will still intensify for the next few hours. However, the snow should taper off by morning.'

'By morning!' Lindsay exclaimed.

Gil said nothing. He didn't think urging Lindsay to give up would be effective. The hardheaded woman would probably refuse to do so because she didn't want to give in to a man's advice. He understood a woman's resistance to male domination, but not in the face of common sense.

'Lindsay, the snow's almost half a foot deep now. We're not going to be able to go much farther. Don't you want to look for shelter while we can?' he finally asked.

She said nothing, leaning farther over the steering wheel, her gaze glued to the road in front of them.

Gil sighed.

Abruptly, she put on her blinker light, taking him by surprise. 'You're stopping?' he asked.

Though her face remained grim, she nodded. 'There's a small town here, according to that sign. I guess we'd better stop while we can.'

'Good thinking,' he agreed, as if it had been her idea. He didn't care who got credit for stopping, as long as they did so.

The exit road was downhill and they skidded several times negotiating it. When they reached the bottom, they discovered another sign, pointing out that the small town they'd sought was another four miles down the road.

'Rats!' Lindsay exclaimed, frowning fiercely.

'We can make it,' Gil assured her. Four miles on

level road would be a hell of a lot better than trying to go uphill to get back on the freeway.

'We don't have much choice,' she muttered, not looking at him.

'Want me to drive?'

She glared at him. 'No.'

He drew a deep breath and leaned back, trying to give the impression of complete relaxation.

Half an hour later, they reached the city limits of Witherspoon.

'Where is it?' Lindsay demanded in frustration.

'I think I see a few buildings. Keep going.'

He was right. They discovered a filling station, obviously shut down, a Dairy Queen, no lights on, a couple of houses and finally the red fluorescent light appeared through the snow, flashing OTEL.

'I think we can assume that should say motel,' he said with a chuckle.

'I hope you're right.' She turned off the road into the parking lot.

Gil studied as much as he could see of the motel and figured they'd be lucky to get a room. The parking lot was almost full.

'There's the office,' he said, pointing to their right.

She eased the car through the crunchy snow and stopped as close to the office door as she could.

'If you'd like, I'll go see what they've got available. I've already got my coat out,' he offered, careful to couch his idea as a suggestion.

'Thank you. I'd appreciate it.'

Surprised by her acquiescence without argument, he hurriedly got out into the storm before she could change her mind.

The cold sting of the snow attacked his exposed skin as he hurried toward the door, trying not to slip.

As soon as he got inside, closing the door behind him, he shook off the snow that covered him and stepped to the counter.

No one appeared to be on duty, but there was a button to push for assistance. After he'd followed directions, he heard footsteps. Then, a door behind the counter opened and an elderly man appeared.

'Evening. Didn't hear anyone arrive. Sorry to keep you waiting,' he said, a genial smile on his face. 'We don't usually do this much business.'

Gil would guess not. So far he hadn't seen anything in Witherspoon that would attract travelers. Of course, he hadn't seen much in the snowstorm, so he could be wrong.

'You're in luck,' the man said. 'I've got one room left. You want it?'

Gil frowned. 'Only one room? We need two.'

'Sorry, young man. But one's all I got. If you don't want it, someone else will probably come along.'

Gil felt sure he was right. 'Is there another motel in town?'

'Nope. This is it.'

The sound of another vehicle on the road just barely penetrated the room above the sound of the wind. Gil didn't want to do any more driving in the storm. He hurriedly agreed to the one room, pulling out his credit card.

'We, uh, had to up the price a little, because of the storm, you know. Had to hire extra help to get all the rooms ready.' The man avoided Gil's cynical gaze.

He wasn't surprised to discover price-gouging. It

happened all the time. In fact, he figured the man had a hard time making a living wage most days.

He waited for the man to run his credit card, thinking about the reaction he was bound to receive when he announced to Lindsay Crawford that they were going to share a motel room.

The man handed over an old-fashioned key. None of those fancy plastic cards that the hotels used these days. Gil almost smiled as he pocketed the key. Just as he put his hand on the door to venture out into the storm, he looked over his shoulder. 'This room does have two beds, doesn't it?'

The man stared at him, and Gil got a sinking feeling in his stomach.

CHAPTER THREE

LINDSAY shivered as the wind swirled around the car, making visibility impossible. She was glad they'd stopped, but she wished they could continue on. She wished she had her coat out of the trunk. She wished... A blur of movement stopped her thoughts.

Suddenly the passenger door opened and Gil slid into the car, bringing with him snow and wind. She shivered again.

'Okay,' he said, not looking at her. 'We need to turn right. Room number nine.'

Without speaking, she followed his directions, forcing her car to push its way through the snow. They could barely make out the numbers on the doors of the single story structure. There was a parking space in front of number nine and she pulled her car into it.

Then it occurred to her that he'd only given her the number of one room.

'Is this your room or mine?'

Dead silence. He didn't even look at her.

'Gil? Is this—'

'Our room.'

It was her turn to be silent.

His gaze met hers. 'He only had one room left. We can't go on, and we can't stay in the car. I didn't know what to do but take the room. I promise you you're in no danger from me.'

She believed him. And she should've been grateful.

She *was* grateful, she hurriedly assured herself. But he needn't make it sound so easy.

All afternoon, closed up in her small car, his male aura had kept her aware, tense…interested, no matter how much she told herself she wasn't attracted to him.

Now she was going to share a motel room with him?

And he assured her that wouldn't be a problem.

What could she say? He was right. They couldn't go any farther. And neither of them could stay in the car. He'd done the only practical thing. After drawing a deep breath, she said, 'Thanks, I appreciate your assurance.'

He stared at her, as if her reaction differed from what he'd expected. 'You mean you're not going to insist I sleep in the car?'

'And have your death on my hands? Of course not. I can share a room with you for the night.' So he'd be sleeping a few feet away. Maybe she'd have trouble getting to sleep, but she was tired. She'd manage.

'Great. We'd better take these blankets I borrowed from Kathy. We might need them.'

Normal, practical words. So why was he avoiding her gaze? Why was she waiting for the other shoe to drop? Something wasn't right, but for the life of her, she couldn't imagine what it could be.

'Okay. Did the clerk mention anything about where we could get supper?'

'He's got a small grocery attached to the office. Not a lot of selection, but I'll go back and find something as soon as we get settled in the room. And there's a microwave we can use, too.'

'In the room?' she asked, surprised by a modern convenience like a microwave in a 1950s motel.

He grinned. 'Nope. In the office. The food will probably be cold before I can get it to the room, but hopefully it won't be frozen. There is a coffee machine in the room, though.'

'I'll start a pot at once,' she promised. 'Can you get the blankets and your bag? I need to get my bag and coat out of the trunk.'

'Sure. Need some help?'

'No, thank you.'

By the time she'd struggled through the wind and snow, retrieved her belongings and made it to the door of their room, she wished she hadn't been quite so fiercely independent. She could admit to herself, if not to her companion, that it would've been really nice to run for the door and leave the carrying to Gil's strong shoulders.

He was waiting for her and immediately closed the door behind her, shutting out the storm.

She covered her face with her hands, grateful to feel the warmth against her chilled cheeks. 'Thanks,' she muttered, leaning against the wall.

'It's brutal out there. And you didn't get your coat on.'

'It seemed easier just to gather it up and run,' she said, raising her head and smiling wearily at Gil.

Over his shoulder, she took in the room.

'I see our room is as out of date as—'

When her gaze focused on the major piece of furniture in the small room, she couldn't continue. She just stared at it instead.

Then she stared at Gil.

'You're not surprised,' she accused.

He turned to look at the double bed. As if to remind himself of what she'd discovered. 'No, I'm not. The clerk told me there was only one bed. But I was hoping for king-size.'

'What are we going to do?' Sudden visions of sharing the bed with Gil, a large man, and sexy as could be, left her mouth dry.

'We're going to get some sleep. And I promise that's all we're going to do, so don't give me any virginal protests. You're safe.'

Of course she was. The dratted man had made it more than clear he had no interest in her. But was she safe from herself?

'You could sleep on the floor,' she suggested, finding the air suddenly thin.

'So could you. I thought you were a feminist, wanting to prove you're as strong as any guy. Want to draw for the bed?'

The immediate outrage that filled her had her reconsider her reaction. He was right. She'd fought for being equal to her brothers, but when things got difficult she wanted special treatment?

'No. There's no point in either of us being uncomfortable. We'll share.' If he could control himself, she was sure she could do the same. She hoped. It wasn't as if she had an uncontrollable libido. In fact, she'd never understood others' fascination with sex.

But the itchiness she'd been feeling all afternoon in the car, because of this man, had her reevaluating her previous experience.

'The bathroom is, uh, pretty small, too,' Gil said, as if giving her the rest of the bad news now that she'd remained calm about the bed.

She moved to the door just past the bed and peeked into the bath. Gil had understated its size. Postage stamp might be more accurate. No tub. Only a small shower, sink and toilet. So much for the thought of a hot, soaking bath.

More shivers brought her attention to another disappointment. The room wasn't warm.

'Is the heater on? Can we turn it up? I'm still cold,' she said, looking around the room.

'It's a lot warmer than outside, but definitely not toasty,' Gil agreed. He crossed the room to the small controls on the wall by the door. Sighing, he turned to face her. 'I'm afraid it's on high.'

Lindsay moaned in disappointment.

Damn, she had to stop making that noise. It made Gil think of long nights of mindless sex. Which warmed him up a little in spite of the inadequacies of the furnace.

He turned his mind to food, a safer subject than sex. Especially since he'd given his word that he'd keep his hands off of her. He hoped he hadn't been overly optimistic. After all, she was a beauty.

She'd surprised him with her calm acceptance not only of the one room but also the one bed. He'd expected a tantrum, like Amanda had been capable of. She'd demanded luxury no matter what the circumstances.

'Want to give me some idea of what you want for dinner?' he asked, waiting for a long list of preferences.

She actually grinned at him. 'I don't eat liver. I'm not fond of fish—or spinach. Anything else is fine. And I wouldn't say no to a candy bar. Stress makes me crave chocolate.'

He couldn't resist tracing her slim form with his gaze. She must normally live a stress-free life.

Otherwise she'd be several sizes larger. Which made her agreeableness even more amazing. He'd been attracted to her beauty from the beginning. Now, he was drawn to that grin, that twinkle in her hazel eyes.

'I'll see what I can find.'

'Wait!' she called out as he turned to the door.

Before he knew what she intended, she'd looped a red cashmere scarf around his neck. 'I noticed you didn't have a muffler. This will keep your face warm,' she assured him as she tied it.

Her arms were around his neck, securing the scarf and he froze, aware that it wouldn't take much movement to pull her into his embrace, to warm her body with his. But he didn't move. He'd promised.

Against the soft cloth, he muttered, 'I'll be right back.'

He stepped out into the storm, scarcely noting the frigid conditions. It reminded him of that song, 'Let It Snow,' with the words that said the singer would stay warm if he got a hug before he left.

He'd always laughed at that silliness, but even the thought of an embrace from Lindsay had him steaming.

He returned a few minutes later with a variety of food, none of it gourmet. He'd nuked several prepackaged hamburgers in the microwave, picked up the last two egg salad sandwiches wrapped in cellophane, grabbed a couple of bags of chips and selected several chocolate candy bars.

Lindsay deserved any treat he could find.

When he burst into the motel room, slamming the door behind him, he was immediately assailed by the aroma of hot coffee. 'You made the coffee!' he exclaimed.

'I said I would,' she replied. 'I figured it might be the only way we'll get warm tonight. In fact, I might even soak my feet in coffee later on. They feel like blocks of ice.'

He swallowed his 'told you so' thought about the shoes she'd chosen to wear. No point in starting an argument when they had an entire night to get through together. 'Want to see what's for dinner?'

'Yes,' she said, coming around the bed.

He pulled the two hamburgers from inside his coat. 'These are still warm, but we'd better eat them fast. These sandwiches are the second course. Chips to accompany either or both. And, ta-da,' he called, as if presenting the pièce de résistance, 'chocolate for dessert.'

'Bless you,' she said, taking her share of his offerings.

Gil hadn't believed she'd be pleased with his selections. Pleased? Hell, he'd expected her to turn her nose up at all of it.

She surprised him even more when she put her food down and returned to the other side of the bed to pour both of them a cup of coffee before starting to eat.

'Warm is more than I expected. With the coffee, they might even taste hot.' She set his cup on the lamp table, then moved down the length of the bed and sat down.

Neither bothered with conversation while they ate. By the time Gil took the last bite of his hamburger, it was cold, but the coffee was still warm. And the egg salad sandwich helped satisfy his hunger.

Lindsay handed him the second half of hers. 'I'm saving room for the chocolate. You finish mine off.'

'Don't mind if I do,' he said with a grin. Before he

ate any of it, however, he added, 'Thanks for being such a good sport about all this, Lindsay.'

She looked surprised. 'Why not be a good sport? None of it is your fault. In fact, if I'd stopped when you first suggested it, our accommodations might be a little more...spacious.' She shrugged her shoulders. 'You're the one who should be complaining.'

Rather than argue about who was responsible for their situation, he smiled and finished off her sandwich.

'Do you think we'll be able to get any reception on the television?' she asked, eyeing the set against the wall.

'Maybe. It looks remarkably new compared to everything else in the room.' He set down his coffee cup and crossed over to the television. When he turned it on, Lindsay cheered as a clear picture filled the screen.

'All right! My favorite show comes on tonight,' she said.

Gil changed the channel, only to discover that only one station got reception. 'Then I hope it's on this channel.'

'Me, too. If you don't mind, I'm going to take a turn in the bathroom.'

With a nod, he watched her grab her suitcase and open it, extracting several articles. Then she tucked it away and disappeared into the bath.

All he could think about was Lindsay emerging in something from Victoria Secret. A man could dream, couldn't he?

When Lindsay finally opened the door, she was completely dressed in a velour warm-up suit, with thick socks on her feet. She sent him a nervous grin.

'Not the latest style in pj's, but this is the warmest I have.'

'I think you look very stylish,' he assured her. When she frowned at him, he asked, 'What?'

'Is that a slam?'

'Why would you think that?'

'You said your ex-wife always had to be in style.'

Gil was at a loss at what to say. His first reaction was to tell her his wife wouldn't have been caught dead in a sweat suit—unless she was modeling it in a fashion show. But that response wouldn't do. The alternative was to tell her that he thought she'd look stylish in a trash bag, because all he'd be able to think about was what was underneath.

That *definitely* wouldn't do.

'Uh, I was teasing you. Being warm is a lot more important than being stylish.'

She smiled and picked up two of the candy bars. Then she returned to the side of the bed closest to the bathroom and pulled down the covers. 'I'm getting under the covers to watch television.'

He stood and moved his candy bars to the lamp table. 'Good idea. Want a refill on the coffee? I think there's just enough for both of us.'

'Sure, thanks.'

After filling their cups, he gathered his duffel bag and, with a nod of his head in the direction of the bathroom, he walked past her, closing the door behind him.

Lindsay drew a deep breath when she was finally alone. The man, with his sexy grin, was tough to resist. She couldn't even suggest he sleep in the tub tonight, because there wasn't one.

Oh, well. She could share the bed with him. After all, he'd brought her chocolate. She unwrapped the candy and took a big bite. Then she turned her pillow on end and sank into it, focusing her gaze on the television.

If there had been more covers, so she could really get warm, Lindsay thought she might've even drifted off to sleep, though it was barely eight o'clock. But the two thin blankets on the bed didn't provide much warmth.

When the bathroom door swung open and Gil came back into her view, she felt the room get suddenly a little warmer. He was still dressed in jeans, but he'd changed his cotton shirt to a flannel one, left open over a white T-shirt.

'You're going to sleep in jeans?' she asked, frowning.

He cocked one eyebrow at her. 'I only brought jeans.'

She thought about his words as he pulled back the covers on his side of the bed. She knew he'd be uncomfortable, but he could sleep if he was really tired. She'd done it before when she'd been camping out with the family.

'You'll probably need them. These blankets aren't much help.'

He snapped his fingers. 'I forgot about the ones I borrowed from Kathy.' He reached for the blankets that he'd dumped in a corner of the room and spread them out over the bed.

Lindsay immediately felt the difference. 'Oh, thank you for thinking of them. That helps a lot.'

Even more effective at raising her temperature was Gil's entry into the bed. His body heat was like a personal furnace, even though he maintained the foot of distance that the size of the bed allowed.

Twelve inches. And those twelve inches were possible only because she'd scooted to the edge of the bed. Gil's broad shoulders took up more than his half of the bed. The temptation to press her body against his, resting her head on his shoulder, was almost overpowering.

'You're not going to fall off the bed, are you?'

She snapped her head around. 'Of course not! But I wanted you to have enough room.'

'I appreciate it,' he assured her with a grin that could compete with Mel Gibson's any day.

She forced her gaze back to the television. A movie had just started. It wasn't the show she'd anticipated, but it was one she hadn't seen. Beggars couldn't be choosers. At least it might distract her from the sexy man next to her.

Two hours later, the movie ended, and Lindsay tried to unobtrusively wipe away the tears that had filled her eyes. She was always a sucker for sad stories. Or happy ones. She even cried over Hallmark commercials.

'You okay?' a quiet, tender voice asked.

'Of course!' she exclaimed, irritated that he'd noticed her tears. She shoved back the covers and jumped out of bed. 'But I have to brush my teeth before I can go to sleep.' She grabbed her toothbrush and toothpaste and disappeared into the bathroom, shutting the door behind her.

Gil lay back against his pillow, missing the heat from Lindsay's body almost at once. The room wasn't much warmer than when they'd first entered it. He supposed there was too much demand for heat from the system.

Not that he'd been cold. No, with Lindsay in bed beside him, so close, he'd been warm. Aroused, but warm. He now had the answer about how long her hair was. When she'd come out of the bathroom, he'd been too distracted by the total picture to pay attention to detail. But she'd taken all the pins out and brushed it and it hung in silken strands to her shoulders. The urge to stroke it was very distracting.

Maybe that was why it had taken him a while to realize she was crying over the sentimental film. At first he'd been amused. Then touched. Suddenly, the need to hold her, comfort her, had turned to raging hormones. The thought of pulling her into his arms was too tempting.

Good thing she'd gone to brush her teeth.

When she came back out, he took his turn in the bathroom. If he stayed in there long enough, maybe she'd fall asleep before he came back.

It was too cold and uncomfortable to stay in the bathroom longer than five minutes. He cautiously opened the door, flicking off the light quickly so it wouldn't shine in Lindsay's eyes.

But she'd left the bedside lamp on for him. He stared at her rigid form, strictly on her side of the bed. She definitely wasn't asleep.

'The coffee keeping you awake?' he whispered.

'Um, I don't think so. I used decaffeinated. It's probably the chocolate. It has caffeine, too, you know.'

Now she told him. He'd have limited her to one candy bar if he'd thought of that. He rounded the bed and slipped beneath the covers again. His side of the bed had grown cold, but he could feel Lindsay's heat.

'Are you still cold?' she whispered as a shiver racked him.

'I'll warm up in a minute. It doesn't take long for the bed to get cold, does it?' His own words reminded him of his marriage. Once the ring was on Amanda's finger, her eagerness to share a bed with him had vanished. She'd made it very clear she was more interested in his bankroll than his body right away. In fact, their marriage bed had been colder every night than the one he shared with Lindsay tonight.

'Do you have enough room?' she asked, still whispering.

'Yeah.' He'd like less room. He'd like Lindsay snuggled up next to him, with no space between. But he'd promised. Gradually, the heat the two of them generated helped him relax.

Until he turned over and found himself facing her, her features barely visible in the dark. 'Uh, good night.'

'Good night,' she said softly.

He turned back over, unable to face her, knowing only inches separated their lips. Hell, it was going to be a long night!

CHAPTER FOUR

WHEN Lindsay first stirred the next morning, a sigh of contentment sifted through her and she burrowed her face against Gil's chest, hoping to postpone the inevitable. She didn't want to leave her nice, warm cocoon.

Then she realized what she was lying on. Gil's chest.

She gasped and shoved on the big, warm body that cradled her against him. 'Gil!' she snapped.

Accusations stopped up in her throat as he came awake. How could she accuse him of anything when he was still sleeping?

'What?' he muttered, his eyes still closed. In fact, he pulled her closer to him. 'Don't move. You're letting in a draft.'

She scrambled away from him, pushing against his hands. 'Gil! We—you were supposed to stay on your side!'

He slowly opened his eyes, their bright blue a little foggy, as if he awoke slowly. 'My side?'

She said nothing, waiting until her words pierced his head.

He frowned, staring at her. Suddenly he jerked his hands from her body and she felt cold.

'Uh, I didn't know. I mean, I must've—it was cold.'

His ridiculous words made her reaction seem a little over the top. With a grimace, she said, 'So I've heard.'

'Really, I know I promised, but I didn't—'

'It's okay, Gil,' she said, a calm settling over her.

'What time is it?' Even as she asked, she looked at her watch. Nine o'clock!

She looked up to tell him how late they'd slept, only to find him staring at her, shock on his face.

'What? Is my hair standing on end?'

As if he couldn't help himself, he reached out and stroked a strand of hair behind her ear. 'No. It's beautiful.'

Lying in bed with a man who touched her hair with such awe made her nervous. Because she wanted to return the favor. His dark hair wasn't smooth and in place. But the idea of running her fingers through it held a lot of appeal.

'Um, I'll take first turn in the bathroom. Okay?'

He nodded and she slipped out from under the covers. Away from Gil.

The bed wasn't nearly as warm without Lindsay curled up against him. Or as exciting.

Better stow that thought away. He was going to have to abandon the covers that hid his reaction to waking up with his arms wrapped around Lindsay. He checked his own watch. A little after nine. He hadn't slept that late in years.

But he'd gladly stay in bed all day if she were with him.

He shook his head in disgust. It was only lust. He hadn't been with a woman since his divorce. He'd have to start getting out more. That would take care of the problem.

The bathroom door opened and Lindsay walked back in the room, wearing what she'd slept in.

'Your turn,' she said brightly, as if she were the social director for a cruise line.

'Thanks. You going to wear that today?'

Her cheeks flushed, making her look that much more tempting. 'Yes. I have a limited wardrobe and this is the warmest thing I brought.'

'Hey, I wasn't complaining,' he said at once. 'I think it's a smart decision. I'm doing the same thing.' He headed for the bathroom before he could say anything else he shouldn't.

When he came back out, Lindsay was on the phone. 'Sorry for the delay, Mom, but we should be there this evening, kind of late.'

She said her goodbyes and hung up the phone.

'Your mom was worried about you?'

'I suppose, though she seldom shows it. I guess that comes from raising five boys before she got to me.'

He chuckled. 'You must've been a real shock.'

She smiled back. 'Why do you think I was the last child? My brothers always claimed my parents stopped because they were afraid they might have another girl, and one was all they could handle.'

He shook his head at her silliness. 'I'd better call Rafe, too. I talked to him before I left Kathy's, but he'll be wondering about me.'

After he hung up the phone, she asked, 'Who's Rafe?'

'My manager. My teacher. I could already ride, but I didn't know much about running a ranch when I first came back to Oklahoma.'

'From New York City?'

'Yeah.'

'That was quite a change of vocation, from stock-broker to rancher.'

He nodded, but he didn't give any explanation.

'You ready to go? We probably should get on the road, if it's open.'

'Will the man in the office know?'

'Probably.'

They loaded their bags back into the car. Another two inches had fallen during the night, but Lindsay managed to get her car started and inch their way to the office.

When she opened her car door as he did his, he looked at her. 'Are you coming in?'

'Yes. I have to pay.'

'I told you I'd pay the expenses of the trip if you'd let me come with you.'

'But you didn't know it would be this long a trip. There's no need—'

'Stay here,' he ordered. 'I'll ask about the roads.'

Assuming she would obey, he got out of the car.

When he heard the other car door slam, he knew he'd miscalculated.

She'd actually begun to like him! But now he'd resorted back to that typical male behavior. Me, Tarzan, you Jane, and you do what I say!

She beat him to the office door. Or maybe he'd let her beat him. She didn't care, as long as she was the first one inside.

'Morning, Miss. You wantin' a room?' the clerk asked, a smile on his weathered face.

'No, I have a room. We were in number nine last night.'

'Oh, right, a'course. I recognize the mister,' he said, nodding in Gil's direction.

'Are the roads open this morning?' she asked,

ignoring his acknowledgment of her traveling companion.

'Yes, Ma'am. Heard the snowplow go by about seven. Which direction you heading?'

'South,' Gil answered before she could.

'No problem, then. Not much snow fifty miles south of here. You'll be fine.'

She opened her purse to pull out her credit card as relief filled her. She didn't think she could stand another hour in that small room with Gil.

'Shall I charge it to your card?' the man asked.

Both Gil and she answered with a yes, until she realized what he meant. He was referring to the card Gil had used last night.

'No, I mean, I have my card.'

'Don't need but one,' the man said calmly.

Gil took her arm. 'Don't be difficult, Lindsay. Let's just get on the road.'

She glared at him, but there was no relenting in his gaze and the man behind the counter thought she was crazy. She jerked her arm from Gil's hold and stomped to the door.

'Any place for a hot breakfast nearby?' Gil asked before he followed her.

'There's a real good café just down the road. Stay on the side road for another mile. The Roadrunner Café.'

'Thanks.'

Back in the car, still angry about his high-handedness, Lindsay pulled out onto the highway, keeping her gaze straight ahead.

'If you don't mind, I'd like some breakfast before we get started.'

She shot him a dark look. 'Aren't you going to order me to stop?'

'Nope. If you want to starve to death, I suppose I can keep you company.' He crossed his arms across his chest and stared straight ahead.

She knew she was being ridiculous. 'Fine, we'll stop for breakfast. But I'm paying for our food since you paid for the room. And for dinner last night.'

'Lady, you may regret that. I like a big breakfast.' Instead of arguing, he grinned at her.

'Room nine, please.'

The clerk scratched his head. 'Uh, sorry, but they checked out about ten minutes ago.'

He wondered if the person had hung up, since the caller said nothing. Then the man growled, 'They?'

'Yep. There was two of 'em.'

'Two women?'

'Nope, a man and his missus. A pretty blonde.' He looked at the credit card slip. 'A Mr. Daniels.'

'I'll kill him,' the man exclaimed and slammed down the phone.

'Mercy, I'm glad those people are gone. Don't want no trouble around here.' He settled back into his lumpy chair to watch the television.

Lindsay still hadn't warmed up to her companion by the time they'd finished their meal. True, he'd ordered an enormous amount of food. And remained cheerful in spite of her silence.

A lowering thought occurred to her. Was she trying to build a barrier between them, to help her pretend last night hadn't happened? Was she that much of a coward?

'You going to eat that last piece of bacon?' he asked, piercing her thoughts.

She stared at him. 'You can't still be hungry?'

'Well, not hungry exactly,' he confessed, his gaze sweeping over all the empty plates around him, 'but I hate to see a piece of good bacon go to waste.'

She silently shoved her plate in his direction. He reminded her of her brothers again. A vacuum cleaner when it came to food.

But she hadn't been thinking of her brothers when she'd awakened this morning wrapped in his arms. In fact, what she'd been thinking would have her father and brothers up in arms. According to them, she should reach her thirtieth birthday unkissed. Then they'd take a vote on allowing her within a mile of any man.

When she realized her gaze had settled on Gil's firm lips, she hurriedly looked away. The couple at the next table drew her attention. The man was hiding behind a newspaper. His wife, or at least she assumed the woman was his wife, was frantically attending to four children, ranging in age from two to maybe ten.

Even as she watched, the two-year-old slid down from his chair and made good his escape, his route bringing him right by Lindsay and Gil. The mother shouted an order, which, of course, the child promptly ignored. However, it alerted Gil to the situation. As junior sped by, he extended his big arm and scooped the child into his lap.

'Whoa, little guy! Where are you heading?'

The child squirmed, but was unable to free himself. Gil's grin seemed to reassure him, though, so the scream of outrage Lindsay expected didn't materialize.

The woman immediately left her chair to claim her

child. 'Oh, thank you so much. Buster doesn't like to sit still for long.' The woman, once pretty, looked tired and too busy to concern herself with her appearance.

The man lowered the paper and scowled at all of them. 'Alice, can't you control these kids?'

'Of course, dear,' the woman muttered. Then she thanked Gil again and returned to her table, Buster in tow.

'That man should be shot,' Lindsay whispered. She hated men who didn't participate in raising the children they'd fathered.

'Yeah.'

Her gaze jerked to Gil's face. She hadn't expected him to agree with her.

Correctly interpreting her response, he said in a low voice, 'Why does that surprise you?'

'I didn't think— You seem irritated by my "feminist" reactions.'

He grinned. 'That's because sometimes you get carried away. But a man should take care of his children.'

While she might want to argue his first statement, she didn't because of his second. She couldn't agree more. 'Are you—do you want children?'

His gaze hardened. 'No. I wouldn't mind having kids, but that requires a wife. And I won't go down that road again.'

Ah, yes. The wife. The one she reminded him of. Somehow that thought hurt more than it had the first time she'd heard it. 'Too bad,' she said. 'You'd make a great daddy.'

'Was your father a good daddy?'

'The best,' she assured him, a smile on her lips. Then her expression darkened. 'Until I became a teenager. Then he and all my brothers became jailers rather than family.'

He wiped his mouth with his napkin. 'Maybe a slight exaggeration,' he suggested.

Before she could argue, the waitress appeared at their table. 'Anything else, folks? More coffee?'

'I wouldn't mind a cup to go,' Gil suggested. 'How about you, Lindsay? Coffee?'

'Yes, a cup to go would be nice. And the ticket, please.' She was ready to get on the road, to concentrate on her driving instead of the man across from her. To forget about waking in his arms.

They sat silently until the waitress returned, two foam cups and the ticket in her hands. In spite of Lindsay's having asked for it, the woman presented it to Gil with a smile.

'I'll take that,' Lindsay insisted, reaching for the ticket. The waitress looked surprised, but Gil didn't protest at all.

Lindsay put the piece of paper with her credit card and handed it to the woman, ignoring the way her eyebrow went up in question. She muttered something and hurried away.

'What did she say?'

Gil sent her a teasing look. 'You're not going to like it. Why don't you just forget she said anything.'

Which, of course, only made her more determined to know the waitress's comment. 'Tell me.'

He straightened his shoulders. 'She said she guessed I was worth it.'

Lindsay knew he was teasing, pretending to be proud that the waitress rated him worth the price of breakfast. She wanted to turn the tables on him. 'So she thinks you're a gigolo?'

He was just as quick. 'So she thinks you have to pay to have a man want you?'

'Maybe she realizes I like to be in control,' she said, staring down her nose at him.

The waitress returned and Lindsay quickly signed the charge slip, handed it to the waiting woman and slid out of the booth.

Gil joined her. 'In control, huh?' he said under his breath. Then, as the waitress turned away, he pulled Lindsay against him and kissed her.

The warmth of his lips against hers melted something deep inside her. Before Lindsay could respond, as she realized with humiliation she would've done, he released her and said, 'Thanks for the breakfast, darlin'.'

Then he walked out of the café.

Gil called himself all kinds of a fool for giving in to temptation. First of all, because he might have lost his ride back to Oklahoma. Lindsay might be so mad at him she'd leave him standing in the snow outside the Roadrunner Café.

But the biggest reason he shouldn't have touched her was because it only made him hungrier to touch her again. To hold her as he had all through the night. What a shame to have wasted all that time sleeping.

She swept past him like a film star and unlocked the car.

He stood there waiting for her reaction.

'I'm leaving,' she snapped. 'If you're coming with me, you'd better shake a leg.'

He didn't waste any time. As soon as he'd fastened his seat belt, she backed the car out of the parking space and headed for the interstate.

*   *   *

Six hours later, they'd exchanged few words. He figured she still hadn't forgiven him. But he'd watched her as she'd driven, noticing the exhaustion that was gradually claiming her.

'I offered to help with the driving. Want me to take over now?' he finally said, figuring she'd never ask for any help.

'Take over?' she repeated stiffly, irritation still in her voice.

'Poor choice of words,' he said immediately. 'I meant, do you want me to spell you. You've done all the driving so far, and it's still another four or five hours 'til we get home.'

'I'm fine,' she assured him, never looking his way. 'There's a town coming up. Want to see if they have a fast-food place to get some lunch?'

They'd made one stop for fuel since breakfast and he was ready to eat, and stretch his legs. The small car was turning into a torture chamber. And not just because of lack of legroom. The woman was too close to him. He couldn't escape her scent, her warmth, the temptation of touching her.

'Yeah, that'd be good.'

He convinced her to go into a small café rather than hit a drive-through window. If she was determined to do all the driving, she needed a break now and then.

'I'm surprised we found something open on Thanksgiving Day,' she said after they were seated.

A cheerful waitress greeted them. 'We're open every day of the year, honey. We got regulars who wouldn't have any place to go. You two going home for the holidays?'

'Yes,' Lindsay replied.

'That's nice. What can I get ya? We got the Thanksgiving Day special, turkey and all the trimmings.'

'That will be fine;' Lindsay said with a tired smile.

'Me, too,' Gil agreed. He was concentrating on Lindsay instead of the food. After the waitress left, he leaned forward. 'How you feeling?'

'I'm fine.' She didn't look at him.

'Will it help if I apologize?'

Her gaze collided with his before she looked away. 'Apologize for what?'

'For kissing you at breakfast. I shouldn't have done that.'

'Because it reminded you of your ex-wife, your marriage?'

He could hear the bitterness in her voice, which surprised him. But what surprised him even more was the fact that thoughts of his wife had never entered his head.

For the past two years, any woman he encountered had been compared to Amanda. And neither had come out smelling like a rose. He'd been filled with distaste.

Thoughts of Lindsay filled him with hunger. And no reminders of Amanda. 'No. No, because I shouldn't have taken advantage of you.'

Her tense shoulders sagged just a little and he was encouraged.

'I shouldn't have suggested you were a gigolo.'

He smiled. 'I've been called worse.'

The waitress returned with two plates filled with steaming turkey and dressing and green beans. 'I'll be right back with your coffee.'

Lindsay stared at her plate, not moving.

'You okay?' Gil asked, concern filling him. Had she pushed herself too far? Was she getting sick?

She met his gaze briefly and he was dismayed to see tears in her eyes. Shaking her head, she picked up her fork.

'Lindsay? What's wrong? Did I say something I shouldn't have?' he asked, trying to think if he'd offended her in some way.

The waitress brought the coffee. 'You folks need anything else right now?'

He hurriedly assured her they didn't.

'Well, save room for pie 'cause it comes with the meal. Besides, Joe makes the best pecan pie you've ever tasted.'

When she'd left the table, a sob escaped Lindsay.

Gil shot out a hand and grabbed her wrist. 'Lindsay, what's wrong?'

'Nothing! Nothing, I'm being silly.'

'Tell me,' he ordered, but his tone was gentle.

After a moment's hesitation, she burst out, 'I thought I'd be home today, sharing turkey with my family.'

Relief filled him as he released her wrist. 'That's it? You're homesick?'

She gave a definite sniff and glared at him. 'You needn't make it sound so stupid. I know—'

'Baby, I didn't mean—'

'Don't call me that!' she snapped, dabbing at her eyes with her napkin.

He hadn't even realized he'd used his pet name for his little sister. Damn. More carefully, he tried again. 'Lindsay, I don't think it's stupid. But I was afraid you were getting sick, or something was really wrong.'

She didn't look at him, picking up her fork again and taking a bite of turkey. 'Probably I'm just hungry.'

'I know I am,' he assured her, taking a bite, too, and finding it surprisingly good.

But the hunger he was feeling wasn't for food.

And it wasn't likely he'd be able to satisfy it any time soon.

CHAPTER FIVE

BACK on the road again, Lindsay seemed somewhat revived by their meal. But she'd still refused his second offer to do any driving. He figured she wouldn't relinquish the wheel all the way to Oklahoma, no matter how tired she became.

Hardheaded woman.

At least she'd forgiven him for the kiss. His gaze fastened onto her mouth, noting the generous bottom lip he'd tasted earlier. It had been wonderfully soft, inviting. In fact, he'd been surprised she hadn't hauled off and leveled him.

She must be too much a lady to brawl in public. Something else different from Amanda. She had enjoyed the attention public argument gave her. She considered herself a diva.

'Do you have a herd of cattle on your place?'

Gil looked at her in surprise. They hadn't bothered with much friendly conversation during the drive. 'Yeah, I've got a herd of Charolais.'

'Oh. I thought you might be raising horses. There are several horse ranches around Apache.'

'Yeah. And I am. That's what I'm really interested in, but we have a lot of acreage. I didn't see any point in letting it go to waste.' And Rafe loved the breed. In fact, as a bonus last year, he'd given Rafe a number of heifers and free breeding rights to his bull. They'd branded Rafe's cattle and run them in with the main herd.

'What kind of horses?'

'Cutting horses.' No showy breeds for him. Working horses, so vital to the operation of a ranch. He and Rafe worked together on training the animals. He'd even begun to build a reputation for the training of them.

Lindsay asked several more detailed questions, showing her knowledge of ranch life. Gil found himself relaxing, expanding on his hopes, his plans for the future.

'Hey,' he said after going on for several minutes, 'I'm probably boring you silly.'

'No, I'm enjoying it. You remind me so much of my dad and brothers. They never think of anything else but ranching.'

'And ordering around their little sister?'

'That, too,' she agreed with a smile. 'They've probably gotten a lot more done in the past year and a half since I've been gone.'

'I bet they've gotten out of the habit of bossing you around and you'll find yourself with all kinds of freedom this visit.' He couldn't imagine any man forgetting Lindsay Crawford, but maybe her brothers could.

She sighed. 'I wish, but I think they were born being bossy, or they learned it at Daddy's knee.'

'Aren't any of them married? That would take their attention off you.'

'Only Logan. He moved to Texas a couple of years ago and married his boss. Abby is wonderful. She encouraged me to—to become my own woman.'

'He married his boss? Didn't he find that, uh, awkward?' Gil couldn't imagine working for a woman *and* bedding her, too.

Lindsay grinned. 'That's what my other brothers

said. But Logan actually bought in as a partner. They're very happy.'

Lindsay's brother's name struck a chord of memory. 'Where in Texas?'

'Near Wichita Falls. Only a couple of hours from our place.'

'I visited a place near there. There's a trainer, Jed Davis. I talked to him about training horses.'

Lindsay beamed at him, and he caught his breath. Her radiance left him speechless.

'That's Abby's brother-in-law! Her younger sister Beth's husband. What a small world. Logan and Abby's home is just across the road.'

'I guess it *is* a small world,' he said, unable to come up with anything more original. Not when he was still basking in the warmth of her smile. Lordy, a man would do most anything to bring that look to her face again.

'Beth and Jed have a little boy three years old, and Abby told me they're expecting again. And Abby's other sister, Melissa, and her husband, Rob, have a boy just a little younger. And Abby and Logan have a girl. You should see Logan with his daughter—she's got him wrapped around her little finger just like Abby does.' She finished with a deep sigh of happiness.

'When I was there, Jed's son was a toddler.'

'He's grown a bit. He has lots of children to play with when you include Rob and Melissa's seven children.'

'Seven? She must've had triplets or something.' He'd seen Beth. She wasn't very old. In fact, Jed had said something about his child bride, joking about doing whatever she wanted.

Lindsay chuckled, a sound that warmed Gil's blood.

'No, not at all. Rob already had a daughter, Terri. She's fifteen now. And Melissa started a foster home for siblings. She was given two little girls, sisters, who were abandoned.' Looking at Gil, she said, 'You should see them, Gil. They're such precious little girls. And their parents just left them! How could anyone be so cruel?'

'I don't know, baby,' he said softly, then hurriedly corrected himself. 'I mean, Lindsay.'

She pretended she hadn't heard his slip, but he knew she had by the sidelong glance she gave him.

'Anyway, they're darling. Then a neighbor and his wife were killed in a car crash. Melissa took in their three children so they wouldn't have to be separated and sent to different homes. And now they have one of their own.'

'That's a lot of kids.'

'Yeah,' she agreed, but Gil could read the pleasure on her face. She wanted to be a mother. Some women seemed to have the nesting instinct. Others, like Amanda, never thought beyond themselves and should never have children. Not that she would have agreed to a child anyway, as he had learned to his own dismay. He cleared his throat. 'You planning on a big family?'

She gave him another sidelong look. 'Yes.' Her chin rose, as if she thought he'd challenge her decision.

'In Chicago?'

Several minutes passed, and he wondered if he'd asked the wrong question.

Finally, she said, 'That depends on my husband, and—and where my career takes me.'

'What kind of career are we talking about, here? What do you do in Chicago?'

'I'm an assistant buyer at Bloomingdale's, in the housewares department.'

'I figured they'd put you in fashion. You have the looks for it.' Well, not quite. While she had a terrific figure, from a man's point of view, and curves in all the right places, she didn't have the reed-thin body of a model.

He was celebrating those curves, salivating over them, when he caught Lindsay's glare.

'Uh, what?'

'You think a woman can't look good *and* care about her house?'

'I didn't say that!' he protested at once. 'I mean, I thought you'd—you seem to know a lot about fashion.'

'How would you know?'

He shrugged his shoulders. 'I saw you yesterday.'

'I minored in retailing,' she admitted, 'concentrating in fashion, but the only opening they had at the time was housewares. And I wanted to get away from home.'

No need to ask why. She'd made it clear her family was way too protective. So, in spite of being raised on a ranch, she was a city girl by choice. Like Amanda, who had come from a small Indiana town. She had headed to New York City as soon as she could, conveniently forgetting her roots.

And Lindsay would stay a city girl. Assistant buyers at Bloomingdale's wouldn't find any opportunities hanging on the trees on an Oklahoma ranch.

Abruptly, he asked a question that had been bothering him since yesterday. 'Who gave you your ring?' Not that he was interested in any future with Lindsay Crawford, but it was a good idea to have all the facts.

She sent him a startled look. 'My parents, for my twenty-first birthday. Why?'

'No reason. Just curious.' Curious to know if some man had legitimate claims. Curious to know if she let men give her expensive presents. Curious to find out more about Miss Lindsay Crawford. For no reason.

Gil settled back in his car seat and told her he thought he'd take a nap. Before he tripped over any more land mines, or said something he shouldn't.

Lindsay looked at her watch. It was after six. They could stop for a meal, but they were only a couple of hours away. She knew her mother would have something waiting for them, and she was anxious to get home. But she wasn't sure she could keep going.

Her gaze shifted to the man beside her. He'd actually gone to sleep, his head pillowed against one of his hands on the window. She looked back to the road as he began to stir. Had he realized she was staring at him?

Shifting in his seat, he lifted his head and then rubbed his face. 'Wow, I didn't think I'd go to sleep. How are you doing?'

'Feeling envious.'

'Pull over and I'll give you the same opportunity.'

She hadn't intended to let him drive, to leave him in control while she slept. But they'd shared more than twenty-four hours. And much to her surprise, she trusted him.

So she pulled over.

Only to find him staring at her, disbelief on his face. 'You're actually going to let me drive?'

'Did you mean it when you—'

'Of course I did. But I didn't think you'd trust me.'

She shrugged her shoulders. Better not tell him that

letting him drive was nothing compared to sharing a bed with him. She'd prefer he think their closeness hadn't bothered her at all.

When she opened the door, after checking for oncoming traffic, she noticed the air was warmer than the last time she'd gotten out of the car. Not comfortable without a coat but a lot better than frozen Chicago.

She and Gil met at the back of the car. 'You are alert, aren't you? Do you need some time to wake up?'

'Nope, I'm fine. I can't believe I slept. I haven't taken a nap in years.' He circled around her to reach the driver's side.

When she got into the passenger's seat, she found it still warm from Gil's body. She shivered at the thought.

'You cold?' he asked, proving he'd been watching her. 'My coat's in the back seat. Why don't you pull it over you?'

She hesitated. 'I don't think I'll go to sleep.'

'Maybe not, but you should get comfy. Use it as a pillow if you want.'

She reached back for his coat, then fastened her seat belt. When she'd done that, Gil pulled out into traffic, handling her car as if he'd driven it forever.

She should've known he'd be a good driver. He seemed to do everything well. Snuggling down inside his coat, letting his scent surround her, her eyes drifted shut. They were tired from staring at the road. She'd just rest them for a few minutes.

Gil threw Lindsay a look. She was sleeping. Her beautiful face looked as angelic as a small child's when it was relaxed in sleep. And it also reminded him of this morning. He wished he'd been the first to awaken.

But he suspected the fact that he was asleep when she awoke made it easier for her to accept his apology. Her immediate trust in him had made him feel pretty good. She had regressed during the day, but at least she had trusted him enough to drive.

He passed a sign showing twenty miles to Oklahoma City. From there, they only had another hour to go. He even knew how to reach her home. When he'd been slouched down in his seat, his eyes closed, he realized he'd met several of her brothers at one of the local rodeos.

Once he'd even gone to their ranch to look at a young colt they had for sale. He'd bought the youngster and the horse was turning into one of his favorite rides. That day he'd even met Caleb Crawford himself, Lindsay's father. A big, burly, jovial man, he'd welcomed Gil warmly, offered any help he needed with his new place.

Rafe knew the entire family. Said they were good people. If he'd told Rafe who he was driving back with, he probably would've been able to tell him even more details about the family.

He stamped down any desire to find out more about Lindsay. She was heading back to Chicago in a few days. If he was fortunate, he'd forget about her before she even left Oklahoma.

He sighed as he realized that wasn't a possibility. Having spent the night holding her against him, sharing all this time with her—kissing her—he'd be lucky if he'd forgotten her by *next* Thanksgiving.

Definitely he needed to develop a social life. Rafe had been telling him he was too young to spend all his time at the ranch, with only his manager for company.

He looked at Lindsay again. Too bad she'd be gone

so quickly. He could've taken her to dinner a couple of times. Shown her his ranch. She knew enough about ranching to appreciate the work he'd done. To ask intelligent questions. She would make the perfect rancher's wife.

Except that she was a city girl. Besides, while he was glad she had shown some trust in him, he had to admit he didn't offer that quality often himself. He had naively placed his heart in Amanda's hands and had it thoroughly trampled. He had vowed never to be that foolish again.

No, it was a good thing she was leaving. That kept him from getting addicted to her presence.

She shifted in her seat, as if trying to find a more comfortable spot. With an eagerness that worried him, he reached out his right arm and pulled her head against his shoulder. With a sigh, she settled into him, a smile on her lips.

'Oh, baby,' he muttered, drawing in her scent, feeling her soft hair brush his jaw. Yeah, it was a good thing she was leaving.

Gil turned down a dirt road that he was pretty sure led to the Crawford ranch. Now that they'd left the freeway with its bright lights, and even the farm-to-market road, the interior of the car was darker, more intimate.

Lindsay had shifted several times in her sleep. The last time, she'd turned more in to him and rested her hand across his stomach. Her touch burned into him, and left him both praying and fearing that it might slip just a little farther south.

He dropped his lips to her brow again. Several times he'd caressed her gently, needing to touch her somehow. He didn't think she'd object to such benign kisses. Of course, he wasn't going to test that theory by telling her. Nope, he wasn't an idiot.

But desire had been building inside him. For over an hour he'd held her against him, one hand on her and one on the steering wheel.

The ranch house came into view, a light flooding the area near it. The intimacy of the car was about to be invaded. He'd surrender Lindsay to her family and never see her again.

The pain that shot through him was jolting, unexpected. Okay, so he was attracted to the woman. A man would have to be made out of concrete not to respond to Lindsay's body, her warmth, her mind, her smile.

But he'd forget her. Of course he would.

He stopped the car near the front door, putting it in park. Before he cut the motor, he decided he deserved a little reward…and a goodbye.

Pulling Lindsay closer, he tipped her head up and covered her wonderful lips with his. A goodbye kiss. He felt her coming awake in his arms, but she didn't pull away. In fact, her arms slid up his chest to encircle his neck.

A jealous surge made him question who she thought she was kissing. Whoever it was had the right to be angry with him, but he didn't care. Nothing could make him call a halt to the wonderful exchange of passion that would keep him warm for many a night.

Until the car door opened and strong hands jerked Gil from the car and Lindsay's arms.

'Hey!' Gil protested.

He was spun around and just had time to notice his assailant had friends before a big fist collided with his chin.

*   *   *

'Daddy!' Lindsay shrieked, her voice piercing the pain that shot through Gil.

Great. He was being attacked by Lindsay's father. There went his intention of retaliating. Even if he wanted to, he couldn't hit an old man.

He shook his head to clear it, and the forms of four men became clear. The older man, Caleb Crawford, was preparing to hit him again.

'Hey, Dad, you've had your shot. It's our turn now,' one of the men said.

So he was to become a punching bag for the Crawford clan? He didn't think so. He took hold of Caleb's hand, still clutching his shirt, and shoved it away.

'I—' he began, about to announce his intention to fight back, when Lindsay stopped him.

'If anyone touches him, you'll have to fight me next!' she insisted, her voice hot with rage. She shoved her way out of the car, past Gil, and stepped in front of him.

He put his hands on her shoulders to move her out of danger, but she whirled around to face him. 'What are you doing?'

'I'm trying to get you out of firing range of these maniacs,' he said with a growl.

She turned back around. 'These maniacs are my family. They won't hit *me*.'

'Not on the chin, young lady,' Caleb assured her, his voice a deep burr, 'but you may have trouble sitting down for a while.'

Gil could feel her stiffen in shock as she took in her father's words.

'Mr. Crawford—' he began, unsure what to say. He'd figured Lindsay had exaggerated the behavior of the male members of her family, but now he wasn't so sure. If a kiss upset them this much, he'd hate to think what his fantasies would generate.

'We'll deal with you in a minute,' the man snapped. 'Lindsay, get in the house.'

That the man expected immediate obedience was obvious to everyone. Lindsay, however, didn't move. Not exactly a surprise to Gil.

'No,' she said firmly.

'Young lady, did you hear me? You get in the house right now. I don't want you seeing what's going to happen next.'

'What's going to happen next, Dad, is I'm getting back in my car and heading back to Chicago, and taking Gil with me.'

'But you just got here!'

'Yes, but there's no point in staying with the welcome you've given me.'

Gil heard the hurt in her voice. The desire to comfort her, to wrap his arms around her and tell her— what? He didn't know what to say.

'Hell, girl, did you expect me to congratulate this bastard for seducing my little girl? For taking advantage of you? I told you to be careful up there in Chicago. You can't trust those city men!'

Lindsay proved she didn't need Gil's comfort. She slapped her hands on her hips and roared back at her father. 'This city man lives in Apache! And all he did was kiss me! Since when is that a crime? Are you telling me you've attacked every woman my brothers have kissed? Because if you did I figure there wouldn't be any women left in the county!'

'Here, now, Lindsay, don't be yelling at me,' Caleb ordered, but Gil could hear uneasiness in his voice.

'I'm only yelling because you are. When you're ready to speak in a reasonable tone of voice, so will I. But I won't be ordered around like a rag doll, and I won't let you beat up poor Gil.'

Poor Gil? Gil didn't much appreciate that tag. 'I can defend myself, Lindsay. I don't need your protection.'

She whirled around again. 'Don't you dare go all macho on me, Gil Daniels. This is ridiculous!'

'Gil? Gil Daniels, is that you?' one of the voices in the foursome asked.

Several others chimed in, and even Caleb stared at him. 'The one who bought that colt?'

'Yeah, it's me,' Gil acknowledged, but he kept his voice stern. He'd have a bruise tomorrow, which didn't put him in a forgiving mood.

'What are you doing with Lindsay? How'd she connect up with you?' Pete Crawford asked.

'Do you mind if we have this conversation after I put on my coat?' Gil asked. The wind was blowing right through him, and he noticed Lindsay was shivering.

'We'll go in the house, Gil,' Lindsay said. 'But there's no need for any conversation with these animals. You don't owe them any explanation.' She took her coat as Gil handed it to her and shrugged into it.

'Listen here, little girl,' Caleb said, anger still in his voice, 'don't think you can bring your city ways back home. I don't know what you've been up to in Chicago, but back here, you'll abide by our rules.'

'So kissing is against the rules?' she challenged, her chin up.

Gil couldn't hold back a grin. She was a fighter.

'No,' her father snapped. 'But sleeping with a man you're not married to sure is!'

CHAPTER SIX

LINDSAY thought of several responses to her father's statement. But she didn't give any of them. Instead, she took Gil's arm and started toward the house.

Her father and three of her brothers were on their heels, as if herding them. Only the back door opening and her mother's call of welcome kept her going. The urge to run, as she'd done when she left for Chicago, filled her. Nothing had changed. Nothing ever would.

Her mother's warm hug brought tears to her eyes, but she knew that warmth wouldn't solve her problems. 'Mom, this is Gil Daniels. He drove down from Chicago with me.'

Gil greeted her mother with perfect manners, but Lindsay recognized her mistake at once. Her mother thought she'd invited Gil home with her for the holidays.

'No, Mom,' she said, before her mother could speak. 'Gil isn't an unexpected guest. At least, not for long. He lives in Apache. He was visiting his sister in Chicago and got caught by the snowstorm and a canceled flight. He asked for a ride.' She turned to glare at her father. 'Though I suspect he'd prefer the snow to the kind of welcome he received here.'

Her father glared back. 'I won't apologize for trying to protect my daughter.'

'Protect me from what? I'm twenty-five, Dad. If I want to kiss a man, I think I'm old enough.'

'I'm not just talking about kissing. You slept together, didn't you?' The level of his accusation rose as he spoke, until he finished with a roar.

'No!' Lindsay shouted back.

'Yes,' Gil said calmly.

Lindsay spun around to stare at Gil. 'What did you say?'

'You know what I said. I have no intention of lying to your father.'

She gasped. Her gaze flickered to her father's enraged features and then back to Gil. 'Nothing happened!'

'I know. But we did sleep together.'

'But we didn't have sex, you idiot!' She was almost as mad at Gil as she was at her father. His claim of honesty had just made things worse.

'Maybe you'd better explain, Daniels,' Caleb Crawford said forcefully.

'Sure, I'll—'

'You'll do no such thing!' Lindsay snapped. She was old enough not to be interrogated about her personal behavior. She decided she should begin as she meant to go on.

'Lindsay, darling, have you and Gil eaten anything? I have some turkey saved for you.' Her mother took her arm to urge her toward the kitchen.

'Mom, I'm not going to abandon Gil to them. He's already been slugged once. They might—'

With a stern look in her husband's direction, Carol said, 'Your father isn't going to do any more hitting tonight. Right, Caleb? Or your brothers, Lindsay. Now come help me fix a couple of plates for you and Gil.'

Before she conceded to her mother's orders, she looked at Gil one more time. 'Don't say a word.' Then she headed for the kitchen.

*   *   *

Gil knew better than to obey Lindsay's order. He could sympathize with Caleb Crawford, though he didn't appreciate being the recipient of all that anger.

'Look, Mr. Crawford, if you'll let me explain—'

'Go ahead. But be prepared for the consequences,' the older man said with a growl.

'Lindsay and my sister are neighbors in Chicago. When my flight got canceled, I offered to pay the expenses and help with the driving if Lindsay would give me a ride home. We got caught in the blizzard. When she finally agreed to stop for the night, the only motel within our reach had one room left. With one bed. We shared the bed, but we didn't have sex.'

Caleb stared at him, as if weighing his tale for its truthfulness. Gil had said his piece. He stood there in silence, awaiting the man's decision.

He'd told an abbreviated version of the past twenty-four-plus hours. There was no mention of the sexual hunger his companion had inspired. Or the two kisses they'd shared.

Caleb Crawford didn't deserve that much honesty.

'You sure that's the truth, Daniels?' Caleb asked.

Gil stiffened. He wasn't used to his honesty being questioned. 'Yes, Mr. Crawford. That's the truth.'

The kitchen door swung open and Lindsay and her mother entered.

Mrs. Crawford smiled at Gil. 'Come here to the table, Gil. You must be starved. Caleb, boys, do you want coffee? I've got some pie left, too. Everyone come sit down.'

Pete, one of the brothers Gil had met before, stepped closer to his father. 'If Gil says that's the truth, Dad, you can trust him. His word is good.'

Caleb nodded and moved toward the table.

Just as Gil let himself relax, with a nod of gratitude toward Pete, Lindsay exploded.

'So that's it? You accept a stranger's word, but your own daughter's isn't good enough, Dad? What did he tell you? Did he reveal something that convinced you to believe him, but not me? Or am I just a second-class citizen, like I've always been?'

Even her mother protested those harsh words. 'Lindsay!'

'Don't you ever get tired of it, Mom?' she asked, whirling to stare at the woman behind her. 'They want you to cook and clean for them, but you get no say in anything!'

'That's not true, dear,' her mother said calmly.

'It certainly is not!' Caleb denied, his face turning red again.

Gil decided it was time to exit this family confrontation. 'Pete, if I can use the phone, I'll get my ranch manager to come get me.'

Pete, and the other two young men bearing a striking resemblance to him, looked uneasily at his parents and sister. 'Uh, why don't I give you a ride? It'll be faster and I bet you're tired.'

'Sure, that'd be great,' he agreed. He didn't have any place in the middle of Lindsay's family argument.

She must have thought differently. In the angry glare she cast his way, he also saw hurt, as if she thought he was abandoning her without offering her any help. 'Lindsay—' he began.

But she didn't wait. Without saying a word, she walked from the room and slammed the door behind her.

Gil wanted to chase her, to pull her into his arms and assure her he hadn't meant to disappoint her. But he had no right—and no reason—to do so. After all, they were acquaintances, nothing more. True, they'd spent some trying hours together, but there was no future for them. He was staying in Oklahoma. She was returning to Chicago.

Everyone seemed frozen in shock. He cleared his throat. 'If that offer still stands, Pete, I'd appreciate a lift.'

Pete shook off his immobility. 'Sure thing. You got stuff in Lindsay's car?'

'Yeah, but I think the keys are still in the ignition. I can get them on my way to your truck.'

'But don't you want to eat, Gil?' Carol asked. 'I have the food ready.'

'Thank you, Mrs. Crawford, but I'll grab something at home. Besides, I imagine Lindsay will be glad to see the last of me. She's—she's pretty hurt by everything.' It wasn't his place to rebuke Lindsay's family, but she hadn't received much of a welcome from these people.

Caleb cleared his throat. 'No hard feelings, Daniels? You know how it is, with daughters. You try to protect them—'

'But finally you have to let them grow up.' With a nod, he walked to the door. If he stayed much longer, he might explain to Caleb Crawford what a mistake he was making with his only daughter.

Since he was so experienced with children. The father of so many daughters. Yeah, he'd best get away while he could.

Lindsay woke early the next morning in her old room. The familiarity of it was soothing, until the previous night's events filled her head.

She regretted the way she'd handled everything and everyone last night. She'd fallen right back into the pattern of challenging her father at every turn.

And he, of course, had fought back.

'But he started it,' she muttered to herself. Hearing those childish words only confirmed her condemnation of her behavior. She'd promised herself that this time she'd remain calm. Her father might not have changed, but she'd been sure *she* had.

Her biggest humiliation, and disappointment, she silently confessed to herself, was behaving so poorly in front of Gil. He hadn't been too impressed with her before, telling her she reminded him of his ex-wife. He made it clear that wasn't a compliment. Now he could add immature and spoiled to her resume.

She'd never see him again.

Tears filled her eyes at the thought. They hadn't even had a full two days together. He shouldn't mean anything to her.

But he did.

A soft knock on her door preceded it opening. Her mother said, 'Are you awake, darling? That nice Gil Daniels is on the phone.'

Gil? Calling her? She checked her watch even as she sat up. It was almost eight-thirty. 'Yes, I'm awake. I'm sorry I slept so late, Mom.'

'That's all right, dear. You're a city girl, after all. You don't have to conform to our country ways.' Her mother's smile was warm, but her words hurt.

'City people don't get to sleep late, Mom. I had to be at the store by eight every day.' She knew eight didn't sound early when her brothers and father ate breakfast at six during the spring and summer, but she usually got up at six-thirty.

Grabbing her robe off the end of the bed, she pulled it on as she headed for the door. She had to go to the kitchen to talk to Gil.

She was breathless when she reached the phone. Drawing a deep breath, in an effort to sound calm and relaxed, she said, 'Hello?'

'Lindsay, it's Gil. I wanted to call and thank you again for giving me a ride home.'

His formal words hadn't been what she wanted to hear. 'I appreciated the help in driving.'

Silence.

So all he had to say was a thank-you? Was that all they had to talk about? Truthfully, she couldn't think of anything to say, either, but she didn't want to hang up.

Finally, his voice softened to an intimate level and he asked, 'Are you all right?'

Lindsay leaned against the wall, warmth filling her as she heard the concern in his voice. 'Yes. Are you? Did you have a bruise this morning?'

'A little one. No big deal. Did you work things out with your dad?'

She couldn't hold back the way her body stiffened, her jaw squared. 'No.'

More silence.

'Look, I know you don't have much time here, and if you want to spend it all with your family, I'll understand, but I thought you might like to see my ranch. You seemed interested when I talked about it and...'

'I'd love to. When should I come?'

'I'll come get you.'

'No, I can drive myself. This morning? I mean, when—'

'This morning would be great. I'd like you to meet Rafe, too, my manager. He knows your family.'

Her mother slid a mug of coffee on the cabinet beside her and she smiled her thanks.

'I'd love to meet him. Can you give me directions?'

He did so, then added, 'And plan on staying for lunch, if you'd like. I'm not a great cook, but we can fix ham sandwiches, if that'll do.'

'It'll do fine. I'll see you in about an hour.' She hung up the phone and turned to face her mother. 'Gil invited me to come see his ranch today.'

'How nice. Is it an hour away?'

'No, less than half an hour. But I have to have breakfast and shower. I don't want to go looking like a slob,' she assured her mother. She took a sip of coffee and then headed for the pantry. Her mother had her favorite cereal in its usual place and she began pouring some into a bowl.

'Could you work in a few minutes to speak to your father?' her mother asked softly, pouring herself another cup of coffee and sitting at the table.

Lindsay froze. Then she reminded herself of her game plan. Calm strength. That hadn't been her reaction last night. But with rest and food, she'd be stronger. 'Of course. Is he in the barn?' Even as she asked, she crossed the room and sat down across from her mother with her cereal.

'Yes, he is. He feels badly about last night. You see, he hated not talking to you when you called yesterday morning. So he called the motel to speak with you, but the clerk told him you and your, um, man, had just left. I'm afraid he leapt to conclusions. And they stewed in him all day long.' She hastily held up her hand when Lindsay opened her mouth to protest. 'I'm not defending his behavior, dear, just explaining.'

Calm strength. Lindsay chanted those words in her head like a mantra. 'I understand, Mom,' she finally said, after drawing a deep breath, 'but a little faith in my judgment would be nice.'

'Yes, dear, but you're his only daughter.' Her mother's tolerant smile didn't encourage Lindsay's serenity.

'He would never question the boys' behavior.'

'You'll have to ask your brothers about that,' she said with a chuckle. 'Most of those confrontations occurred in the barn, so you didn't see them.'

'Then how do you know about them?' Lindsay asked.

'Your father told me. Most of *our discussions* occurred in the bedroom, so you weren't privy to them, either,' her mother chided.

Lindsay ducked her head. She wasn't convinced, but she owed her mother an apology. 'I'm sorry I said the things I did last night.'

'And I'm sorry your welcome wasn't all it should've been. We've all missed you so much. Last year, you were hardly here long enough to open presents.'

Lindsay managed to keep the tears at bay and reached out to take her mother's hand. She'd missed them desperately, too. Until last night.

'But we talk on the phone every week,' she reminded her mother.

'Yes, but that's not the same as being together. Your father began to think you'd never come home again.'

'After last night—' Lindsay began, then remembered her plan. With a deep breath, she started over. 'I've missed everyone, too.'

'Good. Tell your father that.'

The sound of the back door opening brought her mother to her feet. 'That will be Mrs. Brown. I meant to make a list for her before I go to town. I've got a meeting at the library at ten o'clock. Do you need anything from town?'

'No, thanks, Mom. I'll have lunch at Gil's and be back later this afternoon.'

Her mother paused on her way out of the kitchen. 'Are you interested in Gil?'

'His sister and I are good friends.' That didn't exactly answer her mother's question, but it was the only answer Lindsay had for her.

She couldn't be interested in Gil. There was no future there. The man had no intention of marrying or having a family. And she reminded him of his ex-wife.

And then there was the evaporation of her own plans.

She'd be heading back to Chicago tomorrow.

With a sigh, she finished her cereal, then greeted Mrs. Brown, her mother's longtime housekeeper, as she entered the kitchen. She had worked for her mother since Lindsay was four. She was a second mother to Lindsay and commiserated often with the inequality of the sexes on the Crawford ranch.

After a shower and the donning of comfortable jeans and shirt, topped with a jean jacket, Lindsay straightened her shoulders, drew a deep breath, and headed for the barn.

'Dad?' she called as she walked into the big structure's shadowy depths. The smell of hay and animals was a scent she was well familiar with. It made her feel at home almost as much as her mother's warm, sunny kitchen.

'Lindsay?' her father called seconds before he emerged from the tack room in the back. 'That you?'

'Yes, Dad.' For the first time, she realized her father felt awkward about this meeting, unsure of what to say. That realization made it easier for her to step forward and hug his neck. His arms tightened around her.

'I'm sorry about last night, Dad.'

'Oh, sweetheart, I am, too,' he said in a rush. 'I was just so worried about you.'

'I'm fine, Dad.' She wanted to argue his lack of faith. She wanted to tell him she'd grown up. She could take care of herself. But she'd promised herself she'd remain calm. Steady. Mature. 'I wanted to tell you I'm going over to see Gil's ranch. He's invited me for lunch. So I'll see you this evening.'

'The whole day? But I wanted to show you— Well, that's fine. I heard he has a nice operation.'

'Maybe you can show me some things in the morning, before I leave.'

'You're leaving that soon? I hoped you'd stay a few days.' The dismay in her father's voice was a solace to her aches.

'Having to drive cut my time short. I'm supposed to be back at work on Monday morning,' she explained.

'I don't know why you don't quit that job and come home. I could use your help here, pay you a salary.'

His dismissal of her job, her work, hurt. But she reminded herself again of her plan. 'I like my job, Daddy. I'll try to plan a longer stay next time.'

To her surprise, her response had the desired effect. He pulled her close for another hug and agreed that

that would be good. Then he warned her to be careful on her drive to Gil's, asked if she knew how to get there. She was tempted to tell him that she'd decided to drive around in circles until she happened upon Gil's ranch. But she refrained.

'Gil gave me directions.'

'Oh, great. He's a good man. Couldn't do better.'

Uh-oh. She knew what those words meant. 'Daddy, Gil isn't interested in me. Don't start getting ideas.'

'He looked pretty interested last night. And he invited you over today.' His chin raised and he challenged her with his gaze.

It suddenly struck her that she might be looking into a mirror. When someone challenged her opinion, she came out of her corner fighting. Never so much as when the challenger was one of her family.

This time she backed away. 'I'll see you this afternoon.' Giving him a kiss on the cheek, she hurried from the barn.

'You keep staring at that road, it's going to disappear on you,' Rafe drawled from behind Gil.

He spun around. 'What are you talking about? I was just checking.'

'Yep. Like you've been doing for the past hour.'

Gil thought about arguing with his manager. But he only spoke the truth. After Lindsay accepted his invitation, Gil had hurriedly straightened up the kitchen, made his bed and headed for the barn. Since then, he'd worn out a path to the barn door to watch for Lindsay.

'She should be here soon, unless she got lost.'

'Not likely. This place is easy to find. I can't wait to meet her. She's the first lady you've shown any interest in since you moved here.'

'Don't be ridiculous! I'm not interested in Lindsay Crawford. I'm simply thanking her for giving me a ride. It's only polite.'

'Uh-huh. Just good manners.' Rafe grinned. 'Your granny would've been proud.'

Rafe, in his fifties now, had worked for Gil's grandmother most of his life. Gil had met him his first summer spent with his grandmother twenty years ago. Gil was used to his teasing.

'Okay, so she's good-looking. It doesn't matter. She's a city girl now, and she's heading back for Chicago right away. But I thought you'd enjoy a little female company before she left.'

'So you were only thinking of me?' Rafe asked, still grinning.

Gil was about to answer him when he heard a car. He spun around and headed for the barn door, completely forgetting the conversation he'd been having.

Rafe leaned against the rake he'd been wielding and waited to see what happened next. He knew about last night. Gil had still been upset when he'd reached the ranch.

For two years, Rafe had worried about Gil. He'd come home from New York a bitter, reserved man. He'd remained on the ranch, avoiding most men and all women. For the first time in two years, he was eager to see a female.

Rafe couldn't wait to meet her.

CHAPTER SEVEN

LINDSAY took note of the excellent condition of Gil's property. The fences were well strung, made from the latest material. His pastures were in excellent shape, still providing good feed for his cattle even this late in the year. The gravel drive that led to the ranch buildings was well maintained.

Having grown up on a ranch, she knew how much effort was required for those results, even if she hadn't been allowed to participate in it on her family's ranch.

The house caught her eye as she pulled to a stop. A large Victorian-style home, it had a covered porch running around three sides of it. She could imagine sitting there in the evening, rocking, discussing the day's events, Gil telling her— No, she didn't mean Gil but some fictitious husband. No one she knew.

Movement caught her attention and she saw Gil emerge from the barn and head toward her car. Excitement zipped through her as she got out. By the time she'd closed her door, he was there, his gaze focused on her lips.

He's going to kiss me! That thought left her breathless, eager, leaning toward him. Then he stuck out his hand.

She stared at it.

'Lindsay? I wanted to welcome you to my place.'

Her cheeks flushed as she prayed he couldn't read her mind. She shook his hand and stepped back, bumping into her car. 'Yes, thank you, it's so nice of you to invite me.'

He reached out to stabilize her. 'Don't trip. We don't want to start our day with an injury. Glad you wore jeans. I started to call back and warn you, because I'm hoping you're up to a little ride. But I decided to take a chance.'

She knew he'd been testing her. She could just as easily have worn a skirt. If she had, he would've labeled her a city girl, through and through. She didn't like taking blind tests.

'I hoped we would do some riding,' she said calmly, but the excitement she'd felt dimmed a little.

'Come meet Rafe.'

He took her arm to guide her to the barn. His touch today set off the alarms as much as it had during their trip. It made her want more. Not a good thing.

'Is he in the barn, working? That's where Dad was, too.'

'You spoke to your father this morning?'

He sounded surprised that she could do the mature thing. Of course, she hadn't shown much maturity last night, but his attitude still irritated her. 'Yes, of course. We both apologized for our behavior. I'm afraid I lost control with the long trip and—and being hungry. I wasn't at my best.'

'None of us were. I hope you ate some dinner before you went to bed. Rafe made me a big sandwich and we shared a pot of coffee while I caught up on everything.'

So, he'd had a warm welcome. The kind she hadn't been offered. Good for him. That made Rafe a special man. She couldn't wait to meet him.

Since they were entering the barn, she didn't have

to tell Gil that she'd gone to bed without eating or talking to anyone after their fight. In fact, she'd cried herself to sleep.

But this morning she'd been calm, mature, reasonable. If only she could erase last night and do it over.

An older man stepped forward from the shadows of the barn and offered a warm greeting. His face bore the traces of his mixed heritage, part Mexican-American and she suspected part Indian, but all cowboy.

After a brief chat, one she enjoyed because she was comfortable with cowboys, Gil led her to two horses waiting in a nearby corral, already saddled.

'I guess it is a good thing I wore jeans,' she said with a shrug of her shoulders.

'We could take the truck, if you prefer, but—'

'No! I wasn't complaining. I miss riding. Sometimes in Chicago I go to a stable and hire a horse for an hour, but it's not the same.'

'I know,' Gil agreed with a grin. 'I used to do the same thing in Central Park.'

That shared understanding set the tone for their ride, and Lindsay loved every moment of it. When they returned to the barn several hours later, she was happier than she'd been in several years. Or maybe forever.

'I'm starved,' Gil assured her as they unsaddled their mounts. 'I'll take care of your ride in a minute, baby, I mean, Lindsay. You don't have to—'

'We'll get to eat that much sooner if I help,' she said calmly. She wasn't about to be treated like a sissy, a dude, a doll who sat on a shelf.

'Fair enough,' he agreed with a grin.

When they started for the house, he surprised her

by taking her hand in his. After several hours of leisurely riding, watching his strong body control the
large animal beneath him, Lindsay was already aware
of him. When he touched her, shivers coursed through
her body.

'You cold? It hasn't warmed up much, has it?'

'No, but it's a lot warmer than Chicago,' she assured him, hoping he wouldn't realize the cause for
her reaction.

He tucked her hand, encased in his, in his jacket
pocket. 'Rafe will have the kitchen warm and cozy.
He promised to start making the sandwiches about
noon.'

'Is he the only worker you have?' she asked. They
hadn't covered the entire ranch in the ride, but she
hadn't seen anyone else.

'Nope. I cut back in winter, but there are two other
hands. They're riding fence today on the north side.'

They approached the house that had caught her eye
earlier. His barn was brand-new, with all the latest
equipment. His ranch was up-to-date in every way.
But he'd kept the charming old house.

'I'm glad you didn't tear the house down and re-
build,' she said softly, her gaze tracing the ornate trim
of the porch.

'You like it?'

'Oh, yes, it's wonderful. I can't wait to see inside.'

She turned an eager smile on him but was puzzled
by the way he avoided her gaze.

'It's just a house,' he muttered.

They stepped up on the porch and he reached for
the door, pulling it open and waving her inside.

She understood his reaction as soon as she entered.
The outside of the house had been maintained and

painted recently, its white sides sparkling in the winter sunshine. Inside, the walls were dingy, the floor uneven and stained, the equipment original to the house when it had been built almost a century ago.

She stood still, shocked by the neglect in the midst of the ranch's perfection.

'How was the ride?' Rafe asked from the kitchen counter where he was making sandwiches.

Lindsay stared at him, still trying to recover from the contrast of what she'd seen. 'Uh, fine. Very enjoyable.'

'I told you it was just a house,' Gil muttered, crossing to the sink and washing his hands. 'There's a bath just down the hall if you want to clean up.'

She immediately excused herself, grateful for an opportunity to pull herself together.

'I told you you should fix this place up,' Rafe muttered. 'Didn't you prepare her? She looked kind of shocked.'

Gil dried his hands. 'She said she liked the house. She was glad I left it the way it was.'

'Was that before or after she came inside?'

Not wanting to answer that question, Gil asked, 'Are the sandwiches ready?'

'Yeah. She'll be as impressed with our cooking as she is with our decoratin'.'

Gil ignored Rafe's dig. He'd made a conscious decision when he'd bought the ranch. While he poured any money necessary into the land, buying all the latest equipment, hiring good men to help him and Rafe, buying the start of his herd, horses that he thought would be good cutters, he'd spent nothing on the house.

At first, Rafe had assumed Gil had put off work on the house because of all the outside stuff they had to do. When he suggested some changes as winter approached that first year, Rafe had been shocked to discover Gil had no intention of making improvements in the old home. He still remembered the discussion they had over it.

'But, Gil, this place is drafty. And the hot water isn't very reliable. Cold showers in winter are tough!'

'You getting soft in your old age, Rafe?'

Rafe had stared at him. 'I don't think it's being soft to want to avoid being a Popsicle.'

'I like things the way they are.'

A frown settled on Rafe's face. 'Have we ruined you, boy? Are you broke?'

'No! No, I'm not broke, but I'm not fixing up the house. I don't want a showplace, something the neighbors can ooh and aah over. This is a working ranch.'

And the subject had been closed.

He felt a little guilty now as he realized he could've made life easier for Rafe the past couple of years. His old friend had been patient with his stubbornness.

But after his final break with Amanda, he'd been furious with women, with pretension, with big cities, with everything but the basics of life. So Rafe had suffered.

Lindsay's entrance put an end to his thoughts. 'Hungry?' he asked.

'Yes. A morning ride always sharpens my appetite,' she said with a laugh that invaded Gil's dark thoughts and made him smile in return.

'Good. Rafe said everything's ready.'

She smiled at his friend, and Gil was amazed to feel

a surge of jealousy. No, that couldn't be! He didn't want a woman in his life.

A few minutes later, when their hunger had been satisfied, Rafe leaned back in his chair. 'Gil said you like the house.'

'It's a beautiful old place,' she agreed, still smiling.

Gil was satisfied with her response…until she continued.

'Of course, it needs an incredible amount of work inside, but it would be worth the effort. It's the most beautiful example of Victorian architecture I've ever seen. Why, if you redid it, it would be an even bigger draw than the horses you're training. People love to see these old homes.'

'No!' Gil protested, unable to hold back the distaste building in him.

She leaned toward him. 'I don't mean you have to decorate with doilies and fine china,' she assured him with a laugh. 'You're afraid it would be too feminine for you two tough cowboys, aren't you?' She laughed. 'I promise it doesn't have to be. Why, even a good cleaning would make a big difference. And you'd want to update the plumbing and the electricity, of course and—'

'I don't want to do any of that,' Gil said firmly.

'You're right,' she said.

He sat back with a sigh.

'That would be pretty expensive. You could start off slowly with wallpaper, new paint, polish, and do a lot of the work yourself until you have more money available, but—'

This time Gil didn't leave any doubt of his response. He leapt to his feet and roared, 'No! Nada, nothing! I'm not doing anything to this house. It's fine as it is and I'll thank you to take your ideas and your *fashion sense* out of my house!'

As silence fell, his gaze traveled from Lindsay's shocked face to Rafe's weary stare and back to Lindsay again. 'I didn't mean—' he began, realizing he'd overreacted. But that realization had come too late.

Lindsay was already on her feet. But she didn't stalk out of the room, slamming the door behind her, as she had last night. Instead she looked at Rafe. 'Thank you so much for the lovely lunch, Rafe.'

Then she walked out, without a word to Gil.

Once she was behind the wheel, with the windows tightly closed, Lindsay shared her opinion of the male race with the steering wheel, the radio and the empty seat beside her.

'Men! They are absolutely insane. And so sure they're always right. That had to be about his wife. Every time the word fashion comes up, he's talking about her!' she fumed. Then she added, 'And me.'

With a sigh she told herself what she'd already known. There was no future for her here. She may have hoped everything would have changed, that she could return to the life she loved, but she couldn't. How would she earn any money? And how could she bear her brothers' supervision? Her father was bad enough but at least he was her father. *They* had no right.

Worst of all, how could she live near Gil and not want to be with him? It may have only been two days, but those hours spent together had proven an attraction that could easily develop into something more.

But then she'd be married to someone just like her brothers.

On impulse, she took the long way home, reluctant to return to the ranch and the questions her family would ask. Questions she couldn't answer.

So she drove through Lawton, a larger town than Duncan or Apache that formed a triangle with them. When she passed slowly down one of the main streets, she caught the name of a dress shop and suddenly pulled into a nearby parking place.

Oklahoma Chic. Some people would call that an oxymoron, Lindsay thought with a smile. Probably one of those people would be Gil's ex-wife. But her mother had written her about Kelly Hampton opening a dress shop in Lawton.

She studied the windows of the shop critically. They were attractive, but she thought Kelly could do more with them. When she went in, the shop was almost empty. Which made it easy to surprise her old friend with a hug.

An hour later, Lindsay was feeling much better. Kelly respected her opinion and asked for advice after they'd talked over old times. She saw a lot of possibilities in the shop, but many of her suggestions would cost money.

'I know the old adage that you have to spend money to make money,' Kelly said tiredly, 'but when you don't have any, it doesn't much matter.'

'Things are that bad?'

'Well, I had a lot of bills after Dave's death, and, while I was pregnant with Andrew, I was sick a lot. By the time he was born and I got back on my feet, I was in real trouble. The store kind of hit bottom then.

I'm building it back up slowly, but I don't have any extra money to reinvest.'

'I'm sorry, Kel. I think you have a great location. I'm sure you'll make it. It will just take a little longer.' She gave her friend an encouraging smile.

They'd been best friends since the first grade, in spite of their different backgrounds. Lindsay came from a rich ranching family, one of six children, and Kelly came from a family made up of only her and her mother. Her mother supported them by working two shifts a day at the local diner in Duncan.

'Sure, we'll make it,' Kelly said brightly. 'Will you have time to come see Andrew?'

'Are you busy this evening?' Lindsay asked. 'I know it's Friday night, but I'm going to have to leave tomorrow around noon.'

'Friday night is no different from any other night, Lindsay, when you have a two-year-old,' Kelly assured her with a wry grin.

'Okay. How about I pick up some pizza and meet you at your house?'

'That'd be great unless you're expecting it to be clean.'

Lindsay assured her friend she'd be insulted if Kelly cleaned for her. Then she refused Kelly's offer to pay for half the pizza and said goodbye.

When she was back in her car, Lindsay reminded herself that, compared to Kelly, she had no problems. Maybe her brothers bossed her around. Maybe her father watched her like a hawk. But they loved her.

Maybe she wanted to come home and didn't feel she could. But she had a good job and a nice place to live.

Maybe she wanted Gil to— But she'd survive.

'Lindsay, is that you?' her mother called as she came into the house.

'Yes, Mom,' she replied and moved into the kitchen, the gathering room in their house.

'I've been worried.'

'I told you I'd be back this afternoon.' She checked her watch. It wasn't even three yet.

'But Gil said you left there about one o'clock,' Carol said, a questioning look in her eyes.

'Gil? He called?' She immediately shut down the flutter of her heart at hearing that news. 'Why?'

'He didn't explain, dear. But it seemed awfully important that he talk to you. So I invited him to dinner.' Her mother smiled at her, as if sure she'd be pleased.

'Really. And did he accept?'

'Of course, dear. He said he'd be here at six. I'm fixing roast beef, steamed vegetables, creamed potatoes and an apple pie.' With a wink, she added, 'Mrs. Brown made the pie earlier. I had to fight the boys to save it for tonight.'

'I'm sure you did. I guess the guys won't be here for dinner, since it's Friday night.'

'Only Mike is going out. He's meeting some of his friends from law school. But Joe, Pete and Rick will be here. They were all pleased to hear Gil is coming. They seem to approve—I mean, like him.'

'Good for them. I hope they enjoy themselves.' Lindsay kept moving through the kitchen, trying to hold on to her temper. Her mother was arranging her social life now without even checking with her.

'I hope we all enjoy ourselves,' Carol said, a puzzled look on her face.

'I know I will, Mom, because I've already made plans.'

She was almost out the door before her mother ordered her to halt.

She paused, her hand on the door, and looked over her shoulder. 'Yes?'

'What do you mean you've made other plans? Gil specifically is coming to see you. Of course you'll be here.'

Calm strength, Lindsay reminded herself. 'Mom, Dad has always been the worst about running my life, but you've made arrangements for me before without asking. I've made plans with Kelly, and I won't be home for dinner. Had you asked me before you invited Gil, I would've told you. Sorry.'

'But—but what am I going to tell Gil?'

'Tell him you have apple pie. In fact, you probably should call and invite Rafe, too. I don't think either of them do much cooking. I'm sure he'd appreciate dinner, too. You'll like him.'

'Lindsay, I can't believe you'd be so rude. Please call Gil and tell him you won't be here.'

'No, Mom. I didn't invite him. And I don't want to talk to him.' She attempted to make her escape again, but this time she was halted by her father's entry just as her mother offered another protest.

'What's wrong with Lindsay?' Caleb boomed, his voice filling the kitchen.

'Nothing's wrong with Lindsay,' Lindsay said calmly, smiling at her father. 'I'm just going up to my room.'

'Have a good time at Gil's? Nice operation?'

'Wonderful. You should go visit him.' She kept her smile in place and turned again to leave.

'I should? You telling me something, little girl? Should I ask him about his prospects tonight?'

Calm strength flew out the window. 'Daddy! Don't you dare!' she snapped as she whirled around.

Her big, strong father looked totally bewildered, turning to his wife for help. 'What did I say?'

Lindsay charged across the kitchen. 'There is nothing between me and Gil. Do you hear me? Absolutely nothing! The man has no intention of ever marrying again, and even if he did, I wouldn't have anything to do with him!' She almost added *because he reminds me of you,* but calm strength knocked some sense into her before she did.

'She's not going to be here for dinner,' Carol said softly, her gaze on Lindsay.

'Mom!' Lindsay protested. She knew she wouldn't escape until her father gave her the third degree.

'What? The man's coming to see you and you're not going to be here? Now, little girl, that's no way—'

'I already have plans, Dad. I didn't know he was coming. Mom shouldn't have invited him on my behalf without checking with me first.' She got those words out calmly, but her body was as tight as a new barbed wire fence, stretched between two poles.

'Couldn't you cancel your plans?' her father asked.

'No, I can't.'

Then she finally made her escape from the kitchen.

CHAPTER EIGHT

GIL knocked off work a little early to shower and shave before he left for the Crawfords' for dinner. The blinking light on the answering machine stopped him.

Had Lindsay called to say the invitation was canceled? He wouldn't blame her. He'd been unforgivably rude today at lunch. As Rafe had told him.

Finally, he pushed the play button, holding his breath. Instead of Lindsay, it was Carol, her mother. 'I thought I'd extend the dinner invitation to include Rafe. We'd love to have him join us also. No need to let me know. There'll be plenty of food.'

Gil knew Rafe would enjoy an evening out. As hard as Rafe worked for him, Gil certainly wouldn't deny him dinner with friends. But he didn't want any more lectures. He knew his behavior had been unacceptable.

With a sigh, he went back out to the barn. 'Rafe? You in here?'

Rafe's head popped up from the last stall. 'Yeah, I was just checking on Sugarbaby.'

'How's she doing?'

'Fine. I think we've got another week or two before she drops. Anything wrong?'

'Nope, but Mrs. Crawford left a message inviting you for dinner, too, if you want to come.'

Rafe's eyes brightened. 'Hey, I'd like that. Dinner neither you nor me cooked.' He paused, then asked, 'You don't mind?'

'Of course not. Why would I?'

'Well, I don't want to interfere with your courting Lindsay.'

Gil drew a deep breath, knowing his face was turning beet red as he held back his temper. 'I told you before, I'm not courting anyone! I was just being neighborly.'

'Oh, yeah. Well, then, I'd like to eat with the Crawfords. They're nice people.'

An hour later, they were on their way to the Double C ranch.

'You gonna apologize to Lindsay?' Rafe asked after saying nothing for most of the ride.

'Of course.'

'Good.'

'That's it? No advice on exactly what to say?' Gil growled.

'Nope. I don't like to interfere.'

That blatant lie made Gil laugh. 'Oh, yeah. I forgot.'

'Here, now, boy. You know—'

'I know, Rafe. You're family, even if we're not really related. You can say whatever you want. You know I couldn't manage without you.'

Rafe's cheeks darkened. 'You're the boss,' he protested.

'Yeah,' Gil said with another chuckle. Then, his voice serious, he said, 'I've been doing some thinking about family, since I got home.'

Rafe stared at him. 'Why?'

With a shrug, Gil said, 'Lindsay has some problems with her family. I dismissed them at first, but the way they greeted her the other night...well, I began to understand a little more.'

'They're good people,' Rafe said stubbornly.

'Yeah, they are, but they don't make her feel good about herself.'

'What are you? Some damn psychologist?'

'No, Rafe, but when I got home, you had food ready. You made me feel welcome. You asked about my trip, about Kathy. You made sure I was comfortable.'

'You make me sound like the Beaver's mom,' Rafe said in disgust.

Gil laughed again. 'Yeah. But Lindsay's father yelled at her. He hadn't seen her in almost a year.'

'I bet her mom didn't yell at her.'

'No, and she hugged her, said how good it was to see her. But she didn't stop her husband from showing his anger.'

'What was he angry about?'

Uh-oh. Gil hadn't intended to mention that fact. 'Uh, he'd found out that—that Lindsay and I stopped for the night.'

'He thought you'd driven straight through?' Rafe shook his head. 'Why would he be angry about that? That don't make sense.'

Gil licked his suddenly dry lips. Then he confessed, 'It does when you know that we shared a motel room.'

'Oh.'

'Nothing happened! We had no choice. We couldn't go any farther and there was only one room.'

'You explained that to Crawford?'

'Yeah, and his son, Pete, backed me up.'

'Good.'

'No, that's not good.' When Rafe stared at him, he tried to explain the culmination of the argument. 'What I mean is, he believed me. Not his daughter.

Well, Lindsay didn't exactly explain. She wanted him to trust her. Instead, he trusted me.'

'Aw. How did she react?'

'About how you'd expect. She has a temper like her father.' But she was a hell of a lot prettier. He grinned, knowing she'd condemn that thought.

'That's too bad. She's a nice lady,' Rafe said, rubbing his chin, as if thinking about what he'd heard.

'Yeah. And then I treated her rotten today.'

'It'll be a wonder if she ever comes home again.'

Gil felt his heart sink. Not that it mattered to him, personally, he hurriedly assured himself, but Lindsay deserved better than that.

When he parked at the Crawfords, he didn't see Lindsay's car. But she'd probably put it in one of the barns, out of the way. He hoped he'd have an opportunity to speak to her privately right away. He'd feel better when he'd had a chance to apologize.

Otherwise he might get indigestion.

Mrs. Crawford greeted them at the door, welcoming them warmly. The minute they stepped into the house, Caleb and his sons, three of them at least, did the same. Gil couldn't help but contrast that with Lindsay's welcome the night before.

All the way to Oklahoma, he'd dismissed Lindsay's comments about her family. Maybe he still thought she'd overreacted a little, but he could see her point.

Mrs. Crawford invited them to sit down. She'd prepared some hors d'oeuvres.

Gil and Rafe did so, and Caleb immediately launched into a discussion on winter feed, joined enthusiastically by his sons. Gil remembered Lindsay's comment when he'd talked about his place, that he reminded her of her father and brothers.

Though he kept watching the door for Lindsay's arrival, he talked with the others. After all, he loved ranching, but he could discuss other topics, too.

Lindsay didn't arrive.

When Mrs. Crawford invited them all to the table, he finally asked the question that was driving him crazy.

'Where's Lindsay?'

The two older Crawfords exchanged a look. Then Mrs. Crawford finally said, 'I'm sorry, Gil. But when she got home, Lindsay said she'd already made plans and couldn't cancel. I know I should've called you, but we were looking forward to getting to know you. I hope you don't mind.'

'No, of course not. I'm enjoying the evening,' he said with a smile. Inside, he was tied in knots. Did Lindsay really have plans, or was she so mad at him she wouldn't even eat dinner in the midst of her family?

He suddenly realized Pete was talking.

'She and Kelly have been friends forever.'

'Kelly?' Gil asked. He'd missed the first part of Pete's words. Was Kelly a man or a woman?

Pete cocked one eyebrow. 'Kelly Hampton. The two of them have been best friends since first grade,' he said. 'I never really understood why. They don't have much in common.'

'Me, neither,' Caleb agreed. 'Her mother seems a nice enough lady, but not our kind.'

Carol looked sternly at her husband and son. 'She is a nice lady, and it's not her fault that her husband walked out, leaving her with a baby and no way to make a living except waiting tables.'

Caleb shrugged.

Pete looked at his mother. 'She never brought Kelly around here much. How would we know if she's a nice person?'

'When Lindsay did bring any friends here, you teased them unmercifully, Peter,' Carol said, staring down her son. 'No wonder she didn't want to invite friends over.'

'Aw, Mom, we were just havin' fun.'

Gil watched the interplay, storing away the information. Lindsay had had a lot of benefits from her family, but she'd had some disadvantages, too.

'So, is Kelly male or female?' he asked, trying to make his voice sound casual.

Apparently he failed miserably, since all the Crawfords gave him sympathetic smiles. Pete answered, 'She's a lady, pal. A widow with a little boy.'

Gil didn't know how to respond. He certainly didn't want to give his honest reaction, a sigh of relief. That would give the Crawfords the idea that he cared. Of course, he did, but not—not romantically. He certainly didn't want to raise any expectations in that area.

Fortunately, Carol urged them all to the table which meant he didn't have to respond. Rafe met his gaze and gave him a wink, letting him know he recognized his dilemma. That communication made him feel good, not alone.

Had Lindsay ever experienced that much closeness with her family? He found that a sad thought.

After a pleasant meal, and a little more conversation, Caleb offered to show Gil some horses he had housed in the barn because they were either injured or due to foal any day.

'I'd love to see them, Mr. Crawford, but we've

taken up too much of your evening as it is. We should be going.'

'Don't be silly, boy,' Caleb said with a smile. 'We figured you'd want to stay 'til Lindsay got back. She shouldn't be too much longer. Come on.'

Not leaving him a choice, without being rude, Caleb walked from the room, expecting him to follow. Gil figured he'd already used his quota of rudeness for the day, so he nodded at Rafe, thanked Mrs. Crawford for the wonderful dinner again, and headed to the barn.

He didn't mind waiting for Lindsay's return.

Lindsay hugged Kelly goodbye and hurried out to her car. It had gotten colder since she'd reached Kelly's trailer house.

But they'd had a good evening. She realized how much she missed talking to Kelly. They knew each other better than anyone in the world. It had only taken Kelly a few minutes to figure out something had happened to Lindsay.

Then they'd discussed Gil Daniels nonstop.

But they'd also managed to talk about Kelly's store, and the problems she was facing. Lindsay couldn't help being interested in them. She'd once thought she'd like to have her own store.

In fact, she still wanted to do that. While she'd learned a lot at Bloomingdale's that she'd never learned at school, she still wanted to be in charge. Kelly teased her about always wanting to be the boss.

Maybe she got that from her dad.

Kelly's situation made her sad, too. It had been a real effort for Kelly to attend college. But for three years, she and Lindsay had been roommates. Then Kelly had fallen in love with Dave Hampton and they'd married. Even Lindsay hadn't known her friend was pregnant at the time. Before Andrew was born, Dave had died in a car wreck.

Kelly hadn't been able to return to school, not with the baby and the responsibilities she had then. So she'd opened her store, sinking what savings she had into it.

But she needed an investor, or a partner, Lindsay decided, thinking about it as she drove through the night. Someone to put some money into the operation and also give Kelly a break from the burdens she carried.

Like a lightbulb going on over her head, Lindsay suddenly knew *she* was the one Kelly needed. She could be Kelly's partner. They understood each other. And she had some money.

It would make it possible for her to return to Oklahoma, close to her family, but not be dependent on her parents. Excitement built inside her as she considered every aspect. Of course, she'd have to talk to Kelly about it first. But it was a perfect fit!

She was so distracted when she reached home, she almost didn't notice the strange pickup parked by the house. It couldn't be Gil's, since it was already almost ten o'clock. Ranch folks didn't visit late. The sun came up early.

But who else could it be?

She opened the door to the house, responding to her mother's call. It hadn't come from the kitchen but from the den.

She stepped to the door of the big room and had her answer at once. Both Gil and Rafe were seated among her family.

Before she could even speak, her father leapt to his

feet. 'Rafe, let me show you a book I got last week on the latest breeding techniques.' He grabbed the man by the arm and led him toward the door. ''Bout time you got home, little girl,' he said to Lindsay in passing.

'Boys, I could use some help in the kitchen,' Carol announced. Lindsay watched the shocked expressions on her brothers' faces. Usually Carol chased them out of the kitchen, rather than invite them in.

Gil stood as the others followed Carol. In only seconds Lindsay and Gil were the only occupants in the room.

'Lindsay, I came to apologize for my behavior today,' he said rapidly, as if he figured she wouldn't give him much time.

She fought the relief that filled her. She didn't want to be mad at Gil. But she knew better than to let down her guard. 'Thank you. I appreciate that.'

'I hope you didn't mind my coming to dinner this evening,' he said, watching her.

She returned his gaze, her chin lifting. 'Of course not. Mother is free to ask whomever she pleases to dinner.'

With a small grin, he took a step closer to her. 'You know she asked me here because of you.'

She held her ground. 'Yes, but she didn't ask me. I'm afraid I'd already made plans.'

'I heard. Did you have a good visit?'

His interest surprised her. And relaxed her just a little. 'Yes. Kelly and I are good friends. I've missed her.'

'Yeah. I don't know what I'd do without Rafe.'

Her smile deepened. Maybe he did understand.

'When are you heading back to Chicago?'

That question halted her melting resistance to Gil's charms. And threw her mind into turmoil. 'I'm not sure. I had thought to leave tomorrow, but I may take an extra day or two.'

'That would be great,' he said with a smile.

Why? Did he want her to stay? No, she knew better. He was just being polite. 'We'll see.'

'I'd like to have you come back to the ranch, maybe discuss the ideas you had about fixing up the house. It's time I did something to it.'

She stared at him. Having figured out that his anger had been connected to his ex-wife, she was surprised at his words. 'Why?'

'As I said, it's time. Poor Rafe doesn't handle the cold as well as he used to, and I promised him I'd do something about the drafts.'

He smiled, but Lindsay wasn't fooled. 'Then you probably need to talk to a contractor, instead of me.'

'Sure, I wasn't expecting you to swing a hammer, Lindsay,' he said with a chuckle…and another step closer to her. 'But I thought you might have some good ideas about how to improve the place. After all, your parents' house is up-to-date, well done.'

A little friendly exchange, that's all he wanted. And Lindsay liked to help people out. But she didn't want to spend time with Gil. Not when it would only make her want him more. 'Mom would be the better person to ask. She's great at that kind of thing, and she'll be around.'

'I'd be grateful for her advice, but…I thought it would be nice if you came back to visit before you left. I—I've got some things I'd like to send to Kathy.'

'Have you talked to her since we got here?'

'Nope. We only talk every once in a while. But I'm sure she's okay.' He frowned, as if he felt guilty.

'Not even to wish her a happy Thanksgiving?' She didn't say it, but the thought occurred again. He was just like the men in her family.

'Yeah, I guess I should've done that, but we got here so late, and I was tired. I'll call her first thing in the morning.' He took two steps forward, which brought him almost within reach of Lindsay.

'Good. I think she'd like that.' Kathy talked about her brother a lot.

He nodded in agreement and stepped close enough to catch both her hands in his. 'I enjoyed having you visit today. I'm sorry it ended so badly.'

'I wasn't trying to interfere,' she said softly. 'It's your place. I just got excited about the house.'

'I'm lucky you'd even sit down and eat. It's not in good shape. I—I had a thing about fixing it up because my ex-wife—she wanted to be in *Architectural Digest,* so our apartment was a showplace. I was never comfortable there.'

Lindsay had known his anger was connected to his ex-wife. No wonder he didn't want to associate with any woman. He shouldn't until he'd dealt with his anger. It was a good thing she was going back to Chicago.

'You'll probably want to wait until spring anyway,' she said with a shrug. 'That will give you plenty of time to make a decision.'

'Maybe.' He tugged on her hands, throwing her off balance, until she fell against him. Then he wrapped his arms around her. 'What I can't wait for is to tell you again how sorry I am for my behavior.'

'Really, Gil, it's—'

His lips cut off her dismissal of his second apology.

That connection that only grew stronger each time he touched her encouraged Lindsay to slide her arms around his neck, to open her mouth to his insistent lips, to draw even closer to his strong form. As she did so, he reslanted his mouth over hers and took the kiss to new depths. Even their kiss last night, in the car, hadn't been as deep, as long, as—as passionate as this kiss.

Panicked at the loss of control that was growing by the minute, Lindsay pulled back, sliding her hands to his chest to give her breathing room.

'Gil, I don't think—'

'Good,' he agreed with distraction, his gaze fixed on her lips. 'That's best.' Then he kissed her again.

Lindsay couldn't help herself. Being in Gil's embrace was the most exhilarating thing she'd ever experienced. Being surrounded by his big body, his masculine scent, made reality a distant memory. She'd told herself her feelings for Gil had no future. But she had trouble remembering that when he swept her into his arms.

Gil released her mouth. 'Good thing I hadn't kissed you like that when we shared a bed,' he murmured, his breath shallow and rapid. 'We never would've left the motel.'

She couldn't argue that statement. She didn't believe in promiscuity, but whatever it was that she and Gil shared made good sense too hard to remember.

His mouth lowered again and she met him more than halfway, eager to draw closer to him again. The man was addictive. She never wanted to stop kissing him.

He seemed to feel the same way. His big hands were

stroking her body, encouraging her to get closer, if that were possible. She wanted to touch him, too. Her hand slid into the open neck of his shirt, loving the warmth of his skin, the silkiness of his chest hair. Her other hand began manipulating the buttons on his shirt to allow her more access.

In fact, she was so buried in the desire that spurred her on, she didn't hear the approaching footsteps that normally would've alerted her to someone's presence.

It was only when her father cleared his throat that she vaguely realized they weren't alone.

'Ahem. I guess you two have made up. Maybe you have an announcement to make?' Caleb Crawford asked with great enthusiasm.

CHAPTER NINE

ANGER rose in Gil.

Okay, so it was his fault. He knew what kind of father Caleb Crawford was. He knew kissing Lindsay like he had, in Caleb's house where they could be discovered, was dangerous. He knew he hadn't been able to stop himself.

So he bit his tongue and said nothing. He hated being manipulated. His ex-wife had been an expert at it. But he did realize that Caleb had a right to be protective over his daughter. And he'd rather have the confrontation now than later, because he doubted he could keep himself from kissing Lindsay.

'No!' Lindsay exclaimed, her gaze flicking from her father to Gil and back to her father. 'No, Daddy. We had this discussion last night, remember?'

'Then it seems to me there's an awful lot of kissing going on for no reason.' Caleb Crawford didn't look happy. Then he roared, 'Carol? You'd better get in here!'

Gil leaned closer to Lindsay. 'I'm sorry.'

The look she sent his way didn't show appreciation for his sentiments. In fact, she looked as though she wanted to scratch his eyes out.

'What's wrong?' Carol asked. She was followed by Lindsay's three brothers.

'These two were smooching like nobody's business, but now they don't have anything to tell me,' Caleb protested, frowning at Lindsay and Gil.

The man was formidable. Gil was amazed that Lindsay had stood up to her father as much as she had. He stepped in front of Lindsay, as if to shield her from the heat in her father's glare. 'Mr. Crawford, Lindsay and I share an attraction, but we've only known each other three days.' Even as he said it, he couldn't believe he hadn't had more time with Lindsay. He felt he understood her as he'd never understood a woman. And yet she was still a mystery.

'Then maybe you should think about that before you start kissing her,' Caleb snapped.

Gil wanted to protest, but he decided silence might serve him better.

Lindsay thought differently. 'I'll ask you again, Dad. Do you set down the same rules for your sons? How many women have you kissed, Pete?' she demanded, suddenly swerving her glare from her father to her brother.

'Uh, hey, this isn't about me,' Pete protested. Rick and Joe began backing up, as if hoping to sneak away, before they, too, could be questioned.

'It never is,' Lindsay returned.

Gil heard the bitterness in her answer and wondered that no one else seemed to notice.

'Now, Lindsay, your father is trying to protect you,' Carol said soothingly.

With great dignity, Lindsay turned to face Gil. 'Thank you for your apology. I'm afraid I owe you a larger one for my family's behavior. I'll check on Kathy when I get back to Chicago.' Then she shoved her way past her family and disappeared.

Gil found himself suddenly in enemy territory after being warmly welcomed earlier in the evening. And it made him mad. Lindsay was right. Were her brothers forbidden to kiss a woman unless they were proposing to her?

Lindsay was being treated like a criminal because she exchanged several kisses with someone she was obviously attracted to. No wonder she'd moved all the way to Chicago to get away from the family she loved. She'd told him earlier that she intended to stay an extra day or two. He would guess that her plans had abruptly changed.

Now she would probably leave first thing in the morning.

'Are you people crazy?' Those words burst out of him before he could consider their effect.

'Watch your mouth, boy!' Caleb roared.

'I'm not one of your children, Caleb Crawford,' Gil protested even as Rafe moved over to take his arm and try to lead him from the room. 'If I were and you treated me like you do Lindsay, I'd move far away, too. Don't you understand what you're doing to her?'

'I love my daughter!' Caleb protested.

'Of course you do, dearest,' Carol said, patting her husband's arm. She turned to Gil. 'My husband may be a little overprotective, but it's only because he loves her so much.'

'You have to protect the womenfolk,' Pete added. 'You know how it is. You've got a sister. That's why you went to Chicago, isn't it? To protect her?'

Gil had never thought about his behavior toward Kathy before. Had she resented his trip? His concern?

'Best we leave,' Rafe whispered, still urging him to the door before the discussion went any further.

He remembered Lindsay's dignified retreat. 'Thank you for your hospitality, Mrs. Crawford. I apologize for any—disturbance I've created.' He nodded to the men and he and Rafe left the room. He figured the neighborliness that had been extended would disappear now.

To his surprise, Caleb followed him to the door. 'No hard feelings, Daniels. I know how it is with an attractive woman. Lindsay doesn't understand the temptation she represents.'

Gil's anger bubbled over. 'So now, you're not only condemning her for kissing me, you're making it all her fault? Damn it, man, you're supposed to be loyal to her, not me! *I* initiated the kissing. *I* wrapped my arms around her. *I* persuaded her to kiss me back. Don't you dare blame Lindsay!'

Caleb seemed taken back at Gil's vehemence, but Gil was beyond caring about his relationship with his neighbor. 'Hate me if you want. But don't condemn Lindsay because I kissed her without offering marriage!'

Pete stepped forward. 'So you're saying you were just having fun with my sister? You don't have any serious intentions?'

Gil sighed in exasperation. These people just didn't get it. 'Pete, I'll ask you what Lindsay asked you. Have you ever kissed a woman without offering marriage?'

'Yeah, but she wasn't my sister!' Pete roared. Then he thought about what he'd said. 'Of course I wouldn't kiss my sister. I didn't mean— You know what I mean, damn it!'

'Your sister is a smart, beautiful woman. I think it's about time someone around here recognize that and let her live her own life.'

He didn't wait for a response, afraid if he stayed he'd end up offering to marry Lindsay to get her away from her well-intentioned family. How anyone could mess up so when they intended to help, he didn't know.

Rafe followed him and slid behind the wheel. 'I'll drive. You might run us off the road.'

Gil didn't argue. He was a little upset about the end to the evening. For a lot of reasons.

After ten minutes of silent driving, Rafe drawled, 'Interesting evening.'

Gil's only response was a grunt.

'I see what you mean about Lindsay's family. They don't give her much support, do they?'

'Nope, and they do it in the name of love!' After a pause, he asked, 'Do I do the same thing to Kathy?'

'No, boy. You worry about her, but mostly you leave it up to her to let you know if she's in trouble. You assume the best. Those people assume the worst.'

Gil wasn't sure he deserved Rafe's support this last trip. He'd pretty much assumed the worst when Kathy called him crying.

With a sigh, he said, 'I think tonight's debacle will insure that Lindsay returns to Chicago right away.'

'Didn't you expect that?'

'She said something before, uh, before her dad came in about staying another day or two.'

'Does it matter to you?'

Gil didn't want to answer that question. He didn't want it to matter. He'd promised himself he'd never let another woman get under his skin, cause him pain. He cleared his throat. 'I want Lindsay to be happy.'

'If you asked Caleb, I'm sure he'd say the same thing,' Rafe said with a wry tone.

Gil couldn't argue with him. But he wanted to.

*   *   *

Before she fell into bed that night, Lindsay packed her bags. Even if she talked to Kelly and stayed in Oklahoma, or moved back eventually, she wouldn't be living with her parents.

As much as she loved them, she couldn't remain under her father's roof, to be treated like a witless child.

Then she crawled into bed and stared at the ceiling in the darkness, thinking about those minutes in Gil's arms. She couldn't regret that interlude, even if it had brought another argument with her father.

But she did regret the heartbreak she was facing. How could she fall in love at all with a man like her father, much less fall for him in only three days? Those first few hours in the car, if someone had told her she'd fall for Gil Daniels, she would've laughed. It must be infatuation, she decided. She couldn't have *really* fallen in love.

She'd probably fallen in lust.

The man was a top-notch kisser. He could make Lindsay forget everything. And want more.

So, she determined, she could talk to Kelly about becoming her partner, but she couldn't live at home. And most important of all, she had to avoid Gil Daniels. She'd leave in the morning, stopping on her way to talk to Kelly. Even if they did decide to become partners, she'd have to return to Chicago anyway. But she'd stay away from Gil and her parents. With those resolutions, the pain in her battered heart eased a little. She could handle those two things.

First thing the next morning, she discovered how impossible her resolutions were. When she'd dressed, she gathered her bags to come down to the kitchen. As she entered the room, her mother looked up.

'You're leaving?'

'Yes, Mom. It's a long drive back.'

'But—but your father wanted to show you some things around the ranch.'

'I doubt he still wants to, Mom. After all, we didn't part on good terms last night.' She didn't say any more because she didn't want to think about how her evening had ended.

Before her mother could reply, the phone rang. Since Lindsay was standing near it, she answered.

'Lindsay? Are you okay?'

She recognized Gil's voice at once. 'Haven't we had this conversation before?' she asked, trying to keep her voice light.

'Yes, we have, but what's your answer?' Gil persisted.

'I'm fine.'

'When are you leaving?'

Lindsay bit her bottom lip. She didn't want to lie to him, but he hadn't specifically asked when she was leaving Oklahoma. Just when she was leaving. And she was definitely leaving her family this morning.

'I'm already packed.' That was definitely not a lie.

'You promised you'd take something to Kathy for me,' he reminded her.

Yes, she had. She tried to escape that promise. 'I really don't have time—'

'Why don't you come here and have an early lunch? It will keep you from having to stop for a while. In fact, we'll pack you some sandwiches so you won't have to stop for food at all until in the morning. Please?'

Lindsay sighed, and gave in. 'Okay, I'll be there at eleven. Whatever it is, it's not big, is it? You know how little space I have.'

'I know,' he assured her with a chuckle. 'I didn't think I'd be able to stand up straight after that ride.'

'It wasn't that bad, Gil,' she returned, but she laughed, too.

'Right, I'll see you at eleven.'

'Yes.' After their goodbyes, she hung up the phone and turned to her mother, only to discover she'd disappeared. She'd probably gone to the barn to tell Caleb about his daughter's departure.

Lindsay shrugged. She'd tried. She loved her family, but their attitudes frustrated her so much. It was hard to be happy when you didn't receive any respect from those you loved.

She fixed herself a bowl of cereal and sat down at the breakfast table. Maybe she'd have time for her father to show her around before she left for Gil's. After all, it was only a little after eight o'clock.

A shout penetrated the walls of the kitchen, alarming Lindsay. She leapt to her feet to look out the window that gave a view of the barn. Her brother Rick was racing to the house.

Lindsay ran to meet him. Something was wrong.

'Lindsay, call the doctor. Mom fell and Dad thinks she broke her arm. We're going to take her in.'

Though she wanted to go to her mother, she did as Rick asked. Then she ran upstairs and grabbed a blanket and a pillow, meeting her father and mother just as they got to the car her mother usually drove.

'Should I go with you?' she asked as she wrapped the blanket around her mother and helped her inside the car.

To her surprise, her mother said, 'Yes, please, if you have the time.'

'Of course I have the time, Mom,' she said, ignoring her father's gaze. She settled her mother with the pillow. Then she rounded the car to slide in beside her.

'What happened?' she asked as her father got behind the wheel and slammed his foot on the gas pedal.

With a wince her mother spoke to her husband first. 'Caleb, please slow down. The bumps,' she paused to gasp, 'make my arm hurt more.'

Though he didn't want to, as Lindsay saw the reluctance on his face, he said, 'Yes, dear,' and did as she asked.

'Did you fall?' Lindsay asked.

'Yes. It got below freezing last night and there was a little ice I didn't notice. Before I knew it, my feet flew over my head.'

'But, honey, why were you coming out to the barn?' Caleb asked, frowning as he looked in the rearview mirror.

Carol, her eyes closed, muttered, 'To tell you Lindsay was leaving right away.'

Lindsay bit her bottom lip.

Her father turned his head to stare at her.

'Dad, the road,' she reminded him as the car headed for the ditch alongside the drive.

He jerked his head and the steering wheel, putting the car back on track. 'Were you going to leave without saying goodbye?' he asked angrily.

'No,' Lindsay assured him. 'I intended to come out to the barn to see you. But Gil called and Mom headed for the barn before I hung up.'

'You still mad about last night? I was trying to protect you,' her father insisted.

Lindsay sighed. Her father would never understand.

With that realization came a release of tension. If she accepted that fact, maybe she could stop fighting her father. He was never going to see her as an adult. But that didn't mean she had to stop acting like one whenever they were together.

'No, Dad, I'm not mad. But I'm an adult. Visiting is fine, but I can't come home again.'

'Of course you can!' her mother said sharply. 'We've kept your room for you.'

Lindsay didn't know whether to laugh or cry. As if the only problem was whether there was a place for her to sleep.

'You always have a place with us, little girl,' her father said, using his favorite nickname for her. Which summed up her dilemma.

Both her parents suddenly realized what she'd said. Her mother asked, 'You were thinking of coming home? To stay?'

'Hey, little girl, that'd be—'

'I can't, Dad, Mom. I'm sorry.' She stared out the window, afraid to meet her parents' gazes.

An hour later, Lindsay had to retract her words. Two hours into the morning and she'd already had to recant on both resolutions. She'd agreed to see Gil again. Then, when the doctor took her mother into surgery, saying he had to put a pin in her arm, Lindsay had promised her father she'd stay home until her mother was feeling better.

'What am I going to send to Kathy?' Gil asked Rafe. He'd made up that story last night to insure Lindsay would visit him again before she left for Chicago.

His friend had come in for a second cup of coffee

and was leaning against the kitchen cabinet. 'Why would you send her anything?' Rafe asked.

'Because I told Lindsay I needed her to come pick something up for Kathy.' He rubbed the back of his neck as he paced the room. 'She's coming for lunch at eleven. I told her we'd pack her some supper, too.'

'There goes my plan to check fences this morning,' Rafe said, but he was grinning.

Gil supposed he was pleased because it was a cold morning with the prospect of rain. 'I'll help you with the fences after Lindsay leaves.'

'Why don't you send Kathy your parents' wedding album. You can say you didn't want to mail anything so irreplaceable in case it got lost.'

'You're brilliant, Rafe!' Gil told him, chuckling. 'I'd never have thought of that. Lindsay will believe that story for sure.'

'Yeah. But will Kathy?'

Gil stared at his friend. 'What do you mean?'

'She's never asked for the album. When you go see her in the next week or two, she's bound to ask why you sent it.'

Gil frowned. 'I'm not going to Chicago for Christmas,' he insisted.

Rafe laughed. 'You're going. If Lindsay's up there, you'll be going.'

'You're beginning to sound like Caleb Crawford,' Gil warned.

'Nope, I'm not trying to force you. I'm predicting the future. There's a difference.' Then he set down his coffee cup and began to organize the requirements for sandwiches to pack for Lindsay.

Gil looked at his watch. Then he wished he hadn't. It would be another hour before Lindsay arrived for lunch. Instead of going back out to work, he decided to go upstairs and take a shower, maybe check his stocks. He didn't want to leave the house in case she got there early.

But, of course, her coming wasn't any big deal. Just like her leaving wasn't any big deal.

After all, he knew where she lived. He could go visit his sister anytime he wanted. And see Lindsay.

But probably not before Christmas.

Rafe was way off on that prediction.

Lindsay sat with her father for a few minutes before she realized she'd need to call Gil. She hoped he hadn't fixed any food yet.

'Dad, I have to call Gil. He invited me to lunch on my way back to Chicago.'

'On your way back to Chicago? It's not necessary to go through Apache to get to Chicago.'

'I know, but he asked me to take something back to his sister, and I agreed. To thank me, he offered to feed me an early lunch. I have to let him know I won't be there.'

'All right, but don't be gone long. I don't know when the doctor will be in here.'

Her father tried to hide how worried he was, but Lindsay saw through his pretense. She patted him on the shoulder. 'He said it would take a couple of hours, but that the operation was routine. Mom will be fine.'

Her father blinked rapidly and looked away. 'I don't know what I'd do if she wasn't. She's never been in the hospital before, except when she had you kids.'

'I know,' Lindsay whispered and leaned over to kiss his cheek. 'I'll be right back.'

Lindsay may have realized she couldn't live at

home any longer, but she knew she didn't want to be as far away as Chicago. Her parents had a wonderful marriage. Maybe part of the reason she'd tolerated her father controlling her life was that she knew he loved her, and she knew he loved her mother.

It was the kind of marriage she wanted.

The kind Gil Daniels didn't.

She swallowed the tears that filled her throat. This wasn't the time to worry about Gil Daniels. To give herself a little space, a little distraction, she called Kelly first.

'Hi, it's Lindsay. Mom fell and broke her arm, so I'm going to stay a few extra days to take care of her. And I want to talk to you about an idea I had.'

'I'm sorry about your Mom. And I'd love to get together again,' Kelly assured her. 'Just let me know when. That is, if you don't mind Andrew coming with us. I can't afford any more baby-sitting than I have to have to work.'

'I love having Andrew around. I'll call you tomorrow or Monday.'

'Great. Lindsay, I really am sorry about your Mom, but I'm so glad you're going to be here a little longer.' There was a loneliness in Kelly's voice that wrenched Lindsay's heart. Her staying was the right thing to do for a lot of reasons.

She promised herself she wasn't counting Gil in the positive column. She wasn't masochistic.

But she couldn't wait to hear his voice.

CHAPTER TEN

LINDSAY slid down into the chair beside her mother's bed. She'd sent her father home as soon as the doctor had reported the operation a success and they'd seen Carol in recovery.

He was going to clean up and come back to have dinner with Carol when, hopefully, she'd be awake. Lindsay would go home while her father was here and change so she could spend the night at the hospital with her mother.

Not exactly how she'd expected to spend the day.

'May I come in?'

She straightened in her chair and stared at Gil, standing just inside the door. 'What are you doing here?'

'I brought your mother some flowers,' he said in a quiet voice, lifting a vase filled with colorful hothouse blooms.

'That's very nice of you,' Lindsay said, rising and taking the flowers from him. 'She's still asleep from the anesthesia they gave her,' she said as she set the flowers on a low shelf near the bed.

'Yeah, it usually takes a while to come out of it. But everything went okay?'

'Yes, fine.'

'Where's your father?'

'I sent him home to have a shower. He's going to come back and have dinner with Mom while I go home and change. I'm spending the night here with her.'

'Ah. I brought those sandwiches Rafe made, in case you were stuck here. Or we can throw those away and I'll take you out to eat.'

'Oh, I'm so sorry Rafe went to all that trouble.' When she'd called Gil, he'd assured her she hadn't caused any extra work.

He took her hand. 'Don't worry about it. Will you share dinner with me?'

Before she could remind herself she'd decided to avoid Gil, she'd agreed. A giddiness filled her that was an added warning that she was making a mistake. 'But we should eat the sandwiches Rafe fixed.'

'Okay, we'll have a picnic...in the truck. It's getting colder out there and there's a light rain. They're expecting an ice storm by morning.'

'I can't leave until Dad gets back.'

'I'll go pick up some sodas and something to go with the sandwiches and be back in half an hour. If your dad's not back by then, I'll wait.' He smiled, a slow, warm, all-embracing smile that made her want to fall into his arms. But then he could've frowned and she'd feel the same way.

'Okay,' she agreed, an unusual shyness filling her.

They stood there staring at each other, neither moving. Then Gil pulled her into his arms.

In spite of all those lectures she'd given herself, the magic of his kisses was too hard to resist. Her arms slid around his neck and she leaned in to accommodate him.

She was as lost in his arms now as she'd been the night before. The hospital ceased to exist. Her problems disappeared. All she could think about was Gil.

'K-Kissing again?' a weak voice asked.

They broke apart, both breathing rapidly.

'Mom! You're awake.'

'Yes, I am,' she muttered, her eyes half open. 'Were you wanting to entertain me?'

Lindsay ignored her mother's ridiculous question. 'How are you feeling?'

'Awful.'

'Gil brought you flowers. Aren't they beautiful?' She hoped they distracted her mother's attention from what she'd seen when she woke up.

'Beautiful. Thanks.'

'I'm glad you like them,' Gil responded. 'And I'm sorry you got hurt. Lindsay said the surgery was a complete success.'

'Yes, but I'll be out of commission for at least several weeks and I'll have to wear a cast for another month or two,' Carol wailed, her emotions boiling over.

'It's all right, Mom. I'm going to stay until you get on your feet. I promised Dad.'

She was glad she'd made that decision when she saw relief fill her mother's eyes as well as a few tears. 'Oh, thank you, dear. I was so worried.'

'No problem, Mom.'

'Where is your father?'

'He went home to clean up. He'll be back to have dinner with you. Then I'll be here to stay with you all night.'

'I'm sure that's not necessary—'

'Yes, it is,' Lindsay said with a smile. 'Remember when I had my appendectomy? You stayed with me.'

'But you were a child.'

Lindsay grinned at Gil. 'I was seventeen.'

'Definitely a child,' Gil assured her with a wink.

A nurse bustled into the room. 'You're awake, Mrs. Crawford. How are you feeling?'

'Terrible.'

'Would you two step out for a minute while I check my patient?'

While her words were in a question form, Lindsay and Gil both knew it was an order. They moved out of the room. The long hallway was empty, the hospital quiet.

'She seems to be doing pretty well,' Gil said, his gaze on her face.

She loved his bright blue eyes. And couldn't help thinking of how they'd looked when he first woke up in the morning.

'Don't look at me like that,' he protested with a low groan.

'Like what?' she whispered.

'Like you want to eat me for breakfast,' he muttered and pulled her back into his arms, his lips covering hers.

She wasn't sure how long they stood there, tasting each other, touching, pressing together, but they were again interrupted.

'You two can't stop, can you?' her father growled. 'I don't suppose you want to say anything this time, either?'

With her new acceptance of her father's attitude, Lindsay reluctantly left Gil's embrace and smiled at her father. ''Fraid not, Dad. But Mom's awake and asking for you.'

He forgot about her behavior at once and charged toward the door.

'Wait, Dad, the nurse—'

He didn't stop.

'He loves her very much,' Lindsay said with a sigh.

'Yeah,' Gil said, suddenly sounding uncomfortable.

The reaction dampened Lindsay's enthusiasm. Gil wasn't interested in marriage. Lindsay would have to remember that before she lost her heart to him forever. But she wondered if it wasn't already too late.

The next morning, Lindsay had plenty of time to plan her day. And to review the evening just past. They'd had their picnic, her and Gil, in her mother's kitchen. Something in his voice at the hospital had been another reminder that there was no future with their... feelings.

And she couldn't trust herself to remember that when they were alone.

Her brothers had drifted in and out. Pete even sat down and enjoyed one of the sandwiches. He also took the opportunity to complain about the next few weeks.

'What are we going to do without Mom to cook for us?'

'I said I would stay,' Lindsay reminded him.

'Thanks a lot. We'll all be dead by the time Mom is better.'

In the past, those would've been fighting words. She'd been considered hopeless in the kitchen. Only after she moved to Chicago and began cooking for herself, with no critics looking over her shoulder, had she gained any confidence.

Last night she'd smiled and said, 'Then perhaps you'd better take up cooking.'

Pete had rejected that idea. 'I guess we'll muddle through. We can all eat cereal.'

'Three meals a day?' she'd teased, feeling more

confident now that she'd found a way to deflect all the teasing and disbelief.

She nodded her head. Just thinking about her conversation with Pete made her feel good. Gil, however, was another matter. She was disturbed by her attraction to the man. Even sitting in her mother's kitchen, she had to fight the urge to touch him.

Was she going out of her mind?

By the time her father arrived to take them home, she'd called Kelly and arranged to come over around one, promising to bring lunch with her. If she was going to cook for her family, she might as well include Kelly and Andrew.

Once her mother was settled on one of the large sofas in the den, a coverlet tucked in over her and pillows behind her, Lindsay headed for the kitchen.

When her brothers got in from the community church they all usually attended, they headed for the kitchen, the aroma drawing them like flies to honey.

'Mom cooked!' Rick said with enthusiasm.

'She couldn't have!' Pete contradicted. 'Her arm, remember? Mrs. Brown must've come over, and took pity on us.'

'I don't care who cooked,' Joe announced. 'I'm starved.'

'Me, too,' Michael echoed.

Lindsay stood ready for them, her arms crossed, in front of the table filled with home-fried chicken, mashed potatoes, beans, a tossed salad, and hot rolls.

They came to a screeching halt and stared at their little sister.

'Uh, Lindsay,' Joe said, his gaze going past her to the food. 'Who brought in the food?'

'No one.'

'I told you Mom cooked!' Rick crowed, moving forward, intending to pass Lindsay and grab a plate.

She put out a hand to stop him.

'Mom didn't cook. I did.'

The brothers exchanged looks. Then Pete said, 'I don't believe you.'

'I don't blame you,' she said serenely, 'and I wouldn't eat any of it, if I were you. There's plenty of canned foods in the pantry.'

'Huh?' Mike said, staring at her as if she'd grown two heads.

'I'm going to Kelly's for lunch. Feel free to eat if you want. But I expect the kitchen to be clean and all the leftover food put away when I get back. If it's not, you *will* be reduced to eating cereal and frozen dinners three meals a day until Mom recovers. Understood?'

All four of her brothers nodded, clearly confused by her take-charge air. And distracted by the smell of fried chicken.

She added, 'Mom and Dad are in the den with the football game on. Feel free to join them, but don't forget my warning.'

Then she scooped up a picnic basket she'd already prepared and headed for her car, storing up the sounds of her brothers attacking the food like ravenous bears.

She was getting better at this coming home thing.

About three o'clock, Gil couldn't stand it any longer. He got up from the lumpy sofa and started out of the living room.

'Aren't you gonna watch the second game?' Rafe asked, barely looking away from the television set.

'Uh, no, I think I'll, uh, go visit a neighbor.'

That brought Rafe's gaze sharply to him, and he could feel his cheeks flushing.

'A neighbor over near Duncan, maybe?'

Gil straightened his shoulders. 'It's the only polite thing to do. Mrs. Crawford broke her arm.'

'Right. Give her my regards.' Polite words, but Gil was distracted by Rafe's pointed smile.

'You could come with me.'

'I could. If you need me.'

'Not exactly, but—but it would make it look more—more normal. We could even stop in Lawton and pick up a cake or something.'

'Yeah, that'd be downright neighborly,' Rafe agreed, rising to his feet.

When they'd almost reached the Double C Ranch, Gil cleared his throat. 'Uh, remember, we're just being neighborly.'

'Right. You mean I shouldn't announce that you've got the hots for their daughter and couldn't sit still?'

Gil turned to protest only to discover Rafe grinning like an idiot. 'Thanks a lot, Rafe! I almost ran us off the road.'

'Better than living like a zombie.'

Gil turned to stare at his friend as he parked the car. 'What are you talking about?'

'I'm talking about the way you've been living the past two years, hiding all emotion, not relaxing or having any fun. You've shown more feelings since you came back from Chicago than you have since your divorce.'

Gil frowned. 'I'm not sure that's good. It makes it easier to get hurt.'

'Better hurt every once in a while than dead.'

Gil had no comeback for Rafe's remark.

They got out of the car and approached the house, Gil bearing a large chocolate cake in the plastic container the store provided, and Rafe knocked on the door.

Joe answered the door, his head turned back toward the living room, still watching a play from the game on television. 'Hi, come on in. The Cowboys just scored!'

Rafe didn't hesitate. 'Did they? All right! 'Bout time they found their offense.'

Immediately they were absorbed into the Crawford family with no awkwardness.

But also no Lindsay.

They were offered cold fried chicken if they wanted it, and they handed over their chocolate cake. Several of the brothers took a big piece of cake.

'I don't know how you can eat again, after that huge lunch,' Carol protested.

Gil saw his opening. He hadn't wanted to come right out and ask about Lindsay, and no one had volunteered any information. 'Who cooked?'

'Lindsay,' Rick said, awe in his voice. 'Man, has she changed! Used to, she couldn't boil water without ruining it. She made the best fried chicken I've ever had and—'

'Rick! You love my fried chicken,' Carol protested.

'Aw, Mom, I meant besides yours,' the young man quickly amended.

Gil grinned. Nice save.

'Hey, even her cookies were top-notch,' Pete added. 'I don't know how she found the time to make them, too. Dad said they didn't get home from the hospital until half past ten.'

Trying to keep his voice casual, Gil said, 'That's

great. Uh, where is she now?' The sudden fear that
she might have changed her mind and gone back to
Chicago was filling him.

'Over at Kelly's,' Joe said before another move in
the football game drew their attention back to the television set.

Gil wanted to ask them again to reassure himself
that Kelly was a woman. She was drawing a lot of
Lindsay's attention.

Not that it mattered to him, of course. He was just
there to offer his concern to Mrs. Crawford. Being
neighborly.

He looked up to find Rafe grinning at him again.
Damn it, the man could read his mind. It was a good
thing none of the Crawfords were that perceptive.

The sound of a car approaching had Gil on his feet.
He recognized that vehicle. He'd spent long, torturous
hours in it just a few days ago.

Carol looked up from her recumbent position on the
sofa. 'Is that Lindsay?'

'Yeah, I think so,' he replied, stepping to the window. As soon as he saw her car, he headed for the
door.

'You leaving?' Pete asked, not looking away from
the television.

'No, I thought I'd see if Lindsay needed any help
carrying things.'

All the men in the room, except Rafe, looked at him
in surprise.

'What could she need help carrying?' Rick asked,
bewilderment on his face.

Suddenly, Pete rammed his elbow into his brother's
side and grinned. 'Good idea. Let us know if you need
more muscle.'

Gil took the opportunity and got out of the room, even as he heard Michael ask what Pete meant. Okay, so maybe he'd been obvious. That didn't mean anything.

'Gil! What are you doing here?' Lindsay asked as she saw him. 'I mean, I didn't know you were coming over.'

'The hospital said your mother had checked out and I thought it would be neighborly to— I wanted to see you.' Then, because that remark seemed too obvious, he added, 'You know, to make sure everything was all right.'

'Everything's fine. At least, it will be as soon as I see the kitchen.'

Gil didn't understand her words. 'What do you mean?'

'I told my brothers they'd better clean up after lunch. If they didn't, they'll be eating cereal and frozen dinners for a long time.'

'Kind of like our dinner at the motel?' he asked, a grin on his face. The food had been terrible, but the company had been the best.

'Yeah,' she agreed with a warm smile. Which was hard to do in the cold wind.

'Let's get inside. You got anything you need me to carry?'

She handed him a picnic basket.

'You went on a picnic?' he demanded as he took her arm and hurried into the house.

'No, I took food in it to Kelly's. I had to cook for the family, so I just cooked a little extra.'

'I heard your cookies were great, as well as the chicken.'

Lindsay laughed. 'If you only knew how much they

used to criticize me, making me feel like an incompetent fool. I need to write Abby a thank-you note.'

'Abby, your sister-in-law?'

'Yes. She's the one who told me I had to go away to find myself.'

They'd reached the house. Lindsay stepped into the big room to check on her mother, who was watching the game with her family. Her brothers welcomed her—Mike even paid her a compliment on the food.

Lindsay smiled when Pete kicked him in the ankle. She knew her brothers. The proof wouldn't be in their words but in their actions. If the kitchen was clean and most of the food eaten, she'd know.

Gil followed her into the kitchen, still carrying the picnic basket. Relief flowed through her as she looked at the kitchen table, bare and wiped clean. She'd won! She spun around and grabbed Gil around the neck and kissed him.

He seemed to have no objection to her celebration. Although he did drop the picnic basket. But as his arms came around her, holding her tight against him, she had no complaints. There was nothing breakable in the basket.

'Is everything all— You two are at it again!' Caleb protested. 'Stop that!'

Lindsay drew back from Gil, a shudder going through her. 'Um, sorry, Dad. We thought we were alone.'

Amazingly, those words put her father on the defensive. 'I heard something drop and thought you needed help.'

Gil turned to look at her father. 'I dropped the picnic basket.'

Lindsay stepped closer to her father. She had too

much on her mind right now to even think about her father's attempt to restrain her behavior. 'Dad, I'm glad you came in here.'

Those words surprised both men.

'I need to talk to you. I—I want to buy a building in Lawton. If I can show you the numbers, would you consider making me a loan?'

'Don't be ridiculous!' her father returned, irritation on his face. 'What would you do with a building in Lawton? That's out of the question.'

Lindsay felt her bubble of exhilaration burst. She'd been so excited after her conversation with Kelly, buoyed by her success with her brothers, that she'd jumped in with both feet. She should've known her father would shoot her down.

'I'll loan you the money,' Gil said, moving closer to her.

'The hell you will!' Caleb roared.

CHAPTER ELEVEN

LINDSAY stared at Gil. 'But you haven't even asked any questions,' she pointed out. Neither had her father, but he'd also turned down any hope of a loan.

Gil smiled. 'You're a smart lady. I know you'll explain everything to me.'

Gil's offer proved he trusted her. And trust was more potent than his kisses. Lindsay leaned toward him, awe filling her.

'Here now, none of that. And you're certainly not borrowing money from him!'

Her father's words made her realize what she'd intended to do. She'd already kissed the man once today without warning. She'd better watch herself. It could become habit-forming. 'I will if I want to,' she said calmly, still staring at Gil. 'But I'll probably try a bank first. It would be more professional of me. But, Gil, your offer means a lot. Thanks.'

Her father huffed.

'What's going on?' Joe asked, bringing in his empty cake plate.

'Your sister thinks she's going to buy a building in Lawton. Wanted to borrow money from me. And *he* offered to loan it to her!' He pointed an accusing finger at Gil. By the time he finished his roar, Lindsay's other three brothers had joined them, wanting to know what all the yelling was about.

While her father gave them his version of the conversation, Lindsay picked up the picnic basket and be-

636

gan unloading the dirty dishes into the sink. Then she stored the picnic basket in the pantry.

'You can't be serious, Lindsay,' Mike said. 'There's not going to be a big increase in the real estate market in Lawton. I mean, it's doing well, but you should put your investments in the stock market.'

Lindsay smiled at her brother and rinsed the dishes before putting them in the dishwasher.

'There, that's settled,' Mike said, smiling at his father.

Lindsay turned around, still smiling. 'No, it's not, but it's not really anyone's business but mine, and possibly Gil's if I borrow money from him.'

'Lindsay, I forbid you to even consider such a thing!' Caleb shouted.

'Dad, I'm twenty-five, not fifteen.'

'But you haven't even explained what you're talking about,' he protested.

She cocked her head to one side. 'As I recall, you didn't ask before you summarily rejected the idea of helping me.'

'Well, I— It just sounds crazy.'

'Then it's a good thing you didn't agree, isn't it?'

Gil stepped closer to her. 'Does this mean you're thinking about staying in town? Leaving Chicago?'

Lindsay watched his face carefully as she nodded. The sparks that lit up his eyes encouraged her, making her wish they were alone, instead of in a kitchen with all the male members of her family except Logan.

'Caleb?' Carol called from the other room. 'What's going on?'

'Come in here and tell your mother what you're talking about doing. We can't leave her out,' Caleb insisted.

Everyone trooped after Caleb, Gil included, but he reached out to take Lindsay's hand in his. She smiled warmly, pleased by his support.

Again Caleb filled in the details.

Carol looked at her daughter. 'You're thinking of staying? Here?'

Lindsay quickly said, 'Not here, exactly. It will take some time, and I'll have to find out about costs, but I think I'll be living in Lawton. Close enough to see you more often,' she added hurriedly.

Those words sent her father into another spasm of protests and her brothers delivered a barrage of questions.

Lindsay held up her hand. 'Look, I'll tell everyone what I'm hoping to do if you'll be patient.' She took a deep breath, knowing in advance that the male members of the family would object.

'I have some money I inherited from Great-aunt Agatha that Dad invested for me. I'm going to go into partnership with Kelly in her dress store. But I think we'd be better off buying the building...for several reasons. We need to expand, and we can build a living space over the store.'

She'd expected the negative response from her father and brothers. But Gil's horrified expression stopped her cold.

'Gil? What's wrong?'

'I didn't know you wanted the money to have a career in fashion, Lindsay.' He stood stiff and cold, staring at her.

She shook her head at her own silliness. She knew how he felt about fashion, because of his wife. And yet she'd believed him when he said he supported her.

With a painful smile, she said, 'Then I guess the

loan idea is off. Thanks anyway.' With a deep breath, she added, 'Well, I guess I've interrupted football long enough. Thanks, guys, for cleaning up the kitchen. I'll see you later.'

Without looking at Gil, she headed for the stairs and the sanctuary of her old bedroom.

It was another silent drive, this one taking them home. Rafe let Gil drive this time, a good sign, Gil supposed, since it meant he thought Gil wouldn't run them off the road because he was upset.

Gil wasn't so sure. To hear that Lindsay was planning to stay in the area, which thrilled him, only to learn that she intended to involve herself in the fashion industry, sent him on a downward spiral. He had, of course, vowed never to get near a woman who considered her appearance more important than her life.

But he couldn't help remembering the disappointment on Lindsay's face. It reminded him of the times early in his marriage when he had turned to his wife, excitement filling him, and shared an idea with her. But Amanda had rejected everything unless it was her own idea. He had done the same thing to Lindsay. He had erased that excitement from her face and voice.

'You gonna sell any cows in the spring?' Rafe asked.

Gil stared at him. Where had that subject come from? 'Of course we'll sell the young bulls at the end of the summer. Not before then.'

'Uh-huh. Guess you and Lindsay will be in the same business then.'

Gil almost stood on the brakes. 'What are you talking about?' Rafe wasn't making any sense.

'You'll both be selling a product. Sounds the same to me.'

Gil picked up speed. 'It's not the same. Fashion is all about ego. It's an unnecessary thing that only creates problems.'

'Vegetarians might say the same thing about raising beef. Or at least some of those things. They sure wouldn't be in favor of it.'

'I suppose not, but they're in the minority. All they have to do is not buy beef, instead of trying to convert the world to their way of thinking.' He'd wanted to concentrate on his anger, to think about Lindsay's betrayal...about the way he'd betrayed *her*...not discuss fanatics with Rafe.

'Fashion sure cheers up a lot of ladies. And the men who are watching 'em, too,' Rafe said, staring straight ahead, not looking at his companion.

Gil immediately pictured Lindsay in her teal suit with that short skirt that showed off her killer legs. 'But it's not necessary.'

'Lots of things aren't necessary. But I'd sure miss a good steak...or a beautiful woman.'

'Rafe, you can't justify what Lindsay's doing! It's unacceptable!' Gil was sure he was right. She knew how he felt. If she had any interest— What was he thinking about? Of course there was nothing between them. Friendship, that's all it was. And he didn't have to be friends with her.

They reached Gil's ranch and he got out of the truck with relief. When they went in the house, though, Rafe stopped him one more time.

'This isn't about fashion, Gil,' Rafe muttered.

He spun around and stared at Rafe. 'Of course it is!'

'Nope. This is about whether you trust Lindsay not to leave you. Pure and simple, that's all it comes down to.'

Gil stared at him, the truth slapping him in the face. But he couldn't say anything.

'Women leave men all the time. And men leave women. The reasons change. Bottom line is trust. Does she love me enough to be there for me? Do I love her enough to be there for her? Even if it means a sacrifice. If the answer is yes, then you should get married. If it's not, then you move on down the road.'

Rafe walked past Gil and disappeared, not waiting for a response.

A good thing. Gil's heart ached. Rafe was right, but Gil didn't want to admit it. Because he didn't have the answer. He didn't know for sure how he felt about Lindsay.

He knew he wanted her.

But for forever? When she was involved in the one industry that had ruined his first marriage?

Though, according to Rafe, that wasn't accurate.

And how did she feel about him? When he'd offered to loan her the money, the look she'd bestowed on him had sent champagne bubbles through him. Her look before she'd left the room had almost destroyed him.

What was he going to do now?

Lindsay spent a lot of time on the phone Monday morning. She'd talked with the only bank in town. The president had agreed to listen to her pitch, but he hadn't made any promises.

He would definitely consider the loan if her father would co-sign. That much he could promise her now.

Lindsay wasn't about to beg her father to do that. Not when he didn't have any faith in her. She thought of Gil's lovely offer, later withdrawn. In that moment, when he'd offered his trust to her, she'd felt she could leap tall mountains in a single bound.

Now she was an ordinary person with big dreams.

'Lindsay?' her mother called from the sofa. Her father had carried her down this morning after Lindsay had helped her clean up and change into a fresh nightgown. The doctor had suggested Carol stay in bed for several days.

'Coming, Mom,' she said, hurrying to her side.

When she reached the living room, she expected her mother to ask for a drink, or something to eat, or more blankets. Instead she asked Lindsay to sit down.

'Are you lonely, Mom? I'm sorry, I was just—'

'I heard you.'

'What?'

'Calling the bank. Charlie Jones wouldn't agree to the loan?'

'He gave me an appointment for tomorrow morning to hear what I have to say. That's fair enough,' she said with a smile that she knew didn't reach her eyes. 'I'm working on my numbers now.'

'We've banked there for forty years. What's wrong with that man?' Carol protested.

Lindsay shrugged her shoulder. 'I don't have your resources, Mom. It's me asking for a loan, not you or Dad.'

Carol stared at her. 'So he'll give it to you if your father co-signs?'

Lindsay didn't want to answer that question. 'We'll see after I talk to him tomorrow.'

'I liked your ideas, what you've shared with me,'

Carol said. She'd asked Lindsay some questions this morning while Lindsay helped her. 'I know you want to do this on your own, but if Charlie is stubborn, I'll give him a piece of my mind, and then *I'll* co-sign the papers.'

Some of the amazement from Gil's offer was repeated in Lindsay at that moment. But she wasn't going to put her mother in an argument with her father. 'Mom, I don't want Dad upset with you.'

'Dear, I have my own money, completely in my control. Charlie has been managing it for all these years after your grandparents died. Either I will co-sign, or Charlie will say goodbye to that account.'

Lindsay stared at her mother. She'd had no idea her mother had any money of her own. 'But, Mom—are you sure it won't upset Dad?'

'It might. But I have the right to decide what to do with my money. I believe you'll do well. And I want you back here in Oklahoma, not in Chicago.'

Lindsay leaned over and hugged her mother. 'Thank you. Now I feel confident about giving in my notice on my condo and my job and arranging packers.'

'Good. The sooner you're here to stay, the better.'

'You do understand that I won't live here at home as soon as we get the apartment ready?'

Carol nodded. 'It will be good for Kelly to get her baby out of that house trailer. They're not safe in tornado country.'

'I know. It's going to be good for her to spend more time with Andrew, too. With both of us at the store and him just up the stairs, we're going to manage much better.'

'This is what *you* want to do, isn't it, dear? You're not doing this just for Kelly?'

'No, Mom, I'm not doing it for Kelly. She's just a perk.'

'And Gil?'

'I can't be someone I'm not. If Gil has no interest in me, as I am, then the decision is made.'

Her mother nodded and squeezed her hand in sympathy. 'I think I'll take a nap now. You go make your arrangements.'

Kelly stood, but then she leaned down and kissed her mother's brow. 'Thanks, Mom, for trusting me.'

'I always have, dear, but your father and the boys made it hard for you to realize it. I love you.'

As soon as Lindsay left the room, Carol pulled the phone extension closer to her and dialed the bank's number. 'Mr. Jones, please,' she said, naming the president.

It only took her about two minutes to make her position clear to her old friend. Charlie hurriedly assured her he'd take care of Lindsay tomorrow.

'Thank you, Charlie,' Carol said sweetly. 'I knew you'd be helpful.'

She hung up the phone and lay back with a sigh of contentment. Her baby was coming home.

Caleb and his sons talked a lot that morning as they made sure the animals had feed and they chopped a hole in the ice over the drinking water.

'I think Lindsay might just make it work,' Pete said. 'She's been different since she's come home. More grown up. And she can really cook.'

'She's not opening a café!' Caleb said with scorn. 'She's opening a damned dress store!'

Joe shook his head. 'I'm not in favor of it, but

you've helped all of us try different things, Dad. Why won't you help Lindsay?'

That question seemed to stop the older man. Then he said, 'But I'll take care of her. She doesn't need to take on the worry of her own business.'

Even Rick knew better than to agree with his father. 'It's a new millennium, Dad. Most women don't just sit around. Besides, Lindsay is kin to both you and Mom.'

'Your mother doesn't have a job!' Caleb barked. It had always been a source of pride to him that he'd been able to support his wife.

'No, but she runs the entire town,' Pete said with a grin. 'She could run for mayor and win hands down.'

An hour later, Caleb came back to the house and checked on Carol. She was napping on the couch. He didn't see Lindsay anywhere around. He stepped into the kitchen and picked up the phone and called the bank. When someone answered, he asked to speak to Charlie Jones.

There were chores to be done. They'd been Gil's savior when he'd first bought the ranch. He'd fallen into bed so tired he couldn't think for long about his misery, his failure at his marriage.

Today, he was so tired he couldn't think while he did his chores. He'd lain in bed too long last night thinking about his misery, his failure with Lindsay.

He and Rafe took a break and came into the kitchen for a cup of coffee to warm up. The wind was bitter out there. It wasn't a lot warmer in the house, with all its drafts.

'Sure would be good to fix up the house. Think

Lindsay will give you any tips?' Rafe asked as he poured the coffee.

Gil stared straight ahead. 'I'll call a contractor I know and see how soon he can get to us.'

Rafe stared at him, surprise on his face.

'You're really going to do it?'

'I'm going to get the house shipshape. I'm *not* going to let a decorator get hold of it.'

'Suits me. A big hot-water heater, okay? And a good central heating system? If you have enough money?'

'Rafe, I told you the investments are going well. When I finish, you can furnish your part of the house any way you want. You've got plenty of money, too.' He gave a small grin at Rafe's look of astonishment. 'Haven't you been listening when I told you about your stocks?'

Rafe shook his head. 'It's just a jumble of numbers to me. Besides, I trust you.'

Those words reminded Gil too much of the fiasco he'd made of his life yesterday. Telling Lindsay he supported her. Then ripping that support right out of her hands when she'd needed it most.

He took a sip of coffee, then set it down. 'You think Lindsay will be able to get a loan?'

'Don't know,' Rafe said. 'Bankers don't have much heart. At least that's what I've heard.'

They drank their coffee in silence for several minutes. Then Gil stood up and crossed over to the phone on the wall. He called information. 'First National Bank in Duncan.'

After the operator gave him the number, he dialed it. When the woman's voice announced the name of the bank, he asked who was president. After she gave him the name, he asked to speak to the man.

'What are you doing, Gil?' Rafe asked.

'I'm making sure Lindsay gets her loan.'

It was still cold the next morning, but Lindsay dressed in her teal suit with the gold buttons. It was the only professional outfit she'd brought with her.

She wished she had her leather briefcase to carry, too, but it was in her apartment in Chicago. She'd spent most of the day yesterday figuring her budget, her ability to repay the loan, and the prospects for their shop.

Her mother assured her she'd be fine on the sofa by herself, but Lindsay had called to make sure the housekeeper would be in that day. 'Mrs. Brown should be here any minute, Mom. I'm going to put some cookies and a glass of milk on the table by you, so you'll have a snack.'

'I swear, I'm going to put on weight with your cooking. Everything tastes great.'

After providing the snack, Lindsay leaned over and kissed her mother's cheek. 'Wish me luck.'

'Of course, dear, but I have a feeling you won't need it.'

Lindsay chalked her mother's confidence up to not knowing much about the business world. Banks were notorious about being stingy with their money. Particularly when it came to loaning money to single women.

Her father came in as she was leaving.

'You going somewhere?'

They hadn't discussed anything since Sunday, so Lindsay simply said, 'Yes, I have an appointment.'

Her father nodded. 'You look…very nice,' he said and bent down to kiss her cheek.

'Thanks, Dad,' she muttered, fighting to keep tears from her eyes. Crying wouldn't make her appear professional.

All the way to the bank, she made her arguments over and over in her head. She wanted to have every answer at hand, no matter what the man asked her.

With her head down, she marched toward the front door of the bank and ran into a solid wall of muscle. With a pardon already on her lips, she looked up into Gil's blue eyes.

CHAPTER TWELVE

HAVING run into Gil outside the bank, Lindsay had difficulty pulling her concentration together. He'd said he was there to do some business, but she didn't understand why he'd be in Duncan and not Apache. Or even Lawton.

The receptionist escorted her to Charlie Jones's office at once. She would've preferred a few minutes to gather herself together.

Charlie greeted her warmly and offered her a chair. With a deep breath, she sat down and spread out the papers she'd prepared. Charlie came around the desk and took the chair next to her so he could see what she'd brought.

She launched into her spiel, glad she'd practiced it several times. Though she watched Charlie's face and thought he approved of what she showed him, she held her breath when she'd finished, waiting for his response.

'Damn, I don't know why I got so many phone calls, Lindsay. I thought maybe you didn't know what you were doing,' he said with a big smile.

She stared at him. 'I don't understand what you mean.'

'Well, first your mother called and threatened to skin me if I wasn't kind to her baby girl.'

Lindsay turned a bright red with embarrassment.

'Then your father did the same thing.'

'Dad? Dad asked you to give me the loan?'

'I don't remember asking being a part of it,' Charlie said ruefully. 'And then your young man came in and made a big deposit just so he could tell me how to run my business, too.'

Lindsay froze, staring at the man. *Her young man* could only mean Gil. She'd just seen him outside the bank. And he was the only man in the area she'd even looked at, much less kissed in Oklahoma in a long time.

But Charlie wasn't waiting for her to get up to speed. 'The crazy thing about all this is your presentation would have earned a loan without all those threats.'

Relief flooded Lindsay. 'Really? You would've given me the loan without the phone calls?'

'Why not? You've got everything worked out. You're well-trained and talented. Kelly has already shown that she can make it through tough times.'

'But we're both single women. I thought—'

'Heck, Lindsay, we're not behind the times. What matters is what you've got to offer. And you have a lot to offer.'

Lindsay stuck out her hand to shake his. 'Thank you so much. I wanted to be able to do this on my own. I appreciate the opportunity you're giving me.'

'I'm pleased we can do so. I had my secretary prepare the papers this morning. If you want to go through them and sign them while you're here, we can release the money in about a week.'

'That would be perfect,' she assured him, a big smile on her lips. Inside, her emotions were all jumbled up, anger mixing with excitement, sadness with exhilaration. But she'd deal with all that later. Now she had business to conduct.

*   *   *

Lindsay went straight from the bank to the shop in Lawton. Kelly was waiting on a customer. She ran the shop alone except for a teenager on Thursday evenings and all day Saturday, to keep expenses down.

When two more ladies entered the shop, Lindsay stored her purse behind the counter and offered her assistance. When the three satisfied customers left the store, Lindsay and Kelly high-fived each other.

'Wow, that's a good morning's worth of sales,' Kelly crowed, grinning.

'Even better, I got the loan. We'll get a check next week. I'm going to the real estate office to make an offer on the building.'

'No!' Kelly exclaimed, disbelief on her face.

'Yes! Then I'll call the contractor and get a bid on the work upstairs. If we're lucky, we might be able to move in about the time Mother gets her cast off.'

Kelly hugged her tightly. 'I can't believe it. I feel like Cinderella. Oh, Lindsay, that would be so wonderful.' When she pulled back, she had tears in her eyes. 'We're going to make a great team.'

'Yes, we are. Now, I've got to get home to take care of Mom, after I visit the real estate office. Then I'll call the contractor from home. We've got a lot to do.'

Gil couldn't wait until he heard from Lindsay. *If* he heard from Lindsay. He called the bank president that afternoon.

'Oh, yes, Mr. Daniels. What can I do for you?' Charlie Jones asked with enthusiasm.

He should show some enthusiasm. Gil had opened a large account that morning. 'I wanted to see if you visited with Lindsay Crawford today.'

'I certainly did. And you had nothing to worry about. She's a smart businesswoman. Had all her ducks in a row. I would've given her the loan regardless.' Then he hurriedly added, 'Not that we don't appreciate your business, Mr. Daniels. We certainly do. And if there's ever anything I can do to help you in any way, just let me know.'

Gil grimaced. 'Thanks. Glad to hear you're a forward-thinking bank. I appreciate your filling me in,' he said before he hung up.

Lindsay had gotten her loan. She hadn't even needed his help. Which was good, since she didn't know about it anyway. And he'd keep it that way. But he wished he'd been there to celebrate with her.

When he'd seen her this morning, looking terrific in that suit, he'd wanted to offer her whatever money she needed. He'd wanted to tell her the trust he offered was still there. But there was that small voice that suggested she find another line of work. Sell housewares. Go into real estate. Make pottery.

Anything but fashion.

The phone rang. 'Yeah?' he answered, his mind still on Lindsay.

'Oh, Gil!' It was Kathy, crying again.

'Honey, are you all right?' he asked, trying to remember not to expect the worst. To show support, not control. To not be like Lindsay's father.

'Oh, Gil, I'm wonderful! Everything is wonderful!'

She didn't sound wonderful, but he'd take her word for it. Sort of. 'Then why are you crying?'

'Gil, we're going to have a baby! That's why I was crying before Thanksgiving.'

'You were crying because—'

'No, I was crying because my hormones are out of

whack. Brad made me go see a doctor because I've—
well, you know, cried, and it upsets him. Isn't it wonderful?'

'Yes, it is, baby sister. It's absolutely astounding.'

'Are you happy for us?'

'Of course I am. When are you due?'

'Around the first of August. There's only one thing
I'm sad about.'

'What's that?'

'Lindsay's not coming back. I'll miss her terribly.'

Gil didn't know what to say. He didn't want to tell
his sister that he was thrilled Lindsay was staying in
Oklahoma. Kathy might think Lindsay meant something to him. She might get her hopes up that her baby
would have a cousin some day. That thought stopped
him.

'Um, I know you'll miss her.' What else could he
say? That he was lost in daydreams about a little girl
who looked just like her mother?

'I'm going to call her now and tell her. She'll be
happy for me.'

'I'm sure she will. Look, how about I pay for you
and Brad to fly here for Christmas? It's time I got to
know your husband better. After all, he's going to be
the father of my niece or nephew.'

'Oh, Gil, that would be great, but we can afford
to—'

'Nope. Part of my Christmas present. Besides, I'm
hoping to have some work done on the house before
Christmas. You can give me some advice when you
get here.'

'You know who's really good at that? Lindsay is
great at pulling a room together. You should ask her
for help.'

'Yeah, good idea. Now, go put your feet up. Got to take good care of that baby.'

'I will. I love you, Gil.'

'I love you, too, baby. Tell Brad hi for me.'

He immediately dialed the number of the contractor he knew. He had no time to waste. He couldn't let his pregnant sister catch a cold in his drafty old house.

'Powell Construction,' a deep voice announced.

'Hey, Jase, don't tell me business is so slow you're answering the phones these days,' Gil teased. He and Jason Powell had become good friends when Jason had built his barn for him.

Jason chuckled. 'Not hardly. Secretary's on her coffee break. In fact, business is great right now. How are you, Gil?'

'Good. But I've got a project for you. My house.'

With a whistle, Jason said, 'That's not a small project.'

'Nope.'

'Can it wait?'

'My sister's coming for Christmas. I'd at least like a good heating system and enough work to limit the drafts by then. You got something else cooking?'

'Yeah, but I can handle both jobs. Lindsay Crawford just hired me to remodel a building in Lawton. You probably don't know her but—'

'I know her.'

'Ah.' There was a pause. Then Jason said, 'Good-looking woman.'

Gil ground his teeth. 'Yeah.'

He knew his friend recognized the tension in his voice. But he didn't intend to explain anything.

'Can I come out to your place after lunch tomorrow?'

'Come for lunch. Rafe and I aren't gourmet cooks, but we'll fix something.'

'Great, see you then.'

Lindsay had a million things to do. All she could think about was Gil. She'd decided to write him a note, thanking him for his attempt to help her.

She'd already thanked both her parents. The anger that had filled her at their lack of faith had been resolved. She could even admit that if her child had been facing a challenge, she would be tempted to ease the way. But she knew that wasn't the best thing to do.

She could appreciate their support, though. She and her father actually had a long talk. He explained that it wasn't his lack of faith in her abilities, but the fact that he wanted to take care of her, as he did her mother.

Lindsay had hidden a grin at that remark. She was beginning to have a much better appreciation of her mother's skills. Not only was she one of the most influential people in town, on every board of every business and charity, but she also managed to convince her husband that she was a lady of leisure, totally dependent on him.

After only being home a week, Lindsay was pleased that she understood her parents better, dealt with her brothers' teasing, and felt appreciated for what she'd accomplished.

And all she could think about was Gil.

Once, all those accomplishments would've been enough. Once, finding a new career and forming a partnership with her best friend would've thrilled her.

Once, she hadn't known Gil.

With a sigh, she reread the stiffly worded note, then

signed her name, sealed it and put a stamp on the envelope. The fact that he made the effort even when he was against her going into fashion was impressive. She wanted him to know she appreciated it.

She also wanted him to know their thing, whatever it had been, was over. She wasn't going to give up her business for his outdated ideas, his hang-ups.

But she'd miss him.

Lindsay flew back to Chicago to talk to Bloomingdale's and pack more suitcases. Her limited wardrobe had gotten old quickly.

She spent one evening with Kathy and Brad, celebrating their coming parenthood with them. Kathy promised to water her plants until she could come pick them up and arrange for a mover. She had until the end of December.

Then she returned home. Her mother was up and around now, but not able to fix meals. So Lindsay spent her days at the store, organizing, selling, planning with Kelly and supervising the work done on the building. In the evenings she cooked, but her brothers did the cleanup, much to Carol's surprise.

Joe asked her to bake something for the church's bake sale, but he agreed to come into the kitchen and help. Mike asked her to go shopping with him. He needed to look more professional. Rick asked advice about a young woman he'd started dating. Even Pete showed appreciation for his little sister's abilities.

Her father still called her little girl, but he didn't try to make decisions for her. Well, not often. She even asked his advice on the remodeling. Her mother visited the store frequently, doing all her shopping there.

'I swear, our sales totals have doubled since your

mom started shopping here,' Kelly said one day. 'I feel like we're taking advantage of her.'

'But she looks good,' Lindsay assured her friend with a grin. 'She's great advertising, anyway. She goes everywhere, and she always tells everyone where she buys her clothes.'

'I know. Do you think we should—'

Kelly stopped and stared over Lindsay's shoulder. Curious, she turned around. In the midst of all their elegant garments, feminine attire, stood a big cowboy, his hat in his hand.

'Gil! What—can I help you?' Lindsay asked, trying to keep her voice professional. What she really wanted to do was run into his arms. But she couldn't do that. He wouldn't want her to do that.

'I got your note.'

He didn't look particularly pleased about receiving it, she noted. 'Good. I appreciated the effort—especially in the circumstances.'

There was an awkward silence. Lindsay could tell he'd interpreted her words as she'd meant them. Their—whatever it had been, madness, infatuation, longing—was over.

Finally he said, 'Um, I thought I'd buy something for Kathy.'

'Of course.' He wasn't here to see her. He was shopping. 'Do you have any idea what you'd like?'

'Nope. I was hoping you could pick something out for me.'

Lindsay tried to focus on Gil's sister, but all she could see was Gil. She turned to look around the store for inspiration and knew immediately what she would sell him.

'Is this for a special occasion?' It had suddenly occurred to her that Gil might not know about the baby.

'It's to celebrate the baby.'

Now that that was cleared up, she led him across the store to a new shipment they'd just gotten in. 'This would be perfect,' she said, lifting one of the jumpers from the rack. 'It's the latest style, but it has a relaxed fit. She'll be able to wear it for quite a while, but it's not maternity clothes.'

Gil looked at the jumper and then her. 'But it's denim. I figured you'd sell me something silk.'

'I can, if you want, but I think Kathy would like this. Denim is very popular.'

'And washable,' Kelly added, standing nearby. 'As a mother, I can tell you that becomes very important.'

'Okay, I'll take it. And you might pick out a few more things for her for Christmas. She and Brad are coming here for the holidays.'

'That's wonderful!' Lindsay exclaimed. 'I'd love to—I mean, please tell her to call me when she gets to town,' she finished, tempering her enthusiasm. After all, Gil hadn't contacted her since a week ago. He didn't want her in his life.

'Yeah. I've started renovations on my house.'

'Jason said you did,' she said with a smile. 'That's a wonderful idea.'

He shuffled his boots, an amazing reaction from the confident, sexy Gil. Then he looked at her. 'Kathy said you'd be the best one to give me ideas about fixing up the house.'

Oh, how she wanted to. She'd love to be a part of Gil's life, to share ideas, interests, to— But she couldn't. 'There are lots of people who can help you. Jason works with a decorator who's very good.'

'No! Never mind. You've got a nice place here,' he said, more to Kelly than her. Then he took his package and left.

'You were kind of tough on him,' Kelly said. 'He seems so unhappy.'

Lindsay said nothing.

Two days later, Gil returned to the shop. He'd overnighted Kathy's present to her and she'd loved it. He felt it would only be polite to thank Lindsay. Rafe agreed with him. Of course, he'd given him that knowing smile, but Gil ignored it.

'Gil!' Lindsay said as she turned away from helping a customer. 'I didn't see you come in.'

'You busy?'

There was no one else in the store, so he figured she couldn't claim the need to tend to customers. And Kelly was there.

'Um, I have a lot to do, but I can wait on you.'

'I wanted to take you out for a cup of coffee.'

She opened her mouth and he read refusal in her eyes. But Kelly intervened.

'Good,' Lindsay's partner said, stepping over. 'And I'll let you stay gone longer if you'll promise to bring me back a cup.'

'That's a deal,' Gil said, taking Lindsay's arm. It was the first time he'd touched her in two weeks. His heart beat faster.

Lindsay stared first at him and then at Kelly. Finally, she said, 'I have to get my coat.'

Once they were seated at the local coffee bar, she made small talk, asking about Rafe and the work on his house. Gil patiently waited her out. When she'd finally run out of anything to say, he muttered, 'I'm going crazy.'

Her head snapped up and she stared at him. 'What did you say?'

'You heard me. Rafe says I'm useless. I can't seem to concentrate on work.' It was interesting that her cheeks flamed with color at his confession. 'I keep thinking about you.'

Instead of expressing similar feelings, which had been his hope, she said, 'I have to get back to work.'

His hand shot out to catch hers. 'Wait! I know I— I didn't stand by you. I have—had a hang-up about— you know. But I don't want to give up our—our friendship.' He couldn't call it what he thought it really was. A courtship. He wanted her in his life. But she'd really freak out, then.

'Gil, we don't have a friendship,' she told him, her features stiff with rejection.

'Could we? Have a friendship, I mean?'

Then he waited, holding his breath 'til she answered.

Lindsay's heart sank. Friendship with Gil. She wished life could be that simple. But it couldn't be. They'd gone beyond the friendship stage when he kissed her. Things had broken down before they'd gotten to the next stage. The one where she could throw herself in his arms whenever she wanted. Paradise.

She shook her head and started to rise, tugging on her hand.

'Lindsay, I can't let you go.'

'You don't have the right to say that,' she protested. She managed to get to her feet, but Gil stood also and pulled her against him. 'Gil, we're right in the middle of town. Everyone will see—'

Apparently he didn't care, since his lips covered hers. Lindsay tried to resist his magic, but that was one thing she hadn't succeeded in accomplishing since her return. Her arms slid around his neck.

'You two are going to have to stop that!' Caleb roared, calling even more attention to the two of them. 'Unless you've got something to tell me,' he added, a grin on his face.

Lindsay jerked away from Gil. 'No! No, there's nothing to tell.'

'Yes, sir, you're right. We have something to tell you,' Gil contradicted.

Lindsay stared at him in shock. What was he doing? Letting her father manipulate him?

'I want to marry your daughter,' Gil continued, as if they were sitting down, chatting. 'If she'll have me.'

Lindsay stiffened. 'Rafe is right. You are crazy!' Then she ran out of the coffee shop.

Gil wanted to chase after her. But he figured he needed to mend a few fences with her father, first.

'You serious?' Caleb asked.

'Oh, yeah. I tried to fight it, but I can't stay away from her. She—she completes me.'

Caleb nodded, a smile on his face. 'Yeah. Her mother does the same for me. Well, good. You'll get her out of the dress shop and back in a home, where she belongs.'

Gil knew he'd prefer to have Lindsay at home, with her life centered around him. But he also wanted her to be happy—and to make her own decisions. He had learned a few lessons since Thanksgiving. Particularly the part about respecting her decisions, especially if her decision was to choose him. 'No, sir. Lindsay will keep the store, if that's what she wants.'

'Now, boy, you need to begin as you mean to go on, and a man has to be boss in his house,' Caleb warned, not looking pleased.

'I intend to,' Gil said with a smile. 'Do we have your blessing?'

'Of course you do. I'm happy my daughter is going to marry a rancher. Best thing for her.'

'I hope she will. She didn't say yes.'

'She will,' Caleb assured him.

Gil wished he was as confident.

'Gil must not be getting much work done on his ranch these days,' Kelly teased as she saw the cowboy heading for their shop again. He'd been in every day for the past week. At first Lindsay had ignored him. Finally, on Wednesday, she'd gone for coffee again. And yesterday, too. He'd kept the conversation on easy topics. Kathy's pregnancy. The remodeling. Rafe's behavior.

Today, Gil strode into the shop at lunchtime. 'Morning, ladies.'

Kelly greeted him cheerfully. Lindsay frowned at him.

He leaned over and kissed her. A brief salute that had her heart racing.

'I thought I'd take you to lunch today and maybe out to the ranch to see the progress we've made on the house,' he said.

'I can't do that!' she exclaimed, drawing away from him. 'I can't leave Kelly alone. We have Andrew here. It takes two of us—'

'Actually,' Kelly said, grinning, 'Mom is coming in a few minutes to pick up Andrew and take him home with her. She's thinking about cutting back on her work hours and spending more time with her grandson.'

'Then we could use the time with both of us here, to go over those latest bills. And to plan the trip to the Spring Market in Dallas.'

'Later,' Kelly said, easily dismissing Lindsay's suggestion.

Gil stood patiently waiting.

Lindsay looked at her friend and then Gil. Suddenly she said, 'You're conspiring against me!'

Kelly stepped over and hugged her. 'We're trying to get you to relax, have a little fun. You've been a major workaholic since we got the loan.'

Lindsay felt a little hurt by Kelly's words. 'Fine. I'll take the rest of the day off. But that doesn't mean I'm going to your place!' she snapped at Gil.

Gil shrugged his shoulders, as if her decision didn't matter, but he said, 'Okay, but Rafe will be real disappointed. He made lunch for you.'

'Gil Daniels, you're trying to blackmail me!'

'Yeah. Is it working?' he asked with his biggest smile.

Lindsay wanted to give in so badly. She was dying to see how the house was coming along. She'd asked a few casual questions of Jason, but she couldn't ask too much or he'd get suspicious.

She enjoyed Rafe and she'd like to see him again.

Most of all, she wanted to be in Gil's arms. But there was a price to pay for that luxury. Her father had mentioned something last night about her being in her rightful place, a man's kitchen, when, not if, she married Gil.

'I am not giving up my shop.'

Her words seemed to surprise Gil and Kelly.

'Of course not,' Kelly said hurriedly.

'Why would you?' Gil asked.

'My father said—he insinuated that I should marry you and stay home barefoot and pregnant!'

Gil grinned. 'I don't have a problem with either of those conditions,' he said, his gaze drifting to her feet, 'but only if that's what you want. I'll admit I'd kind of miss the professional Miss Crawford in her business suits, in that case.'

'You would?' she asked, suspicious in spite of the thrill that ran through her.

'Oh, yeah. Killer legs like yours are too good to be covered up.'

'But I work in fashion,' she pointed out.

'Yeah. And I think you're going to be a big success. I heard two ladies talking yesterday, claiming your shop was the only place in Lawton to get great clothes.'

Kelly and Lindsay exchanged exultant looks.

'We're just getting started,' Lindsay said, warning in her voice.

'I figured.'

Lindsay stared at him, unsure what to think. He'd been so adamant against any involvement in fashion, she hadn't thought he could ever accept what she did for a living.

'Sweetheart, Rafe explained it to me.'

'Rafe? You discussed our—you talked with Rafe?'

'Hell, no! He talked, I listened. He said the only real question was whether I trusted you to stay.' He put his hands on her shoulders. 'I watched you come back to your family, even though they didn't treat you right, and fight for a relationship with them. I've watched you and Kelly join together, renewing your friendship. Why wouldn't I trust you to stay…if you loved me?'

She fought the urge to fall into his arms. 'We haven't known each other very long.'

'No, we haven't, though I realized I was in trouble when I woke up in that motel with you in my arms.' He grinned when Kelly gasped. 'Her father's reaction was a little more volatile.'

'I can imagine,' Kelly said with a laugh. 'Um, maybe I'd better dust the front windows.' She moved away to give them some privacy.

'Gil, I don't—'

He kissed her. 'Don't think, sweetheart. When I think, I let all kinds of silly reasons come between us. But we're right together.' He kissed her again. 'I'll wait as long as it takes for you to agree. But come with me today, so I can show you what your new home is going to look like.'

'And you wouldn't insist I leave the store? You wouldn't get upset if I wore silk or lace or—'

'As long as I get to take it off of you, you can wear whatever you like,' he assured her, his lips returning to hers.

Lindsay slid her arms around his neck and opened to him, delighted to have found the home she'd longed for, where she could be herself and so much more. She'd become her own woman. Now she could be Gil's woman, too.

EPILOGUE

'THERE you go again, always kissing her!' Caleb complained as he entered the kitchen. 'Can't you two find somewhere private?'

'Well, my bedroom's not crowded,' Lindsay suggested with a grin, knowing what her father's reaction would be.

'No!' Caleb roared. 'You're getting married in two days. I think you can wait that long.' He grabbed the pitcher of tea and hurried out of the room.

'I think your dad is going to be glad when we're married,' Gil murmured, nuzzling her neck, his arms still holding her close.

'I don't think he's the only one,' she said with a hopeful smile. Gil's response was all she could've wanted. But since they'd promised to wait before they headed for a bedroom, she finally drew back. 'I can't wait either.'

'Yeah,' Gil said, his gaze fixed on her lips, his voice husky.

'I'm glad you and Brad are getting along so well.'

He rolled his eyes. 'He's fine. I just hadn't spent any time with him.'

'He's fitting in well here. And I'm glad Rafe came, too. He's okay about staying in the house with us, isn't he? You convinced him?' Rafe had offered to move out as soon as they married, but both she and Gil had protested. Gil had changed his plans with Jason Powell, making Rafe a self-contained apartment on the ground floor, so he'd have some privacy. And they would, too.

'Yeah, everything is going just the way it should.'

'Or it will be in two more days,' she added.

'Yeah. Christmas Eve. You just wanted to get more presents, that's why you agreed to that date for the wedding,' he teased.

'It made sense. Abby and Logan would be here, with their baby. Kathy and Brad were already coming. I wanted all the family around us.'

'Yeah, and it meant we didn't have to wait too long,' Gil added, grinning. ''Cause I should tell you, lady, once I get you in my bed, I may not let you out of it for at least a month.'

'A week is all you get, cowboy, before I have to be back at the store. But every night, I'm all yours, for as long as you want.'

'I can't ask for anything more, sweetheart,' he assured her as his lips covered hers once more.

Modern Romance™
...seduction and
passion guaranteed

Tender Romance™
...love affairs that
last a lifetime

Sensual Romance™
...sassy, sexy and
seductive

Blaze
...sultry days and
steamy nights

Medical Romance™
...medical drama on
the pulse

Historical Romance™
...rich, vivid and
passionate

27 new titles every month.

With all kinds of Romance for every kind of mood...

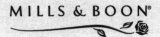

MILLS & BOON®

MILLS & BOON®

1102/59/MB58

**USE THIS COUPON TO GET 50P OFF YOUR NEXT
PURCHASE OF ANY MILLS & BOON® SERIES BOOK.**

*Vibrant, compelling, entertaining stories that
capture the timeless adventure of falling in love.*

To the consumer: This coupon can be redeemed for
£0.50 off any Mills & Boon series book at any retail store in
the UK or Eire. Only one coupon can be redeemed against
each purchase of any Mills & Boon series book. Please do
not attempt to redeem this coupon against any other
product. Not valid for Reader Service™ books.

To the retailer: Harlequin Mills & Boon will redeem this
coupon for £0.50, provided ONLY that it has been used
against the purchase of Mills & Boon series books.
Harlequin Mills & Boon reserves the right to refuse
payment against misused coupons. Please submit coupons
to Series Book Offer, NCH, Corby, Northants NN17 1NN.

Valid only until 28th February 2003.

9 904170 370509

Don't miss *Book Four* of this BRAND-NEW 12 book collection 'Bachelor Auction'.

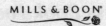